Praise for #1 bestselling author Lee Child
and his Jack Reacher series

"If you're a thriller fan and you're not reading the Reacher series, you're not a thriller fan."
—*Chicago Tribune*

"The indomitable Reacher burns up the pages of every book in Child's series."
—*USA Today*

"If there were such a thing as a writer-magician, Lee Child would be the face above the cloak."
—Associated Press

"Lee Child [is] the current poster-boy of American crime fiction."
—*Los Angeles Times*

"Jack Reacher is a tough guy's tough guy."
—*Santa Monica Mirror*

"Reacher's just one of fiction's great mysterious strangers."
—*Maxim*

"Jack Reacher is one of the best thriller characters at work today."
—*Newsweek*

By Lee Child

LEE CHILD

No Middle Name

THE COMPLETE COLLECTED

Jack Reacher

STORIES

Dell • New York

2018 Dell Mass Market Edition

Copyright © 2017 by Lee Child
"Too Much Time" copyright © 2017 by Lee Child
"Second Son" copyright © 2011 by Lee Child
"High Heat" copyright © 2013 by Lee Child
"Deep Down" copyright © 2012 by Lee Child
"Small Wars" copyright © 2015 by Lee Child
"James Penney's New Identity" copyright © 1999 by Lee Child
"Everyone Talks" copyright © 2012 by Lee Child
"Not a Drill" copyright © 2014 by Lee Child
"Maybe They Have a Tradition" copyright © 2016 by Lee Child
"Guy Walks into a Bar" copyright © 2009 by Lee Child
"No Room at the Motel" copyright © 2015 by Lee Child
"The Picture of the Lonely Diner" copyright © 2015 by Lee Child
Excerpt from *The Midnight Line* by Lee Child copyright © 2017 by Lee Child

Published in the United States by Dell, an imprint of Random House, a division of Penguin Random House LLC, New York.

DELL and the HOUSE colophon are registered trademarks of Penguin Random House LLC.

Originally published in hardcover in the United States by Delacorte Press, an imprint of Random House, a division of Penguin Random House LLC, in June 2017.

ISBN 978-0-399-59359-8
Ebook ISBN 978-0-399-59358-1
International edition ISBN 978-0-525-61832-4

Cover design: Carlos Beltrán
Type design: Tim Green, Faceout Studio

Printed in the United States of America

randomhousebooks.com

9 8 7 6 5 4 3 2 1

Dell mass market edition: January 2018

Contents

No Middle Name

Too Much Time

Sixty seconds in a minute, sixty minutes in an hour, twenty-four hours in a day, seven days in a week, fifty-two weeks in a year. Reacher ballparked the calculation in his head and came up with a little more than thirty million seconds in any twelve-month span. During which time nearly ten million significant crimes would be committed in the United States alone. Roughly one every three seconds. Not rare. To see one actually take place, right in front of you, up close and personal, was not inherently unlikely. Location mattered, of course. Crime went where people went. Odds were better in the center of a city than the middle of a meadow.

Reacher was in a hollowed-out town in Maine. Not near a lake. Not on the coast. Nothing to do with lobsters. But once upon a time it had been good for something. That was clear. The streets were wide, and the buildings were brick. There was an air of long-gone

prosperity. What might once have been grand bou-
tiques were now dollar stores. But it wasn't all doom
and gloom. Those dollar stores were at least doing some
business. There was a coffee franchise. There were
tables out. The streets were almost crowded. The weather
helped. The first day of spring, and the sun was shining.

Reacher turned in to a street so wide it had been
closed to traffic and called a plaza. There were café
tables in front of blunt red buildings either side, and
maybe thirty people meandering in the space between.
Reacher first saw the scene head-on, with the people
in front of him, randomly scattered. Later he realized
the ones that mattered most had made a perfect shape,
like a capital letter T. He was at its base, looking
upward, and forty yards in the distance, on the crossbar of the T, was a young woman, walking at right
angles through his field of view, from right to left ahead
of him, across the wide street, direct from one sidewalk to the other. She had a canvas tote bag hooked
over her shoulder. The canvas looked to be medium
weight, and it was a natural color, pale against her
dark shirt. She was maybe twenty years old. Or even
younger. She could have been as young as eighteen.
She was walking slow, looking up, liking the sun on
her face.

Then from the left-hand end of the crossbar, and
much faster, came a kid running, head-on toward
her. Same kind of age. Sneakers on his feet, tight black
pants, sweatshirt with a hood on it. He grabbed the
woman's bag and tore it off her shoulder. She was sent
sprawling, her mouth open in some kind of breathless
exclamation. The kid in the hood tucked the bag under

his arm like a football, and he jinked to his right, and he set off running down the stem of the T, directly toward Reacher at its base.

Then from the right-hand end of the crossbar came two men in suits, walking the same sidewalk-to-sidewalk direction the woman had used. They were about twenty yards behind her. The crime happened right in front of them. They reacted the same way most people do. They froze for the first split second, and then they turned and watched the guy run away, and they raised their arms in a spirited but incoherent fashion, and they shouted something that might have been *Hey!*

Then they set out in pursuit. Like a starting gun had gone off. They ran hard, knees pumping, coattails flapping. Cops, Reacher thought. Had to be. Because of the unspoken unison. They hadn't even glanced at each other. Who else would react like that?

Forty yards in the distance the young woman scrambled back to her feet, and ran away.

The cops kept on coming. But the kid in the black sweatshirt was ten yards ahead of them, and running much faster. They were not going to catch him. No way. Their relative numbers were negative.

Now the kid was twenty yards from Reacher, dipping left, dipping right, running through the broken field. About three seconds away. With one obvious gap ahead of him. One clear path. Now two seconds away. Reacher stepped right, one pace. Now one second away. Another step. Reacher bounced the kid off his hip and sent him down in a sliding tangle of arms and legs. The canvas bag sailed up in the air and the

kid scraped and rolled about ten more feet, and then
the men in the suits arrived and were on him. A small
crowd pressed close. The canvas bag had fallen about
a yard from Reacher's feet. It had a zipper across the
top, closed tight. Reacher ducked down to pick it up,
but then he thought better of it. Better to leave the
evidence undisturbed, such as it was. He backed away
a step. More onlookers gathered at his shoulder.

The cops got the kid sitting up, dazed, and they
cuffed his hands behind him. One cop stood guard
and the other stepped over and picked up the canvas
bag. It looked flat and weightless and empty. Kind
of collapsed. Like there was nothing in it. The cop
scanned the faces all around him and fixed on Reacher.
He took a wallet from his hip pocket and opened it
with a practiced flick. There was a photo ID behind a
milky plastic window. Detective Ramsey Aaron, county
police department. The picture was the same guy, a
little younger and a lot less out of breath.

Aaron said, "Thank you very much for helping us
out with that."

Reacher said, "You're welcome."

"Did you see exactly what happened?"

"Pretty much."

"Then I'll need you to sign a witness statement."

"Did you see the victim ran away afterward?"

"No, I didn't see that."

"She seemed OK."

"Good to know," Aaron said. "But we'll still need
you to sign a statement."

"You were closer to it all than I was," Reacher said.

"It happened right in front of you. Sign your own statement."

"Frankly, sir, it would mean more coming from a regular person. A member of the public, I mean. Juries don't always like police testimony. Sign of the times."

Reacher said, "I was a cop once."

"Where?"

"In the army."

"Then you're even better than a regular person."

"I can't stick around for a trial," Reacher said. "I'm just passing through. I need to move on."

"There won't be a trial," Aaron said. "If we have an eyewitness on the record, who is also a military veteran, with law enforcement experience, then the defense will plead it out. Simple arithmetic. Pluses and minuses. Like your credit score. That's how it works now."

Reacher said nothing.

"Ten minutes of your time," Aaron said. "You saw what you saw. What's the worst thing could happen?"

"OK," Reacher said.

It was longer than ten minutes, even at first. They hung around and waited for a black-and-white to come haul the kid to the police station. Which showed up eventually, accompanied by an EMS truck from the firehouse, to check the kid's vital signs. To pronounce him fit for processing. To avoid an unexplained death in custody. Which all took time. But in the end the kid went in the back seat and the uniforms in the front, and the car drove away. The rubberneckers went back to meandering. Reacher and the two cops were left standing alone.

The second cop said his name was Bush. No relation to the Bushes of Kennebunkport. Also a detective with the county. He said their car was parked on the street beyond the far corner of the plaza. He pointed. Up where their intended stroll in the sun had begun. They all set out walking in that direction. Up the stem of the T, then a right turn along the crossbar, the cops retracing their earlier steps, Reacher following the cops.

Reacher said, "Why did the victim run?"

Aaron said, "I guess that's something we'll have to figure out."

Their car was an old Crown Vic, worn but not sagging. Clean but not shiny. Reacher got in the back, which he didn't mind, because it was a regular sedan. No bulletproof divider. No implications. And the best legroom of all, sitting sideways, with his back against the door, which he was happy to do, because he figured the rear compartment of a cop car was very unlikely to spontaneously burst open from gentle internal pressure. He felt sure the designers would have thought of that consideration.

The ride was short, to a dismal low-built concrete structure on the edge of town. There were tall antennas and satellite dishes on its roof. It had a parking lot with three unmarked sedans and a lone black-and-white cruiser all parked in a line, plus about ten more empty spaces, and the stove-in wreck of a blue SUV in one far corner. Detective Bush drove in and parked in a slot marked D2. They all got out. The weak spring sun was still hanging in there.

"Just so you understand," Aaron said. "The less money we put in our buildings, the more we can put in catching the bad guys. It's about priorities."

"You sound like the mayor," Reacher said.

"Good guess. It was a selectman, making a speech. Word for word."

They went inside. The place wasn't so bad. Reacher had been in and out of government buildings all his life. Not the elegant marble palaces of D.C. necessarily, but the grimy beat-up places where government actually happened. And the county cops were about halfway up the scale, when it came to luxurious surroundings. Their main problem was a low ceiling. Which was simple bad luck. Even government architects succumbed to fashion sometimes, and back when *atomic* was a big word they briefly favored brutalist structures made of thick concrete, as if the 1950s public would feel reassured the forces of order were protected by apparently nuclear-resistant structures. But whatever the reason, the bunker-like mentality too often spread inside, with cramped airless spaces. Which was the county police department's only real problem. The rest was pretty good. Basic, maybe, but a smart guy wouldn't want it much more complicated. It looked like an OK place to work.

Aaron and Bush led Reacher to an interview room on a corridor parallel to the detectives' pen. Reacher said, "We're not doing this at your desk?"

"Like on the TV shows?" Aaron said. "Not allowed. Not anymore. Not since 9/11. No unauthorized access to operational areas. You're not authorized until your name appears as a cooperating witness in an official printed file. Which yours hasn't yet, obviously. Plus our insurance works best in here. Sign of the times. If you were to slip and fall, we'd rather there was a camera in the room, to prove we were nowhere near you at the time."

"Understood," Reacher said.

They went in. It was a standard facility, perhaps made even more oppressive by a compressed, hunkered-down feeling, coming from the obvious thousands of tons of concrete all around. The inside face was unfinished, but painted so many times it was smooth and slick. The color was a pale government green, not helped by ecological bulbs in the fixtures. The air looked seasick. There was a large mirror on the end wall. Without doubt a one-way window.

Reacher sat down facing it, on the bad-guy side of a crossways table, opposite Aaron and Bush, who had pads of paper and fistfuls of pens. First Aaron warned Reacher that both audio and video recording were taking place. Then Aaron asked Reacher for his full name, and his date of birth, and his Social Security number, all of which Reacher supplied truthfully, because why not? Then Aaron asked for his current address, which started a whole big debate.

Reacher said, "No fixed abode."

Aaron said, "What does that mean?"

"What it says. It's a well-known form of words."

"You don't live anywhere?"

"I live plenty of places. One night at a time."

"Like in an RV? Are you retired?"

"No RV," Reacher said.

Aaron said, "In other words you're homeless."

"But voluntarily."

"What does that mean?"

"I move from place to place. A day here, a day there."

"Why?"

"Because I like to."

"Like a tourist?"

"I suppose."

"Where's your luggage?"

"I don't use any."

"You have no stuff?"

"I saw a little book in a store at the airport. Apparently we're supposed to get rid of whatever doesn't bring us joy."

"So you junked your stuff?"

"I already had no stuff. I figured that part out years ago."

Aaron stared down at his pad of paper, unsure. He said, "So what would be the best word for you? Vagrant?"

Reacher said, "Itinerant. Distributed. Transient. Episodic."

"Were you discharged from the military with any kind of diagnosis?"

"Would that hurt my credibility as a witness?"

"I told you, it's like a credit score. No fixed address is a bad thing. PTSD would be worse. Defense counsel might speculate about your potential reliability on the stand. They might knock you down a point or two."

"I was in the 110th MP," Reacher said. "I'm not scared of PTSD. PTSD is scared of me."

"What was the 110th MP?"

"An elite unit."

"How long have you been out?"

"Longer than I was in."

"OK," Aaron said. "But this is not my call. It's about the numbers now, pure and simple. Trials happen inside laptop computers. Special software. Ten thousand simulations. The majority trend. A couple of points either way could be crucial. No fixed address isn't ideal, even without anything else."

"Take it or leave it," Reacher said.

They took it, like Reacher knew they would. They could never have too much. They could always lose some of it later. Perfectly normal. Plenty of good work got wasted, even on slam-dunk successful cases. So he ran through what he had seen, carefully, coherently, completely, beginning to end, left to right, near to far, and afterward they all agreed that must have been about all of it. Aaron sent Bush to get the audio typed and printed, ready for Reacher's signature. Bush left the room, and Aaron said, "Thank you again."

"You're welcome again," Reacher said. "Now tell me your interest."

"Like you saw, it happened right in front of us."

"Which I'm beginning to think is the interesting part. I mean, what were the odds? Detective Bush parked in the D2 slot. Which means he's number two on the detective squad. But he drove the car and now he's doing your fetching and carrying. Which means you're number one on the detective squad. Which means the two biggest names in the most glamorous division in the whole county police department just happened to be taking a stroll in the sun twenty yards behind a girl who just happened to get robbed."

"Coincidence," Aaron said.

Reacher said, "I think you were following her."

"Why do you think that?"

"Because you don't seem to care what happened to her afterward. Possibly because you know who she is. You know she'll be back soon, to tell you all about it. Or you know where to find her. Because you're blackmailing her. Or she's a double agent. Or maybe she's one of your own, working undercover. Whichever, you trust her to look out for herself. You're not worried about her. It's the bag you're interested in. She was violently robbed, but you followed the bag, not her. Maybe the bag is important. Although I don't see how. It looked empty to me."

"Sounds like a real big conspiracy going on, doesn't it?"

"It was your choice of words," Reacher said. "You thanked me for my help. My help in what exactly? A spontaneous split second emergency? I don't think you would have used that phrase. You would have said, Wow, that was something, huh? Or an equivalent. Or just a raised eyebrow. As a bond, or an icebreaker. Like we're just two guys, shooting the shit. But instead you thanked me quite formally. You said, Thank you very much for helping us out with that."

Aaron said, "I was trying to be polite."

Reacher said, "But I think that kind of formality needs a longer incubation. And you said *with that*.

With what? For you to internalize something as *that*, I think it would need to be a little older than a split second. It would need to be previously established. And you used a continuous tense. You said I was *helping you out*. Which implies something ongoing. Something that existed before the kid snatched the bag and will continue afterward. And you used the plural pronoun. You said thanks for helping *us* out. You and Bush. With something you already own, with something you're already running, and it just came off the rails a little bit, but ultimately the damage wasn't too bad. I think it was that kind of help you were thanking me for. Because you were extremely relieved. It could have been much worse, if the kid had gotten away, maybe. Which is why you said thank you *very much*. Which was way too heartfelt for a trivial mugging. It seemed more important to you."

"I was being polite."

"And I think my witness statement is mostly for the chief of police and the selectmen, not a computer game. To show them how it wasn't your fault. To show them how it wasn't you who just nearly screwed up some kind of long-running operation. That's why you wanted a regular person. Any third party would do. Otherwise all you would have is your own testimony, on your own behalf. You and Bush, watching each other's back."

"We were taking a stroll."

"You didn't even glance at each other. Not a second thought. You just chased after that bag. You'd been thinking about that bag all day. Or all week."

Aaron didn't answer, and got no more opportunity

to discuss it, because at that moment the door opened and a different head stuck in. It gestured Aaron out for a word. Aaron left and the door snicked shut behind him. But before Reacher could get around to worrying about whether it was locked or not, it opened up again, and Aaron stuck his head back in and said, "The rest of the interview will be conducted by different detectives."

The door closed again.

Opened again.

The guy who had stuck his head in the first time led the way. He had a similar guy behind him. Both looked like classic New England characters from historic black-and-white photographs. The product of many generations of hard work and stern self-denial. Both were lean and wiry, all cords and ligaments, almost gaunt. They were wearing chino pants, with checked shirts under blue sport coats. They had buzzed haircuts. No attempt at style. Pure function. They said they worked for the Maine Drug Enforcement Agency. A statewide organization. They said state-level inquiries outbid county-level inquiries. Hence the hijacked interview. They said they had questions about what Reacher had seen.

They sat in the chairs Aaron and Bush had vacated. The one on the left said his name was Cook, and the one on the right said his name was Delaney. It looked like he was the team leader. He looked set to do all the talking. About what Reacher had seen, he said again. Nothing more. Nothing to be concerned about.

But then he said, "First we need more information on one particular aspect. We think our county colleagues went a little light on it. They glossed right over it, perhaps understandably."

Reacher said, "Glossed over what?"

"What exactly was your state of mind, in terms of intention, at the moment you knocked the kid down?"

"Seriously?"

"In your own words."

"How many?"

"As many as you need."

"I was helping the cops."

"Nothing more?"

"I saw the crime. The perpetrator was fleeing straight toward me. He was outrunning his pursuers. I had no doubt about his guilt or innocence. So I got in his way. He wasn't even hurt bad."

"How did you know the two men were cops?"

"First impressions. Was I right or wrong?"

Delaney paused a beat.

Then he said, "Now tell me what you saw."

"I'm sure you were listening in, the first time around."

"We were," Delaney said. "Also to your continued conversation afterward, with Detective Aaron. After Detective Bush left the room. It seems you saw more than you put in your witness statement. It seems you saw something about a long-running operation."

"That was speculation," Reacher said. "It didn't belong in a witness statement."

"As an ethical matter?"

"I suppose."

"Are you an ethical man, Mr. Reacher?"

"I do my best."

"But now you can knock yourself out. The statement is done. Now you can speculate to your heart's content. What did you see?"

"Why ask me?"

"We might have a problem. You might be able to help."

"How could I help?"

"You were a military policeman. You know how this stuff works. Big picture. What did you see?"

Reacher said, "I guess I saw Aaron and Bush following the girl with the bag. Some kind of surveillance operation. Surveillance of the bag, principally. When the thing happened they ignored the girl completely. Best guess, maybe the girl was due to hand the bag off to an as-yet-unknown suspect. At a later stage. In a different place. Like a delivery or a payment. Maybe it was important to eyeball the exchange itself. Maybe the unknown suspect is the last link in the chain. Hence the high-status eyewitnesses. Or whatever. Except the plan failed because fate intervened in the form of a random purse-snatcher. Sheer bad luck. Happens to the best of us. And really no big deal. They can run it again tomorrow."

Delaney shook his head. "We're in murky waters. People like we're dealing with here, if you miss a rendezvous, you're dead to them. This thing is over."

"Then I'm sorry," Reacher said. "But shit happens. Best bet would be get over it."

"Easy for you to say."

"Not my monkeys," Reacher said. "Not my circus. I'm just a guy passing by."

"We need a word about that, too. How could we get

ahold of you, if we needed to? Do you carry a cell phone?"

"No."

"Then how do folks get ahold of you?"

"They don't."

"Not even family and friends?"

"No family left."

"No friends, either?"

"Not the kind you call on the phone every five minutes."

"So who even knows where you are?"

"I do," Reacher said. "That's enough."

"You sure?"

"I haven't needed rescuing yet."

Delaney nodded. Said, "Let's go back to what you saw."

"What part?"

"All of it. Maybe it ain't over yet. Could there be another interpretation?"

"Anything's possible," Reacher said.

"What kind of thing would be possible?"

"I used to get paid for this kind of discussion."

"We could trade you a cup of county coffee."

"Deal," Reacher said. "Black, no sugar."

Cook went to get it, and when he got back Reacher took a sip and said, "Thank you. But on balance I think it was probably just a random event."

Delaney said, "Use your imagination."

Reacher said, "Use yours."

"OK," Delaney said. "Let's assume Aaron and Bush didn't know where or when or who or how, but eventually they were expecting to see the bag transferred into someone else's custody."

Reacher said, "OK, let's assume."

"And maybe that's exactly what they saw. Just a little earlier than anticipated."

"Anything's possible," Reacher said again.

"We have to assume secrecy and clandestine measures on the bad guys' part. Maybe they gave a decoy rendezvous and planned to snatch the bag along the way. For the sake of surprise and unpredictability. Which is always the best way to beat surveillance. Maybe it was even rehearsed. According to you the girl gave it up pretty easily. You said she went down on her butt, and then she sprang back up and ran away."

Reacher nodded. "Which means you would say the kid in the black sweatshirt was the unknown suspect. You would say he was due to receive the bag all along."

Delaney nodded. "And we got him, and therefore the operation was in fact a total success."

"Easy for you to say. Also very convenient."

Delaney didn't answer.

Reacher asked, "Where is the kid now?"

Delaney pointed to the door. "Two rooms away. We're taking him to Bangor soon."

"Is he talking?"

"Not so far. He's being a good little soldier."

"Unless he isn't a soldier at all."

"We think he is. And we think he'll talk, when he comes to appreciate the full extent of his jeopardy."

"One other major problem," Reacher said.

"Which is?"

"The bag looked empty to me. What kind of a delivery or a payment would that be? You won't get a conviction for following an empty bag around."

"The bag wasn't empty," Delaney said. "At least not originally."

"What was in it?"

"We'll get to that. But first we need to loop back around. To what I asked you at the very beginning. To make sure. About your state of mind."

"I was helping the cops."

"Were you?"

"You worried about liability? If I was a civilian rendering assistance, I get the same immunity law enforcement gets. Plus the kid wasn't hurt anyway. Couple of bruises, maybe. Maybe a scrape on his knee. No problem. Unless you got some really weird judges here."

"Our judges are OK. When they understand the context."

"What else could the context be? I witnessed a felony. There was a clear desire on the part of the police department to apprehend the perpetrator. I helped them. Are you saying you've got an issue with that?"

Delaney said, "Would you excuse us for a moment?"

Reacher didn't answer. Cook and Delaney got up and shuffled out from behind the crossways table. They stepped to the door and left the room. The door snicked shut behind them. This time Reacher was pretty sure it locked. He glanced at the mirror. Saw nothing but his reflection, gray tinged with green.

Ten minutes of your time. What's the worst thing could happen?

Nothing happened. Not for three long minutes. Then Cook and Delaney came back in. They sat down again, Cook on the left and Delaney on the right.

Delaney said, "You claim you were rendering assistance to law enforcement."

Reacher said, "Correct."

"Would you like to revisit that statement?"

"No."

"Are you sure?"

"Aren't you?"

"No," Delaney said.

"Why not?"

"We think the truth is very different."

"How so?"

"We think you were taking the bag from the kid. The same way he took it from the girl. We think you were a second surprising and unpredictable cutout."

"The bag fell on the ground."

"We have witnesses who saw you bend down to pick it up."

"I thought better of it. I left it there. Aaron picked it up."

Delaney nodded. "And by then it was empty."

"Want to search my pockets?"

"We think you extracted the contents of the bag, and handed them off to someone in the crowd."

"What?"

"If you were a second cutout, why wouldn't there be a third?"

"Bullshit," Reacher said.

Delaney said, "Jack-none-Reacher, you are under arrest for felonious involvement with a racketeer-influenced corrupt organization. You have the right to remain silent. Anything you say can be used against you in a court of law. You have the right to the presence of an attorney before further questioning. If you cannot afford an attorney, then one will be appointed for you, on the taxpayers' dime."

Four county cops came in, three with handguns drawn and the fourth with a shotgun held at port arms across his body. Across the table Cook and Delaney merely peeled back their lapels to show off Glock 17s in shoulder holsters. Reacher sat still. Six against one. Too many. Dumb odds. Plus nervous tension in the air, plus trigger fingers, plus a completely unknown level of training, expertise, and experience.

Mistakes might be made.

Reacher sat still.

He said, "I want the public defender."

After that, he said nothing at all.

They handcuffed his wrists behind his back and led him out to the corridor, and around two dogleg corners, and through a locked steel door in a concrete frame, into the station's holding area, which was a miniature cell block with three empty billets on a narrow corridor, all ahead of a booking table that was currently unoccupied. One of the county cops holstered his weapon and stepped around. Reacher's handcuffs were removed. He gave up his passport, his ATM card, his toothbrush, seventy bucks in bills, seventy-five cents in quarters, and his shoelaces. In exchange he got a shove in the back and sole occupancy of the first cell in line. The door clanged shut, and the lock tripped like a hammer hitting a railroad spike. The cops looked in for a second more, like people at the zoo, and then they about-turned and walked back past the booking table and out of the room, one after the other. Reacher heard the steel door close after the last of them. He heard it lock.

He waited. He was good at waiting. He was a patient man. He had nowhere to go, and all the time in the world to get there. He sat on the bed, which was a cast concrete structure, as was a little desk, with an integral stool. The stool had a little round pad, made of the same thin vinyl-covered foam as the mattress on the bed. The toilet was steel, with a dished-in top to act as a basin. Cold water only. Like the world's lousiest motel room, further stripped back to the unavoidable minimum requirements, and then reduced in size to the barely bearable. The old-time architects had used even more concrete than elsewhere. As if prisoners trying to escape might exert more force than atom bombs.

Reacher kept track of time in his head. Two hours ticked by, and part of a third, and then the youngest of the county uniforms came by for a status check. He looked in the bars and said, "You OK?"

"I'm fine," Reacher said. "A little hungry, maybe. It's past lunchtime."

"There's a problem with that."

"Is the chef out sick?"

"We don't have a chef. We send out. To the diner

down the block. Lunch is authorized up to four dollars. But that's the county rate. You're a state prisoner. We don't know what they pay for lunch."

"More, I hope."

"But we need to know for sure. Otherwise we could get stuck with it."

"Doesn't Delaney know? Or Cook?"

"They left. They took their other suspect back to their HQ in Bangor."

"How much do you spend on dinner?"

"Six and a half."

"Breakfast?"

"You won't be here for breakfast. You're a state prisoner. Like the other guy. They'll come get you tonight."

An hour later the young cop came back again with a grilled cheese sandwich and a foam cup of Coke. Three bucks and change. Apparently Detective Aaron had said if the state paid less than that, he would cover the difference personally.

"Tell him thanks," Reacher said. "And tell him to be careful. One favor for another."

"Careful about what?"

"Which mast he nails his colors to."

"What does that mean?"

"Either he'll understand or he won't."

"You saying you didn't do it?"

Reacher smiled. "I guess you heard that before."

The young cop nodded. "Everyone says it. None of you ever did a damn thing. It's what we expect."

Then the guy walked away, and Reacher ate his meal, and went back to waiting.

Another two hours later the young cop came back for the third time. He said, "The public defender is here. She's going through the case on the phone with the state guys. They're still in Bangor. They're talking right now. She'll be with you soon."

Reacher said, "What's she like?"

"She's OK. One time my car got stole and she helped me out with the insurance company. She was in my sister's class in high school."

"How old is your sister?"

"Three years older than me."

"And how old are you?"

"Twenty-four."

"Did you get your money back for your car?"

"Some of it."

Then the guy went and sat on the stool behind the booking table. To give the impression of proper prisoner care, Reacher supposed, while his lawyer was in the house. Reacher stayed where he was, on the bed. Just waiting.

Thirty minutes later the lawyer came in. She said hello to the cop at the desk, in a friendly way, like a person would to an old high school classmate's kid brother. Then she said something else, lawyer-like and quietly, about client confidentiality, and the guy got up and left the room. He closed the steel door behind him. The cell block went quiet. The lawyer looked in the bars at Reacher. Like a person at the zoo. Maybe at the gorilla house. She was medium height and medium weight, and she was wearing a black skirt suit. She had short brown hair with lighter streaks, and brown eyes, and a round face, with a downturned mouth. Like an upside-down smile. As if she had suffered many disappointments in her life. She was carrying a leather briefcase too fat to zip. There was a yellow legal pad poking out the top. It was covered with handwritten notes.

She left the briefcase on the floor and went back and dragged the stool out from behind the booking table. She positioned it outside Reacher's cage and climbed up on it, and got comfortable, with her knees pressed tight together, and the heels of her shoes hooked over the rail. Like a regular client meeting, one person either side of a desk or a table, except there was no desk or table. Just a wall of thick steel bars, closely spaced.

She said, "My name is Cathy Clark."

Reacher said nothing.

She said, "I'm sorry I took so long to get here. I had a closing scheduled."

Reacher said, "You do real estate, too?"

"Most of the time."

"How many criminal cases have you done?"

"One or two."

"There's a large percentage difference between one and two. How many exactly?"

"One."

"Did you win?"

"No."

Reacher said nothing.

She said, "You get who you get. That's how it works. There's a list. I was at the top today. Like the cab line at the airport."

"Why aren't we doing this in a conference room?"

She didn't answer. Reacher got the impression she liked the bars. He got the impression she liked the separation. As if it made her safer.

He said, "Do you think I'm guilty?"

"Doesn't matter what I think. It matters what I can do."

"Which is?"

"Let's talk," she said. "You need to explain why you were there."

"I have to be somewhere. They need to explain why I would have given up my co-conspirator. I delivered him right to them."

"They think you were clumsy. You intended merely to grab the bag, and you knocked him over by mistake. They think he intended to keep on running."

"Why were county detectives involved in a state operation?"

"Budgets," she said. "Also sharing the credit, to keep everyone sweet."

"I didn't grab the bag."

"They have four witnesses who say you bent down to it."

Reacher said nothing.

She said, "Why were you there?"

"There were thirty people in that plaza. Why were any of them there?"

"The evidence shows the boy ran straight toward you. Not toward them."

"Didn't happen that way. I stepped into his path."

"Exactly."

"You think I'm guilty."

"Doesn't matter what I think," she said again.

"What do they claim was in the bag?"

"They're not saying yet."

"Is that legal? Shouldn't I know what I'm accused of?"

"I think it's legal for the time being."

"You think? I need more than that."

"If you want a different lawyer, go right ahead and pay for one."

Reacher said, "Is the kid in the sweatshirt talking yet?"

"He claims it was a simple robbery. He claims he thought the girl was using the bag as a purse. He claims he was hoping to get cash and credit cards. Maybe a cell phone. The state agents see that as a rehearsed cover story, just in case."

"Why do they think I didn't run, too? Why would I stick around afterward?"

"Same thing," she said. "A rehearsed cover story. As soon as it all went wrong. You saw them grab your pal, so you both switched to plan B, instantly. He was a mugger, you were helping law enforcement. He would get a trivial sentence, you would get a pat on the head. They anticipate a certain level of sophistication from both of you. Apparently this is a big deal."

Reacher nodded. "How big of a deal, do you think?"

"It's a major investigation. It's been running a long time."

"Expensive, do you think?"

"I imagine so."

"At a time when budgets seem to be an issue."

"Budgets are always an issue."

"As are egos and reputations and performance reviews. Think about Delaney and Cook. Put yourself in their shoes. A long-running and expensive investigation falls apart due to random chance. They're back to square one. Maybe worse than that. Maybe there's no way back in. Lots of red faces all around. So what happens next?"

"I don't know."

"Human nature," Reacher said. "First they shouted and cussed and punched the wall. Then their survival instinct kicked in. They looked for ways to cover their ass. They looked for ways to claim the operation was in fact a success all along. Agent Delaney said exactly that. They dreamed up the idea the kid was a part of the scam. Then they listened in when Aaron was talking to me. They heard me say I don't live anywhere. I'm a vagrant, in Aaron's own words. Which gave them an even better idea. They could make it a twofer. They could claim they bagged two guys and ripped the heart out of the whole damn thing. They could get pats on the back and letters of commendation after all."

"You're saying their case is invented."

"I know it is."

"That's a stretch."

"They double-checked with me. They made sure.

They confirmed I don't carry a cell phone. They confirmed no one keeps track of where I am. They confirmed I'm the perfect patsy."

"You agreed with the idea the kid was more than a mugger."

"As a hypothetical," Reacher said. "And not very enthusiastically. Part of a professional discussion. They flattered me into it. They said I know how this stuff works. I was humoring them. They were making shit up, to cover their ass. I was being polite, I guess."

"You said it was possible."

"Why would I say that, if I was involved?"

"They think it was a double bluff."

"I'm not that smart," Reacher said.

"They think you are. You were in an elite MP unit."

"Wouldn't that put me on their side?"

The lawyer said nothing. Just squirmed on her stool a little. Uneasiness, Reacher figured. Lack of sympathy. Distrust. Even revulsion, maybe. A desire to get away. Human nature. He knew how this stuff worked.

He said, "Check the timing on the tape. They heard me say I have no address, and the mental cogs started turning, and pretty soon after that they had hijacked the interview and were in the room with me. Then they left again later, just for a minute. For a private chat. They were confirming with each other whether they had enough. Whether they could make it work. They decided to go for it. They came back in and arrested me."

"I can't take that to court."

"What can you take?"

"Nothing," she said. "Best I can do is try for a plea bargain."

"Are you serious?"

"Completely. You're going to be charged with a very serious offense. They're going to present a working theory to the court, and they're going to back it up with eyewitness testimony from regular Maine folk, all of whom are either literally or figuratively friends and neighbors of the jury members. You're an outsider with an incomprehensible lifestyle. I mean, where are you even from?"

"Nowhere in particular."

"Where were you born?"

"West Berlin."

"Are you German?"

"No, my father was a Marine. Born in New Hampshire. West Berlin was his duty station at the time."

"So you've always been military?"

"Man and boy."

"Not good. People thank you for your service, but deep down they think you're all screwed up with trauma. There's a substantial risk you'll be convicted, and if you are, you'll get a long custodial sentence. It will be far safer to plead guilty to a lesser offense. You'd be saving them the time and expense of a contested trial. That counts for a lot. It could be the difference between five years and twenty. As your lawyer I would be delinquent in my duty if I didn't recommend it."

"You're recommending I do five years for an offense I didn't commit?"

"Everyone says they're innocent. Juries know that."

"And lawyers?"

"Clients lie all the time."

Reacher said nothing.

His lawyer said, "They want to move you to Warren tonight."

"What's in Warren?"

"The state pen."

"Terrific."

"I petitioned to have you kept here a day or two. More convenient for me."

"And?"

"They refused."

Reacher said nothing.

His lawyer said, "They'll bring you back tomorrow morning for the arraignment. The courthouse is in this building."

"So I'm going there and back in less than twelve hours? That's not very efficient. I should stay here."

"You're in the system now. That's how it works. Nothing will make sense ever again. Get used to it. We'll discuss your plea in the morning. I suggest you think about it very seriously overnight."

"What about bail?"

"How much can you pay?"

"About seventy bucks and change."

"The court would regard that as an insult," she said. "Better not to apply at all."

Then she slid down off her stool and picked up her overstuffed bag and walked out of the room. Reacher heard the steel door open and close. The cell block went quiet again.

Ten minutes of your time. What's the worst thing could happen?

———

Another hour went by, and then the young cop came back in. He said the state had authorized the same six dollars and fifty cents for dinner that the county would have spent. He said that would get most anything on the diner's menu. He recited a list of possibilities, which was extensive. Reacher thought about it for a moment. Chicken pot pie, maybe. Or pasta. Or an egg salad. He mused out loud between those three alternatives. The cop recommended the chicken pie. He said it was good. Reacher took his word for it. Plus coffee, he added. Lots of it, he emphasized, a really serious quantity, in a flask to keep it warm. With a proper china cup and saucer. No cream, no sugar. The cop wrote it all down on a slip of paper with a stub of a pencil.

Then he said, "Was the public defender OK?"

"Sure," Reacher said. "She seemed like a nice lady. Smart, too. She figures it's all a bit of a misunderstanding. She figures those state guys get a bit over-enthusiastic from time to time. Not like you county people. No common sense."

The young cop nodded. "I guess it can be like that sometimes."

"She says I'll be out tomorrow, most likely. She says I should sit tight and trust the system."

"That's usually the best way," the kid said. He tucked the slip of paper in his shirt pocket, and then he left the room.

Reacher stayed on his bed. He waited. He sensed the building grow quieter, as the day watch went home and the night watch came in. Fewer people. Budgets.

A rural county in an underpopulated part of the state. Then eventually the young cop came back with the food. His last duty of the day, almost certainly. He was carrying a tray with a china plate with a metal cover, and a white fluted fat-bellied plastic coffee flask, and a saucer topped with an upside-down cup, and a knife and a fork wrapped in a paper napkin.

The plastic flask was the key component. It made the whole assemblage too tall to fit through the horizontal pass-through slot in the bars. The kid couldn't lay the flask down on its side on the tray. It would roll around and the coffee would spill out all over the pie. He couldn't pass it upright on its own through a regular part of the bars, because they were too close together for its fat-bellied shape.

The kid paused, unsure.

Twenty-four years old. A rookie. A guy who knew Reacher as nothing worse than a placid old man who spent all his time on his bed, apparently relaxed and resigned. No shouting, no yelling. No complaints. No bad temper.

Trusting the system.

No danger.

He would balance the tray one-handed on steepled fingers, like a regular waiter. He would take his keys off his belt. He would unlock the gate and slide it open with his toe. His holster was empty. No gun. Standard practice everywhere in the world. No prison guard was ever armed. To carry a loaded weapon among locked-up prisoners would be just asking for trouble. He would step into the cell. He would hook his keys back on his belt and juggle the tray back into two hands. He would turn away, toward the concrete desk.

Which relative positioning would offer a number of different opportunities.

Reacher waited.

But no.

The kid was the kind of rookie who got his car stolen, but he wasn't totally dumb. He put the tray on the floor outside the cell, just temporarily, and he took the coffee pot off it, and the cup and saucer, and he placed them all on the tile on the wrong side of the bars, and then he picked up the tray again and fed it through the slot. Reacher took it. To get a drink, he would have to put his wrists between the bars and pour on the outside. The cup would fit back through. Maybe not on its saucer, but then, he wasn't dining at The Ritz.

The kid said, "There you go."

Not totally dumb.

"Thanks," Reacher said anyway. "I appreciate it."

The kid said, "Enjoy."

Reacher didn't. The pie was bad and the coffee was weak.

An hour later a different uniform came by to collect the empties. The night watch. Reacher said, "I need to see Detective Aaron."

The new guy said, "He isn't here. He went home."

"Get him back. Right now. It's important."

The guy didn't answer.

Reacher said, "If he finds out I asked but you didn't

call him, he'll kick your ass. Or take your shield. I hear there are budget issues. My advice would be don't give him an excuse."

"What's this all about?"

"A notch on his belt."

"You going to confess?"

"Maybe."

"You're a state prisoner. We're county. We don't care what you did."

"Call him anyway."

The guy didn't answer. Just carried the tray away and closed the steel door behind him.

The guy must have made the call, because Aaron showed up ninety minutes later. About halfway through the evening. He was wearing the same suit. He looked neither eager nor annoyed. Just neutral. Maybe a little curious. He looked in through the bars.

He said, "What do you want?"

Reacher said, "To talk about the case."

"It's a state matter."

"Not if it was a simple mugging."

"It wasn't."

"You believe that?"

"It was a credible way to beat surveillance."

"What about me as the second secret ingredient?"

"That's credible, too."

"It would have been a miracle of coordination. Wouldn't it? Exactly the right place, at exactly the right time."

"You could have been waiting there for hours."

"But was I? What do your witnesses say?"

Aaron didn't reply.

Reacher said, "Check the timing on the tape. You and me talking. Picture the sequence. Delaney got a hard-on for me because of something he heard."

Aaron nodded. "Your lawyer already passed that on. The homeless patsy. Didn't convince me then, doesn't convince me now."

"Beyond a reasonable doubt?" Reacher asked.

"I'm a detective. Reasonable doubt is for the jury."

"You happy for an innocent man to go to prison?"

"Guilt and innocence are for the jury."

"Suppose I get acquitted? You happy to see your case go down in flames?"

"Not my case. It's a state matter."

Reacher said, "Listen to the tape again. Time it out."

"I can't," Aaron said. "There is no tape."

"You told me there was."

"We're the county police. We can't record a state interview. Not our jurisdiction. So the recording was discontinued."

"It was before that. When you and I were talking."

"That part got screwed up. The previous stuff got erased when the recording was stopped."

"It got?"

"Accidents happen."

"Who pressed the stop button?"

Aaron didn't answer.

"Who was it?" Reacher said.

"Delaney," Aaron said. "When he took over from me. He apologized. He said he wasn't familiar with our equipment."

"You believed him?"

"Why wouldn't I?"

Reacher said nothing.

"Accidents happen," Aaron said again.

"You sure it was an accident? You sure they weren't making a silk purse out of a pig's ear? You sure they weren't covering their tracks?"

Aaron said nothing.

Reacher said, "You never saw such a thing happen?"

"What do you want me to say? He's a fellow cop."

"So am I."

"You were, once upon a time. Now you're just a guy passing by."

"One day you will be, too. You want all these years to count for nothing?"

Aaron didn't answer.

Reacher said, "Right back at the beginning you told me juries don't always like police testimony. Why would that be? Are those juries always wrong?"

No response.

Reacher said, "Can't you remember what we said on the tape?"

"Even if I could, it would be my word against the state. And it ain't exactly a smoking gun, is it?"

Reacher said nothing. Aaron gazed through the bars a minute more, and then he left again.

Reacher lay on his back on the narrow bed with one elbow jammed against the wall and his head resting on his cupped hand. *Check the timing on the tape,* he had said. He ran through what he remembered of his first conversation with Aaron. In the green bunker-like room. The witness statement. The preamble. Name, date of birth, Social Security number. Then his address. No fixed abode, and so on and so forth. He pictured Delaney listening in. A tinny loudspeaker in another room. *In other words you're homeless,* Aaron had said. Delaney had heard him say it. Loud and clear. How long did he take to spot his opportunity and come barging in?

Too long, Reacher thought.

There had been the bravura bullshit about PTSD and the 110th, and some lengthy dickering from Aaron about whether his testimony would be helpful or hurtful, and then the testimony itself, careful, composed, coherent, detailed, clear, and slow. Then the private chat afterward. After Bush had left the room. The speculation, and the semantic analysis backing it up. *You said, Thank you very much for helping us out with that.* And so on. All that stuff. Altogether seven minutes, maybe. Or eight, or nine.

Or ten.

Too much time.

Delaney had reacted to something else.

Something he heard later.

At ten o'clock in Reacher's head there was the heavy tramp of footsteps in the corridor outside the steel door. The door opened and people came in. Six of them. Different uniforms. State police. Prisoner escorts. They had Mace and pepper spray and Tasers on their belts.

Handcuffs and shackles and thin metal chains. They knew what they were doing. They made Reacher back up against the bars and stick his hands out behind him, through the meal slot. They cuffed his wrists, and held tight to the link, and squatted down and put their hands in through the bars, the same way he had poured his coffee, but in reverse. They put shackles around his ankles, and linked them together, and ran a chain up to his handcuffs. Then they unlocked his gate and slid it open. He shuffled out, small clinking steps, and they stopped him at the booking desk, where they retrieved his possessions from a drawer. His passport, his ATM card, his toothbrush, his seventy bucks in bills, his seventy-five cents in quarters, and his shoelaces. They put them all in a khaki envelope and sealed the flap. Then they escorted him out of the cell block, three ahead, three behind. They walked him around the dog-leg corners, under the low concrete ceilings, and out to the lot. There was a gray-painted school bus with wire on the windows parked next to the wrecked SUV in the far corner. They pushed him inside and planted him on a bench seat in back. There were no other passengers. One guy drove and the other five sat close together up front.

They got to Warren just before midnight. The prison was visible from a mile away, with bright pools of arc light showing through the mist. The bus waited at the gate, idling with a heavy diesel clatter, and spotlights played over it, and the gate ground open, and the bus drove inside. It waited again for a second gate, and then shut down in a brightly lit space near an iron door marked *Prisoner Intake*. Reacher was led through it, and down the right-hand spur of a Y-shaped junction, to the holding pen for inmates as yet unconvicted. His cuffs and chains and shackles were removed. His possessions in their khaki envelope were filed away, and he was issued with a white jumpsuit uniform and blue shower shoes. He was led to a cell more or less identical to the one he had just left. The gate was slid shut, and the key was turned. His escort left, and a minute later the light clicked off and the block was plunged into noisy and restless darkness.

The lights came back on at six in the morning. Reacher heard a guard in the corridor, unlocking one gate after another. Eventually the guy showed up at Reacher's door. He was a mean-looking man about thirty. He said, "Go get your breakfast now."

Breakfast was in a large low room that smelled of boiled food and disinfectant. Reacher lined up with about twelve other guys. The kid in the black sweatshirt was not among them. Still in Bangor, Reacher figured, at the state DEA's office. Maybe talking, maybe not. Reacher arrived at the serving station and got a spoonful of bright yellow mush that might have been scrambled eggs, served on a slice of what might have been white bread, with a melamine mug half-full of what might have been coffee. Or the water left over from washing the previous night's dishes. He sat on a bench at an empty table and ate. The inmates all around him were a mixed bunch, mostly squirrelly and furtive. The back part of Reacher's brain ran an automatic threat assessment, and found nothing much to worry about, unless tooth decay was contagious.

When breakfast was over they were all corralled out for a compulsory hour of early-morning exercise. The jail part of the installation was much smaller than the prison part, and therefore it had a correspondingly smaller yard, about the size of a basketball court, separated from the general population by a high wire fence. The fence had a gate with a bolt but no lock. The guard who had led them out took up station in front of it. Beyond him a wan spring dawn was coming up in the sky.

The bigger part of the yard was full of men in jumpsuits of a different color. Hundreds of them. They were milling about in groups. Some of them looked like desperate characters. One of them was a huge guy about six-seven and three hundred pounds. Like a caricature of an old Maine lumberjack. All he needed was a plaid wool shirt and a two-headed axe. He was bigger than Reacher, which was a statistical rarity. He was twenty feet away, looking in through the wire. Looking at Reacher. Reacher looked back. Eye to eye. The guy came closer. Reacher kept on looking. Dangerous etiquette, in prison. But looking away was a slippery slope. Too submissive. Better to get any kind of hierarchy issues straightened out right from the get-go. Human nature. Reacher knew how these things worked.

The guy stepped close to the fence.

He said, "What are you looking at?"

A standard gambit. Old as the hills. Reacher was supposed to get all intimidated and say *nothing*. Whereupon the guy would say *you calling me nothing?* Whereupon things would go from bad to worse. Best avoided.

So Reacher said, "I'm looking at you, asshole."

"What did you call me?"

"An asshole."

"You're dead."

"Not yet," Reacher said. "Not the last time I checked."

At which exact moment a big commotion started up in the far corner of the big yard. Later Reacher realized it was precisely timed. Whispers and signals had been passed through the population, diagonally, man to man. There was distant shouting and yelling and fighting. Searchlights sparked up in the towers and swung in that direction. Radios crackled. Everyone rushed over. Including the guards. Including the guard at the small yard's gate. He slipped through and ran into the crowd.

Whereupon the big guy moved the opposite way. In through the unattended gate. Into the smaller yard. Straight toward Reacher. Not a pretty sight. Black shower shoes, no socks, an orange jumpsuit stretched tight over bulging muscles.

Then it got worse.

The guy snapped his arm like a whip and a weapon appeared in his hand. From up his sleeve. A prison shiv. Clear plastic. Maybe a toothbrush handle sharpened on a stone, maybe six inches long. Like a stiletto. A third of its length was wrapped with surgical tape. For grip. Not good.

Reacher kicked off his shower shoes.

The big guy did the same.

Reacher said, "All my life I've had a rule. You pull a knife on me, I break your arms."

The big guy said nothing.

Reacher said, "It's completely inflexible, I'm afraid. I can't make an exception just because you're a moron."

The big guy stepped closer.

The other men in the yard stepped back. Reacher heard the fence clink as they pressed up tight against it. He heard the distant riot still happening. Manufactured, therefore a little halfhearted. Couldn't last forever. The searchlights would soon swing back. The guards would regroup and return. All he had to do was wait.

Not his way.

"Last chance," he said. "Drop the weapon, and get down on the ground. Or I'll hurt you real bad."

He used his MP voice, honed over the years to a thing of chill and dread, all floating on the unhinged psycho menace he had been as a kid, brawling in back streets all over the world. He saw a flicker of something in the big guy's eyes. But nothing more. Wasn't going to work. He was going to have to fight it out.

Which he was suddenly very happy about.

Because now he knew.

Ten minutes of your time. You saw what you saw.

He didn't like knives.

He said, "Come on, fat boy. Show me what you got."

The guy stepped in, rotating on the way, leading with the shiv. Reacher feinted to his left, and the shiv jerked in that direction, so Reacher swayed back to his right, inside the trajectory, and aimed his left hand inside-out for the guy's wrist, but mistimed it a little and caught the guy's hand instead, which was like gripping a softball, and he pulled on it, which turned the guy more, and he slammed a triple right jab to the guy's face, *bang bang bang,* a blur, all the while crushing the guy's right hand as hard as possible, shiv and all. The guy pulled back, and the sweat on Reacher's palm greased his exit, until Reacher had nothing but the shiv in his grip, which was OK, because it was a pick not a blade, sharp only at the point, and it was plastic, so Reacher put the ball of his thumb where the tape ended and snapped it like turning a door handle.

So far so good. At that point, about three seconds in, Reacher saw his main problem as how the hell he was going to make good on his promise to break the guy's arms. They were huge. They were thicker than most people's legs. They were sheathed and knotted with slabs of muscle.

Then it got worse again.

The guy was bleeding from the nose and the mouth, but the damage seemed only to energize him. He braced and roared like the kind of guy Reacher had seen on strongman shows on afternoon cable in motel rooms. Like he was psyching himself up to pull a semi truck in a harness or lift up a rock the size of a Volkswagen. He was going to charge like a water buffalo. He was going to knock Reacher down and pummel him on the ground.

The lack of shoes didn't help. Kicking barefoot was

strictly for the health club or the Olympic Games. Rubbery shower shoes were worse than none at all. Which Reacher supposed was the point of making prisoners wear them. So kicking the guy was off the menu. Which was a sad limitation. But knees would still work, and elbows.

The guy charged, roaring, arms wide as if he wanted to catch Reacher in a bear hug. So Reacher charged, too. Straight back at him. It was the only real alternative. A collision could be a wonderful thing. Depending on what hit who first. In this case the answers were Reacher's forearm and the big guy's upper lip. Like a wreck on the highway. Like two trucks crashing head-on. Like getting the guy to punch himself in the head.

The prison sirens blared to life.

Big picture. What did you see?

The searchlights swung back. The riot was over. The prison yard went suddenly quiet. The big guy couldn't resist. Human nature. He wanted to look. He wanted to know. He turned his head. Just a tiny spasm. An instinct, instantly crushed.

But enough. Reacher hit him on the ear. All the time in the world. Like hitting a speedball hanging down from a tree. And no one has muscles on his ear. All ears are pretty much equal. The smallest bones in the body are right there. Plus all kinds of mechanisms for maintaining balance. Without which you fall over.

The guy went down hard.

The searchlights hit the fence.

Reacher took the big guy's hand. As if to help him

up. But no. Then as if to shake respectfully, and congratulate him warmly on a valiant defeat.

Not that, either.

Reacher drove the broken shiv through the guy's palm, and left it sticking out both sides, and then he stepped away and mingled with the others by the door. A second later a searchlight beam came to rest on the guy. The sirens changed their note, to lockdown.

Reacher waited in his cell. He expected the wait to be short. He was the obvious suspect. The others from the small yard were half the big guy's size. So the guards would come to him first. Probably. Which could be a problem. Because technically a crime had been committed. Some would say. Others would say offense was the best kind of self-defense, which was still mostly legal. Purely a question of interpretation.

It would be a delicate argument to make.

What's the worst thing could happen?

He waited.

He heard boots in the corridor. Two guards came straight to his cell. Mace and pepper spray and Tasers on their belts. Handcuffs and shackles and thin metal chains.

One said, "Stand by to turn around on command and stick your wrists out through the meal slot."

Reacher said, "Where are we going?"

"You'll find out."

"I'd appreciate sooner rather than later."

"And I'd appreciate half a chance to use my Taser. Which one of us is going to get what he wants today?"

Reacher said, "I guess neither would be best for both of us."

"I agree," the guy said. "Let's work hard to keep it that way."

"I still want to know."

The guy said, "You're going back where you came from. You have your arraignment this morning. You have half an hour with your lawyer beforehand. So put your street clothes on. You're innocent until you're proven guilty. You're supposed to look the part. Or we ain't being constitutional. Or some such thing. They say jail uniforms look like you're already guilty. That's where prejudice comes from, you know. The judicial system. It's right there in the word."

He led Reacher out of the cell, small clinking steps, and his partner crowded in from behind, and they met a team of two state prisoner escorts, in an airlock lobby, halfway in and halfway out of the place, where responsibility was handed over from one team to the other, who then led Reacher onward, out to a gray prison bus, the same kind of thing he had ridden in on. He was pushed down the aisle and dumped on the rearmost bench. One of the escorts got in behind the wheel to drive, and the other sat sideways behind him with a shotgun in his lap.

They retraced the journey Reacher had made in the opposite direction less than twelve hours previously. They covered every yard of the same pavement. The two escorts talked all the way. Reacher heard some of the conversation. It depended on the engine note. Some of the words were lost. But he got plenty of gossip about the big guy found knocked down in the small yard that morning. No one was yet implicated in the incident. Because no one could understand it. The big guy was a month away from his first parole hearing. Why would he fight? And if he didn't fight, who would fight him? Who would fight him and win and drag him back to the small yard like some kind of trophy?

They shook their heads.

Reacher said nothing.

The drive back took the same duration, just shy of two hours, the same night and day, because their speed was not limited by visibility or traffic, but by a slow-revving engine and a short gearbox, good for stopping and starting in cities and towns, but not so good for the open road. But eventually they pulled into the lot Reacher recognized, next to the stove-in wreck of the blue SUV, and Reacher was beckoned down the aisle, and off the bus, and in through the same concrete door he had come out of. Inside was a lobby, lockable both ends, where his chains and cuffs were taken off, and where he was handed over to a two-person welcoming committee.

One person was Detective Bush.

The other person was the public defender, Cathy Clark.

The two prisoner escorts turned around and left double quick. Anxious to get going. Back later. Couldn't keep a bus standing idle. They gave the impression they had many different jobs that day. Many bits and pieces. Maybe they did. Or maybe they liked a long lazy lunch. Maybe they knew somewhere good to go.

Reacher was left alone with Bush and the lawyer.

Just for a second.

He thought, *You got to be kidding me.*

He tapped Bush high on the chest, just a polite warning to the solar plexus, like a wake-up call, enough to cause a helpless buzzing in all kinds of retaliatory muscles, but no real pain anywhere else. Reacher stuck his hand in Bush's pocket and came out with car keys. He put them in his own pocket, and shoved the guy in the chest, quite gently, as considerately as possible, just enough to send him staggering backward a pace or two.

Reacher didn't touch the lawyer at all. Just pushed past her and walked away, head up and confident, under the low ceilings, through the dogleg corridors, and out through the front door. He went straight to Bush's car, in the D2 slot. The Crown Vic. Worn but not sagging, clean but not shiny. It started first time. It was already warmed up. The prisoner escorts were already beyond it. They were on their way to their bus. They didn't look back.

Reacher took off, just as the first few *wait a damn minute* faces started showing at doors and windows. He turned right and left and left again, on random streets, aiming at first for what passed for downtown. The first squad car was more than two whole minutes behind him. Starting out from the station house itself. A disgrace. Others were worse. It was not the county police department's finest five minutes.

They didn't find him.

Reacher called on the phone, just before lunch. From a pay phone. The town still had plenty. Cell reception was poor. Reacher had quarters, from under café tables. Always a few. Enough for local calls at least. He had the number, from a business card pinned up behind the register in a five-and-dime even cheaper than the dollar stores. The card was one of many, as if together they made a defensive shield. It was from Detective Ramsey Aaron, of the county police department. With a phone number and an e-mail address. Maybe some kind of neighborhood outreach. Modern police did all kinds of new things.

Evidently the number on the card rang through to Aaron's desk. He answered first ring.

He said, "This is Aaron."

Reacher said, "This is Reacher."

"Why are you calling me?"

"To tell you two things."

"But why me?"

"Because you might listen."

"Where are you?"

"I'm a long way out of town by now. You're never going to see me again. I'm afraid your uniformed division let you down badly."

"You should give yourself up, man."

"That was the first thing," Reacher said. "That ain't going to happen. We need to get that straight from the get-go. Or we'll waste a lot of energy on the back-and-forth. You'll never find me. So don't even try. Just give it up gracefully. Spend your time on the second thing instead."

"Was that you at the prison? With the parolee that got beat up?"

"Why would a parolee be in prison?"

"What's the second thing?"

"You need to find out exactly who the girl with the bag was, and exactly who the kid in the sweatshirt was. Names and histories. And exactly what was in the bag."

"Why?"

"Because before you tell me, I'm going to tell you. When you see I'm right, maybe you'll start paying attention."

"Who are they?"

Reacher said, "I'll call again later."

He was in the diner down the block. Where his lunch and his dinner had come from. The safest place to be, amid all the panic. No one in there had ever seen him before. No cop was going to come in for a coffee break. Not right then. Out of the question. And the police station was the eye of the storm, which meant for a block all around the squad cars were either accelerating hard to get away and go search some other distant place, or braking hard as they came back in again, all negative and disappointed and frustrated. In other words there was visual drama and emotion, but therefore not very much patient looking out through the car windows at the immediate neighborhood surroundings.

The phone was on the wall of a corridor in the back of the diner, with restrooms left and right, and a fire door at the end. Reacher hung up and walked back to his table. He was one of six people sitting alone in the shadows. No one paid him attention. He got the feeling strangers were not rare. At least as a concept. There were old photographs on the wall. Plus old-time artifacts hung up on display. The town had been in the lumber business. Fortunes had been made. People had been in and out constantly for a hundred years, hauling loads, selling tools, putting on all kinds of mock outrage about prices.

Maybe some part of the town was still working. A lone sawmill here or there. Maybe some people were still coming by. Not many, but enough. Certainly no one stared in the diner. No one hid behind a newspaper and surreptitiously dialed a phone.

Reacher waited.

He called again, a random number of minutes after the first hour had gone by. He cupped his hand over his mouth, so the background noise wouldn't sound the same twice. He wanted them to think he was always on the move. If they thought he wasn't, they would start to ask themselves where he was holed up, and Aaron seemed a smart enough guy to figure it out. He could step right in and pull up a chair.

The phone was answered on the first ring.

Aaron said, "This is Aaron."

Reacher said, "You need to ask yourself a transportation question. Six guys took me to Warren last night. But only two guys brought me back this morning. Six guys was a lot of overtime in one evening. Overkill, some might say, for one prisoner in a bus. Especially when budgets are an issue. So why did it happen that way?"

"You were an unknown quantity. Better safe than sorry."

"Then why didn't I get the same six guys again this morning? They don't know me any better now than they did last night."

Aaron said, "I'm sure you're going to tell me why."

"Two possibilities. Not really competing. Kind of interlinked."

"Show me."

"They really, really wanted to get me there last night. It was important I went. My lawyer put in a reasonable request. They said no. They signed off on an unnecessary round-trip that did nothing but waste gas and man-hours. They assigned six guys to make sure I got there safe and sound."

"And?"

"They didn't expect me to leave again this morning. So they didn't assign escorts. So when it came to it they had to scramble an odd-job crew who already had a bunch of other stuff to do today."

"That doesn't make sense. Everyone expected you to leave again this morning. For the arraignment. Standard procedure. Common knowledge."

"So why the scramble?"

"I don't know."

"They weren't expecting me to leave."

"They knew you had to."

"Not if I was in a coma in the hospital. Or dead in the morgue. Which normally would be a surprise event. But they knew well in advance. They didn't arrange round-trip transportation."

Aaron paused a beat.

He said, "It was you up at the prison."

Reacher said, "The guy didn't even know me. We had never crossed paths before. Yet he came straight for me. While his pals staged a diversion far away. He was coming up for parole. My guess is Delaney was the guy who busted him, way back in the day. Am I right?"

"Yes, as it happens."

"So they made a deal. If the big guy took care of me, under the radar, then Delaney would speak up for him at his parole board hearing. He would say he was a reformed character. Who better to know than the arresting officer? People assume some kind of a mystical connection. Parole boards love all that shit. The guy would have walked. Except he didn't get the job done. He underestimated his opponent. Possibly he was badly briefed."

"You're admitting felony assault."

"You'll never find me. I could be in California tomorrow."

Aaron said, "Tell me who the girl was. And the boy in the sweatshirt. Show me you know what you're talking about here."

"The boy and the girl were both stooges. Both blackmailed into playing a part. Probably the girl had just gotten busted. Maybe her second time. Maybe even her first. By the state DEA. By Delaney. She thinks he's making up his mind about whether to drop it. He proposes a deal. All she has to do is carry a bag. He proposes a similar deal to the boy. A minor bust could go away. He could get back to Yale or Harvard or wherever he's from with his record unblemished. Daddy need never know. All he has to do is run a little and grab a bag. The boy and the girl don't know each other. They're from different cases. Am I right so far?"

Aaron said, "What was in the bag?"

"I'm sure the official report says it was either meth or Oxycontin or money. One or the other. A delivery, or a payment."

"It was money," Aaron said. "It was a payment."

"How much?"

"Thirty thousand dollars."

"Except it wasn't. Think about it. What makes me exactly the same as the boy and the girl, and what makes me completely different?"

"I'm sure you're going to tell me."

"Three people in the world could testify that bag was empty all along. The girl and the boy, because they had to carry it, so they knew it was light as a feather, and then later me, because it sailed up in the air a yard from my face, and I could see there was nothing in it. It was obvious."

"How are you different?"

"He controls the boy and the girl. But he doesn't control me. I'm a wild card running around in public saying the bag was empty. That's what he heard. On the tape. That's what he reacted to. He couldn't let me say that. No one else was supposed to know the bag was empty. It could ruin everything. So he deleted the tape and then he tried to delete me."

"You're arguing ahead of the facts."

"That's why he asked how people get ahold of me. He found out he could put me in a potter's field and no one would ever know."

"You're speculating."

"There's only one way this thing works. Delaney stole the thirty grand. He knew it was coming through. He's DEA. He thought he could get away with it if he staged a freak accident. I mean, accidents happen, right? Like if your house sets on fire, and the money is all in the sofa. It's an operating loss. It's a rounding error. It's the cost of doing business for these guys. They don't trust their mothers, but they know that shit happens eventually. One time I read in the paper where some guy lost nearly a million dollars, all eaten up by mice in his basement. So Delaney figured he could get away with it. Without getting his legs broken. All he had to do was put on a bold face and stick to his story."

"Wait," Aaron said. "None of that makes sense."

"Unless."

"That's ridiculous."

"Say it out loud. See how ridiculous it sounds."

"None of that makes sense, because OK, Delaney might know thirty grand is coming through, but how does he get access to it? How does he dictate who carries what in a bag? And when and where and by which route?"

"Unless," Reacher said again.

"This is crazy."

"Say it."

"Unless Delaney is walking on the dark side of the street."

"Don't hide behind flowery language. Say it out loud."

"Unless Delaney is himself a link in the chain."

"Still kind of flowery."

"Unless Delaney is secretly a drug dealer as well as a DEA agent."

"Thirty grand might be about right for the kind of franchise fee he has to pay. For the kind of dealer he is. Which is not big. But not small-time, either. Probably medium-sized, with a relatively civilized clientele. The work is easy. He's well placed to help himself out with legal problems. He makes a decent living from it. Better than his pension is going to be. It was all good. But even so, he started to get greedy. This time he wanted to keep all the money for himself. He only pretended to pass along his boss's share. The bag was empty from the get-go. But no one would know that. The police report would list thirty grand missing. Any gossip about what eyewitnesses saw would make it sound exactly like a freak robbery. His boss might write it off as genuine. Maybe Delaney planned to do it once a year. Kind of randomly. As an extra little margin."

"Still makes no sense," Aaron said. "Why would the bag be empty? He would have used a wad of cut-up newspaper."

"I don't think so," Reacher said. "Suppose the kid had blown it? Suppose he missed the tackle? Or chickened out beforehand. The girl might have gotten all the way through. The real people might have taken the bag. Newspaper would be hard to explain. It's the kind of thing that could sour a relationship. Whereas an empty bag could be claimed as reconnaissance. A dry run, looking for surveillance. An excess of caution. The bad guys couldn't complain about that. Maybe they even expect it. Like employee of the month competitions."

Aaron said nothing.

Reacher said, "I'll call again soon," and he hung up the phone.

This time he moved on. He went out the back of the diner, and across one exposed street corner, and into an alley between what might once have been elegant furniture showrooms. He scouted out a phone on the back wall of a franchise tire shop. Maybe where you called a cab, if the shop didn't have the right tires.

He backed into a doorway, and waited. The police station was now two blocks away. He could still hear cars driving in and out. Speed and urgency. He gave it thirty more minutes. Then he headed for the tire shop. For the phone on the wall. But before he got there a guy came out the back of the building. From where the customers waited for their cars, on mismatched chairs, with a pay machine for coffee. The guy had buzzed hair and a blue sport coat over a checked shirt, with tan chino pants below.

The guy had a Glock in his hand.

From his shoulder holster.

Delaney.

Who pointed the gun and said, "Stop walking."

Reacher stopped walking.

Delaney said, "You're not as smart as you think."

Reacher said nothing.

Delaney said, "You were in the police station. You saw how basic it was. You gambled they couldn't trace a pay phone location in real time. So you talked as long as you wanted."

"Was I right?"

"The county can't do it. But the state can. I knew where you were. From the start. You made a mistake."

"That's always a theoretical possibility."

"You made one mistake after another."

"Or did I? Because think about it for a minute. From my point of view. First I told you where I was, and then I gave you time to get here. I had to hang around for hours. But never mind. Because here you are. Finally. Maybe I'm exactly as smart as I think."

"You wanted me here?"

"Face to face is always better."

"You know I'm going to shoot you."

"But not yet. First you need to know what I said to Aaron. Because I gambled again. I figured you would know where the phone was, but I figured you couldn't tap in and listen. Not instantly and randomly anywhere in the state. Not without warrants and subpoenas. You don't have that kind of power. Not yet. So you knew about the call but you didn't hear the conversation. Now you need to know how much more damage control will be necessary. You hope none at all. Because getting rid of Aaron will be a lot harder than me. You'd rather not do it. But you need to know."

"Well?"

Reacher said, "Let's talk about county police technology. Just for a moment. I was safe as long as I was talking. They're basic, but it's not exactly the Stone Age in there. At least they can get the number after the call is over. Surely. They can find out who owns it. Maybe they even recognize it. I know they call that diner from time to time."

"So?"

"So my guess is Aaron knew where I was pretty early. But he's a smart guy. He knows why I'm yapping. He knows how long it takes to drive from Bangor. So he sits tight for an hour or two, just to see what comes out of the woodwork. Why not? What's he got to lose? What's the worst thing could happen? And then you show up. A crazy theory is proved right."

"You saying you got reinforcements here? I don't see any."

"Aaron knew I was in the diner. Now he knows I'm a block or two away. It's all about where the pay phones are. I'm sure he figured that out pretty early. My guess is he's watching us right now. His whole squad is watching us, probably. Lots of people. It's not just you and me, Delaney. There are lots of people here."

"What is this? Some kind of psy-ops bullshit?"

"It's what you said. It's a gamble. Aaron is a smart guy. He could have picked me up hours ago. But he didn't. Because he wanted to see what would happen next. He's been watching for hours. He's watching right now. Or, maybe he isn't. Because maybe he's actually a dumb guy all along. Except did he look dumb to you? That's the gamble. I have to tell you, personally,

I'm betting on smart. My professional advice would be close your mouth and lie down on the ground. There are witnesses everywhere."

Delaney glanced left, at the back of the tire shop. Then right, at the derelict showroom. Ahead, at the narrow alley between. Doors and windows all around, and shadows.

He said, "There's no one here."

Reacher said, "Only one way to be sure."

"Which is?"

"Back up to one of the windows and see if someone grabs you."

"I ain't doing that."

"Why not? You said no one is here."

Delaney didn't answer.

"Time to cast your vote," Reacher said. "Is Aaron smart or dumb?"

"He's going to see me shoot a fugitive. Doesn't matter if he's smart or dumb. As long as he spells my name right, I'll get a medal."

"I'm not a fugitive. He sent Bush and the lawyer to meet me. It was an invitation. No one chased after me. He wanted me gone. He wanted some bait in the water."

Delaney paused a beat.

He glanced left. Glanced right.

He said, "You're full of shit."

"That's always a theoretical possibility."

Reacher said nothing more. Delaney glanced all around. Old brick, gone rotten from soot and rain. Doorways. And windows. Some glassed and whole, some punched out and ragged, some just blind holes in the wall, with no frames left at all.

One such was on the ground floor of the nearby derelict showroom. Chest-high above the sidewalk. About nine feet away. A little behind Delaney's left shoulder. It was a textbook position. The infantry would love it. It commanded most of the block.

Delaney glanced back at it.

He edged toward it, crabwise, his gun still on Reacher, but looking back over his shoulder. He got close, and he sidled the last short distance, diagonally, craning backward, trying to keep an eye on Reacher, trying to catch a glimpse inside the room, both at once.

He arrived at the window. Still facing Reacher. Backing up. Glancing over his shoulders, left and right. Seeing nothing.

He turned around. Fast, like the start of a quick there-and-back glance. For a second he was face-on to the building. He went up on his toes, and he put his palms on the sill, Glock and all, temporarily awkward, and he levered himself up as high as he could and he bent forward and stuck his head inside for a look.

A long arm grabbed him by the neck and reeled him in. A second arm grabbed his gun hand. A third arm grabbed his coat collar and tumbled him over the sill into the darkness inside.

Reacher waited in the diner, with coffee and pie all paid for by the county police department. Two hours later the rookie uniform came in. He had driven to Warren to get the khaki envelope with Reacher's stuff in it. His passport, his ATM card, his toothbrush, his seventy bucks in bills, his seventy-five cents in quarters, and his shoelaces. The kid accounted for it all and handed it over.

Then he said, "They found the thirty grand. It was in Delaney's freezer at home. Wrapped up in aluminum foil and labeled steak."

Then he left, and Reacher laced his shoes again and tied them off. He put his stuff in his pockets and drained his cup and stood up to go.

Aaron came in the door.

He said, "Are you leaving?"

Reacher said yes, he was.

"Where are you going?"

Reacher said he had no idea at all.

"Will you sign a witness statement?"

Reacher said no, he wouldn't.

"Even if I ask you nicely?"

Reacher said no, not even then.

Then Aaron asked, "What would you have done if I hadn't put guys in that window?"

Reacher said, "He was nervous by that point. He was about to make mistakes. Opportunities would have presented themselves. I'm sure I would have thought of something."

"In other words you had nothing. You were gambling everything on me being a good cop."

"Don't make a whole big thing out of it," Reacher said. "Truth is, I figured it would be about fifty-fifty at best."

He walked out of the diner, away from town, to a left-right choice on a county road, north or south,

Canada one way and New Hampshire the other. He chose New Hampshire and stuck out his thumb. Eight minutes later he was in a Subaru, listening to a guy talk about the pills he got to ease his back. Nothing like them. Best thing ever, the guy said.

Second Son

1

On a hot August Thursday in 1974, an old man in Paris did something he had never done before: he woke up in the morning, but he didn't get out of bed. He couldn't. His name was Laurent Moutier, and he had felt pretty bad for ten days and really lousy for seven. His arms and legs felt thin and weak and his chest felt like it was full of setting concrete. He knew what was happening. He had been a furniture repairman by trade, and he had become what customers sometimes brought him: a wormy old heirloom weakened and rotted beyond hope. There was no single thing wrong with him. Everything was failing all at once. Nothing to be done. Inevitable. So he lay patient and wheezing and waited for his housekeeper.

She came in at ten o'clock and showed no great shock or surprise. Most of her clients were old, and they came and went with regularity. She called the doctor, and at one point, clearly in answer to a question about his age, Moutier heard her say "Ninety," in a re-signed yet satisfied way, a way that spoke volumes, as if it was a whole paragraph in one word. It reminded him of standing in his workshop, breathing dust and glue and varnish, looking at some abject crumbly cabinet and saying, "Well now, let's see," when really his mind had already moved on to getting rid of it.

A house call was arranged for later in the day, but then as if to confirm the unspoken diagnosis the housekeeper asked Moutier for his address book, so she could call his immediate family. Moutier had an address book but no immediate family beyond his only daughter, Josephine, but even so she filled most of the book by herself, because she moved a lot. Page after page was full of crossed-out box numbers and long strange foreign phone numbers. The housekeeper dialed the last of them and heard the whine and echo of great distances, and then she heard a voice speaking English, a language she couldn't understand, so she hung up again. Moutier saw her dither for a moment, but then as if to confirm the diagnosis once again, she left in search of the retired schoolteacher two floors below, a soft old man who Moutier usually dismissed as practically a cretin, but then, how good did a linguist need to be to translate *ton père va mourir* into *your dad is going to die*?

The housekeeper came back with the schoolteacher, both of them pink and flushed from the stairs, and the guy dialed the same long number over again, and asked to speak to Josephine Moutier.

"No, *Reacher*, you idiot," Moutier said in a voice

that should have been a roar, but in fact came out as a breathy tubercular plea. "Her married name is Reacher. They won't know who Josephine Moutier is."

The schoolteacher apologized and corrected himself and asked for Josephine Reacher. He listened for a moment and covered the receiver with his palm and looked at Moutier and asked, "What's her husband's name? Your son-in-law?"

"Stan," Moutier said. "Not Stanley, either. Just Stan. Stan is on his birth certificate. I saw it. He's Captain Stan Reacher, of the United States Marine Corps."

The schoolteacher relayed that information and listened again. Then he hung up. He turned and said, "They just left. Really just days ago, apparently. The whole family. Captain Reacher has been posted elsewhere."

2

The retired schoolteacher in Paris had been talking to a duty lieutenant at the Navy base on Guam in the Pacific, where Stan Reacher had been deployed for three months as Marine Corps liaison. That pleasant posting had come to an end and he had been sent to Okinawa. His family had followed three days later, on a passenger plane via Manila, his wife Josephine and his two sons, fifteen-year-old Joe and thirteen-year-old Jack. Josephine Reacher was a bright, spirited, energetic woman, at forty-four still curious about the world and happy to be seeing so much of it, still tolerant of the ceaseless moves and the poor accommodations. Joe Reacher at fifteen was already almost full grown, already well over six feet and well over two hundred pounds, a giant next to his mother, but still quiet and studious, still very much Clark Kent, not Superman. Jack Reacher at thirteen looked like an engineer's napkin sketch for something even bigger and even more ambitious, his huge bony frame like the scaffolding around a major construction project. Six more inches and a final eighty pounds of beef would finish the job, and they were all on their way. He had big hands and watchful eyes. He was quiet like his brother, but not studious. Unlike his brother he was always called by his last name only. No one knew why, but the family was Stan and Josie, Joe and Reacher, and it always had been.

Stan met his family off the plane at the Futenma air station and they took a taxi to a bungalow he had found half a mile from the beach. It was hot and still inside and it fronted on a narrow concrete street with ditches either side. The street was dead straight and lined with small houses set close together, and at the end of it was a blue patch of ocean. By that point the family had lived in maybe forty different places, and the move-in routine was second nature. The boys found the second bedroom and it was up to them to decide whether it needed cleaning. If so, they cleaned it themselves, and if not, they didn't. In this case, as usual, Joe found something to worry about, and Reacher found nothing. So he left Joe to it, and he headed for the kitchen, where first he got a drink of water, and then he got the bad news.

3

Reacher's parents were side by side at the kitchen counter, studying a letter his mother had carried all the way from Guam. Reacher had seen the envelope. It was something to do with the education system. His mother said, "You and Joe have to take a test before you start school here."

Reacher said, "Why?"

"Placement," his father said. "They need to know how well you're doing."

"Tell them we're doing fine. Tell them thanks, but no thanks."

"For what?"

"I'm happy where I am. I don't need to skip a grade. I'm sure Joe feels the same."

"You think this is about skipping a grade?"

"Isn't it?"

"No," his father said. "It's about holding you back a grade."

"Why would they do that?"

"New policy," his mother said. "You've had very fragmented schooling. They need to check you're ready to advance."

"They never did that before."

"That's why it's called a new policy. As opposed to an old policy."

"They want *Joe* to take a test? To prove he's ready for the next grade? He'll freak out."

"He'll do OK. He's good with tests."

"That's not the point, Mom. You know what he's like. He'll be insulted. So he'll make himself score a hundred percent. Or a hundred and ten. He'll drive himself nuts."

"Nobody can score a hundred and ten percent. It's not possible."

"Exactly. His head will explode."

"What about you?"

"Me? I'll be OK."

"Will you try hard?"

"What's the pass mark?"

"Fifty percent, probably."

"Then I'll aim for fifty-one. No point wasting effort. When is it?"

"Three days from now. Before the semester starts."

"Terrific," Reacher said. "What kind of an education system doesn't know the meaning of a simple word like *vacation*?"

4

Reacher went out to the concrete street and looked at the patch of ocean in the distance up ahead. The East China Sea, not the Pacific. The Pacific lay in the other direction. Okinawa was one of the Ryukyu Islands, and the Ryukyu Islands separated the two bodies of water.

There were maybe forty homes between Reacher and the water on the left-hand side of the street, and another forty on the right. He figured the homes closer to him and further from the sea would be off-post housing for Marine families, and the homes further from him and nearer the water would be locally owned, by Japanese families who lived there full-time. He knew how real estate worked. *Just steps to the beach.* People competed for places like that, and generally the military let the locals have the best stuff. The DoD always worried about friction. Especially on Okinawa. The air station was right in the center of Ginowan, which was a fair-sized city. Every time a transport plane took off, the schools had to stop teaching for a minute or two, because of the noise.

He turned his back on the East China Sea and walked inland, past identical little houses, across a four-way junction, into a perfect rectilinear matrix of yet more identical houses. They had been built quick and cheap, but they were in good order. They were meticulously maintained. He saw small doll-like local ladies on some of the porches. He nodded to them politely, but they all looked away. He saw no local Japanese kids. Maybe they were in school already. Maybe their semester had already started. He turned back and a hundred yards later found Joe out on the streets, looking for him.

Joe said, "Did they tell you about the test?"

Reacher nodded. "No big deal."

"We have to pass."

"Obviously we'll pass."

"No, I mean we have to really *pass* this thing. We have to crush it. We have to knock it out of the park."

"Why?"

"They're trying to humiliate us, Reacher."

"Us? They don't even know us."

"People like us. Thousands of us. We have to humiliate them back. We have to make them embarrassed they even thought of this idea. We have to piss all over their stupid test."

"I'm sure we will. How hard can it be?"

Joe said, "It's a new policy, so it might be a new kind of test. There might be all kinds of new things in it."

"Like what?"

"I have no idea. There could be anything."

"Well, I'll do my best with it."

"How's your general knowledge?"

"I know that Mickey Mantle hit .303 ten years ago. And .285 fifteen years ago. And .300 twenty years ago. Which averages out to .296, which is remarkably close to his overall career average of .298, which has to mean something."

"They're not going to ask about Mickey Mantle."

"Who, then?"

Joe said, "We need to know. And we have a right to know. We need to go up to that school and ask what's in this thing."

Reacher said, "You can't do that with tests. That's kind of opposite to the point of tests, don't you think?"

"We're at least entitled to know what part or parts of which curriculum is being tested here."

"It'll be reading and writing, adding and subtracting. Maybe some dividing if we're lucky. You know the drill. Don't worry about it."

"It's an insult."

Reacher said nothing.

5

The Reacher brothers walked back together, across the four-way junction, and into the long concrete street. Their new place was ahead and on the left. In the distance the sliver of sea glowed pale blue in the sun. There was a hint of white sand. Maybe palm trees. Between their place and the sea there were kids out on the street. All boys. Americans, black and white, maybe two dozen of them. Marine families. Neighbors. They were clustered outside their own places, at the cheap end of the street, a thousand steps from the beach.

Reacher said, "Let's go take a look at the East China Sea."

Joe said, "I've seen it before. So have you."

"We could be freezing our butts off in Korea all winter."

"We were just on Guam. How much beach does a person need?"

"As much as a person can get."

"We have a test in three days."

"Exactly. So we don't have to worry about it today."

Joe sighed and they walked on, past their own place, toward the sliver of blue. Ahead of them the other kids saw them coming. They got up off curbstones and stepped over ditches and kicked and scuffed their way to the middle of the road. They formed up in a loose arrowhead, facing front, arms folded, chests out, more than twenty guys, some of them as young as ten, some of them a year or two older than Joe.

Welcome to the neighborhood.

The point man was a thick-necked bruiser of about sixteen. He was smaller than Joe, but bigger than Reacher. He was wearing a Corps T-shirt and a ragged pair of khaki pants. He had fat hands, with knuckles that dipped in, not stuck out. He was fifteen feet away, just waiting.

Joe said quietly, "There are too many of them."

Reacher said nothing.

Joe said, "Don't start anything. I mean it. We'll deal with this later, if we have to."

Reacher smiled. "You mean after the test?"

"You need to get serious about that test."

They walked on. Forty different places. Forty different welcomes to forty different neighborhoods. Except that the welcomes had not been different. They had all been the same. Tribalism, testosterone, hierarchies, all kinds of crazy instincts. Tests of a different kind.

Joe and Reacher stopped six feet from the bruiser and waited. The guy had a boil on his neck. And he smelled pretty bad. He said, "You're the new kids."

Joe said, "How did you figure that out?"

"You weren't here yesterday."

"Outstanding deduction. You ever thought of a career with the FBI?"

The bruiser didn't answer that. Reacher smiled. He figured he could land a left hook right on the boil. Which would hurt like hell, probably.

The bruiser said, "You going to the beach?"

Joe said, "Is there a beach?"

"You know there's a beach."

"And you know where we're going."

"This is a toll road."

Joe said, "What?"

"You heard. You have to pay the toll."

"What's the toll?"

"I haven't decided yet," the bruiser said. "When I see what you've got, I'll know what to take."

Joe didn't answer.

The guy said, "Understand?"

Joe said, "Not even a little bit."

"That's because you're a retard. You two are the retard kids. We heard all about you. They're making you take the retard test, because you're retards."

Reacher said, "Joe, now *that's* an insult."

The big guy said, "So the little retard talks, does he?"

Joe said, "You seen that new statue in the square in Luzon?"

"What about it?"

"The last kid who picked a fight with my brother is buried in the pedestal."

The guy looked at Reacher and said, "That doesn't sound very nice. Are you a psycho retard?"

Reacher said, "What's that?"

"Like a psychopath."

"You mean do I think I'm right to do what I do and feel no remorse afterward?"

"I guess."

Reacher said, "Then yes, I'm pretty much a psychopath."

Silence, except for a distant motorbike. Then two motorbikes. Then three. Distant, but approaching. The big kid's gaze jumped to the four-way junction at the top of the street. Behind him the arrowhead formation broke up. Kids wandered back to the curbs and their front yards. A bike slowed and turned in to the street and puttered slowly along. On it was a Marine in BDUs. No helmet. An NCO, back from the base, his watch finished. He was followed by two more, one of them on a big Harley. Disciplinarian dads, coming home.

The big kid with the boil said, "We'll finish this another time."

Joe said, "Be careful what you wish for."

Reacher said nothing.

6

Stan Reacher was a quiet man by nature, and he was quieter than ever at breakfast on the fourth morning of his new command, which was turning out to be a tough gig. Back in the States the presidency had changed hands a little prematurely, and the Joint Chiefs had scrambled to present the new guy with a full range of options for his review. Standard practice. The start of every new administration was the same. There were plans for every imaginable theoretical contingency, and they had all been dusted off. Vietnam was effectively over, Korea was a stalemate, Japan was an ally, the Soviet Union was the same as ever, so China was the new focus. There had been a lot of public hoo-hah about détente, but equally there had been a lot of private planning for war. The Chinese were going to have to be beaten sooner or later, and Stan Reacher was going to have to play his part. He had been told so on his second morning.

He had been given command of four rifle companies and he had been handed a top-secret file defining their mission, which was to act as the tip of an immense spear that would land just north of Hangzhou and then punch through clockwise to isolate Shanghai. Tough duty. Casualty estimates were frightening. But ultimately a little pessimistic, in Stan's opinion. He had met his men and he had been impressed. On Okinawa it was always hard to avoid mental comparisons with the ghosts of the freak Marine generation that had been there thirty years before, but the current crop was good. Real good. They all shared Stan's personal allegiance to the famous old saying: *War is not about dying for your country. It's about making the other guy die for his.* For the infantry it all came down to simple arithmetic. If you could inflict two casualties for every one you took, you were ahead. If you could inflict five, you were winning. Eight or ten, the prize was in the bag. And Stan felt his guys could do eight or ten, easy.

But China's population was immense. And fanatical. They would keep on coming. Men, and then boys. Women, too, probably. Boys no older than his own sons. Women like his wife. He watched them eat, and imagined husbands and fathers a thousand miles away doing the same thing. A Communist army would draft a kid Joe's age without a second thought. Reacher's age, even, especially a big kid like that. And then the women. And then the girls. Not that Stan was either sentimental or conflicted. He would put a round through anyone's head and sleep like a baby. But these were strange times. That was for damn sure. Having kids made you think about the future, but being a combat Marine made the future a theory, not a fact.

He had no real plans for his sons. He wasn't that kind of a father. But he assumed they would stay military. What else did they know? In which case Joe's brains would keep him safe. Not that there weren't plenty of smart guys on the front lines. But Joe wasn't a fighter. He was like a rifle built without a firing pin. He was all there physically, but there was no trigger in his head. He was like a nuclear launch console instead, full of are-you-really-sure failsafes and interlocks and sequenced buttons. He thought too much. He did it quickly, for sure, but any kind of delay or hesitation was fatal at the start of a fight. Even a split second. So privately Stan figured Joe would end up in Intelligence, and he figured he would do a pretty good job there.

His second son was a whole different can of worms.

The kid was going to be huge. He was going to be an eighth of a ton of muscle. Which was a frightening prospect. The kid had come home bruised and bloodied plenty of times, but as far as Stan knew he hadn't actually lost a fight since he was about five years old. Maybe he had never lost a fight. He had no trigger, either, but not in the same way as his big brother. Joe was permanently set to safe, and Reacher was permanently jammed wide open on full auto. When he was grown, he was going to be unstoppable. A force of nature. A nightmare for somebody. Not that he ever started anything. His mother had trained him early and well. Josie was smart about things like that. She had seen the danger coming. So she had taught him never, ever, ever to start trouble, but that it was perfectly OK to react if someone else started it first. Which was a sight to see. The smart money brings a gun to a knife fight. Reacher brought a hydrogen bomb.

But the kid could think, too. He wasn't academic like Joe, but he was practical. His IQ was probably about the same, but it was a get-the-job-done type of street smart IQ, not any kind of for-the-sake-of-it cerebral indulgence. Reacher liked facts, for sure, and information, too, but not theory. He was a real-world character. Stan had no idea what the future held for the guy. No idea at all, except he was going to be too big to fit inside a tank or an airplane cockpit. So it was going to have to be something else.

But anyway, the future was still far off, for both of them. They were still kids. They were still just his fair-haired boys. Stan knew that right then Joe's horizons stretched no further than the start of the new semester, and Reacher's stretched no further than a fourth cup of coffee for breakfast. Which the kid got up and poured, right on cue. And also right on cue Joe said, "I'm going to walk up to the school today and ask them about this test."

"Negative on that," Stan said.

"Why not?"

"Two reasons. First, never let them see you sweat. Second, I put in a requisition form yesterday and I'm expecting a delivery today."

"Of what?"

"A telephone."

"Mom will be here."

"I won't," Josie said. "I have errands to run."

"All day?"

"Probably. I have to find a store cheap enough to feed you the eight pounds of protein you seem to need at every meal. Then I have to go have lunch with the other mothers at the Officers' Club, which will probably tie me up all afternoon, if Okinawa is still the same as it was last time we were here, which it probably is."

"Reacher can wait home for the telephone," Joe said. "He doesn't need a babysitter."

"That's beside the point," Stan said. "Go swimming, go play ball, go chase girls, but don't go ask about the test. Just do your best when it rolls around."

7

At that moment it was very late in the previous evening in Paris, and the retired schoolteacher was back on the phone with the Navy station on Guam. Laurent Moutier's housekeeper had whispered to him that they *really ought* to try to get hold of the old man's daughter. But the schoolteacher was getting nowhere. The duty lieutenant on Guam had no personal insight into the Pentagon's plans for China, but Stan Reacher's new posting was classified as secret, so no foreign citizen was going to hear a thing about it. Not from the Navy. No, sir. No way, no how.

Moutier heard the audible half of the back-and-forth from his bed. He could understand English a little. Enough to get by, and just enough to hear things between the lines. He knew exactly how the military worked. Like practically every other twentieth-century male human in Europe he had been in the service. He was already thirty years old when World War One broke out, but he volunteered immediately and survived all four years, Verdun and the Somme included, and he came out the other end with a chestful of medals and no scars longer than his middle finger, which was statistically the same thing as completely unscathed. On his day of demobilization a lugubrious one-armed, one-eyed brigadier wished him well and then added, apropos of nothing, "Mark my words,

Moutier, a great war leaves a country with three armies: an army of cripples, an army of mourners, and an army of thieves."

And Moutier found all three immediately, on his return to Paris. There were mourners everywhere. Mothers, wives, fiancées, sisters, old men. Someone said that if you gave every dead soldier a one-page obituary, just one lousy page to list all his hopes and dreams, then the resulting pile of paper would still stand taller than the Eiffel Tower itself.

Thieves were everywhere, some solo, some in mobs or gangs, some with a political tint. And Moutier saw cripples all day long, some in the natural course of events, but many more at work, because his furniture repair operation had been commandeered by the government and told to make wooden legs for the next ten years. Which Moutier did, out of parts of tables bought up cheap from bankrupt restaurants. It was entirely possible there were veterans in Paris stumping around on the same furniture they had once dined off.

The ten-year government contract expired a week before the Wall Street crash, and the next ten years were hard, except that he met the woman who quickly became his wife, a beauty foolish enough to take on a battered forty-five-year-old wreck like him. And a year later they had their only child, a mop-haired girl they called Josephine, who had grown up and married a Marine from New Hampshire in America, and who was currently completely uncontactable, despite the vast array of technological innovations Moutier had witnessed in his lifetime, many of them invented by the Americans themselves.

8

Stan Reacher pulled his field cap low and walked away to work. A minute later Josie headed out shopping, with a big bag and a thin purse. Reacher sat on the curb, waiting for the kid with the boil to come out to play. Joe stayed inside. But not for long. Thirty minutes later he came out with combed hair and a jacket. He said, "I'm going to take a walk."

"To the school?" Reacher asked.

"Least said, soonest mended."

"They're not humiliating you. You're humiliating yourself. How does scoring a hundred percent make you feel good when you already asked what the questions were?"

"It's a matter of principle."

"Not my principle," Reacher said. "My principle is they set these things so average people can pass them, which gives me enough of a chance that I don't feel I have to get my panties in a wad beforehand."

"You want people to think you're average?"

"I don't care what people think."

"You know you have to wait here for the delivery, right?"

"I'll be here," Reacher said. "Unless the fat smelly kid comes out with so many friends I end up in the hospital."

"Nobody's coming out with anybody. They all went

to a ballgame. This morning, in a bus. I saw them. They'll be gone all day."

9

The telephone delivery arrived while Reacher was eating lunch. He had made himself a cheese sandwich and a pot of coffee and was halfway through both when the delivery guy knocked on the door. The guy unpacked the box himself and handed Reacher the phone. He said he had to keep the box. Apparently there was a shortage of boxes on the island.

The phone was a weird instrument. It was like no phone Reacher had seen before. He put it on the countertop next to the remains of his sandwich and looked at it from all angles. It was definitely foreign, and probably about thirty years old. From some beaten nation's wartime warehouses, then. Mountains of stuff had been inherited. A hundred thousand typewriters here, a hundred thousand binoculars there. A hundred thousand telephones, rewired and reissued. At the right time, too. Turning tents and Quonset huts all over the world into permanent brick and stone buildings must have put a lot of pressure on a lot of people. Why wait for Bell Labs or GE when you can just back up a truck to a warehouse in Frankfurt?

Reacher found the jack on the kitchen wall and plugged in the phone and checked for dial tone. It was there. So he left the phone on the countertop and headed out to the beach.

10

It was a great beach. Better than most Reacher had seen. He took off his shirt and his shoes and took a long swim in warm blue water, and then he closed his eyes and lay in the sun until he was dry again. He opened his eyes and saw nothing but white-out and glare from the sky. Then he blinked and turned his head and saw he was not alone. Fifteen feet away a girl was lying on a towel. She was in a one-piece bathing suit. She was maybe thirteen or fourteen. Not all grown up, but not a kid, either. She had beads of water on her skin and her hair was slick and heavy.

Reacher stood up, all crusted with sand. He had no towel. He used his shirt to brush himself off, and then he shook it out and put it on. The girl turned her head and asked, "Where do you live?"

Reacher pointed.

"Up the street," he said.

"Would you let me walk back with you?"

"Sure. Why?"

"In case those boys are there."

"They're not. They're gone all day."

"They might come back early."

"Did they give you that toll road crap?"

She nodded. "I wouldn't pay."

"What did they want?"

"I don't want to tell you."

Reacher said nothing.

The girl asked, "What's your name?"

Reacher said, "Reacher."

"Mine's Helen."

"I'm pleased to meet you, Helen."

"How long have you been here?"

"Since yesterday," Reacher said. "You?"

"A week or so."

"Are you staying long?"

"Looks like it. You?"

"I'm not sure," Reacher said.

The girl stood up and shook out her towel. She was a slender thing, small but long-legged. She had nail polish on her toes. They walked off the sand together and into the long concrete street. It was deserted up ahead. Reacher asked, "Where's your house?"

Helen said, "On the left, near the top."

"Mine's on the right. We're practically neighbors." Reacher walked her all the way, but her mom was home by then, so he wasn't asked in. Helen smiled sweetly and said thanks and Reacher crossed the street to his own place, where he found hot still air and nobody home. So he just sat on the stoop and whiled away the time. Two hours later the three Marine NCOs came home on their motorbikes, followed by two more, then two more in cars. Thirty minutes after that a regular American school bus rolled in from the ballgame, and a crowd of neighborhood kids spilled out and went inside their homes with nothing more than hard stares in Reacher's direction. Reacher stared back just as hard, but he didn't move. Partly because he hadn't seen his target. Which was strange. He looked all around, once, twice, and by the time the diesel smoke cleared he was certain: the fat smelly kid with the boil had not been on the bus.

11

Eventually Joe came home, silent and preoccupied and uncommunicative. He didn't say where he had been. He didn't say anything. He just headed for the kitchen, washed his hands, checked the new phone for dial tone, and then went to take a shower, which was unusual for Joe at that time of day. Next in, surprisingly, was their father, also silent and preoccupied and uncommunicative. He got a glass of water, checked the phone for dial tone, and holed up in the living room. Last in was their mother, struggling under the weight of packages and a bouquet of flowers the women's welcoming committee had produced at lunch. Reacher took the packages from her and carried them to the kitchen. She saw the new phone on the countertop and brightened a little. She never felt good until she had checked in with her dad and made sure he had her latest contact information. France was seven hours behind Japan, which made it mid-morning there, which was a good time for a chat, so she dialed the long number and listened to it ring.

She got the housekeeper, of course, and a minute later the hot little house on Okinawa was in an uproar.

12

Stan Reacher got straight on the new phone to his company clerk, who leaned on a guy, who leaned on another guy, like dominoes, and within thirty minutes Josie had a seat on the last civilian flight of the evening to Tokyo, and within forty she had an onward connection to Paris.

Reacher asked, "Do you want company?"

His mother said, "Of course I would like it. And I know your grandpa Moutier would love to see you again. But I could be there a couple of weeks. More, perhaps. And you have a test to take, and then school to start."

"They'll understand. I don't mind missing a couple of weeks. And I could take the test when I get back. Or maybe they'll forget all about it."

His father said, "Your mother means we can't afford it, son. Plane tickets are expensive."

And so were taxicabs, but two hours later they took one to the airport. An old Japanese guy showed up in a big boxy Datsun, and Stan got in the front, and Josie and the boys crowded together in the back. Josie had a small bag. Joe was clean from the shower, but his hair was no longer combed. It was back to its usual tousled mess. Reacher was still salty and sandy from the beach. No one said much of anything. Reacher remembered his grandfather pretty well. He had met him three times. He had a closet full of artificial limbs. Apparently the heirs of deceased veterans were still officially obliged to return the prostheses to the manufacturer, for adjustment and eventual reissue. Part of the deal, from back in the day. Grandpa Moutier said every year or so another one would show up at his door. Sometimes two or three a year. Some of them were made from table legs.

They got out at the airport. It was dark and the air was going cold. Josie hugged Stan, and kissed him, and she hugged Joe, and kissed him, and she hugged Reacher, and kissed him, and then she pulled him aside and whispered a long urgent sentence in his ear. Then she went on alone to the check-in line.

Stan and the boys went up a long outside staircase to the observation deck. There was a JAL 707 waiting on the tarmac, spotlit and whining and ringed with attendant vehicles. It had stairs rolled up to its forward door, and its engines were turning slowly. Beyond the runway was a nighttime view of the whole southern half of the island. Their long concrete street lay indistinguishable in the distance, miles away to the south and the west. There were ten thousand small fires burning in the neighborhood. Backyard bonfires, each one flickering bright at its base and sending thin plumes of smoke high in the air.

"Trash night," Stan said. Reacher nodded. Every island he had ever been on had a garbage problem. Regulated once-a-week burning was the usual solution, for everything, including leftover food. Traditional, in every culture. The word *bonfire* came from *bone fire*. General knowledge. He had seen a small wire incinerator behind the hot little house.

"We missed it for this week," Stan said. "I wish we'd known."

"Doesn't matter," Joe said. "We don't really have any trash yet."

They waited, all three of them, leaning forward, elbows on a rail, and then Josie came out below them, one of about thirty passengers. She walked across the tarmac and turned at the bottom of the stairs and waved. Then she climbed up and into the plane, and she was lost to sight.

13

Stan and the boys watched the takeoff, watched the jet bank and climb, watched its tiny lights disappear, waited until its shattering noise was gone, and then they clattered down the long staircase three abreast. They walked home, which was Stan's usual habit when Josie wasn't involved and the distance was less than eight miles. Two hours' quick march. Nothing at all, to a Marine, and cheaper than the bus. He was a child of the Depression, not that his family's flinty New England parsimony would have been markedly different even in a time of plenty. Waste not, want not, make do and mend, don't make an exhibition of yourself. His own father had stopped buying new clothes at the age of forty, feeling that what he owned by that point would outlast him, and to gamble otherwise would be reckless extravagance.

The bonfires were almost out when they arrived at their street. Layers of smoke hung in the air, and there was the smell of ash and scorched meat, even inside the hot little house. They went straight to bed under thin sheets, and ten minutes later all was silent.

14

Reacher slept badly, first dreaming about his grandfather, the ferocious old Frenchman somehow limbless and equipped with four table legs, moving and rearing like a piece of mobile furniture. Then he was woken in the early hours by something stealthy in the back yard, a cat or a rodent or some other kind of scavenger, and then again much later when the new phone rang twice. Too soon for his mother to have arrived in Paris, too late for a report of a fatal accident en route to Tokyo. Something else, obviously, so he ignored it both times. Joe got up at that point, so Reacher took advantage of the solitude and rolled over and slept on, until after nine o'clock, which was late for him.

He found his father and his brother in the kitchen, both of them silent and strained to a degree he found excessive. No question that Grandpa Moutier was a nice old guy, but any ninety-year-old was by definition limited in the life expectancy department. No big surprise. The guy had to croak sometime. No one lives forever. And he had already beaten the odds. The guy was already about twenty years old when the Wright brothers flew, for God's sake.

Reacher made his own coffee, because he liked it stronger than the rest of his family. He made toast, poured cereal, ate and drank, and still no one had spoken to him. Eventually he asked, "What's up?"

His father's gaze dipped and swiveled and traversed like an artillery piece, and came to rest on a point on the tabletop, about a foot in front of Reacher's plate. He said, "The phone this morning."

"Not Mom, right?"

"No, not that."

"Then what?"

"We're in trouble."

"What, all of us?"

"Me and Joe."

Reacher asked, "Why? What happened?"

But at that point the doorbell rang, so there was no answer. Neither Joe or his father looked like moving, so Reacher got up and headed for the hallway. It was the same delivery guy as the day before. He went through the same ritual. He unpacked a box and retained it and handed Reacher a heavy spool of electric cable. There must have been a hundred yards of it. The spool was the size of a car tire. The cable was for domestic wiring, like Romex, heavy and stiff, sheathed in gray plastic. The spool had a wire cutter attached to it by a short chain.

Reacher left it on the hallway floor and headed back

to the kitchen. He asked, "Why do we need electric cable?"

"We don't," his father said. "I ordered boots."

"Well, you didn't get them. You got a spool of wire."

His father blew a sigh of frustration. "Then someone made a mistake, didn't they?"

Joe said nothing, which was very unusual. Normally in that kind of a situation he would immediately launch a series of speculative analyses, asking about the nature and format of the order codes, pointing out that numbers can be easily transposed, thinking out loud about how QWERTY keyboards put alphabetically remote letters side by side, and therefore how clumsy typists are always a quarter-inch away from an inadvertent jump from, say, footwear to hardware. He had that kind of a brain. Everything needed an explanation. But he said nothing. He just sat there, completely mute.

"What's up?" Reacher said again, in the silence.

"Nothing for you to worry about," his father said.

"It will be unless you two lighten up. Which I guess you're not going to anytime soon, judging by the look of you."

"I lost a code book," his father said.

"A code book for what?"

"For an operation I might have to lead."

"China?"

"How did you know that?"

"Where else is left?"

"It's theoretical right now," his father said. "Just an option. But there are plans, of course. And it will be very embarrassing if they leak. We're supposed to be getting along with China now."

"Is there enough in the code book to make sense to anyone?"

"Easily. Real names plus code equivalents for two separate cities, plus squads and divisions. A smart analyst could piece together where we're going, what we're going to do, and how many of us are coming."

"How big of a book is it?"

"It's a regular three-ring binder."

"Who had it last?" Reacher asked.

"Some planner," his father said. "But it's my responsibility."

"When did you know it was lost?"

"Last night. The call this morning was a negative result for the search I ordered."

"Not good," Reacher said. "But why is Joe involved?"

"He isn't. That's a separate issue. That was the other call this morning. Another three-ring binder, unbelievably. The test answers are missing. Up at the school. And Joe went there yesterday."

"I didn't even see the answer book," Joe said. "I certainly didn't take it away with me."

Reacher asked, "So what exactly did you do up there?"

"Nothing, in the end. I got as far as the principal's office and I told the secretary I wanted to talk to the guy about the test. Then I thought better of it and left."

"Where was the answer book?"

"On the principal's desk, apparently. But I never got that far."

"You were gone a long time."

"I took a walk."

"Around the school?"

"Partly. And other places."

"Were you in the building across the lunch hour?"

Joe nodded.

"And that's the problem," he said. "That's when they think I took it."

"What's going to happen?"

"It's an honor violation, obviously. I could be excluded for a semester. Maybe the whole year. And then they'll hold me back a grade, which will be two grades by then. You and I could end up in the same class."

"You could do my homework," Reacher said.

"This is not funny."

"Don't worry about it. We'll have moved on by the end of the semester anyway."

"Maybe not," their father said. "Not if I'm in the brig or busted back to private and painting curbstones for the rest of my career. We all could be stuck on Okinawa forever."

And at that point the phone rang again. Their father answered. It was their mother on the line, from Paris, France. Their father forced a bright tone into his voice, and he talked and listened, and then he hung up and relayed the news that their mother had arrived safely, and that old man Moutier wasn't expected to live more than a couple of days, and that their mother was sad about it.

Reacher said, "I'm going to the beach."

15

Reacher stepped out through the door and glanced toward the sea. The street was empty. No kids. He took a snap decision and detoured to the other side and knocked on Helen's door. The girl he had met the day before. She opened up and saw who it was and crowded out next to him on the stoop and pulled the door all the way closed behind her. Like she was keeping him secret. Like she was embarrassed by him. She picked up on his feeling and shook her head.

"My dad is sleeping," she said. "That's all. He sat up and worked all night. And now he's not feeling so hot. He just flaked, an hour ago."

Reacher said, "You want to go swimming?"

She glanced down the street, saw no one was there, and said, "Sure. Give me five minutes, OK?" She crept back inside and Reacher turned and watched the street, half hoping that the kid with the boil would come out, and half hoping he wouldn't. He didn't. Then Helen came out again, in a bathing suit under a sundress. She had a towel. They walked down the street together, keeping pace, a foot apart, talking about where they'd lived and the places they'd seen. Helen had moved a lot, but not as much as Reacher. Her dad was a rear echelon guy, not a combat Marine, and his postings tended to be longer and more stable.

The morning water was colder than it had been the

afternoon before, so they got out after ten minutes or so. Helen let Reacher use her towel, and then they lay on it together in the sun, now just inches apart. She asked him, "Have you ever kissed a girl?"

"Yes," he said. "Twice."

"The same girl two times or two girls once each?"

"Two girls more than once each."

"A lot?"

"Maybe four times each."

"Where?"

"On the mouth."

"No, *where*? In the movies, or what?"

"One in the movies, one in a park."

"With tongues?"

"Yes."

She asked, "Are you good at it?"

He said, "I don't know."

"Will you show me how? I've never done it."

So he leaned up on an elbow and kissed her on the mouth. Her lips were small and mobile, and her tongue was cool and wet. They kept it going for fifteen or twenty seconds, and then they broke apart.

He asked, "Did you like it?"

She said, "Kind of."

"Was I good at it?"

"I don't know. I don't have anything to compare it with."

"Well, you were better than the other two I kissed," he said.

"Thank you," she said, but he didn't know what she was thanking him for. The compliment or the trial run, he wasn't sure.

16

Reacher and Helen walked back together, and they almost made it home. They got within twenty yards of their destination, and then the kid with the boil stepped out of his yard and took up a position in the middle of the road. He was wearing the same Corps T-shirt and the same pair of ragged pants. And he was alone, for the time being.

Reacher felt Helen go quiet beside him. She stopped walking and Reacher stopped a pace ahead of her. The big kid was six feet away. The three of them were like the corners of a thin sloping triangle. Reacher said, "Stay there, Helen. I know you could kick this guy's ass all by yourself, but there's no reason why both of us should be exposed to the smell."

The big kid just smiled.

He said, "You've been to the beach."

Reacher said, "And we thought Einstein was smart."

"How many times have you been?"

"You can't count that high."

"Are you trying to make me mad?"

Reacher was, of course. For his age he had always been a freakishly big kid, right from birth. His mother claimed he had been the biggest baby anyone had ever seen, although she had a well-known taste for the dramatic, so Reacher tended to discount that information. But even so, big or not, he had always fought two or three classes up. Sometimes more. With the result that one on one, ninety-nine percent of the time, he had been the small kid. So he had learned to fight like a small kid. All things being equal, size usually wins. But not always, otherwise the heavyweight championship of the world would be decided on the scale, not in the ring. Sometimes, if the small guy is faster and smarter, he can get a result. And one way of being smarter is to make the other guy dumber, which you can do by inducing a rage. An opponent's red mist is the smaller guy's best friend. So yes, Reacher was trying to make the smelly kid mad.

But the smelly kid wasn't falling for it. He was just standing there, taking it, tense but controlled. His feet were well placed, and his shoulders were bunched. His fists were ready to come up. Reacher took one pace forward, into the miasma of halitosis and body odor. Rule one with a guy like that: don't let him bite you. You could get an infection. Rule two: watch his eyes. If they stayed up, he was going to swing. If they dropped down, he was going to kick.

The guy's eyes stayed up. He said, "There's a girl here. You're going to get your butt kicked in front of a girl. You won't be able to show your face. You'll be the neighborhood retard pussy. Maybe I'll charge the toll every time you come out of your house. Maybe I'll expand the zone all over the island. Maybe I'll charge a double toll. From you and your retard brother."

Rule three with a guy like that: upset the choreography. Don't wait, don't back off, don't be the challenger, don't be the underdog, don't think defensively.

In other words, rule four: hit him first.

And not with a predictable little left jab, either.

Because rule five: there are no rules on the back streets of Okinawa.

Reacher snapped a vicious straight right into the guy's face and caught him square on the cheek.

That got his attention.

The guy rocked back and shook his head and popped a straight right of his own, which Reacher had expected and was ready for. He leaned left and let the fat fist buzz past his ear. *Smarter and faster.* Then the guy was all tangled up in the follow-through and could do nothing but step back and crouch and start over. Which he got well into doing.

Until he heard the sound of a motorbike. Which was like the bell at the end of a round to him. Like Pavlov's dog. He hesitated for a fatal split second.

Reacher hesitated, too. But for a shorter time. Purely because of geometry. He was facing up the street, toward the four-way junction. His eyes flicked up and he saw a bike heading north to south, keeping straight on the main road, passing by, not turning in. He processed that information and deleted it even before the bike was gone, just as soon as its speed and position had made a turn impossible. Whereupon his gaze came straight back to his opponent.

Who was at a geometric disadvantage. He was facing down the street, toward the sea. He had nothing to go on but sound. And the sound was loud and diffuse. Not specific. No spatial cues. Just an echoing roar. So like every other animal on earth with better sight than hearing, the guy yielded to a basic instinct. He started to turn his head to look behind him. Irresistible. Then a split second later the auditory input went unambiguous when the roar got trapped behind buildings, and the guy came to his conclusion and stopped his move and started to turn his head back again.

But by then it was far too late. By then Reacher's left hook was halfway through its travel. It was scything in, hard and fast, every sinew and ropy muscle in his greyhound's frame unspooling in perfect coordination, with just one aim in sight: to land that big left fist on the guy's neck.

Total success. The blow landed right on the boil, crushing it, crushing flesh, compressing bone, and the guy went down like he had run full speed into a clothesline. His legs came out from under him and he thumped more or less horizontally on the concrete, just sprawling, tangled and stunned like a pratfall stunt in a silent movie.

Next obvious move was for Reacher to start kicking him in the head, but he had an audience with feminine sensibilities, so he resisted the temptation. The big guy got his face off the floor and he looked nowhere in particular and said, "That was a sucker punch."

Reacher nodded. "But you know what they say. Only suckers get sucker punched."

"We're going to finish this."

Reacher looked down. "Looks kind of finished already."

"Dream on, you little punk."

"Take an eight count," Reacher said. "I'll be back."

17

Reacher hustled Helen up to her house and then he jogged across the street to his own. He went in the door and ran through to the kitchen and found his father in there, alone.

"Where's Joe?" Reacher asked.

"Taking a long walk," his father said.

Reacher stepped out to the back yard. It was a square concrete space, empty except for an old patio table and four chairs, and the empty incinerator. The incinerator was about the size of a big round garbage can. It was made of diagonal steel mesh. It was up on little legs. It was faintly gray with old ash, but it had been emptied and cleaned after its last use. In fact, the whole yard had been swept. Marine families. Always meticulous.

Reacher headed back to the hallway. He crouched over the spool of electric cable and unwound six feet of wire and snipped it off with the cutters.

His father asked, "What are you doing?"

"You know what I'm doing, Dad," Reacher said. "I'm doing what you intended me to do. You didn't order boots. You ordered exactly what arrived. Last night, after the code book went missing. You thought the news would leak and Joe and I would get picked on as a result. You couldn't bring us Ka-Bar knives or knuckledusters, so you thought of the next best thing."

He started to wind the heavy wire around his fist, wrapping one turn after another, the way a boxer binds his hands. He pressed the malleable metal and plastic flat and snug.

His father asked, "So has the news leaked?"

"No," Reacher said. "This is a previous engagement."

His father ducked his head out the door and looked down the street. He said, "Can you take that guy?"

"Does the Pope sleep in the woods?"

"He has a friend with him."

"The more the merrier."

"There are other kids watching."

"There always are."

Reacher started wrapping his other hand.

His father said, "Stay calm, son. Don't do too much damage. I don't want this family to go three for three this week, as far as getting in trouble is concerned."

"He won't rat me out."

"I know that. I'm talking about a manslaughter charge."

"Don't worry, Dad," Reacher said. "It won't go that far."

"Make sure it doesn't."

"But I'm afraid it will have to go a certain distance. A little farther than normal."

"What are you talking about, son?"

"I'm afraid this time I'm going to have to break some bones."

"Why?"

"Mom told me to. In a way."

"What?"

"At the airport," Reacher said. "She took me aside,

remember? She told me she figures this place is driving you and Joe crazy. She told me I had to keep an eye on you and him both. She said it's up to me."

"Your mother said that? We can look after ourselves."

"Yeah? How's that working out so far?"

"But this kid has nothing to do with anything."

"I think he does," Reacher said.

"Since when? Did he say something?"

"No," Reacher said. "But there are other senses apart from hearing. There's smell, for instance."

And then he jammed his bulbous gray fists in his pockets and stepped out to the street again.

18

Thirty yards away there was a horseshoe gaggle of maybe ten kids. The audience. They were shifting from foot to foot and vibrating with anticipation. About ten yards closer than that the smelly kid was waiting, with a sidekick in attendance. The smelly kid was on the right, and the sidekick was on the left. The sidekick was about Reacher's own height, but thick in the shoulders and chest, like a wrestler, and he had a face like a wanted poster, flat and hard and mean. Those shoulders and that face were about ninety percent of the guy's armory, Reacher figured. The guy was the type that got left alone solely because of his appearance. So probably he didn't get much practice, and maybe he even believed his own bullshit. So maybe he wasn't really much of a brawler.

Only one way to find out.

Reacher came in at a fast walk, his hands still in his pockets, on a wide curving trajectory, heading for the sidekick, not slowing at all, not even in the last few strides, the way a glad-handing politician approaches, the way a manic church minister walks up to a person, as if delivering an eager and effusive welcome was his only aim in life. The sidekick got caught up in the body language. He got confused by long social training. His hand even came halfway up, ready to shake.

Without breaking stride Reacher head-butted him full in the face. *Left, right, bang.* A perfect ten, for style and content, and power and precision. The guy went over backward and before he was a quarter of the way to the floor Reacher was turning toward the smelly kid and his wrapped hands were coming up out of his pockets.

In the movies they would have faced off, long and tense and static, like the O.K. Corral, with taunts and muttered threats, hands away from their sides, up on their toes, maybe circling, narrowed eyes on narrowed eyes, building the suspense. But Reacher didn't live in the movies. He lived in the real world. Without even a split second's pause he crashed his left fist into the smelly guy's side, a vicious low blow, the second beat in a fast rhythmic *one-two* shuffle, where the *one* had been the head butt. His fist must have weighed north of six pounds at that point, and he put everything he had into it, and the result was that whatever the smelly kid was going to do next, he was going to do it with three busted ribs, which put him at an instant disadvantage, because busted ribs hurt like hell, and any kind of violent physical activity makes them hurt worse. Some folks with busted ribs can't even bear to sneeze.

In the event the smelly kid didn't do much of anything with his busted ribs. He just doubled over like a wounded buffalo. So Reacher crowded in and launched a low clubbing right and busted some more ribs on the other side. Easy enough. The heavy cable wrap made his hands like wrecking balls. The only problem was that people don't always go to the hospital for busted ribs. Especially not Marine families. They just tape them up and gut it out. And Reacher needed the guy in a hospital cot, with his whole concerned family all around him. At least for one evening. So he dragged the guy's left arm out from its midsection clutch, clamping the guy's wrist in his own left hand, clumsy because of the wire, and he twisted it through a 180 turn, so the palm was up and the soft side of the elbow was down, and then he smashed his own right fist clean through the joint and the guy howled and screamed and fell to his knees and Reacher put him out of his misery with an uppercut under the jaw.

Game over.

Reacher looked left to right around the silent semicircle of spectators and said, "Next?"

No one moved.

Reacher said, "Anyone?"

No one moved.

"OK," Reacher said. "Let's all get it straight. From now on, it is what it is."

And then he turned and walked back to his house.

19

Reacher's father was waiting in the hallway, a little pale around the eyes. Reacher started unwrapping his hands, and he asked, "Who are you working with on this code book thing?"

His father said, "An Intelligence guy and two MPs."

"Would you call them and ask them to come over?"

"Why?"

"All part of the plan. Like Mom told me."

"They should come here?"

"Yes."

"When?"

"Right now would be good." Reacher saw he had the word *Georgia* stamped backward across one of his knuckles. Must have been where the wire was manufactured. Raised lettering on the insulation. A place he had never been.

His father made the call to the base and Reacher watched the street from a window. He figured with a bit of luck the timing would be perfect. And it was, more or less. Twenty minutes later a staff car pulled up and three men in uniform got out. And immediately an ambulance turned in to the street behind them and maneuvered around their parked vehicle and headed on down to the smelly kid's house. The medics loaded the kid on board, and his mother and what looked like a younger brother rode along as passengers. Reacher figured the kid's father would head straight for the hospital, on his motorbike, at the end of his watch. Or earlier, depending on what the doctors said.

The Intelligence guy was a major, and the MPs were warrant officers. All three of them were in BDUs. All three of them were still standing in the hallway. All three of them had the same expression on their faces: *why are we here?*

Reacher said, "That kid they just took away? You need to go search his house. Which is now empty, by the way. It's ready and waiting for you."

The three guys looked at each other. Reacher watched their faces. Clearly none of them had any real desire to nail a good Marine like Stan Reacher. Clearly all of them wanted a happy ending. They were prepared to clutch at straws. They were prepared to go the extra mile, even if that involved taking their cues from some weird thirteen-year-old kid.

One of the MPs asked, "What are we looking for?"

"You'll know it when you see it," Reacher said. "Eleven inches long, one inch wide, gray in color."

The three guys stepped out to the street, and Reacher and his father sat down to wait.

20

It was a reasonably short wait, as Reacher had privately predicted. The smelly kid had demonstrated a degree of animal cunning, but he was no kind of a criminal mastermind. That was for damn sure. The three men came back less than ten minutes later with a metal object that had been burned in a fire. It was ashy gray as a result. It was a once-bright alloy fillet eleven inches long and one inch wide, slightly curved across its shorter dimension, with three round appendages spaced along its length.

It was what is left when you burn a regular three-ring binder.

No stiff covers, no pages, no contents, just scorched metal.

Reacher asked, "Where did you find it?"

One of the MPs said, "Under a bed in the second bedroom. The boys' room."

No kind of a criminal mastermind.

The major from Intelligence asked, "Is it the code book?"

Reacher shook his head.

"No," he said. "It's the test answers from the school."

"Are you sure?"

"Positive."

"So why call us?"

"This has to be handled by the Corps. Not by the school. You need to go up to the hospital and talk to the kid and his father together. You need to get a confession. Then you need to tell the school. What you do to the kid after that is your business. A warning will do it, probably. He won't trouble us again anyway."

"What exactly happened here?"

"It was my brother's fault," Reacher said. "In a way, anyway. The kid from down the street started hazing us, and Joe stepped up and did really well. Smart mouth, fast answers, the whole nine yards. It was a great performance. Plus, Joe is huge. Gentle as a lamb, but the kid didn't know that, obviously. So he decided to duck the physical route, in terms of revenge. He decided to go another way. He figured out that Joe was uptight about the test. Maybe he had heard us talking. But anyway, he followed Joe up to the school yesterday and stole the answers. To discredit him."

"Can you prove that?"

"Circumstantially," Reacher said. "The kid didn't go to the ballgame. He wasn't on the bus. So he was in town all day. And Joe washed his hands and took a shower when he got back. Which is unusual for Joe, in the afternoon. He must have felt dirty. And my guess is he felt dirty because he had been smelling that kid's stink all day, from behind him and around corners."

"Very circumstantial," the major said.

"Ask the kid," Reacher said. "Lean on him, in front of his dad."

"Then what happened?"

"The kid made up a scenario where Joe memorized

the answers and then burned the book. Which would be plausible, for a guy who wanted to cheat on a test. And it was trash night, which was convenient. The plan was the kid would burn the book in his own back yard, and then sneak into ours during the night and dump the metal part in our incinerator, among our ashes, so the evidence would be right there. But we had no ashes. We missed trash night. We had to be up at the airport instead. So the kid had to abort the plan. He just snuck away again. And I heard him. Early hours of the morning. I thought it was a cat or a rat."

"Any trace evidence?"

"You might find footprints out there," Reacher said. "The yard was swept at some point, but there's always dust. Especially after trash night."

The MPs went away and took a look at the yard, and then they came back with quizzical expressions on their faces, as if to say, *the kid could be right.*

The Intelligence major got a look on his own face, like *I can't believe I'm about to say this to a thirteen-year-old,* and then he asked, "Do you know where the code book is, too?"

"No," Reacher said. "Not for sure. But I could make a pretty good guess."

"Where?"

"Help my brother out with the school, and then we'll talk."

21

The three Marines came back ninety minutes later. One of the MPs said, "You busted that kid up pretty good, didn't you?"

"He'll live," Reacher said.

The other MP said, "He confessed. It went down like you figured. How did you know?"

"Logic," Reacher said. "I knew Joe wouldn't have done it, so clearly someone else did. It was just a question of who. And how, and why."

The Intelligence major said, "We squared things away with the school. Your brother is in the clear." Then the guy smiled. He said, "But there's one unfortunate consequence."

"Which is what?"

"They don't have the answers anymore, so the test has been canceled."

"That's a shame."

"Every silver lining has a cloud."

"Did you see the questions?"

The major nodded. "Reading, writing, adding, subtracting. Nothing out of the ordinary."

"No general knowledge?"

"No."

"No baseball?"

"Not even a hint."

"No statistics?"

"Percentages, maybe, in the math section. Odds and probabilities, that sort of thing."

"Which are important," Reacher said. "As in, what are the odds of a Marine officer losing a code book?"

"Low."

"What are the odds of a *good* Marine officer like my dad losing a code book?"

"Lower still."

"So the probability is the book isn't lost at all. The probability is there's another explanation. Therefore time spent chasing the notion it's lost is time wasted. Time spent on other avenues would be more fruitful."

"What other avenues?"

"When did President Ford take over from President Nixon?"

"Ten days ago."

"Which must have been when the Joint Chiefs started dusting off all the options. And I'm guessing the only real live one is China. Which is why we got the transfer here. But we're the combat phase. So a little earlier than us the planners must have been brought in. A week or so ago, maybe. They must have been told to nail everything down double quick. Which is a lot of work, right?"

"Always."

"And what's the last phase of that work?"

"Revising the code books to match the updated plans."

"What's the deadline?"

"Theoretically we have to be ready to go at midnight tonight, should the president order it."

"So maybe somewhere there's a guy who worked

on the codes all through the night. A rear echelon guy who got here about a week ago."

"I'm sure there is. But we already checked all over the base. That's the first thing we did."

"Maybe he worked off post."

"That would be unauthorized."

"But it happens."

"I know. But even if it did in this case, he would have been back on the base hours ago, and the book would have been back in the safe hours ago."

"Suppose he wore himself out and fell asleep? Suppose he hasn't gotten up yet? Suppose the code book is still on his kitchen table?"

"Where?"

"Across the street," Reacher said. "Knock on the door and ask for Helen."

22

Joe got back from his long walk an hour later and he and his brother and his father headed for the beach and took a swim. The water was warm, the sand was white, and the palms were swaying. They loitered and strolled until the sun dipped low, and then they headed home to the hot little house at the top of the concrete street, where an hour later the new phone rang again and Josie told them that her father had died. Old Laurent Moutier was gone, at the age of ninety, taking with him like everyone does a lifetime of unknown private hopes and dreams and fears and experiences, and leaving behind him like most people do a thin trace of himself in his living descendants. He had never had a clear idea of what would become of his beautiful mop-haired daughter and his two handsome grandsons, nor did he really want one, but like every other twentieth-century male human in Europe he hoped they would live lives of peace, prosperity, and plenty, while simultaneously knowing they almost certainly wouldn't. So he hoped they would bear their burdens with grace and good humor, and he was comforted in his final moments by the knowledge that so far they always had, and probably always would.

High Heat

The man was over thirty, Reacher thought, and solid, and hot, obviously. He had sweated through his suit. The woman face to face with him could have been younger, but not by much. She was hot, too, and scared. Or tense, at least. That was clear. The man was too close to her. She didn't like that. It was nearly half past eight in the evening, and going dark. But not cooling off. A hundred degrees, someone had said. A real heat wave. Wednesday, July 13, 1977, New York City. Reacher would always remember the date. It was his second solo visit.

The man put the palm of his hand flat on the woman's chest, pressing damp cotton against her skin, the ball of his thumb down in her cleavage. Not a tender gesture. But not an aggressive gesture, either. Neutral, like a doctor. The woman didn't back off. She just froze in place and glanced around. Without seeing much. New York City, half past eight in the evening, but the street was deserted. It was too hot. Waverly Place, between Sixth Avenue and Washington Square. People would come out later, if at all.

Then the man took his hand off the woman's chest, and he flicked it downward like he wanted to knock a bee off her hip, and then he whipped it back up in a big roundhouse swing and slapped her full in the face, hard, with enough power for a real *crack,* but his hand and her face were too damp for pistol-shot acoustics, so the sound came out exactly like the word: *slap.* The woman's head was knocked sideways. The sound echoed off the scalding brick.

Reacher said, "Hey."

The man turned around. He was dark-haired, dark-eyed, maybe five-ten, maybe two hundred pounds. His shirt was transparent with sweat.

He said, "Get lost, kid."

On that night Reacher was three months and sixteen days shy of his seventeenth birthday, but physically he was pretty much all grown up. He was as tall as he was ever going to get, and no sane person would have called him skinny. He was six-five, two-twenty, all muscle. The finished article, more or less. But finished very recently. Brand-new. His teeth were white and even, his eyes were a shade close to navy, his hair had wave and body, his skin was smooth and clear. The scars and the lines and the calluses were yet to come.

The man said, "Right now, kid."

Reacher said, "Ma'am, you should step away from this guy."

Which the woman did, backward, one step, two, out of range. The man said, "Do you know who I am?"

Reacher said, "What difference would it make?"

"You're pissing off the wrong people."

"People?" Reacher said. "That's a plural word. Are there more than one of you?"

"You'll find out."

Reacher looked around. The street was still deserted.

"When will I find out?" he said. "Not right away, apparently."

"What kind of smart guy do you think you are?"

Reacher said, "Ma'am, I'm happy to be here alone, if you want to take off running."

The woman didn't move. Reacher looked at her.

He said, "Am I misunderstanding something?"

The man said, "Get lost, kid."

The woman said, "You shouldn't get involved."

"I'm not getting involved," Reacher said. "I'm just standing here in the street."

The man said, "Go stand in some other street."

Reacher turned and looked at him and said, "Who died and made you mayor?"

"That's some mouth, kid. You don't know who you're talking to. You're going to regret that."

"When the other people get here? Is that what you mean? Because right now it's just you and me. And I don't foresee a whole lot of regret in that, not for me, anyway, not unless you've got no money."

"Money?"

"For me to take."

"What, now you think you're going to mug me?"

"Not mug you," Reacher said. "More of a historical

thing. An old principle. Like a tradition. You lose a war, you give up your treasure."

"Are we at war, you and me? Because if we are, you're going to lose, kid. I don't care how big of a corn-fed country boy you are. I'm going to kick your ass. I'm going to kick it bad."

The woman was still six feet away. Still not moving. Reacher looked at her again and said, "Ma'am, is this gentleman married to you, or related to you in some other way, or known to you either socially or professionally?"

She said, "I don't want you to get involved." She was younger than the guy, for sure. But not by much. Still way up there. Twenty-nine, maybe. A pale-colored blonde. Apart from the vivid red print from the slap she was plenty good looking, in an older-woman kind of a way. But she was thin and nervous. Maybe she had a lot of stress in her life. She was wearing a loose summer dress that ended above her knees. She had a purse hooked over her shoulder.

Reacher said, "At least tell me what it is you don't want me to get involved in. Is this some random guy hassling you on the street? Or not?"

"What else would it be?"

"Domestic quarrel, maybe. I heard of a guy who busted one up, and then the wife got real mad with him afterward, for hurting her husband."

"I'm not married to this man."

"Do you have any interest in him at all?"

"In his welfare?"

"I suppose that's what we're talking about."

"None at all. But you can't get involved. So walk away. I'll deal with it."

"Suppose we walk away together?"

"How old are you, anyway?"

"Old enough," Reacher said. "For walking, at least."

"I don't want the responsibility. You're just a kid. You're an innocent bystander."

"Is this guy dangerous?"

"Very."

"He doesn't look it."

"Looks can be deceptive."

"Is he armed?"

"Not in the city. He can't afford to be."

"So what's he going to do? Sweat on me?"

Which did the trick. The guy hit boiling point, aggrieved at being talked about like he wasn't there, aggrieved at being called sweaty, even though he manifestly was, and he came in at a charge, his jacket flapping, his tie flailing, his shirt sticking to his skin. Reacher feinted one way and moved another, and the guy stumbled past, and Reacher tapped his ankles, and the guy tripped and fell. He got up again fast enough, but by then Reacher had backed off and turned around and was ready for the second maneuver. Which looked like it was going to be an exact repeat of the first, except Reacher helped it along a little by replacing the ankle tap with an elbow to the side of the head. Which was very well delivered. At nearly seventeen Reacher was like a brand-new machine, still gleaming and dewy with oil, flexible, supple, perfectly coordinated, like something developed by NASA and IBM on behalf of the Pentagon.

The guy stayed down on his knees a little longer than the first time. The heat kept him there. Reacher figured the hundred degrees he had heard about must have been somewhere open. Central Park, maybe. Some little weather station. In the narrow brick canyons of the West Village, close to the huge stone sidewalk slabs, it must have been more like a hundred and twenty. And humid. Reacher was wearing old khakis and a blue T-shirt, and both items looked like he had fallen in a river.

The guy stood up, panting and unsteady. He put his hands on his knees.

Reacher said, "Let it go, old man. Find someone else to hit."

No answer. The guy looked like he was conducting an internal debate. It was a long one. Clearly there were points to consider on both sides of the argument. Pros, and cons, and pluses, and minuses, and costs and benefits. Finally the guy said, "Can you count to three and a half?"

Reacher said, "I suppose."

"That's how many hours you got to get out of town. After midnight you're a dead man. And before that, too, if I see you again." And then the guy straightened up and walked away, back toward Sixth Avenue, fast, like his mind was made up, his heels ringing on the hot stone, like a brisk, purposeful person on a just-remembered errand. Reacher watched until he was lost to sight, and then he turned back to the woman and said, "Which way are you headed?"

She pointed in the opposite direction, toward Washington Square, and Reacher said, "Then you should be OK."

"You have three and a half hours to get out of town."

"I don't think he was serious. He was hauling ass, trying to save face."

"He was serious, believe me. You hit him in the head. I mean, Jesus."

"Who is he?"

"Who are you?"

"Just a guy passing through."

"From where?"

"Pohang, at the moment."

"Where the hell is that?"

"South Korea. Camp Mujuk. The Marine Corps."

"You're a Marine?"

"Son of a Marine. We go where we're posted. But school's out, so I'm traveling."

"On your own? How old are you?"

"Seventeen in the fall. Don't worry about me. I'm not the one getting slapped in the street."

The woman said nothing.

Reacher said, "Who was that guy?"

"How did you get here?"

"Bus to Seoul, plane to Tokyo, plane to Hawaii, plane to LA, plane to JFK, bus to the Port Authority. Then I walked." The Yankees were out of town, in Boston, which had been a major disappointment. Reacher had a feeling it was going to be a special year. Reggie Jackson was making a difference. The long drought might be nearly over. But no luck. The stadium was dark. The alternative was Shea, the Cubs at the Mets. In principle Reacher had no objection to Mets baseball, such as it was, but in the end the pull of downtown music had proven stronger. He had figured he would swing through Washington Square and check out the girls from NYU's summer school. One of them might be willing to go with him. Or not. It was worth the detour. He was an optimist, and his plans were flexible.

The woman said, "How long are you traveling?"

"In theory I'm free until September."

"Where are you staying?"

"I just got here. I haven't figured that out yet."

"Your parents are OK with this?"

"My mother is worried. She read about the Son of Sam in the newspaper."

"She should be worried. He's killing people."

"Couples sitting in cars, mostly. That's what the papers say. Statistically unlikely to be me. I don't have a car, and so far I'm on my own."

"This city has other problems, too."

"I know. I'm supposed to visit with my brother."

"Here in the city?"

"Couple hours out."

"You should go there right now."

Reacher nodded. "I'm supposed to take the late bus."

"Before midnight?"

"Who was that guy?"

The woman didn't answer. The heat wasn't letting up. The air was thick and heavy. There was thunder coming. Reacher could feel it, in the north and the west. Maybe they were going to get a real Hudson Valley thunderstorm, rolling and clattering over the slow water, between the high cliffs, like he had read about in books. The light was fading all the way to purple, as if the weather was getting ready for something big.

The woman said, "Go see your brother. Thanks for helping out."

The red handprint on her face was fading.

Reacher said, "Are you going to be OK?"

"I'll be fine."

"What's your name?"

"Jill."

"Jill what?"

"Hemingway."

"Any relation?"

"To who?"

"Ernest Hemingway. The writer."

"I don't think so."

"You free tonight?"

"No."

"My name is Reacher. I'm pleased to meet you." He stuck out his hand, and they shook. Her hand felt hot and slick, like she had a fever. Not that his didn't. A hundred degrees, maybe more, no breeze, no evaporation. Summer in the city. Faraway to the north the sky flickered. Heat lightning. No rain.

He said, "How long have you been with the FBI?"

"Who says I am?"

"That guy was a mobster, right? Organized crime? All that shit about his people, and getting out of town or else. All those threats. And you were meeting with him. He was checking for a wire, when he put his hand on you. And I guess he found one."

"You're a smart kid."

"Where's your backup? There should be a van, with people listening in."

"It's a budget thing."

"I don't believe you. The city, maybe, but the feds are never broke."

"Go see your brother. This isn't your business."

"Why wear a wire with no one listening?"

The woman put her hands behind her back, low down, and she fiddled and jiggled, as if she was working something loose from the waistband of her underwear. A black plastic box fell out below the hem of her dress. A small cassette recorder, swinging knee-high, suspended on a wire. She put one hand down the front of her dress, and she pulled on the wire behind her knees with her other hand, and she squirmed and she wriggled, and the recorder lowered itself to the sidewalk, followed by a thin black cable with a little bud microphone on the end.

She said, "The tape was listening."

The little black box was dewed with perspiration, from the small of her back.

Reacher said, "Did I screw it up?"

"I don't know how it would have gone."

"He assaulted a federal agent. That's a crime right there. I'm a witness."

The woman said nothing. She picked up the cassette recorder and wound the cord around it. She slid her purse off her shoulder and put the recorder in it. The temperature felt hotter than ever, and steamy, like a hot wet towel over Reacher's mouth and nose. There was more lightning in the north, winking slow, dulled by the thick air. No rain. No break.

Reacher said, "Are you going to let him get away with that?"

The woman said, "This really isn't your business."

"I'm happy to say what I saw."

"It wouldn't come to trial for a year. You'd have to come all the way back. You want to take four planes and two buses for a slap?"

"A year from now I'll be somewhere else. Maybe nearer."

"Or further away."

"The sound might be on the tape."

"I need more than a slap. Defense lawyers would laugh at me."

Reacher shrugged. Too hot to argue. He said, "OK, have a pleasant evening, ma'am."

She said, "Where are you going now?"

"Bleecker Street, I think."

"You can't. That's in his territory."

"Or nearby. Or the Bowery. There's music all over, right?"

"Same thing. All his territory."

"Who is he?"

"His name is Croselli. Everything north of Houston and south of 14th is his. And you hit him in the head."

"He's one guy. He won't find me."

"He's a made man. He has soldiers."

"How many?"

"A dozen, maybe."

"Not enough. Too big of an area."

"He'll put the word out. All the clubs and all the bars."

"Really? He'll tell people he's frightened of a sixteen-year-old? I don't think so."

"He doesn't need to give a reason. And people will bust a gut to help. They all want brownie points in the bank. You wouldn't last five minutes. Go see your brother. I'm serious."

"Free country," Reacher said. "That's what you're working for, right? I'll go where I want. I came a long way."

The woman stayed quiet for a long moment.

"Well, I warned you," she said. "I can't do more than that."

And she walked away, toward Washington Square. Reacher waited where he was, all alone on Waverly, head up, head down, searching for a breath of air, and then he followed after her, about two minutes behind, and he saw her drive away in a car that had been parked in a tow zone. A 1975 Ford Granada, he thought, mid-blue, vinyl roof, a big toothy grille. It took a corner like a land yacht and drove out of sight.

Washington Square was much emptier than Reacher had expected. Because of the heat. There were a couple of unexplained black guys hanging around, probably dealers, and not much else. No chess players, no dog walkers. But way over on the eastern edge of the square he saw three girls go into a coffee shop. Coeds for sure, long hair, tan, lithe, maybe two or three years older than him. He headed in their direction, and looked for a pay phone on the way. He found a working instrument on his fourth try. He used a hot damp coin from his pocket and dialed the number he had memorized for West Point's main switchboard.

A singsong male voice said, "United States Military Academy, how may I direct your call?"

"Cadet Joe Reacher, please."

"Hold the line," the voice said, which Reacher thought was appropriate. West Point was in the business of holding the line, against all kinds of things, including enemies foreign and domestic, and progress, sometimes. West Point was Army, which was an unusual choice for the elder son of a Marine, but Joe's heart had been set on it. And he claimed to be enjoying it so far. Reacher himself had no idea where he would go. NYU, possibly, with women. The three in the coffee shop had looked pretty good. But he didn't make plans. Sixteen years in the Corps had cured him of that.

The phone clicked and buzzed as the call was transferred from station to station. Reacher took another hot wet coin from his pocket and held it ready. It was a quarter to nine, and dark, and getting hotter, if such a thing was possible. Fifth Avenue was a long narrow canyon running north ahead of him. There were flashes of light in the sky, low down on the horizon, way far in the distance.

A different voice said, "Cadet Reacher is currently unavailable. Do you have a message?"

Reacher said, "Please tell him his brother is delayed twenty-four hours. I'm spending the night in the city. I'll see him tomorrow evening."

"Roger that," the new voice said, with no interest at all, and the line went dead. Reacher put the second coin back in his pocket, and he hung up the phone, and he headed for the coffee shop on the eastern edge of the square.

An air conditioner over the coffee shop's door was running so hard it was trembling and rattling, but it wasn't making much difference to the temperature of the air. The girls were together in a booth for four, with tall soda glasses full of Coke and melting ice. Two of them were blondes and one was a brunette. All of them had long smooth limbs and perfect white teeth. The brunette was in short shorts and a sleeveless button-front shirt, and the blondes were in short summer dresses. They all looked quick and intelligent and full of energy. Storybook Americans, literally. Reacher had seen girls just like them in greasy old out-of-date copies of *Time* and *Life* and *Newsweek* at Mujuk and every other base he had lived on. They were the future, the stories had said. He had admired them from afar.

Now he stood at the door under the roaring air conditioner and admired them from a whole lot closer. But he had no idea what to do next. Life as a Corps kid taught a guy plenty, but absolutely nothing about bridging a fifteen-foot door-to-table distance in a New York City coffee shop. Up to that point his few conquests had not really been conquests at all, but mutual experiments with Corps girls just as isolated as himself, and just as willing and enthusiastic and desperate. Their only negatives had been their fathers, who were all trained killers with fairly traditional views. The three students in front of him were a whole different can of worms. Much easier from the parental point of view, presumably, but much harder in every other way.

He paused.

Nothing ventured, nothing gained.

He moved on, fifteen feet, and he approached their table, and he said, "Do you mind if I join you?"

They all looked up. They all looked surprised. They were all too polite to tell him to get lost. They were all too smart to tell him to sit down. New York City, in the summer of 1977. The Bronx, burning. Hundreds of homicides. The Son of Sam. Irrational panic everywhere.

He said, "I'm new here. I was wondering if you could tell me where to go, to hear some good music."

No answer. Two pairs of blue eyes, one pair of brown, looking up at him.

He said, "Are you headed somewhere this evening?"

The brunette was the first to speak.

She said, "Maybe."

"Where to?"

"Don't know yet."

A waitress came by, barely older than the coeds themselves, and Reacher maneuvered himself into a spot where her approach gave him no choice but to sit down. As if he had been swept along. The brunette scooted over and left an inch between her thigh and his. The vinyl bench was sticky with heat. He ordered a Coke. It was way too hot for coffee.

There was an awkward silence. The waitress brought

Reacher's Coke. He took a sip. The blonde directly opposite asked him, "Are you at NYU?"

"I'm still in high school," he said.

She softened a little, as if he was a rare curiosity.

"Where?" she asked.

"South Korea," he said. "Military family."

"Fascist," she said. "Get lost."

"What does your dad do for a living?"

"He's a lawyer."

"Get lost yourself."

The brunette laughed. She was an inch shorter than the others, and her skin was a shade darker. She was slender. Elfin, almost. Reacher had heard the word. Not that it meant much to him. He had never seen an elf.

The brunette said, "The Ramones might be at CBGB. Or Blondie."

Reacher said, "I'll go if you go."

"It's a rough area."

"Compared to what? Iwo Jima?"

"Where's that?"

"It's an island in the Pacific."

"Sounds nice. Does it have beaches?"

"Lots of them. What's your name?"

"Chrissie."

"Pleased to meet you, Chrissie. My name is Reacher."

"First or last?"

"Only."

"You have only one name?"

"That anyone uses."

"So if I go to CBGB with you, do you promise to stick close by?"

Which was pretty much a do-bears-sleep-in-the-woods type of a question, in Reacher's opinion. Is the Pope a Catholic? He said, "Sure, count on it."

The blondes on the opposite side of the table started fidgeting with dubious body language, and immediately Reacher knew they wouldn't come, too. Which was dead-on A-OK with him. Like a big green light. A one-on-one excursion. Like a real date. Nine o'clock in the evening, Wednesday, July 13, New York City, and his first civilian conquest was almost upon him, like a runaway train. He could feel it coming, like an earthquake. He wondered where Chrissie's dorm was. Close by, he guessed.

He sipped his Coke.

Chrissie said, "So let's go, Reacher."

Reacher left money on the table for four Cokes, which he guessed was the gentlemanly thing to do. He followed Chrissie out through the door, and the night heat hit him like a hammer. Chrissie, too. She held her hair away from her shoulders with the backs of her hands and he saw a damp sheen on her neck. She said, "How far is it?"

He said, "You've never been?"

"It's a bad area."

"I think we have to go east about five blocks. Past Broadway and Lafayette to the Bowery. Then about three blocks south to the corner with Bleecker."

"It's so hot."

"That's for sure."

"Maybe we should take my car. For the AC."

"You have a car?"

"Sure."

"Here in the city?"

"Right there." And she pointed, to a small hatch-back car on the curb about fifty feet away. A Chevrolet Chevette, Reacher thought, maybe a year old, maybe baby blue, although it was hard to tell under the yellow street lights.

He said, "Doesn't it cost a lot to keep a car in the city?"

She said, "Parking is free after six o'clock."

"But what do you do with it in the daytime?"

She paused a beat, as if unraveling the layers of his question, and she said, "No, I don't live here."

"I thought you did. Sorry. My mistake. I figured you were at NYU."

She shook her head and said, "Sarah Lawrence."

"Who's she?"

"It's a college. Where we go. In Yonkers. North of here. Sometimes we drive down and see what's going on. Sometimes there are NYU boys in that coffee shop."

"So we're both out-of-towners."

"Not tonight," Chrissie said.

"What are your friends going to do?"

"About what?"

"About getting home tonight."

"I'm going to drive them," Chrissie said. "Like always."

Reacher said nothing.

"But they'll wait," Chrissie said. "That's part of the deal."

The Chevette's air conditioner was about as lousy as the coffee shop's, but something was better than nothing. There were a few people on Broadway, like ghosts in a ghost town, moving slow, and a few on Lafayette, slower still, and homeless people on the Bowery, waiting for the shelters to open. Chrissie parked two blocks north of the venue, on Great Jones Street, between a car with its front window broken and a car with its back window broken. But it was under a working street light, which looked to be about as good as it got, short of employing a team of armed guards, or a pack of vicious dogs, or both. And the car would have been no safer left on Washington Square, anyway. So they got out into the heat and walked to the corner through air thick enough to eat. The sky was as hot and hard as an iron roof at noontime, and it was still flickering in the north, with the kind of restless energy that promised plenty and delivered nothing.

There was no line at the door of the club, which Chrissie felt was a good thing, because it meant there would be spots to be had at the front near the stage, just in case it really was the Ramones or Blondie that night. A guy inside took their money, and they moved past him into the heat and the noise and the dark, toward the bar, which was a long low space with dim light and sweating walls and red diner stools. There were about thirty people in there, twenty-eight of them kids no older than Chrissie, plus one person Reacher already knew, and another person he was pretty sure he was going to get to know, pretty well and pretty soon. The one he knew was Jill Hemingway, still thin and blonde and nervous, still in her short summer dress.

The one he felt he would get to know looked a lot like Croselli. A cousin, maybe. He was the same kind of size and shape and age, and he was wearing the same kind of clothes, which were a sweated-through suit and a shirt plastered tight against a wet and hairy belly.

Jill Hemingway saw Reacher first. But only by a second. She moved off her stool and took a step and immediately the guy in the suit started snapping his fingers and gesturing for the phone. The barkeep dumped the instrument in front of him and the guy started dialing. Hemingway pushed her way through the thin crowd and came up to Reacher face to face and said, "You idiot."

Reacher said, "Jill, this is my friend Chrissie. Chrissie, this is Jill, who I met earlier this evening. She's an FBI agent."

Beside him Chrissie said, "Hi, Jill."

Hemingway looked temporarily nonplussed and said, "Hi, Chrissie."

Reacher said, "Are you here for the music?"

Hemingway said, "I'm here because this is one of the few places Croselli doesn't get total cooperation. Therefore this is one of the few places I knew he would have to put a guy. So I'm here to make sure nothing happens to you."

"How did you know I would come here?"

"You live in South Korea. What else have you heard of?"

Chrissie said, "What exactly are we talking about?"

Croselli's guy was still on the phone.

Reacher said, "Let's sit down."

Hemingway said, "Let's not. Let's get you the hell out of here."

Chrissie said, "What the hell is going on?"

There were tiny café tables near the deserted stage. Reacher pushed through the crowd, left shoulder, right shoulder, and sat down, his back to a corner, most of the room in front of him. Chrissie sat down next to him, hesitant, and Hemingway paced for a second, and then she gave it up and joined them. Chrissie said, "This is really freaking me out, guys. Will someone please tell me what's going on?"

Reacher said, "I was walking down the street and I saw a guy slap Agent Hemingway in the face."

"And?"

"I hoped my presence would discourage him from doing it again. He took offense. Turns out he's a mobster. Jill thinks they're measuring me for concrete shoes."

"And you don't?"

"Seems oversensitive to me."

Chrissie said, "Reacher, there are whole movies about this stuff."

Hemingway said, "She's right. You should listen to her. You don't know these people. You don't understand their culture. They won't let an outsider disrespect them. It's a matter of pride. It's how they do business. They won't rest until they fix it."

Reacher said, "In other words they're exactly the same as the Marine Corps. I know how to deal with people like that. I've been doing it all my life."

"How do you plan to deal with them?"

"By making the likely cost too high. Which it already is, frankly. They can't do anything in here, because they'd be arrested, either by you or the NYPD. Which is too high of a cost. It would mean lawyers and bribes and favors, which they won't spend on me. I'm not worth it. I'm nobody. Croselli will get over it."

"You can't stay in here all night."

"He already tried it on the street, and he didn't get very far."

"Ten minutes from now he'll have six guys out front."

"Then I'll go out the back."

"He'll have six guys there, too."

Chrissie said, "You know when I asked you to stick close by me?"

Reacher said, "Sure."

"You can forget that part now, OK?"

Reacher said, "This is nuts."

Hemingway said, "You hit a made man in the head. What part of that don't you understand? That just doesn't happen. Get used to it, kid. And right now you're in the same room as one of his goons. Who just got off the phone."

"I'm sitting next to an FBI agent."

Hemingway said nothing in reply to that. Reacher thought: *NYU. Sarah Lawrence.* Hemingway had never confirmed it either way. He had asked her: How long have you been with the FBI? She had answered: Who says I am?

He said, "Are you or are you not?"

She said nothing.

"It's not real hard. It's a yes or no answer."

"No," she said. "It really isn't."

"What does that mean?"

"It's yes and no. Not yes or no."

Reacher paused a beat.

"What, you're freelancing here?" he said. "Is that it? This isn't really your case? Which is why there was no backup van? Which is why you were using your little sister's tape player?"

"It was my tape player. I'm suspended."

"You're what?"

"Medical grounds. But that's what they always say. What it means is they took my badge, pending review."

"Of what?"

"Like you said. The lawyers and the bribes and the favors. They're weighing me in the balance. Me against all the good stuff."

"This was Croselli?"

Hemingway nodded. "Right now he's fireproof. He had the investigation shut down. I figured I might get him to boast about it, on the tape. I might have gotten something I could use. To make them take me back."

"Why wasn't Croselli armed in the city?"

"Part of the deal. They all can do what they want in every other way, but the homicide figure has to come down. Give and take. Everyone's a winner."

"Does Croselli know you're suspended?"

"Of course he does. He made them do it."

"So in fact the goon in the same room as me knows it, too, right? Is that what we're saying here? He knows you're not about to pull a badge. Or a gun. He knows you're just a member of the public. Legally, I mean. In terms of your powers of arrest, and so on. And less than that, in terms of your credibility. As a witness against Croselli's people, I mean."

"I told you to go see your brother."

"Don't get all defensive. I'm not blaming you. I need to make a new plan, that's all. I need to understand the parameters."

Chrissie said, "You shouldn't have gotten involved in the first place."

"Why not?"

"At Sarah Lawrence we would say it was uncomfortably gender normative behavior. It was patriarchal. It spoke to the paternalistic shape of our society."

"You know what they would say in the Marine Corps?"

"What?"

"They would point out you asked me to stick close by, because you think the Bowery is dangerous."

"It is dangerous. Twelve guys are about to show up and kick your butt."

Reacher nodded. "We should go, probably."

"You can't," Hemingway said. "The goon won't let you. Not until the others get here."

"Is he armed?"

"No. Like I said."

"You sure?"

"Hundred percent."

"Do we agree one opponent is better than twelve?"

"What are you talking about?"

"Wait here," Reacher said.

Reacher walked across the dim room, as graceful as a bulked-up greyhound, with all the dumb confidence a guy gets from being six-five and two-twenty and sixteen years old. He moved on through the bar, toward the restroom corridor. He had been in relatively few bars in his life, but enough to know they were superbly weapons-rich environments. Some had pool cues, all neatly lined up in racks, and some had martini glasses, all delicate and breakable, with stems like stilettos, and some had champagne bottles, as heavy as clubs. But the CBGB bar had no pool table, and its customers were apparently indifferent to martinis and champagne. The most numerous local resource was long-neck beer bottles, of which there were plenty. Reacher collected one as he walked, and out of the corner of his eye he saw Croselli's guy get up and follow him, no doubt worried about rear exits or bathroom windows. There was in fact a rear exit, at the end of the restroom corridor, but Reacher ignored it. Instead he stepped into the men's room.

Which was perhaps the single most bizarre place he had ever seen, outside of a military installation. The walls were bare brick covered in dense graffiti, and there were three wall-hung urinals and a lone sit-down toilet all exposed up on a step like a throne. There was a two-hole metal sink, and unspooled toilet rolls everywhere. No windows.

Reacher filled his empty beer bottle with water from the faucet, for extra weight, and he wiped his palm on his T-shirt, which neither dried his hand nor made his shirt appreciably wetter. But he got a decent grip on the long glass neck, and he held the bottle low down

by his leg and he waited. Croselli's guy came in seconds later. He glanced around, first amazed by the decor,
then reassured by the lack of windows, which told
Reacher all he really needed to know, but at sixteen he
still played it by the book, so he asked anyway. He said,
"Do we have a problem, you and me?"

The guy said, "We're waiting for Mr. Croselli. He'll
be here in a minute. Which won't be a problem for me.
But it will be for you."

So Reacher swung the bottle, the water kept in by
centrifugal force, and it caught the guy high on the
cheekbone and rocked him back, whereupon Reacher
whipped the bottle down again and smashed it on the
lip of a urinal, glass and water flying everywhere, and
he jabbed the jagged broken circle into the guy's thigh,
to bring his hands down, and then again into his face,
with a twist, flesh tearing and blood flowing, and then
he dropped the bottle and shoved the guy in the chest,
to bounce him off the wall, and as he came back
toward him he dropped a solid head butt straight to
the guy's nose. Which was game over, right there,
helped a little by the way the guy's head bounced off
the urinal on his way to the floor, which all made a
conclusive little head-injury trifecta, bone, porcelain,
tile, good night and good luck.

Reacher breathed in, and breathed out, and then he
checked the view in the busted mirror above the sink.
He had diluted smears of the guy's blood on his forehead. He rinsed them off with lukewarm water and
shook like a dog and headed back through the bar into
the main room. Jill Hemingway and Chrissie were on
their feet in the middle of the dance floor. He nodded

them toward the exit. They set off toward him and he waited to fall into step. Hemingway said, "Where's the goon?"

Reacher said, "He had an accident."

"Jesus."

They hustled on, through the bar one more time, into the lobby corridor, fast and hot.

Too late.

They got within ten feet of the street door, and then it opened wide and four big guys in sweated-through suits stepped in, followed by Croselli himself. All five of them stopped, and Reacher stopped, and behind him Chrissie and Jill Hemingway stopped, eight people all in a strung-out, single-file standoff, in a hot narrow corridor with perspiration running down the bare brick walls.

From the far end of the line Croselli said, "We meet again, kid."

Then the lights went out.

Reacher couldn't tell if his eyes were open or closed. The darkness was total and profound, like the next stop after nothing. And the darkness was completely silent, way down at some deep primeval level, all the low subliminal hum of modern life suddenly gone, leaving nothing in its place except blind human shufflings and a kind of whispered eerie keening that seemed to come up from ageless rocks below. From the twentieth century to the Stone Age, at the flick of a switch.

From behind him Reacher heard Chrissie's voice say, "Reacher?"

"Stand still," he said.

"OK."

"Now turn around."

"OK."

He heard her feet on the floor, shuffling. He searched his last retained visual memory for where the first of Croselli's guys had stopped. *The middle of the corridor, facing dead ahead, maybe five feet away.* He planted his left foot and kicked out with his right, hard, blindly, aiming groin-high into the pitch-black emptiness ahead. But he hit something lower, making contact a jarring split second before he expected. A kneecap, maybe. Which was fine. Either way the first of Croselli's guys was about to fall down, and the other three were about to trip over him.

Reacher spun around and felt for Chrissie's back, and he put his right arm around her shoulders, and with his left hand he found Hemingway, and he half pulled and half pushed them back the way they had come, to the bar, where a feeble battery-powered safety light had clicked on. Which meant it hadn't been the flick of a switch. The whole building had lost power.

He found the restroom corridor and pushed Chrissie ahead of him and pulled Hemingway behind him, to the rear door, and they barged through it, out to the street.

Which was way too dark.

They hustled onward anyway, fast, out in the heat again, muscle memory and instinct compelling them to put some distance between the door and themselves, compelling them to seek the shadows, but it was all shadows. The Bowery was a pitch-dark and sullen ditch, long and straight both ways, bordered by pitch-dark and sullen buildings, uniformly massive and gloomy, their unlit bulk for once darker than the night sky. The skyline sentinels forty blocks north and south weren't there at all, except in a negative sense, because at the bottom of the sky there were dead fingers where inert buildings were blocking the glow of starlight behind thin clouds.

"The whole city is out," Hemingway said.

"Listen," Reacher said.

"To what?"

"Exactly. The sound of a billion electric motors not running. And a billion electric circuits switched off."

Chrissie said, "This is unbelievable."

Hemingway said, "There's going to be trouble. Give it an hour or so, and there's going to be rioting, and arson, and a whole lot of looting. So you two, right now, head north as far and as fast as you can. Do not go east or west. Do not use the tunnels. Do not stop until you're north of 14th Street."

Reacher said, "What are you going to do?"

"I'm going to work."

"You're suspended."

"I can't stand by and do nothing. And you have to get your friend back where you found her. I think those are our basic obligations." And then she ran, south toward Houston Street, and was lost in the dark within seconds.

The street light on Great Jones was no longer working, but the blue Chevette was still under it, gray and formless in the dark, as yet unmolested. Chrissie opened it up, and they got in, and she started the motor and put it in gear. She didn't turn on the lights, which Reacher understood. Disturbing the massive darkness didn't seem right. Or possible, even. The great city felt stunned and passive, an immense organism laid low, implacable and indifferent to tiny scurrying humans. Of which there was a growing number within view. Windows were opening, and folks on lower floors were walking downstairs and coming out, standing near their doors and peering about, full of wonder and apprehension. The heat was still way up there. It wasn't cooling down at all. A hundred degrees, maybe more, clamping down and now smug and settled and supreme, unchallenged by fans or air-conditioning or any other kind of man-made mediation.

Great Jones Street was one-way west, and they crossed Lafayette and Broadway, and continued on West Third, Chrissie driving slow and tentative, not much faster than walking pace, a dark car in the dark, one of very few about. Maybe drivers had felt compelled to pull over, as part of the general paralysis. The traffic lights were all out. Each new block was newly weird, still and silent, blank and gray, absolutely unlit. They turned north on LaGuardia Place, and went counterclockwise around the bottom right-hand corner of Washington Square, back to the coffee shop. Chrissie parked where she had before, and they got out into the soupy air and the silence.

The coffee shop was dark, obviously, with nothing

to see behind its dusty glass window. The air conditioner above the door was silent. And the door was
locked. Reacher and Chrissie cupped their hands and
pressed them to the glass and peered through, and saw
nothing except vague black shapes in the dark. No
staff. No customers. Maybe a health board thing. If
the refrigerators went out, maybe they had to abandon
ship.

Reacher said, "Where will your friends have gone?"

Chrissie said, "No idea."

"You said there was a plan."

"If one of us gets lucky, we meet back here at
midnight."

"I'm sorry you didn't get luckier."

"I feel OK now."

"We're still south of 14th Street."

"They won't find you in the dark, surely."

"Will we find your friends in the dark?"

"Why would we want to? They'll get back by midnight. Until then we should hang out and experience
this. Don't you think? This is pretty amazing."

And it was. There was a hugeness to it. Not just a
room or a building or a block, but the entire city, slumped
inert and defeated all around them, as if it was ruined,
as if it was dead, like a relic from the past. And maybe
it was more than just the city. There was no glow on
any horizon. Nothing from across either river, nothing
from the south, nothing from the north. Maybe the
whole Northeast was out. Maybe all of America. Or
the whole world. People were always talking about secret weapons. Maybe someone had pulled a trigger.

Chrissie said, "Let's go look at the Empire State Building. We may never see it like this again."

Reacher said, "OK."

"In the car."

"OK."

They went up University, and used Ninth Street across to Sixth Avenue, where they turned north. Sixth Avenue was nothing at all. Just a long black hole, and then a small rectangle of night sky where it ended at Central Park. There were a few cars on it. All were moving slow. Most had their lights off. Like the Chevette. Instinctive, somehow. A shared assumption. Crowd behavior. Reacher caught a sudden whiff of fear. *Hide in the dark. Don't stand out. Don't be seen.*

Herald Square had people in it. Where Broadway cut across, at 34th Street. Most of them were out in the middle of the triangle, away from the buildings, trying to see the sky. Some of them were formed up in moving bunches, like sports fans leaving the stadium after a win, with the same kind of boisterous energy. But Macy's windows were all intact. So far.

They kept going all the way to West 38th, crawling past the dead traffic lights and the cross streets, unsure every time whether they should yield or keep on going, but it turned out there was no real danger of either fender benders or confrontation, because everyone was moving slow and acting deferential, all *after you, no, after you.* Clearly the spirit so far was cooperation. On the roads, at least. Reacher wondered how long it would last.

They went east on 38th and turned on Fifth four blocks north of the Empire State. Nothing to see. Just a broad dark base, like both sides of every other block, and then nothing above. Just spectral darkness. They parked on the Fifth Avenue curb, on the block north of 34th Street, and got out for a closer look. Thirty-fourth was a double-wide street, with a clear view east and west, dark all the way, except for an orange glow in the far distance above what must have been Brooklyn. Fires were burning there.

"It's starting," Reacher said.

They heard a cop car coming north on Madison, and they saw it cross the six-lane width of 34th Street one block over. Its lights looked amazingly bright. It drove on out of sight, and the night went quiet again. Chrissie said, "Why did the power go out?"

"Don't know," Reacher said. "Overload from all the AC, or a lightning strike somewhere. Or the electromagnetic pulse from a nuclear explosion. Or maybe someone didn't pay the bill."

"Nuclear explosion?"

"It's a known side effect. But I don't think it happened. We'd have seen the flash. And depending where it was, we'd have been burned to a crisp."

"What kind of military are you?"

"No kind at all. My dad's a Marine, and my brother is going to be an army officer, but that's them, not me."

"What are you going to be?"

"I have no idea. Probably not a lawyer."

"Do you think your FBI friend was right about riots and looting?"

"Maybe not so much in Manhattan."

"Are we going to be OK?"

Reacher said, "We're going to be fine. If all else

fails, we'll do what they did in the olden days. We'll wait for morning."

They turned onto 34th Street and drove over as close as they could get to the East River. They stopped on a trash-strewn triangle half under the FDR Drive, and they stared through the windshield over the water to the dark lands beyond. Queens dead ahead, Brooklyn to the right, the Bronx way far to the left. The fires in Brooklyn looked pretty big already. There were fires in Queens, too. And the Bronx, but Reacher had been told there were always fires in the Bronx. Nothing behind them, in Manhattan. Not yet. But there were plenty of sirens. The darkness was getting angry. Maybe because of the heat. Reacher wondered how Macy's windows were doing.

Chrissie kept the engine running, for the AC. The gas was about half full. The tails of her shirt hid her shorts completely. She looked like she was wearing nothing else. Just the shirt. Which looked great. She was very pretty. He asked, "How old are you?"

She said, "Nineteen."

"Where are you from?"

"California."

"You like it here?"

"So far. We get seasons. Heat and cold."

"Especially heat."

She asked, "How old are you?"

"I'm legal," he said. "That's really all you need to know."

"Is it?"

"I hope so."

She smiled, and turned off the engine. She locked her door, and leaned over to lock his. She smelled of hot clean girl. She said, "It's going to get warm in here."

"I hope so," he said again. He put his arm around her shoulders and pulled her close and kissed her. He knew how to do it. He had more than three years of practice. He put his free hand on the curve of her hip. She was a great kisser. Warm, wet, plenty of tongue. Closed eyes. He pushed her shirt up a little and ducked his hand under it. She was lean and firm. Hot, and a little damp. She brought her spare hand over and put it under his shirt. She smoothed it up over his side, over his chest, and down to his waist. She put the tips of her fingers under his waistband, which he took to be an encouraging sign.

They came up for air, and then they started again. He moved his free hand to her knee, and slid it up the wondrous smooth skin of her thigh, on the outside, with his thumb on the inside, to the hem of her shorts, and back again, to the other knee, and up her other leg, just as smooth and luscious, his fingers on the inside this time, his thumb on the outside, all the time trying to imagine anything more splendid than the feel of a warm girl's skin, and failing. And this time he went a little further, until his leading finger was jammed against the hard seam between her legs, at the bottom of her zip. She clamped hard on his hand, which at first he took as an admonition, but then he realized she had another purpose in mind, so he kept his hand there, pushing hard as she ground away, almost lifting her off the seat. Then she sighed and gasped and went all rubbery, and they came up for air again, and he moved his crushed hand to the buttons on her shirt, and he tried to make his fingers work. Which they did, reasonably well, one button, two, three, all the way down until her shirt fell open.

They kissed again, the third marathon, and his free hand went to work in a different area, first outside a silky bra, and then inside, from below, until it was all pushed up and her small damp breasts were his. He moved his mouth to her neck, and then to her nipples, and he put his hand back where it had been before, and she started grinding again, long and slow, long and slow, breathing hard, until for a second time she sighed and gasped and fell against him, as if she had no bones in her body.

Then she put a hand on his chest and pushed him away, back toward his window, which again he took as a reproach, until she smiled like she knew something he didn't, and unbuttoned his pants. Slim brown fingers took care of his zip, at which exact point for the first time in his life he truly understood the phrase *died and gone to heaven*. Her head went down into his lap, and he felt cool lips and a tongue, and he closed his eyes, and then he opened them again and stared about, determined to remember every last detail of his situation, the where and the when, and the how, and the who and the why, especially the why, because his conscious mind could find no logical path between the Port Authority Bus Terminal and what had to be some kind of enchanted kingdom. *New York, New York. It's a wonderful town.* That was for damn sure. So he stared around, locking it all in, the river, the formless boroughs beyond, the distant fires, the wire fences, the bleak concrete pillars holding up the road above.

He saw a man standing thirty yards away in the dark, silhouetted against the glow coming off the water. Mid-twenties, maybe, judging by his posture, medium height, thick in the upper body, a geeky shape to his head, because of uncooperative hair. He had the kind of hair that should have been cut much shorter, but it was 1977. He was holding something in his right hand.

Chrissie was still busy. She was unquestionably the best ever. No comparison. None at all. He wondered if Sarah Lawrence was coed. He could go there. Just as good as NYU. Not that they were likely to get married or anything. But maybe she had friends. Or a sister. In fact he knew she had friends. The two blondes. *They'll wait. That's part of the deal.* They had two hours until midnight, which suddenly seemed like nothing at all.

The guy moved in the dark. He rolled around a pillar, light on his feet, staying covered, checking the blind spot at ninety degrees, checking the other direction, and then moving forward, fast and straight to the next pillar.

Toward the Chevette.

The guy eased around the new pillar, just to check his new blind spot, and then he pulled back and merged with the concrete, barely visible again, all the time being very careful with the thing in his hand, as if it was valuable or especially fragile.

Chrissie was still busy. And she was doing a fine, fine job. Died and gone to heaven wasn't even close. It was an underestimate of the most serious kind. Egregious, even. It was the kind of faint praise that could cause a diplomatic incident.

The guy moved again. He went through the same routine, reflexively, glance, glance, move, to the next pillar, closer still to the Chevette, and he blended in, bringing his right arm to rest last, solicitous of the thing he was holding, taking care not to bring it into contact with the concrete.

Thereby bringing it separately through the river's glow, all by itself.

Reacher knew what it was.

It was an upside-down revolver, swinging by the trigger guard on the guy's right-hand index finger. A squat shape, thick in the upper body like the guy himself, rounded in the grips, a two-and-a-half-inch barrel, smooth, with few projections. Could have been a Charter Arms Bulldog, a five-shooter, sturdy, most often chambered for the .44 Special. Double action. Easy to service. Not a target shooter's gun. But good close up.

Chrissie was still busy. The guy moved again. Closer still to the Chevette. He stared right at it. Before he had gotten on the bus in Pohang Reacher's mother had made him read her newspapers. New York City. A killing spree. The Son of Sam. Named from his crazy letters. But before the letters came he had been called something else. He had been called the .44 Caliber Killer. Because he used .44 caliber bullets. From a revolver.

Specifically, the NYPD said, from a Charter Arms Bulldog.

Chrissie was still busy. And this was no kind of a time to stop. No kind of a time at all. In fact stopping was not a possibility. Physically, mentally, every other way. It was absolutely not on the agenda. It was in a whole different hemisphere than the agenda. Maybe a whole different universe. It was a biological fact. It was not going to happen. The guy stared. Reacher stared back. *He's killing people. Couples sitting in cars.* Way to go, Reacher thought. Do it now. I'll go out on a high note. The highest possible note in the whole history of high notes. *Jack Reacher, RIP. He died young, but he had a smile on his face.*

The guy made no move. He just stared.

Reacher stared back.

The guy made no move.

Couples sitting in cars.

But they weren't. Not from an exterior perspective. Chrissie's head was in his lap. Reacher was alone in the car. Just a driver, off the road in the emergency, waiting in the passenger seat, for the extra legroom. The guy stared. Reacher stared back. Chrissie was still busy. The guy moved on. To the next pillar, and the next, and then he was lost to sight.

And then Chrissie's work was done.

Afterward they repaired the damage as well as they could, straightening and zipping and buttoning and combing. Chrissie said, "Better than Blondie?"

Reacher said, "How could I tell?"

"Better than Blondie live onstage at CBGB, I mean."

"A lot better. No real comparison."

"You like Blondie, right?"

"Best ever. Well, top five. Or ten."

"Shut up." She started the engine again and put the air on max. She slid down in her seat and lifted her shirt tails so the vents blew straight up against her skin.

Reacher said, "I saw someone."

"When?"

"Just now."

"Doing what?"

"Peering into this car."

"Who?"

"Some guy."

"For real? That's kind of creepy."

Reacher said, "I know. And I'm real sorry, but I have to go find Jill Hemingway. I should tell her first. She needs some favors."

"Tell her what?"

"What I saw."

"What did you see?"

"Something she should know about."

"Was it one of Croselli's guys?"

"No."

"So how is it important?"

"She might be able to use it."

"Where is she?"

"I have no idea. Let me out in Washington Square and I'll walk. I bet she's north of Houston."

"You would be going right back in there, where we got chased out before."

"Let's call that phase our reconnaissance."

"What would you do this time?"

"Fastest way to find Hemingway is to look for Croselli."

"I'm not going to let you."

"How could you stop me?"

"I would tell you not to. I'm your girlfriend. At least until midnight."

"Is this what they teach you at Sarah Lawrence?"

"Pretty much."

"Works for me," Reacher said. "We'll just hang out, see if she comes by."

"Really?"

"I mean it."

"Why?"

"Laws of physics. A random encounter doesn't get more likely just because both parties are moving."

"OK, where?"

"Let's say the corner of Bleecker and Broadway. That might make the encounter less random."

"That's way down there."

"It's a block from Houston. We can break out south if we need to."

"We?"

"Was it you who wanted me to stick close by?"

"This is a whole different type of crazy."

Reacher nodded.

"I understand," he said. "I really do. It's your choice. You can let me out in Washington Square. That would be fine. Don't think I'll ever forget you."

"Really?"

"If I'm done before midnight, I'll come say goodbye."

"I mean, really, you won't forget me? That's very sweet."

"Also very true. As long as I live."

Chrissie said, "Tell me more about the guy you saw."

Reacher said, "I think it was the Son of Sam."

"You *are* crazy."

"I'm serious."

"And you just sat there?"

"Seemed like the best thing to do."

"How close did he get?"

"About twenty feet. He had a good look, and he walked away."

"The Son of Sam was twenty feet from me?"

"He didn't see you. I think that's why he walked away."

She glanced all around in the dark and put the car in gear. She said, "The Son of Sam is an NYPD case, not the FBI."

Reacher said, "Whoever passes on a tip gets a brownie point. I imagine that's how it works."

"What's the tip?"

"The way he moved."

There were more sirens behind them. First Avenue, Second Avenue, uptown, downtown, crosstown, there were plenty of cops on the streets. The mood was changing. Reacher could taste it on the air.

"I'll come with you," Chrissie said. "For the experience. These are the big things we'll always remember."

They used 34th Street again, back toward the center of the island, back toward the heart of darkness. The city was still pitch black, still dead, like a giant creature fallen on its back. There were broken windows. There were people roaming in groups, carrying stuff. There were police cars and fire trucks speeding through the streets, all lit up and whooping and barking, but their lights didn't make much impression on the blackness, and their sirens didn't seem to worry the roaming people. They merely scuttled into doorways as the cars and trucks passed. The people reminded Reacher of tiny nighttime organisms working on a corpse, penetrating its skin, exploring it, disassembling it, feeding off it, recovering its nutrients, recycling its components, like a dead whale feeds a million sea creatures on the ocean bed.

They turned south on Fifth Avenue at the Empire State Building and drove slowly in the middle lane, passing knots of people in the roadway, two of whom were carrying a rolled-up carpet, three of whom were loading the trunk of a big battered car with something in boxes. They veered left onto Broadway at 23rd Street, past the ghostly Flatiron Building, and they continued south, around Union Square, across 14th Street, into enemy territory, and onward. The mayhem got a little worse the further south they went. Broadway looked narrow, like a dark trench through a dark landscape, and there were busted windows, and people everywhere, moving in groups, fast and furtive and silent, barely visible at all, except for the glow of cigarettes. They passed 4th Street, and 3rd, where they had been before, and Chrissie started to slow the car, and Reacher said, "Change of plan. I think Sixth Avenue and Bleecker might be better."

Chrissie said, "Why?"

"What is Croselli worried about right now?"

"Getting his stuff ripped off. Like anyone. If he has stuff."

"I think he does. I mean, how does he earn money between Houston and 14th? Maybe protection rackets and hookers and so on, but dope for sure. He must have a stash somewhere. But where? Not in an ancestral home in Little Italy, because that's way south of Houston."

"You know the geography pretty well."

"I've studied it from afar. And he walked west from Waverly. After the slapping incident. Toward Sixth Avenue. Obviously he was heading back to make his phone calls. About me. So his HQ must be west of Waverly."

"You think Hemingway knows where it is?"

"I'm sure she does. And I'm sure she's watching it, right now. I'm assuming no one gave her an actual role tonight, because she's suspended. So she's still freelancing. I bet she's hoping some bunch of guys busts down Croselli's door, so she can get a record of what's inside. Maybe she'll even get Croselli defending it, which would be pretty much a slam dunk, wouldn't it? Doesn't matter what kind of deal he made. Some things can't be ignored."

"It will be more than just Croselli defending it. He's got twelve guys."

"Ten now," Reacher said. "Two of them are in the

hospital. Or trying to get there. But we'll keep out of their way. It's Hemingway we want."

"Hard to find one woman in the dark."

"All we can do is try."

So they rolled onward, toward Houston Street, past a big stereo store with two busted windows and not much left inside, and they made the right and crept west, past the dark wasteland streets of SoHo coming in from the left, Mercer, and Greene, and Wooster, and West Broadway, and Thompson, and Sullivan, and MacDougal. Then they turned right on Sixth, and headed north a block to where Bleecker and Downing and Minetta all met in an untidy little six-way split. Retail was down-market and scruffy in that location, some of it too scruffy even for looters, some of it already busted wide open and stripped. Looking north, Sixth was the same long black hole it had been before, with the same slim upright rectangle of night sky at the end of it.

Chrissie said, "Should I park here?"

Reacher said, "Let's cruise a few blocks."

"You said we would hang out and let her come to us."

"Mission creep. Occupational hazard. Like the Navy transporting the Marines."

"I'm an English major."

"Just five minutes, OK?"

"OK," she said.

But they didn't need five minutes. They were done in barely sixty seconds. They made the tight left onto Downing, and a right on Bedford, and a right on Carmine, back toward Bleecker again, and in a doorway on the right side of the street Reacher caught a flash of pale skin and blonde hair, and he pointed, and Chrissie jammed to a stop, and Jill Hemingway stepped out of the dark and bent down to Reacher's window, like a Seoul streetwalker talking to an enlisted man.

Reacher expected Hemingway to be mad at his reappearance, but she wasn't. He figured she felt exposed. Or caught out in her own obsession. Which she was, basically. And she looked a little sheepish about it.

He asked, "Is his place near here?"

She pointed through the car at a pair of large blank doors across the street. They were tall and wide. Like a wagon entrance, from long ago, big enough for a cart and a team of horses. In the daylight the paint might have looked dark green. Set into the right-hand door was a Judas gate, big enough for a person. Presumably the doors would lead to an interior ground-floor yard. It was a two-story building. Offices above, possibly. Or storerooms. Behind the building was a bigger building, blank and dark and massive. A brick church of some kind, maybe.

Reacher asked, "Is he in there?"

Hemingway nodded.

Reacher asked, "With how many others?"

"He's alone."

"Really?"

"He runs protection rackets. Among other things. So now he has to deliver. His guys are all out, watching over his clients."

"I didn't know protection rackets worked that way. I thought they were just extortion, plain and simple."

"They are, basically. But he needs to maintain some kind of credibility. And he needs to keep his best cash cows in business. There's a lot of damage being done tonight. Plenty of places are going to go under. No more payoffs from them. And a wise man keeps an eye on his cash flow."

Reacher turned and looked at the doors. "You hoping someone will break in?"

"I don't know what's taking them so long. That's the problem with junkies. No get-up-and-go."

"What has he got in there?"

"A little of everything. He keeps his inventory low because he's got the New Jersey Turnpike and the Holland Tunnel for rapid resupply, which is apparently what they teach you in business school now, but still, I bet there's a week's worth in there."

"Are we in the way? Should we go park somewhere else?"

"You should go home. This isn't your business."

"I need to talk to you."

"About what?"

"The Son of Sam."

"Croselli isn't enough for you?"

"I saw him."

"Who?"

"I saw a man carrying a Charter Arms Bulldog and peering into cars."

"Are you serious?"

"It was our car he peered into."

"Where?"

"The East River, at 34th Street."

Hemingway said, "You know guns, right? Being a Marine and all?"

"Son of a Marine," Reacher said. "It was the right gun."

"It's pitch dark."

"The moon and the stars and the water."

Hemingway ducked down another inch and looked across Reacher at Chrissie. "Did you see it, too?"

Chrissie said, "No."

"How come?"

"I wasn't looking."

Hemingway said, "I don't know what to do. OK, let's say we have a confirmed sighting, but so what? We already know the Son of Sam is in New York. That's the point of the guy. It adds no new information. You'd need something more. You'd need to know who he is. Do you?"

"No," Reacher said. "But I know what he used to be."

They parked on Bleecker, intending to walk back and join Hemingway in her doorway hideout, but suddenly Bleecker had people on it, some of them in groups, some of them in pairs, some of those groups and pairs carrying stuff too heavy for comfort, and therefore consequently looking for alternative modes of transportation, such as small hatchback cars, each one apparently ideal for hauling a large television. Reacher and Chrissie were a yard out of the Chevette, with the doors closed but not locked, when the staring match started. Two guys, staggering under an enormous box, with Sony written on it upside down. They came in a straight line, eyeballing the Chevette all the way, and Reacher said, "Keep walking, guys."

The guy on the left was a shadowy grunting figure, and he said, "Suppose we don't?"

"Then I'll kick your butt and steal your television."

"Suppose you drive us?"

"Just keep walking," Reacher said.

They didn't. They eased the box carefully to the ground and stood up again, breathing deep, two dark figures in the dark. Even from six feet away it was hard to make out detail, but their hands hadn't gone to their pockets yet, which was a good sign. It meant any upcoming combat was likely to be unarmed, which was reassuring. Reacher had grown up in a culture of extreme violence, it being hard to describe the U.S. Marine Corps any other way, and he had taken its lessons on board, with the result that he hadn't lost a fight in more than ten years, against Corps kids from the same culture, and against rivalrous local youth all around the world, who liked to think the U.S. military was nothing special, and who liked to try to prove it by proxy, usually unsuccessfully. Two punks on a blacked-out New York City street were unlikely to prove an unprecedented problem, unless they had knives or guns, which was unknowable at this point.

The guy on the right said, "Maybe we'll take the girl with us. Maybe we'll have ourselves some fun."

The guy on the left said, "Just give us the keys and no one gets hurt."

Which was the moment of decision. Surprise was

always good. Delay was always fatal. Guys who let a situation unfold in its own good time were just stockpiling problems for themselves. Reacher ran at the left-hand guy, two choppy steps, like an infielder charging a grounder, and he didn't slow down. He ran right through the guy, leading with his forearm held horizontal, jerking his elbow into the guy's face, and as soon as he felt the guy's nose burst open he stamped down and reversed direction around the box and went after the second guy, who flinched away and took Reacher's charging weight flat in the back. The guy pitched forward like he had been hit by a truck, and Reacher kicked him in the head, and the guy lay still.

Reacher checked their pockets. No knives, no guns, which was usually the case. But it had been their choice. They could have kept on walking. He hauled the right-hand guy next to the left-hand guy, close together, shoulder to shoulder, and he picked up the heavy box like a strongman in the circus, struggling and tottering, and he took two short steps and dropped it on their heads from waist height.

Chrissie said, "Why did you do that?"

"Rules," Reacher said. "Winning ain't enough. The other guy has to know he lost."

"Is that what they teach you in the Marine Corps?"

"More or less."

"They'll wreck the car when they wake up."

"They won't. They'll throw up and crawl home. By which time you'll be long gone anyway."

So Chrissie locked up, and they walked back through the heat to where Hemingway was waiting on Carmine. Reacher said, "No progress?"

Hemingway said, "Not yet."

"Maybe we should go recruit someone. There are plenty of people on Bleecker."

"That would be suborning a felony."

"Means to an end."

"Tell me what you meant about the guy with the Bulldog."

"Can you use it?"

"Depends what it is."

"It was dark," Reacher said. "Obviously."

"But?"

"He was in his mid-twenties, I would say, medium height, heavy in the chest and shoulders, quite pale, with wavy hair that wouldn't lie down."

"Carrying a .44 Bulldog?"

"Most Bulldogs are .44s. But I don't have X-ray vision."

"How far away was he?"

"Twenty feet, at one point."

"How long were you eyeballing him?"

"Twenty seconds, maybe."

"Twenty seconds at twenty feet," Hemingway said. "In a blackout? That's a tough sell. I bet there have been a thousand reports tonight. People freak out in the dark."

"He was a trained man," Reacher said.

"Trained how?"

"The way he moved through the available cover. He's ex-military. He's had infantry training."

"So have lots of guys. You ever heard of Vietnam?"

"He's too young. This guy was of age six or seven years ago. The draft was winding down. You had to be pretty unlucky. And I don't think he was ever in combat. I've seen lots of people back from Vietnam. They're different. This guy was all theory and training. Second nature, for sure, pretty slick, but he had never lived or died by it. I can guarantee that. And I don't think he was a Marine. They're different, too. I think he was army. And I think he's been in Korea. It was like a fingerprint. I think he did basic, and infantry, with the urban specialization, and I think he served in Seoul. Like a particular combination. That's how he looked. I see it all the time. You ever been there? Seoul teaches you to move a certain way. But he's been out at least two years, because of the hair, and he's had time to get a bit heavy. I think he volunteered at eighteen or nineteen, and I think he served a three-year hitch. That was my impression, anyway."

"That's one hell of a detailed impression."

"You could offer it as a filter. They could see if any persons of interest match up."

"It was twenty seconds in the pitch dark."

"What else have they got?"

"Maybe I could."

"Suppose it worked? Suppose they get the guy? Would that be good for you?"

"Of course it would."

"So what's the downside?"

"Sounding desperate and pathetic."

"Your call."

"You should try it," Chrissie said. "Someone needs to catch the guy."

Hemingway said nothing.

They waited, all crammed together in the doorway opposite Croselli's place, with absolutely nothing happening. They heard sirens, and snatches of conversation from people passing by on Bleecker. Like headline news. It was now only ninety degrees. The lights had gone out at Shea in the bottom of the sixth, with the Mets trailing the Cubs by two to one. Subway riders had spent scary hours trapped underground, but were slowly making their way back to the surface. Cars were using chains and ropes to tear the shutters off stores. Even Brooks Brothers on Madison had been looted. Crown Heights and Bushwick were on fire. Cops had been hurt and arrests had been made.

Then the last of the passersby moved on and Carmine went quiet again and the clock in Reacher's head ticked around toward midnight. He said to Chrissie, "I'll walk you back to your car. Your friends will be waiting."

She said, "Are you staying here?"

"Might as well. I already missed my bus."

"Do you think the roads are open?"

"Wide open. They want people to leave."

"Why?"

"Fewer mouths to feed here."

"Makes sense," Chrissie said. They walked together to the corner, and around it, where the Chevette waited undisturbed. The two guys were still laid out in the roadway, under the box. Like a cartoon accident. They were still breathing.

Reacher said, "Want me to ride with you?"

"No," Chrissie said. "We go back alone. That's part of the deal."

"You know how to go?"

"Up on Sixth and across on 4th. And then it's right there."

"Roger that."

"Take care, OK?"

"I will," Reacher said. "You, too. I'll never forget you."

"You will."

"Check back next year, see if I have."

"OK. Let's see who remembers. Same night, same place. Deal?"

"I'll be there," Reacher said.

She got into the car, and she eased away from the tangle of limbs behind her, and she made the left on Sixth, and she waved through her open window. And then she was gone.

Hemingway said, "I'm going to put it in the system. Your impression, I mean. That's the smart play here. They'll ignore it of course, but it will be in the record. I can say told you so, afterward. If you're right. That's always worth a point or two. Sometimes more. Being right afterward can be a wonderful thing."

"It's a filter," Reacher said. "That's all. It's about efficiency."

"But I still need Croselli."

"The Son of Sam wouldn't get you out of jail?"

"I need Croselli."

"Why?"

"Because he burns me up."

"You ever read a book called *Moby-Dick*?"

"OK, I get it. And I admit it. Croselli is my great white whale. I'm obsessed. But what can I do about it? What could anyone, with a whale pressing on her head?"

"Is that how you feel? Like you have a whale pressing on your head?"

"That's exactly how I feel."

"Then let's trade," Reacher said.

"What for what?"

"I need a ride out of town."

"When?"

"As soon as possible. I'm sure my brother is worrying about me. Which I'm sure is hard on the old guy. I need to put him out of his misery."

"I'm not a taxi dispatcher."

"You have a car."

"I'm not a chauffeur, either."

"You could lend it to me."

"How would I get it back?"

"I don't know."

"Do you even have a license?"

"Not exactly."

"No deal," she said.

"OK," Reacher said.

"What were you going to do for me?"

"Suppose an unknown suspect broke into Croselli's place, and you got a look inside. Then the unknown suspect fled, but you were too busy securing the scene to chase him."

"I've been waiting two hours for that to happen. But it hasn't."

"I could do it."

"You're sixteen years old."

"How is that relevant?"

"Entrapment is bad enough. Entrapment with minors is probably worse."

"Who would ever know, apart from you and me?"

"I have no way of getting you a ride out of town."

Reacher paused a beat, and said, "Maybe we should refine the plan."

"What plan?" Hemingway said. "We don't have a plan."

"Probably better if it's not you who makes the discovery. It could look like a personal vendetta. It could give Croselli's lawyers something to work with. Probably better if it's not even the FBI at all. Better if it's the NYPD. Don't you think? An independent agency, with no axe to grind. If they discover a dope dealer and his stash in their city, then it's out there. It can't be denied. It is what it is. Your people will have to hush up their deal, and they'll have to admit you were right all along, and you can turn your review procedure into a medal ceremony."

"The NYPD is busy tonight."

"They have a narcotics division, surely. Make the call ahead of time. Get a sense of how long they're going to be, and we'll try to time it exactly right. I'll bust in, you hang back and keep an eye on things for a minute until the cops show up, and then we'll both slip away, and you can drive me north. Meanwhile the NYPD will be building your case for you, and by the time you're back in town your bosses will be rolling out the red carpet."

"How far north do you want to go?"

"West Point. It's up the river a ways."

"I know where it is."

"So do we have a deal?"

Hemingway didn't answer.

Hemingway finally agreed about thirty minutes later, close to one o'clock in the morning. But the plan went wrong immediately. First they couldn't find a working phone. They searched up and down Carmine, and they tried the corner of Seventh Avenue, and the corner of Bleecker, and Sixth Avenue, and every pay phone they found was silent. They didn't know if it was the result of the blackout, or just the general abject state of the city. Reacher figured the phone company had its own electricity, in its own wires, so he was all in favor of carrying on the search, but Hemingway was reluctant to foray further, in case she missed something over at Croselli's place. So she walked back to the doorway on Carmine and Reacher went on alone, across Sixth, and on the corner between Minetta Street and Minetta Lane he found a phone with a dial tone.

It was too dark to see the numbers, so he dialed by feel, zero for the operator, and he waited a long time before she answered. He asked for the NYPD's Sixth Precinct, and waited again, even longer, before the call was picked up and a voice barked, "Yes?"

Reacher said, "I want to report illegal narcotics in the West Village."

The voice said, "What?"

"There's a storeroom full of drugs on Carmine just been bust open."

"Any dead bodies?"

"No."

"Anyone currently in the act of getting killed?"

"No."

"Fire?"

"No."

The voice said, "Then stop wasting my time," and the phone went dead. Reacher hung up and hustled back, sweating, ninety degrees at one in the morning, and he relayed the news to Hemingway, who nodded in the dark and said, "We should have seen that coming. I guess they're all hands on deck right now."

"We might have to use your own people."

"Forget it. They wouldn't take my call."

Reacher said, "Still got your little sister's cassette recorder?"

"It's my cassette recorder."

"Still got it?"

"Why?"

"Maybe I can get him to boast on the tape."

"You?"

"Same principle. You can't let this look like a vendetta."

"I can't let you. You and him, face to face? I have a conscience."

"What's he going to do to me?"

"Beat you to death."

"He's a made man," Reacher said. "He has soldiers. Which means he tells other people to do the heavy lifting. Which means he's out of practice. He's all hat and no cattle. He's got nothing. We already saw that on Waverly. Any twelve-year-old in the Philippines could eat his lunch."

"Is this a Marine Corps thing?"

"I'm not a Marine."

"How would you get in?"

"I assume the church behind him is locked."

"Tonight for sure. If not every night."

"I'll figure something out."

"How would the military do it?"

"Marines or army?"

"Army."

"They'd call in artillery support. Or air-to-ground."

"Marines?"

"They'd start a fire, probably. That usually brings them out real fast."

"You can't do that."

"I'm not a Marine," Reacher said again. He looked across the street. The second-story windows were dark, obviously. Which meant Croselli could be right there, watching. But without seeing much. A man in a dark room watching a lit street had an advantage. A man in a dark room watching a dark street might as well have saved himself the eyestrain.

Reacher crossed the dark street, to the double doors. He put his fingertips on them. They felt like sandpaper. Fifty-year-old paint, plus fifty years of smoke and grime and dust. He tapped, first with his fingernails, then gently with his knuckles. The wood felt old and thick and solid, like it had been shipped a hundred years before, from some ancient forest out west. He slid his palms across the surface, until he found the Judas gate. Same paint, same grime, same wood. He felt for the hinges, and didn't find any. He felt for the lock, and rubbed it with his thumb. It seemed to be a small round Yale, worn brass, probably as old as the paint.

He headed back to Hemingway. He said, "The doors are probably two or three inches thick, and the Judas gate is all of a piece. All quality lumber, probably hard as a rock by now."

"Then maybe the army way is the only way."

"Maybe not. The Judas gate opens inward. The lock is an old Yale, put in maybe fifty years ago. I'm guessing they didn't chase out a void in the door. Not in wood that hard. Not back then. People weren't so uptight about security. I bet the lock is surface-mounted on the back. Like an old house. The tongue is in a little surface-mounted box. Two screws, is all."

"There will be another door. Out of the yard, into the building. Might have a newer lock."

"Then I'll knock and rely on charm."

"I can't let you do this."

"It's the least I can do. I screwed you up before. You might have gotten something. You were going to take that slap and keep him talking."

"He had already found the wire."

"But he's arrogant. He's got an ego. He might have carried on regardless, just to taunt you."

"That's what I was hoping."

"Then let me put it right."

———

Reacher turned around and lifted his shirt and bared his back to Hemingway. He felt hot fingers scrabbling at his waistband, gapping it out, fitting the plastic box behind the elastic on his shorts. Then he felt the scrape of a wire, and her hand burrowed up his back, under his shirt, to his shoulder blade, and then on over the top, a curious vertical embrace, her breath on his neck, and then she turned him around again to face her, and her other hand went up the front of his shirt, to find the microphone, to pass it from hand to hand, and to pull it down into place. She stopped with it trapped against his chest, and she kept her hand there, flat, nothing between her palm and his skin except the small pebble of technology.

She said, "I put it in my bra. But you don't have one."

"Imagine that," Reacher said.

"There's nothing to keep it in place."

Reacher felt an immediate film of sweat between his chest and her hand. He said, "Got a Band-Aid in your purse?"

"You're a smart kid," she said, and she went into a one-hand-two-elbows contortion to root through her bag, and as she craned her neck to look downward into it her forehead touched his lips, just briefly, like a kiss. Her hair was limp, but it smelled like strawberries.

She jerked her bag back up on her shoulder and held up something that crackled slightly. A Band-Aid, he assumed, still in its hygienic wrapper. He took it from her and peeled it open in the space between their faces. Then in turn she took it back from him one-handed and used it to tape the microphone in the trench between his chest muscles. She smoothed the adhesive, once, twice, and then she took her hands out from under his shirt and pulled it down into place.

She put her palm on his chest, like Croselli had put his on hers, pressing hard on the damp cotton, and she said, "He'll find it."

"Don't worry," Reacher said. "If he puts his hands on me, I'll beat him to death."

Hemingway said nothing.

Reacher said, "That's a Marine Corps thing."

The darkness didn't help. It didn't help at all. Reacher lined up on the opposite curb, like a sprinter at the start of a race, but he couldn't exactly see where he was heading. Adjustments were going to be necessary as he ran. He took off, slow and clumsy, partly because of the dark, partly because he was a terrible runner, with long lumbering strides, and three paces out he saw the doors, and two paces out he saw the Judas gate, and with one pace to go he saw its lock, and he launched his leading foot in a scything kick, slightly across his body, and he smashed his heel as close to the small Yale circle as he could get, with all his two hundred and twenty pounds behind it, multiplied significantly by the final acceleration of his foot, and by the fact that his whole bulk was moving briskly, if not exactly fast.

But it was enough. The Judas gate exploded inward,

with what felt like no resistance at all, and Reacher hurtled through the resulting blank rectangle into a space so dark he could make out nothing at all. There was the feel of cobblestones under his feet, and the sour smell of garbage, and sheer dark walls rising on his left and his right and ahead.

He felt his way along the right-hand wall to the back corner of the yard, where he found a door. Ridged glass above, a panel below, a smooth steel handle, and a lock that felt newer. The glass was probably tempered and reinforced with wire. The lock was probably chased into the door and the jamb. A whole different proposition.

He waited, to see if Croselli would come down and open it himself. Which he might. He must have heard the crash of the Judas gate. But he didn't come down. Reacher waited three minutes, breathing hard, stretching his eyes wide open, willing them to see something. But they didn't. He stepped up to the door again and traced its shape with his hands. The panel below the glass would be the weak spot. Plywood, probably, maybe three-eighths thick, painted, retained in the frame by quarter-round moldings. Reacher was wearing shoes he had bought in the London airport two deployments ago, stout British things with welts and toecaps as hard as steel. They had busted heads and kneecaps already that night. Plywood wasn't going to be a major problem.

He stepped back and poked forward with his toe to fix his target in his mind. Then he kicked out, *bang, bang,* concentrating on the corners of the panel, viciously and noisily, until the wood splintered and the moldings came loose.

Then he stopped and listened.

No sound from inside the building.

Which was a bitch. Reacher would have preferred to meet Croselli face to face on the ground floor. He didn't relish heading up a flight of stairs toward an alert opponent at the top.

He waited some more.

No sound.

He squatted down with his back against the doorframe and punched out the panel with his elbow, until it folded inward, like a miniature door itself, hinged on a few surviving nails. Then he twisted around and put his arm and his shoulder through the hole and reached up and scrabbled for the knob. Which he found easily enough. He had arms like a gorilla. Every childhood photograph of him featured six inches of bare wrist, at the end of every sleeve.

The door opened and he struggled upright and backed off a yard, just in case. But there was no sound inside. Croselli didn't come out. There was nothing to see. Just darkness. The inside air smelled hot and stale.

Reacher stepped in, to what felt like a narrow lobby with a tiled floor. He slid his feet ahead, one after the other, and he felt a bottom stair. There was a handrail on the left. The opposite wall was less than three feet away. It was painted, and it was damp with condensation.

Reacher went up the stairs, his right hand out in front of him, his left holding the handrail. There was a yard-wide half landing, and then the stairs doglegged and continued upward. At the top was dusty super-heated air and a six-by-three upstairs lobby with a sticky carpet and a door at each end. A front room, and a back room.

Under the back room door was a bar of faint warm light.

Reacher stared at it, like a thirsty man in the desert might stare at a cold drink. It was a candle, probably. It was the first man-made light he had seen in more than three hours.

He put his hand under his shirt at the back and pushed the button Hemingway had showed him. *It's red,* she had said, which hadn't helped, because he didn't have eyes in the back of his head, and it was pitch dark anyway. So he had learned it by feel. He tapped his chest, so that a thump could mark the start of the recording. Then he put his hand on the door-knob.

Reacher twisted the knob and pushed the door, one, two, fast and hard, and he stepped into a room lit by a guttering candle. The flame danced in the rush of air. The room was a twenty-by-twenty space with a dark window in the back wall, and a row of old-fashioned safes on the left, like something out of a black-and-white Western movie about bank robbers, and on the right there was a row of file cabinets and a desk, and sitting at the desk in a leather reclining chair was Croselli. The chair was pushed out and turned sideways, so that he was sitting face-on to the door.

He had a gun in his hand.

It was a Colt M1911, a .45 automatic, standard military issue for sixty-six years, hence the model number. It looked a little scratched and battered. It was all lit up by the candle, which was on the desk, welded to a china plate by a pool of its own wax. A standard household item, a few cents at the hardware store, but it felt as bright as the sun.

Croselli said, "You."

Reacher said nothing.

Croselli had shed his jacket and pulled down his tie, but his shirt was still wet. He said, "I was expecting Hemingway. What are you tonight, her knight in shining armor? Is she sending a boy to do a man's job?"

Is he armed? Reacher had asked. *Not in the city,* Hemingway had said. *He can't afford to be.* Not applicable inside his own premises, apparently. Which was a bitch. Reacher looked at the row of safes. There were six of them, shoulder to shoulder, each one about a yard wide and six feet tall. They had keyholes, not combination locks. The door on the far end was wide open, and the void behind it was empty. Their armory, Reacher guessed. For dire emergencies. Like that very night. Clearly Croselli's soldiers were all armed, all out on the street, all ensuring protection.

"You have a gun," Reacher said, for the tape.

"I'm defending my property," Croselli said.

"This is your place?"

"I'm not a common burglar."

Reacher took a step. The Colt's muzzle rose a degree, to track him. Reacher asked, "Is your name on the title?"

"I'm not that stupid."

"Then this isn't your place."

"Only technically. Believe me, kid, everything you see here is mine."

"What's in the safes?"

"Inventory."

"Yours?"

"I already told you."

"I need to hear it in short simple words."

"Why?"

"We could do business."

"Business?"

"That's what I said."

"You and me?"

"If you're smart," Reacher said.

"You broke down my door."

"Would you have let me in, if I had knocked?"

"What kind of business could we do, you and I?"

"You're using the New Jersey Turnpike and the Holland Tunnel. Which means you're getting supplied out of Miami, all the way up I-95. Which means you're paying over the odds, and you're losing some to unreliable mules, and you're losing some to routine New Jersey State Police patrols. I could help you with all of that."

"How?"

"I bring stuff in direct from the Far East. On military planes. No scrutiny. My dad's a Marine officer."

"What kind of stuff?"

"Anything you want."

"What kind of price, kid?"

"Show me what you've got and tell me what you paid. Then I'll break your heart."

"You hurt two of my men."

Reacher said, "I hope so. I need you to understand. You do not mess with me." He took another step. The Colt's muzzle rose another degree. Reacher said, "Are you buying from Martinez?"

"I never heard of Martinez."

"Then you're way over the odds already. Who are you buying from?"

"The Medellín boys."

"I could save you forty percent."

Croselli said, "I think you're full of shit. I think this is a Hemingway stunt."

"You shut her down."

"For which I paid good money. For which I expected a durable result. Anything else is liable to make me angry."

"This has nothing to do with Hemingway."

"Pull up your shirt."

"Why?"

"I want to see the wire. Before I shoot you."

Reacher thought: *unregistered guns, a deceptive real estate title, a straight-up reference to the Medellín cartel out of Colombia, and a straight-up reference to bribery.* The tape had enough. He took a deep, deep breath and put his hands on the hem of his T-shirt. Then he jerked forward from the waist and blew out the candle.

The room went from softly glowing to blacker than the Earl of Hell's winter coat all in a split second, and Reacher blundered straight ahead, forcing passage between Croselli's chair and the desk, and Croselli whipped the Colt around in the same general direction and fired. But he missed by a mile, and the muzzle flash backlit him perfectly, like a photographer's strobe, so Reacher picked his spot and slammed a straight right into the back of his neck, right where soft turns to hard, and Croselli pitched headfirst out of the chair and landed on his knees. Reacher groped for the chair and lifted it high by the armrests and slammed it down on Croselli's back. He heard the sound of steel on linoleum as the Colt skittered away, and he brushed the chair aside and groped and patted blindly until he found the collar of Croselli's shirt, which he bunched in his left hand while he pounded away with his right, short roundhouse punches to the side of Croselli's head, his ear, his jaw, *one, two, three, four,* vicious clubbing blows, until he felt the steam go out of the guy, whereupon he reached forward and grabbed the guy's wrists and yanked them up behind his back, high and painful, and he clamped them together in his left hand, human handcuffs, a party trick perfected years before, enabled by the freakish strength in his fingers, from which no one had ever escaped, not even his brother, who was of equal size, or his father, who was smaller but stronger. He hauled Croselli to his feet and slapped at his pants pockets until he heard the jingle of keys. Croselli got his second wind and started struggling hard, so Reacher turned him a little sideways and quieted him down again with a pile-driver jab to the kidney.

Then he fished out the keys and held them in his right hand, and he asked, "Where's your book of matches?"

Croselli said, "You're going to die, kid."

"Obviously," Reacher said. "No one lives forever."

"I mean tonight, kid."

Reacher separated a key by feel and pressed the point high on Croselli's cheek. He said, "If so, you won't see it happen. I'll take your eyes out first."

"Matches in the desk drawer," Croselli said.

Reacher turned him again and slammed a short right to his stomach, to fold him over and keep him preoccupied, and he walked him bent over and puking to the desk, and he used his free hand to rattle open the drawers, and to root around, all by feel. There was all kinds of stuff in the drawers. Staplers, pens, rolls of Scotch tape, some in dispensers, pencils, paper clips. And a book of matches, a little limp and damp.

Using a matchbook one-handed was practically impossible, so Reacher turned Croselli toward the window wall, let go of his wrists, and shoved him hard, and used the resulting few undisturbed seconds to detach a match and strike it, all fizzing and flaring in the dark, and to light the candle with it once again, by which time Croselli was shaping up for a charge, so Reacher stepped toward him and dropped him with a right to the solar plexus, just as the room bloomed back to its former cozy glow.

A solar plexus was worth at least a minute, Reacher thought, and he used that minute to cross the room and pick up the Colt, and to dump its magazine, and to eject the shell from its chamber, and to pick up the chair, and to set it back on its casters, and to turn it just so, and to find the Scotch tape, and to pick the guy up, and to dump him in the chair, and to start taping his wrists to the frame.

Scotch tape was weaker than duct tape, but Reacher made up for it with length, around and around, right hand, left hand, until the guy looked like he had two broken wrists, in casts made of some kind of new see-through yellowish plaster. Then came his ankles. In all Reacher used six whole rolls of tape, and after that there was no way the guy was moving.

Then Hemingway came in the door.

She looked at the candle first, and then at Croselli.

Reacher said, "He admits on tape everything here is his."

She said, "I heard a gunshot."

"He missed. It was about twenty degrees off on the port side."

"I was worried."

"It's the godfather who should worry. This is a made man."

"What did he say on the tape?"

"Take it out of my pants and listen for yourself."

Which she did. Reacher felt the hot quick fingers again, and the weird embrace, under his shirt, as the microphone was passed from hand to hand. Then she clicked and waited and clicked again, and a thin tinny version of Croselli's voice filled the room, taking responsibility for everything in it, admitting to the

Medellín connection, admitting to the bribe, and hinting at the size of it.

She said, "You have his keys?"

Reacher said, "Right here in my hand."

"Open the safe doors."

Which he did, starting next to the empty armory, working away from the window, until all of the safes stood open. All of them were full of smooth-packed plastic-wrapped bricks, some brown or green in color, most white or yellow.

She said, "Can you get his keys back in his pocket?"

He did, and said, "What next?"

"Does his phone work?"

He tried it, and said, "Yes."

She gave him a number and said, "It's our internal credible threat hotline."

He called it in, the exact address, without giving his name, and then the call ended, and she said, "Their response time will be more than five minutes but less than ten."

She put her plastic cassette recorder on the floor near Croselli's feet. She said, "We should go. My car is not close."

Reacher said, "Is this enough?"

She said, "More than enough. Medellín is toxic. And the evidence is right here. It's a photograph, Reacher. This is a photogenic prosecution. It doesn't matter who he bribed. No one is ever going to say a word against this one. It's a tidal wave."

"One last thing," Reacher said, and he turned back to Croselli, and he said, "Slapping women is not permitted. You're supposed to be a man, not a pussy."

Croselli said nothing.

Reacher raised his hand. "How would you like it?"

Croselli said, "You wouldn't hit a guy tied to a chair."

Reacher said, "Watch me," and slapped the guy in the face, hard, a real *crack,* wet or not, and the chair went up on its side legs, and balanced, and balanced, and tottered, and then thumped down on its side, with its casters spinning and Croselli's head bouncing around like a pinball.

Then they hit the bricks, and Hemingway's prediction of five-to-ten came true, in that they saw hurrying cars about six minutes out, and then a pair of heavy trucks. A lot of firepower. And why not, for a credible threat?

Hemingway's car was four blocks away, on Sullivan. It was the mid-blue Granada Reacher had seen before, with the vinyl roof and the toothy grille. He said, "You sure this gets you off the hook?"

She said, "Count on it, kid. Being right afterward is a wonderful thing."

"Then give me a ride out of town."

"I should stay."

"Give them time to grieve. Give them time to figure out how it's really their own idea. I've seen this shit before. All organizations are the same. You need to lay low for a day. You need to be out of the spotlight."

"West Point?"

"Take the Thruway and the Tappan Zee."

"How long will I be gone?"

"They're going to roll out the red carpet, Jill. Just give them time to find it first."

They drove a long, long time in the dark, and then they hit neighborhoods with power, with traffic lights and street lights and the occasional lit room. Billboards were bright, and the familiar nighttime background of orange diamonds on black velvet lay all around.

Hemingway said, "I have to stop and call."

Reacher said, "Call who?"

"The office."

"Why?"

"I have to know whether it worked."

"I'm sure it did."

"I have to know."

"So stop. We could get a cup of coffee."

"It's a hundred degrees."

"Got to be less than ninety now."

"Still too hot for coffee." She pulled over to the right-hand lane, and then she took an exit road to what Reacher imagined was a superpower version of the standard type of highway facility, with multiple restrooms, and gas big enough for trucks, and motel rooms for weary drivers, and not just something to eat, but a restaurant big enough to feed Syracuse. And pay phones. There was a long line, right outside the restaurant's extensive and brightly lit windows. Hemingway used one, and hung up smiling, and said, "It's working. Croselli has been arrested."

He asked, "How's the whale?"

She said, "The whale is gone."

She looked dazed for a second, and then she got a big smile on her face, and they hugged, with some kind of relief and ecstasy in her tight embrace. Reacher felt bony ribs, and the flutter of her heart. It was beating fast.

Then she moved to another phone and dialed another number, and she gave her name, and she dictated a long report about a confirmed sighting of the Son of Sam, made by what she called a confidential informant, who had what she called extensive military experience.

Then she hung up again and said, "This will sound crazy, but I really want to rent a room just to take a shower."

Reacher said, "Doesn't sound crazy to me."

"Does it matter what time you get there?"

"Not within a shower or two."

"So let's do it."

"Both of us?"

"It's a mutual benefit."

"Who goes first?"

"I go first."

"OK," Reacher said.

She paid at the motel office, a visible wad of bills, what Reacher figured must be the whole-night rate, and she came back with a key, to room 15, which was located way in back, the last cabin before the woods. Reacher said, "Do you want me to wait in the car?"

Hemingway said, "You can wait in the room."

So they went in together, and found a hot stale space, with the usual features. Hemingway checked the bathroom, and came out with a bunch of towels, and said, "These are yours," and then she went back in and closed the door.

Reacher waited on the bed until she came out again much later, all hot and pink and wrapped in towels. She said, "Your turn," and she crossed the room, a little unsteady on her feet, as if overcome by steam, or exhaustion.

He said, "You OK?"

She said, "I'm fine."

He paused a beat, and then he went in the bathroom, which was as steamy as a sauna, with the mirror all fogged up, showing the swipes and arcs where the maid had cleaned it. He stripped and hung his limp clothes on a hook, and he started the shower and set it warm, and he stepped into the tub and pulled the curtain. He soaped up and used the shampoo, and he scrubbed and rinsed, and he stood under the warm stream for an extra minute, and then he got out.

Getting dry was not really an option, given the temperature and the humidity. He moved the moisture around his skin with a towel, and he put his old clothes back on, damp and snagging, and he combed his hair with his fingers. Then he stepped out in a billow of moisture.

Jill Hemingway was flat on her back on the bed. At first he thought she was sleeping. Then he saw her eyes were open. He took her wrist and felt her pulse.

Nothing there.

He tried her neck.

Nothing there.

Her eyes stared up at him, blank and sightless.

Medical reasons. Her heart, he thought. No doubt a cause of concern. He had felt it racing and fluttering. He had seen her stagger. He crossed the room and stared out the window. Still the dead of night. Through the trees he could see lights from cars on the highway. He could hear their sound, faint and constant. He crossed back to the bed and checked again, wrist, neck, nothing.

He stepped out to the lot and closed the door behind him, and hiked over to the line of pay phones outside the restaurant. He chose one at random and dialed the number she had given him, for the internal hotline. He reported her death, said it looked natural, and gave the location.

He didn't give his name.

Jill Hemingway, RIP. She died young, but she had a smile on her face.

He walked on, to the gas plaza, past the car pumps, past the truck pumps, to the exit road. He kept one foot in the traffic lane, and rested the other on the curb, and he stuck out his thumb. The second car to pass by picked him up. It was a Chevrolet Chevette, baby blue, but it wasn't Chrissie's. It was a whole different car altogether, driven by a guy in his twenties who was heading for Albany. He let Reacher out at an early exit, and a dairyman in a pick-up truck took him onward, and then he walked a mile to the turn that led up to the Academy. He ate in a roadhouse, and he walked another mile, and he saw West Point's lights up ahead, far in the distance. He figured no one would reveille before 0600, which was still two hours away, so he found a bus bench and lay down to sleep.

The day after the blackout power was restored in part of Queens at seven in the morning, followed by part of Manhattan shortly afterward. By lunchtime half the city was back. By eleven in the evening the whole city was back. The outage had been caused by a maintenance error. A lightning strike in Buchanan, New York—part of the long summer storm Reacher had seen in the distance—had tripped a circuit breaker, but a loose locking nut had prevented the breaker from closing again immediately, as it was designed to do. As a consequence, a cascade of trips and overloads had rolled south over the next hour, until the whole city was out. By morning, more than sixteen hundred stores had been looted, more than a thousand fires had been set, more than five hundred cops had been injured, and more than four thousand people had been arrested. All because of a loose nut.

Twenty-eight days after the blackout the Son of Sam was captured outside his home on Pine Street, Yonkers, New York, less than four miles from Sarah Lawrence College. His yearlong killing spree was over. His name was David Berkowitz, and he was twenty-four years old. He was carrying his Charter

Arms Bulldog in a paper sack. He confessed to his crimes immediately. And he confirmed he had volunteered for the U.S. Army at age eighteen, and had served three years, partly inside the continental U.S., but mostly in South Korea.

Deep Down

Reacher's designated handler told him it wasn't going to be easy. There were going to be difficulties. Numerous and various. A real challenge. The guy had no kind of a bedside manner. Normally handlers started with the good news.

Maybe there isn't any, Reacher thought.

The handler was an Intelligence colonel named Cornelius Christopher, but that was the only thing wrong with him. He looked like a decent guy. Despite the fancy name he seemed to have turned out fairly plain and pragmatic. Reacher would have liked him, except he had never met him before. Going undercover with a handler you never met before led to inefficiency. Or worse.

Christopher asked, "How much did they tell you yesterday?"

Reacher said, "I was in Frankfurt yesterday. Which

is in Germany. No one told me anything. Except to get on a plane to Dulles, and then report to this office."

"I see," Christopher said.

"What should they have told me?"

"You really know nothing about this?"

"Some local trouble with staff officers."

"So they did tell you something."

"No one told me anything. But I'm an investigator. I do this stuff for a living. And some things are fairly obvious. I'm a relatively new guy who has so far been posted almost exclusively overseas. Therefore I'm almost certainly unknown to the kind of staff officer who doesn't get out much."

"Out of where?"

"The Beltway, for instance. Call it a two-mile radius from this very office. Maybe they also have a fishing cottage on a lake somewhere. But that's not the kind of place I'm likely to have been."

"You're not very happy, are you?"

"I've had more promising days."

"What's your problem?"

"When does this thing start?"

"This afternoon."

"Well, that's my problem, right there. I've got a handler I never met before and a situation I know nothing about."

"Scared?"

"It's bad workmanship. It's shoddy and confused. It shows no pride. Because you guys are always the same. There's a clue in the title, remember?"

"What title?"

"Your title. Military intelligence. Ideally both of those

words should mean something to you. But surely at least one of them does. One at a time, if you wish. On alternate days, if you want."

"Feel free to give me your honest opinion."

Reacher said, "So what do I need to know?"

And at that same minute a car backed out of a driveway, in a distant location, slowly, a front-wheel-drive car, with a yelp as the tires turned. Not the shriek of speed. The opposite. A suburban sound, rubber on a tended blacktop driveway, like the smell of the sprinkler on the summer air.

Then the car paused and the driver selected a forward gear and the car rolled south, gently over the speed bumps that the driver himself had argued should be put in, for the safety of the children.

Then the car turned a little west, toward the highway, ready to join the mighty flow toward the capital.

Colonel Cornelius Christopher sat forward and made a space on his desk, paired hands coming together back-to-back, and then sweeping apart, pushing clutter aside. The move was emphatic. But purely metaphorical. There was nothing on the desk. No clutter. A good man-manager, Reacher thought. *He let me have my say, and now we're moving right along.*

Christopher said, "There's no danger. It's going to be all talking."

Reacher said, "Talking about what?"

"You were right, it's about staff officers. There are

four of them. One of them is bad. They're all political liaison people. To the House and the Senate. They practically live there. You know the type. Going places, fast track, better not to get in their way."

"Specifically?"

"The army is asking for a new sniper rifle. We're giving evidence to some new pre-committee. Begging, basically. Our legislative overseers. In fact, not even really. They sent senior staffers instead. We're not even talking to elected officials."

"Now you don't sound very happy."

"I'm not here to be happy. The liaison officers are sitting in on these hearings, obviously. And one of them is leaking. Design criteria, load, range, size, shape, weight, and budget."

"Leaking to who?"

"A likely bidder located overseas, we assume. A foreign manufacturer, in other words. Someone that wants the business. Someone that likes a rigged game."

"Is the business worth it? How many sniper rifles do we buy? And how much do we pay for them?"

"It's the implied endorsement. They can sell copies for five grand each to the freak market. The price of a decent used car. As many as they want. Like selling crack."

"Who else is at these hearings?"

"There's our four liaisons and the four staffers we're pitching to, plus our procurement guy and the Marine procurement guy, plus a Ranger sniper and a Marine sniper for color commentary."

"The Marines are involved?"

"In a minority way. They didn't bring their own

liaison, for instance. But it's definitely a joint project. No other way of doing a thing like this."

"So why wouldn't it be the Marines leaking? Their procurement guy or their sniper? Why assume it's our guys?"

"The leaks are via a fax machine inside the Capitol Building. Which is where our liaison guys have their offices."

"How certain are you of that?"

"Completely."

"Could be the staffers. They're in the Capitol Building, presumably."

"Different phone network. Our legislative overseers are on some new super-duper thing. Our offices are still steam-powered."

"OK," Reacher said. "So it's one of our guys."

"I'm afraid so," Christopher said.

"Motive?"

"Money," Christopher said. "Got to be. I can't see anyone forming a deep ideological attachment to a European firearms manufacturer. Can you? And money is always a factor for officers like these. They're mixing with corporate lawyers and lobbyists all the time. Easy to feel like the poor relation."

"Can't we just watch their fax machine?"

"Not inside the Capitol Building. Our legislative overseers don't like surveillance. Too many unintended consequences."

"Are they sending to an overseas fax number?"

"No, it's a local number. But these guys hire local people. As agents and lobbyists."

"So my job is what?"

"To find out which one of our guys is the bad apple. By talking to them."

"Where?"

"In the committee, at first. The Ranger sniper has been recalled. Personal reasons. You're going to take his place."

"As what?"

"Another Ranger sniper."

"With a real Marine sniper in the room? I'll be asked for opinions. He'll nail me in a second."

"So be Delta Force, not Rangers. Be mysterious. Don't say anything. Be all weird and silent. Grow a beard."

"Before this afternoon?"

"Don't worry about it. We've seen your file. You know which end of a rifle is which. We have confidence in you."

"Thank you."

"There's one other thing."

"Which is?"

"Our liaison guys are not guys. They're women."

"All of them?"

"All four."

"Does that make a difference?"

"I sincerely hope so. Some of the talking is going to have to be social. That's easier with women. You can do it one on one. Men always want to drink in groups."

"So I'm here to take women to bars, and ask them what they want to drink, and by the way are they leaking military secrets overseas? Is that the idea?"

"You'll have to be more subtle than that. But yes, it's a kind of interrogation. That's all. Which you're supposed to be good at. You're supposed to do this stuff for a living."

"In which case why not arrest them all and interrogate them properly?"

"Because three of the four are innocent. Where there's smoke there's fire, and so on. Their careers would be hurt."

"That never stopped you before."

"We never had fast-track people before. Not like this. Going places. We wouldn't cripple them all. One of them would survive, and she'd get her revenge."

Reacher said, "I'm just trying to establish the rules of engagement."

"Anything that wouldn't get thrown out of court for blatant illegality."

"Blatant?"

"Flashing red with a siren. That kind of blatant."

"That bad?"

"We can't tolerate this kind of thing. Not with a foreign manufacturer. We have politicians to please, and they have donors to protect. American donors."

"Who like a rigged game."

"There's two different kinds of rigged. Our kind, and their kind."

"Understood," Reacher said.

"There's no danger," Christopher said again. "It's all just talking."

"So what are the difficulties? What's not going to be easy?"

"That's complicated," Christopher said.

The front-wheel-drive car joined the traffic stream on the highway. It became just one of thousands, all heading the same way, all fast and focused and linear and metallic, like giant rounds fired from giant chain gun barrels somewhere far behind them. Which was a mental image the driver liked very much. He was a bullet, implacable and relentless, singular in his purpose. He was heading for his target. His aim was true.

Across the barrier no one was heading in the other direction. The morning flow was all one way, high speed and crowded, toward the distant city.

Christopher did the thing with his hands again, clearing metaphorical clutter off his desk, and out of the conversation. Ready for a new topic. The difficulties. He said, "It's a speed issue. We have to be quick. And at the same time we have to keep things normal for the Marine Corps. We can't let them suspect we have a leak. So we can't stop talking, or they'll guess. But we can't let much more stuff go overseas. So you can't waste time."

Reacher said, "What, this is going to be like speed dating?"

"You're new in town, so why wouldn't you?"

"I would," Reacher said. "Believe me. It would be like a dream come true. But it takes two to tango. And I'm a realistic guy. On a good day I could get a woman to look at me. Maybe. But four women all at once is not very likely."

Christopher nodded.

"That's the complication," he said. "That's the difficulty we were worrying about. Plus, these women are scary. West Pointers, off-the-charts IQs. Fast track. Going places. You can imagine."

"I don't have to imagine. I was at West Point."

"We know. We checked. You didn't overlap with any of them."

"Are any of them married?"

"No, fortunately. Fast-track women don't get married. Not until the time is right."

"Any serious relationships?"

"Same answer."

"Are they older or younger than me?"

"Older. Twenty-nine and thirty."

"Then that's another negative. Most women date older men. And what rank am I going to be?"

"You're going in as a sergeant. Most snipers are."

"Women like that don't want enlisted men."

Christopher nodded again. "I said at the beginning this wasn't going to be easy. But think logically. You might not need to go through all four. You might hit lucky the very first time. Or the second. And you might just know anyway. We have to assume the guilty one will resist any kind of contact. It could be that three say yes and one says no. In which case she's the one."

"They'll all resist contact. They'll all say no."

"Maybe one slightly more emphatically than the others."

"I'm not sure I could tell the difference. It always feels about the same to me. My social antenna must not be very well developed."

"We don't see another way of doing this."

Reacher nodded.

He asked, "Did you get me a uniform?"

"We got you a suit."

"Why?"

"Because you're going to be a Ranger. Or Delta. And they like to show up in civvies. It makes them feel like secret agents."

"It won't fit."

"The suit? It'll fit. Your height and weight are in your file. It was easy. It was like ordering anything. Except bigger."

"Have you got bios on these women?"

"Detailed," Christopher said. "Plus transcripts of everything said at the hearings so far. You should probably read those first. The way they talk will tell you more than the bios."

Five miles west, across the Potomac River, a thirty-year-old woman belted a fanny pack low on her hips and moved it around until it was comfortable, in its accustomed position. Then she bent forward and flipped her hair back and slid a toweling band in place, easing it back, and back, until it was seated just right. Then she kicked the hallway baseboard for luck, left toes, right toes, and then she opened her door and stepped out and ran in place for a moment, just gently, warming up, loosening, getting ready, facing it down.

Five miles.

Thirty minutes.

Possible.

It would depend on the lights, fundamentally. If more than half of the crosswalks were green, she would make it. Fifty-one percent. That was all she needed. Less than that, she wouldn't. Simple arithmetic. A fact of life. No disgrace.

Except it was. Failure was always a disgrace.

She took a breath, and another, and she hit her watch, and she ran down her path, and left onto the sidewalk, and she settled in for the first unbroken stretch. Long, easy strides, relaxed but pushing just a little, breathing well, moving well, her hair swinging behind her in a perfect circular rhythmic pattern, symmetrical, like a metronome.

The first crosswalk was green.

Reacher started with the transcripts. The pre-committee hearings. There were records of two separate sessions, the first two weeks ago, and the second one week ago. Hence the rush. The third session was due.

The transcripts were exactly what transcripts should be. Every vocal sound uttered in the room had been transcribed onto paper. Every *um* and *er* and *you know,* every false start, every repetition, every unfinished sentence, every stutter and stammer, every hopeless tangle and broken train of thought. Reading the pages was almost like hearing the voices. But not quite. There was a semi-real quality. Speech never hit paper just right, however good the transcriber.

The first to speak was one of the Senate staffers. Reacher could picture the guy. Not young. Disrespectful to send a kid, unless the kid was a hotshot, and hotshots didn't get sent to waste time listening for sixteen hours before saying no to the army. So it would be an older guy, solid and substantial and been-there-forever, but a clear B-lister all the same, because A-listers didn't get sent to waste time listening for sixteen hours before saying no to the army, either.

This particular example of a senior B-lister sounded puffed-up and bossy. He started out by making himself chairman of the board. He just announced it. No one objected. Not that Reacher expected anyone to. Presumably the guy had a dynamic of his own going on with the other staffers, and why would the army or the jarheads care which one of the assholes did what? So the guy went ahead and formally recited the purpose of the meeting, which he said was to examine available courses of action in the light of the perceived requirement for a new infantry weapon, namely a sniper rifle.

Reacher didn't like that sentence at all. Because of the word *perceived*. Clearly that was how the argument was going to go. *You don't really need this. Yes, we do. Why?* Which was the big bureaucratic elephant trap, right there. The on-the-ground snipers would drift the wrong way. Had they ever missed a shot because of inferior equipment? Hell no, sir, we *never* miss our shots. Hell, we can use *anything*. Hell, we could make our own damn sniper rifles out of your grand-daddy's old varmint gun and a length of rainwater gutter and a roll of goddamned *duct tape*.

Sir.

And the procurement officers would drift too far the other way, until they started sounding like gun nuts or NRA members writing a letter to Santa Claus. So it was a ritual dance. There was no way of winning. It was 1986 and it was all about planes and missiles and computers and laser-guided integrated systems. Firearms were boring. They were going to lose. But not after their wet-dream sniper rifle specification leaked overseas. The foreign manufacturer could gear up ahead of the next attempt. Or go right ahead and build the thing and sell it to the Soviets.

Reacher turned the pages, and it went pretty much as he had guessed it would. The puffed-up bossy guy asked why they needed the new rifle, and no one answered. The bossy guy asked them to pretend he was an idiot and knew nothing about the subject. Not a big ask, Reacher thought. Then the army procurement guy spoke up and the typist must have nearly worn out his *m* key: *Um. Erm. Umm.* (Pause) *I'm . . . I'm . . . I'm . . .*

The bossy guy said they could come back to that. Then he asked what exactly they were looking for, and things got back on solid ground with long back-and-forths about what qualities a sniper rifle needed. Cold shot accuracy was head of the list, of course. Often a sniper gets just one chance, which by definition will be out of a cold barrel. It has to hit. So the barrel is all about perfectly uniform internal dimensions, and heavy match-grade steel, with the right twist, and maybe some fluting for stiffness and reduced weight, the whole thing properly bedded into the stock, which shouldn't swell or shrink depending on the weather, or be too heavy to carry twenty miles. And so on.

The liaison women spoke often and at length. The first up was identified by the initials *C.R.* She said,

"This is extremely high-tech metalwork we're talking about here. And we'll need groundbreaking optics. Maybe we could incorporate laser range finding. This could be very exciting. It could be a great research opportunity for somebody."

A smart woman. Whole sentences. And good sentences. She was trying to make it radical, not boring, and she was hinting at big dollars getting spent in someone's district, which would be an IOU any senator would be happy to tuck away in his vest pocket. A good tactical approach.

But it didn't work. The chairman of the board asked, "Who's going to pay for all that?"

At which point the transcriber had written: *Pause*.

Reacher switched to the bio stack and found that C.R. was Christine Richardson. From Orange County, California. Private prep school, private high school, West Point. She was thirty years old and already a lieutenant colonel. Fast track, and the political shop was a greased rail anyway. Nice work, if you could get it.

The thirty-year-old woman with the fanny pack and the headband made it through three crosswalks on green and got held up at the next three on red. The seventh turned green before she got there, but it was choked with walkers, and they were slow to get going, so she got hung up behind them, running in place for two whole seconds, then pushing through, dodging left, dodging right, refusing to cut away diagonally, because then the distance would be less than the full five miles, which would be cheating, and she never cheated. At least not with running. She made it through the crowd to the opposite corner, and she turned right, and she logged the junction in her mind as half-red and half-green, which seemed fair to her, and which meant so far she was running exactly fifty-fifty, three and a half green, three and a half red, which was not a catastrophe, but which was not great, either, because she liked to bank plenty of greens well before she got closer to the center, where things were always stickier.

She ran on, another unbroken stretch, her strides still long and easy, still relaxed, but pushing now just a little more, picking up the pace, still breathing well, still moving well, her hair still swinging behind her in its perfect pattern, still symmetrical, still like a metronome.

The next crosswalk was red.

The man in the car got snarled up in traffic where 270 approached the Beltway. Inevitable, and expected. Orderly deceleration by all concerned, the flow hanging together, still like the thousand-round burst from the distant chain gun, but fully subsonic now, slow and fat and stealthy in the air. 355 to Wisconsin Avenue would be jammed, so he decided to stay on until 16th Street, east of Rock Creek Park. It wouldn't be a racetrack, but it would be better. And it would drop him down all the way to Scott Circle, and then Mass Ave ran all the way to the Capitol.

He was a bullet, and he was still on target.

From the other side of the office Cornelius Christopher said, "OK, library hour is over. Go get your suit now. You can take the documents with you, but not out of the building."

The supply office was two floors down, not exactly full of exploding fountain pens or cameras concealed in buttonhole flowers, but full of distantly related stuff, and certainly full of all the items needed to turn an honest man into a fake. The suit was well chosen. Not remotely expensive or up-to-date, but not tacky, either. Some kind of gray sharkskin weave, probably some man-made fiber in there, or a lot, wide lapels like five years ago. Exactly what an enlisted man would wear to a bank interview or a bail hearing. It was artfully creased here and there, from years in an imaginary closet, and there was even room dust on the collar. It looked like it was going to fit, except the arms and the shoulders. Reacher's file figures showed six-five and two-fifty, and he was reasonably in proportion, like a regular guy enlarged, except for arms as long as a gorilla's, and shoulders like basketballs stuffed in a sack.

There was a button-down shirt that was going to be way too small in the neck, but that was OK, because soldiers in suits were supposed to look awkward and uncomfortable. The shirt was blue and there was a red tie with it, with small blue crests on it. It could have come from a rifle club somewhere. It was a good choice. The undershirt and the boxers were standard white PX items, which was fine, because Reacher had never heard of anyone buying that kind of stuff anywhere else. There was a pair of black PX socks, and a pair of black dress-uniform shoes. They looked to be the right size.

The supply guy said, "Try it all on. If there's a problem, we can do some alterations. If not, you should keep it on. Get used to it, and wear it in some. You'd already be on a bus or a plane by now, if you were really coming in from somewhere."

The shirtsleeves ended up half-staff, and the neck couldn't get close to buttoning, but the effect was OK. Every sergeant in civvies Reacher had ever seen wrenched his tie loose after about ten minutes. The suit coat was tight across the shoulders, and the sleeves stopped short of the knobs on the side of his wrists. He stood back and checked a mirror.

Perfect. A sergeant's salary was embarrassingly close to the poverty line. And sergeants didn't read *GQ*. Not usually. The whole ensemble looked exactly like a hundred dollars grudgingly spent at the outlet mall ahead of a sister-in-law's second wedding.

The supply guy said, "Keep it on. It'll do."

Reacher was supposed to supply his own pocket junk, so next up was ID. It had his real name and his photograph on it, but a master sergeant's rank, and an infantry unit sufficiently generic to be plausible for a guy deployed with special forces, shooting individuals one at a time from a mile away.

"How do I communicate with the colonel?" Reacher asked.

"Try the telephone," the supply guy said.

"Sometimes hard to find a phone in a hurry."

"There's no danger," the supply guy said. "It's all just talking."

The woman with the fanny pack and the headband crossed the Potomac on the Francis Scott Key Bridge, high above the water, running hard, die straight, through the hot swampy air, a glorious unbroken sprint, heading for Georgetown but not planning to get there. She was going to turn right on M Street, which became Pennsylvania Avenue, all the way to Washington Circle, and then New Hampshire Avenue to Dupont Circle, and then Mass Ave the rest of the way to the Capitol itself.

A crazy route, geographically, but any other option was either less or more than five miles, and five miles was what she ran. To the inch. Anyone else would have used her car's odometer, on a quiet Sunday morning, but she had bought a surveyor's wheel, a big yellow thing on a stick, and she had walked with it four separate times before she came up with eight thousand eight hundred yards exactly, and not a single step less or more. Precision was important.

She ran on. By that point she could feel a wide sweat stripe all the way down her back, and her throat was starting to burn. Pollution, hanging over the sluggish river, a visible cloud. But she dug in and pushed on, long, long strides, fast cadence, arms pumping. Her headband was soaked. But she was ahead of schedule. Just. Many variables to come, but she had a chance of making it. Five miles in thirty minutes. Eight thousand eight hundred yards in one thousand eight hundred seconds. Fourteen and two-thirds feet a second. Not an international distance, so there was no world record. No national record, no Olympic record. But the greats might have done it in twenty-four minutes. So thirty was acceptable. For her, with traffic, and lights, and office workers in the way.

She pushed on, breathing hard, still moving well, right up there in the zone.

The traffic on 16th Street was stop-start heavy, frustration on every block, past Juniper Street, and Iris, and Hemlock, and Holly, and Geranium, and Floral. Then past Walter Reed, with the park green and serene on the right. The driver was no longer a bullet. He was shrapnel at best, subject to aerodynamic forces, jinking right and left between the lanes to win some fractional advantage on the dead-straight road. A Southern town, built for horses and buggies, perspiring gentlemen in hats and vests flicking mosquitoes away, now sclerotic with jammed vehicles, superheated air shimmering above their hoods, expensive paint winking in the sun.

He still had a long way to go. He was going to be late.

Reacher walked the corridors until he smelled an office with a coffee machine going. He ducked in and helped himself to a cup, practicing a sergeant's manner, on the surface quiet and deferential, with ramrod competence showing underneath. But the office was empty, so his acting was wasted, and the coffee was burnt and stewed. But he took it with him anyway, in one hand, the sheaf of documents in the other, all the way back to Cornelius Christopher's office.

Christopher said, "You look the part."

Reacher said, "Do I?"

"Your file says you're pretty good with a long gun."

"I do my best."

"You could have been a real sniper."

"Too much waiting around. Too much mud. The best snipers are always country boys."

"And you're a city boy?"

"I'm a nowhere boy. I grew up on Marine bases."

"Yet you joined the army?"

"I'm naturally contrary."

"Did you finish your reading?"

"Not yet."

"We checked for financial irregularities," Christopher said. "Or financial excesses, I suppose. But they're all living within their means. Appropriate accommodations, four-cylinder cars, good clothes but small wardrobes, modest jewelry, no vacations, not that they'd take a vacation anyway. Not fast-track people. Not if they want to be Chief of Staff one day. Or a defense industry lobbyist."

Reacher put the thirty-year-old Lieutenant Colonel Christine Richardson to the bottom of the pile, and started in on the second of the women, twenty-nine years old and a mere major, name of Briony Walker, the daughter of a retired naval officer, brought up mostly in Seattle and San Diego, public elementary school, public high school, valedictorian, West Point.

Christopher said, "I hope it's not her."

Reacher said, "Why?"

"The naval connection."

"You like the Navy?"

"Not much, but it's still a military family."

The third candidate was another thirty-year-old light colonel, this one called Darwen DeWitt, and right there Reacher knew she wasn't the product of a military family. Not with a name like that. In fact she was the daughter of a Houston businessman who owned about a hundred dent-repair franchises. Private education all the way, softball star, West Point.

The fourth was Alice Vaz, age thirty, lieutenant colonel, granddaughter of another lieutenant colonel, except this one had been called Mikhail Vasilyevich and he had been a lieutenant colonel in the Red Army. A Soviet. His son, Alice's father, had gotten out of Hungary just in time, with a pregnant wife, and Alice had been born in the United States. A citizen. California, public elementary, public high, West Point.

"Notice anything definitive?" Christopher asked.

Reacher said, "Their names are perfectly alphabetical. Alice, Briony, Christine, and Darwen."

"OK, apart from that."

"Two of them are rich girls. What does that do to your money motive?"

"Maybe taking money is a habit with rich people. Maybe that's how they get rich in the first place. Did you notice anything else?"

"No."

"Neither did we."

The woman with the fanny pack and the headband was on New Hampshire Avenue, gunning hard up the rise, the hubbub of Dupont Circle already visible in the haze ahead. She was up two greens on the crosswalks and she could see it already, reaching the Capitol steps, slamming her hand on her wrist to stop the watch, gasping for air, once, twice, bent over, hands on knees, then raising her head, then bringing her arm up slowly, and blinking the sweat from her eyes and focusing on the pale LCD readout and seeing the magic numbers: twenty-nine something.

She could do it.

She hammered on, striding short because of the gradient, really breathing, really hurting, but still moving well.

The man in the car was still on 16th Street. He had the air on high, but even so he could feel sweat on his back. Vinyl upholstery, and a four-cylinder motor with no power to spare for a big compressor. He was just past Harvard Street, getting to where young and rent-strapped aides were forced to live. No cars for them. They were walking to work, right alongside him, about the same speed.

He watched one, a girl, in pantyhose despite the heat, the nylon scissoring fast, ugly white athletic sneakers on her feet, with tube socks, her dress shoes no doubt in the big bag she was carrying, along with briefing papers and position papers and talking points, maybe with a makeup kit, hoping against hope everyone else would be busy and she would get to go on the television news for a comment.

There were male versions, too, dressed out of a Brooks Brothers sale, heads high, striding out. Every block brought more of them, twos and threes, until both sidewalks were full of them, all heading the same way, power walking, almost an army, an unstoppable force, clean-living and idealistic young people setting out to do good for their country.

They were going to get to work before him. The traffic was awful.

The transcript showed that the second pre-committee hearing had picked up more or less exactly where the first had left off, solidly on the safe grounds of technical discussions, about minutiae like actions and stocks and bedding and triggers and scopes. It was as if a collective but unspoken agreement had been reached, to avoid unpleasant issues, and to run out the clock with the kind of things shooters liked to talk about.

The four liaison women poked and prodded and drew the men out endlessly, going over things again and again, refining details until Reacher could practically see the new weapon in his mind's eye. Three of them were doing it just to keep the ball rolling, and the fourth was lapping it all up, no doubt picturing her contact in a foreign boardroom reading her fax, unable to believe the precision of the specification he was being handed.

Who was the fourth?

Christine Richardson and Darwen DeWitt did most of the talking. The transcript looked like a movie screenplay where C.R. and D.D. were the big stars. They each got plenty of ink. But their approaches were different. Richardson was rah-rah for the army, every question and every point laying a kind of guilt trip on the politicians for not rushing to make the world a safer place. DeWitt showed more concern for the Congressional point of view. She was almost a fifth skeptic. Devil's advocate, maybe, or perhaps her sympathies genuinely lay elsewhere. Perhaps her Houston dent-repair upbringing had made her a fiscal conservative. But wherever she was coming from, she laid bare the details of the secret spec as much as anyone.

Briony Walker and Alice Vaz said less. Walker was all about accuracy. The naval family. She wanted the rifle to be like the guns on her daddy's ships, artillery instruments, infallible when properly aimed. And she was weirdly interested in the end results. She asked about head shots and chest shots, about how it felt to wait while the bullet flew, about what they saw through the scope afterward. The effect was almost pornographic.

Alice Vaz asked mostly wider questions. The others debated rifle stocks made of composite materials, which wouldn't shrink or swell no matter the conditions, and she asked about the conditions. Where in the world was this rifle likely to go? How hot? How cold? How high? How wet? She didn't get clear answers, and after a spell she gave up. There were no A.V. attributions in the last twenty pages of the transcript.

Christopher asked, "Gut feeling?"

Reacher said, "Just from this?"

"Why not?"

"Then I would say it's Christine Richardson. She sounds like the prime mover. She wants everything spelled out every which way. No secrets with that woman."

"I could say she's trying to sell it. I could say she thinks the political guys will find that stuff interesting."

"No, she knows they don't. But she keeps on talking anyway. She won't let them leave anything vague or unspecified. Why is that?"

"Maybe she has OCD."

"What's that?"

"Obsessive-compulsive disorder. Like alphabetizing your underwear."

"How do you alphabetize underwear?"

"Figure of speech."

"So you're happy with Richardson?"

"No," Christopher said. "We think it's her, too. From the externalities in the transcripts, at least. The issue is going to be proving it."

The woman with the fanny pack and the headband was on Mass Ave, approaching Scott Circle, and the man in the car was on 16th Street, approaching Scott Circle. Their average speeds for the last many minutes had been more or less identical, at ten miles an hour, her progress steady and resolute and relentless, his frustratingly stop-start-fast-fast-slow. She was pushing hard, ready for an iconic athletic breakthrough, desperate for it, and he was agitated about the time, anxious about being late, wishing he could have parked and taken the Metro without getting back at the end of the day to find all his wheels had been stolen.

It happened like this: She was on the left-hand sidewalk, on Mass Ave, and he was at right angles to her, in 16th Street's extreme right lane, wanting to come off into the circle. She was looking straight ahead, watching the traffic, watching the upcoming crosswalk lights, trying to time it, suddenly convinced that if she got held up there her bid was over. He was looking beyond the three cars ahead, to the far left, diametrically away from her, watching the traffic coming into the circle, which would have prior right-of-way. He was looking for an upcoming gap, trying to time it, hoping to roll up to the line and squirt on through, one unbroken move.

She sprinted, hard, hard, hard, and he moved up, craning left, looking for the gap that would be his, seeing half a gap, rolling, rolling, the cars ahead of him clearing, the gap tightening, not really a gap at all, but his last chance, so he went for it, hitting the gas, wrenching the wheel, smashing into her as she sprinted into the space she had been sure would remain, because surely no driver would try to use it.

She went up in the air and down on his windshield rail, impossibly loud metallic thumps and crashes, and he braked hard and she spun on the shiny roof and clattered over the inclined tailgate and landed headfirst on the blacktop.

Reacher butted all the paperwork into a neat stack and put it back on Christopher's desk. Christopher said, "Almost time to get down to business. Do you know the committee room number?"

Reacher said, "Yes."

"Do you know where it is?"

"No."

"Good. I'm not going to tell you. I want you wandering around like a little lost country boy. I want everything about this thing to be realistic from the get-go."

"Nothing about this thing is realistic. And nothing about this thing is going to work."

"Look on the bright side. You might get lucky. One of them might be into rough trade. All on the army's dime, too."

Reacher said nothing. He used the door on F Street and turned right and left onto New Jersey Avenue, and then the Capitol Building was right there in front of him, half a mile ahead, big and white and shining in the sun. He looped around into the plaza and went up the steps. A Capitol cop looked at his ID and gave him a barrage of directions so confusing that Reacher knew he would need a couple of refreshers along the way. Which he got, first from another guard, and then from a page.

The designated committee room had an impressive door made from polished mahogany; and inside, it had an impressive table made from the same wood. Around the table were seated four people. One was the transcriber. He was in shirtsleeves and had a court-reporter machine in front of him. The other three were clearly the army procurement officer, and the Marine Corps procurement officer, and the Marine sniper. The two officers were in uniform, and the sniper was in a cheap suit. Probably a Recon Marine. A Delta wannabe. The officers shook hands, and the sniper gave a millimetric nod, which Reacher returned, equally briefly, which for two alleged snipers was effusive, and for a dogface and a jarhead meeting for the first time was practically like rolling around on the floor in an ecstatic bear hug.

There was no one else in the room. No political staffers, none of the liaison women. The clock in Reacher's head said the meeting was due to start inside a minute. The clock on the wall was a minute fast, so the meeting was already under way, according to Capitol time. But nothing was happening. No one seemed to care. The Marine sniper was mute, and the procurement guys were clearly as happy to waste time sitting quiet as to waste it talking up a storm about a lost cause.

The clock ticked. No one spoke. The jarhead stared into space, infinitely still. The officers moved in their chairs and got comfortable. Reacher copied the jarhead.

Then eventually the staffers came in, followed by three women in army Class A uniform. Three women, not four. *Class A uniform, female officer, the nameplate is adjusted to individual figure differences and centered horizontally on the right side between one and two inches above the top button of the coat.* Reacher scanned the black plastic rectangles. DeWitt, Vaz, and Walker were there. Richardson was not. A and B and D were present, but C was missing. No Christine.

The four staffers looked a little upset, and the three women looked very unhappy. They all sat down, in what were clearly their accustomed places, leaving one chair empty, and the guy at the head of the table said, "Gentlemen, I'm afraid we have some very upsetting news. Earlier today Colonel Richardson was struck by a car as she was running to work. At Scott Circle."

Reacher's first thought was: *Running? Why? Was she late?* But then he understood. Jogging, fitness, shower and dress at the office. He had seen people do that.

The guy at the head of the table said, "The driver of the car is a postal worker from the Capitol mail room. Eyewitness accounts suggest risks were taken by both parties."

The army procurement officer asked, "But how is she? How's Christine?"

The guy at the head of the table said, "She died at the scene."

Silence in the room.

The guy said, "Head trauma. From when she hit the windshield rail, or from when she finally fell to the ground."

Silence. No sound in the room, except the patter of the transcriber's machine, as he caught up with what had been said. Then even he went quiet.

The guy at the head of the table said, "Accordingly, I suggest we close down this process and resume it at a more suitable time."

The army procurement officer asked, "When?"

"Let's schedule it for the next round of budget discussions."

"When are those?"

"A year or so."

Silence.

Then Briony Walker said, "No, sir. We have a duty to fulfill. The process must be completed. Colonel Richardson would have wanted it no other way."

No answer.

Walker said, "The army deserves to have its case made properly and its needs and requirements placed in the record. People would quickly forget our reason for abandoning this process. They would assume we had not been truly interested. So I propose we complete our mission by making certain every detail and every parameter have been adequately clarified and accurately recorded. Then at least our legislators will know exactly what they are approving. Or rejecting, as the case may be."

The guy at the head of the table said, "Does anyone wish to speak against the proposal?"

No answer.

"Very well," the guy said. "We will do as Major Walker suggests, and spend the rest of the day going over everything one more time. Just in case there's something we missed."

And go over it they did. Reacher recognized the sequence of individual discussions from the transcripts. They started at the beginning and worked their way through. Most items were simply reiterated and reconfirmed, but there were some lingering live debates. Briony Walker was all out for bolt action. The naval family. The accuracy issue. A bolt action was operated manually, as gently as you liked, so the gun stayed still afterward, with no microscopic tremors running through it. On the other hand a semi-automatic action was operated by gunpowder explosions, and was absolutely guaranteed to put tremors into the gun afterward. Perhaps for a critical length of time.

"How long?" one of the staffers asked.

"Would it be critical?" Walker asked back.

"No, how long do these tremors last?"

"Some fractions of a second, possibly."

"How big are they?"

"Certainly big enough to hurt accuracy at a thousand yards or more."

The staffer looked across the table and said, "Gentlemen?"

The army procurement guy looked at his Marine counterpart, who looked at his sniper, who stared into space. Then everyone looked at Reacher.

Reacher said, "What was the first item you discussed?"

The staffer said, "Cold shot accuracy."

"Which is important why?"

"Because a sniper will often get just one opportunity."

"With a bullet that was chambered when?"

"I think we heard testimony that it can have been several hours previously. Long waits seem to be part of the job."

"Which means any tremors will have disappeared long ago. You could chamber the round with a hammer. If you assume the money shots are always going to be singles, and widely spaced, possibly by hours or even days, then the action doesn't matter."

"So you'd accept a semi-automatic sniper rifle?"

"No, sir," Reacher said. "Major Walker is correct. Possibly the money shots won't always be the first shots. And accuracy is always worth pursuing wherever possible. And bolt actions are rugged, reliable, simple, and easy to maintain. They're also cheap."

So then came a debate about which bolt action was best. The classic Remington had fans in the room, but so did Winchester and Sako and Ruger. And at that point Alice Vaz started up with more of her big-picture questions. She said, "The way to understand our requirements, for not only actions but also stocks and bedding, it seems to me, is to understand where and how this rifle will actually be used. At what altitude? At what barometric pressures? In what extremes of temperature and humidity? What new environments might it face?"

So to shut her up the army procurement guy ran through just about everything in the War Plans locker. No names and no specific details, of course, but all the meteorological implications. High altitude plus freezing mist, extreme dry heat with sand infiltration, rain forest humidity and high ambient temperature, in snow many degrees below zero, in downpours, and so on.

Then one of the staffers insisted that the steel for the barrel had to be domestic. Which was not a huge problem. Then another insisted that the optics had to be domestic, too. Which was a bigger problem. Reacher watched the women seated opposite. Darwen DeWitt wasn't saying much. Which was a surprise after her star turns the first two times out. She was a little more than medium height, and still lithe, like the teenage softball star she had been. She was dark-haired and pale-skinned, with features more likely to be called strong than pretty, but she was spared from being plain by mobile and expressive eyes. They were dark, and they moved constantly but slowly, and they blazed with intelligence and some kind of inner fire. Maybe she was burning off surplus IQ, to stop her head from exploding.

Briony Walker was the Navy daughter, and she looked it, neat and controlled and severe, except for an unruly head of hair, untamed even by what looked like a recent and enthusiastic haircut. She too had an animated face, and she too had a lot going on behind her eyes.

Alice Vaz was the best-looking. Reacher didn't know the word. *Elfin,* maybe? *Gamine?* Probably somewhere in between. She had darker skin than the other two, and a cap of short dark hair, and the kind of eyes that switch between a twinkle and a death ray in, well, the blink of an eye. She was smaller than the other two, and slight, in a European kind of way, and maybe smarter, too. Ultimately she was controlling the conversation, by hemming it in with questions too boring to answer. She was making the others focus.

The meeting dragged on. Reacher made no further contributions beyond an occasional grunt of assent. Eventually conversation dried up and the guy at the head of the table asked if everyone agreed the army's needs and requirements were now properly in the record. All hands went up. The guy repeated the question, this time personally to and directly at Briony Walker, possibly a courtesy, possibly out of spite, her own words fed back to her. But Walker took no offense. She just agreed, yes, she was completely satisfied.

Whereupon the four staffers stood up and left the room, hustling and bustling and without a word, as if to take time out to say goodbye would hopelessly overburden their busy schedules. The women stood up, but the next out of the room was the army procurement guy, who just clapped his Marine buddy on the shoulder and disappeared. Whereupon the Marine clapped his NCO on the shoulder and they walked out together, leaving just Reacher and the women in the room.

But it didn't stay that way for long. The women were already in a huddle. Not exactly leaning in, face to face, a tight little triangle, shoulder to shoulder, touching each other, like regular women. But maybe the West Point version. They drifted in lockstep to the door, there was a polite glance from Alice Vaz, and then they were gone.

Reacher stayed where he was. No big rush. Nothing he could have done about it. Maybe there were guys who could have pulled it off. *Hey, I'm sorry about your dead buddy that I never met, but can I separate you from your grieving pals and take you out and buy you a drink?* Reacher was not one of those guys.

But the women weren't going anywhere. He was sure of that.

He got up and stepped out and saw them where the corridor widened into a lobby. They were still together in their tight huddle. Not going anywhere. Just talking. Lots of social rules. They would end up in a bar, for sure, but not yet.

Reacher drifted back to a bank of pay phones and dialed. He leaned on the wall. He saw Briony Walker glance at him, then glance away. Just the out-of-towner making a call. Maybe to his local buddies, telling them he's done for the day, asking them where the action is at night.

Christopher said, "Yes?"

Reacher said, "Did you hear about Christine Richardson?"

"Yes, we did."

"So it's going to be a little harder now."

"It might be over now. If Richardson was the leak all along."

"Suppose she wasn't?"

"Then it might be easier, not harder. With the other three. Emotion helps. Loose lips sink ships."

"It wasn't a fun afternoon. Romance is on no one's mind. They're talking to each other. There's no way into a conversation like that."

"Exploit any opportunity you can."

"You're not in the Capitol, but you're monitoring their fax line, right?"

"Correct."

"Including tonight?"

"Of course. What do you know?"

"It's not DeWitt."

"How do you know?"

"She was upset. She's thirty years old and she never had anyone die before."

"It's natural to be upset."

"But if she had a secret agenda she'd have gotten over it. To do her work. But she didn't. She hardly said a word. She sat there like the whole thing had no purpose. Which was absolutely the appropriate reaction for anyone without an agenda of her own."

"Had either of the other two gotten over it?"

"Alice Vaz was all over it. Briony Walker likewise. And Walker made a real big fuss about going through it all one more time. With every detail stated for the record."

"So she could check if she missed anything in her last two faxes?"

"That's a possible interpretation."

"What did Vaz do?"

"Same thing she did in the transcripts. Big geography. She should quit and run a travel agency."

"What are you going to do?"

"I don't know yet. Just monitor that fax line for me."

Reacher hung up the phone. The women were still in the lobby, still talking, still not going anywhere. He set off toward them, just strolling, like a man with an hour to kill, like a stranger in town drawn toward the only faces he knew. Plan A was to keep the pretense going, maybe getting into the group via Briony Walker's interest in gunshot wounds. Maybe she was a sniper groupie. He could offer some opinions. Head shot or chest shot? *Well, ma'am, I favor the throat shot. If you hit it just right you can make their heads come off.*

Plan B was to abandon the pretense and come clean as an MP captain undercover for MI, and see where that road led. Which might be all the way home. If he made out Richardson had been the prime suspect, then whoever worked hardest to reinforce that conclusion would be the guilty one. If no one worked hard, then Richardson had been the guilty one all along.

He strolled on.

Plan A or Plan B?

They made the decision for him.

They handed it to him on a plate.

They were civilized women, and reflexively polite in the way that military people always are. He was heading close to them. He wasn't going to pass by on the other side. So he had to be acknowledged. Briony Walker looked straight at him, but Darwen DeWitt was the first to speak. She said, "We weren't introduced. I guess it wasn't that kind of an afternoon."

"No, ma'am," Reacher said. "I guess it wasn't." He said his name. He saw each of the three file it away in her memory.

He said, "I was sorry to hear about Colonel Richardson."

DeWitt nodded. "It was a shock."

"Did you know her well?"

"We all came up together. We expected to carry on together."

"Brother officers," Reacher said. "Or sisters, I guess."

"We all felt that way."

Reacher nodded. They could all afford to feel that way. No rivalry. Not yet. They faced no significant bottleneck until the leap from brigadier general to major general. From one star to two. Then a little rivalry might bite.

Briony Walker said, "It must have happened to you, sergeant. You must have lost people."

"Ma'am, one or two."

"And what do you do on days like that?"

"Well, ma'am, typically we would go to a bar and toast their journey. Usually starts out quiet, and ends up happy. Which is important. For the good of the unit."

Alice Vaz said, "What unit?"

"I'm not at liberty to say, ma'am."

"What bar?"

"Whatever is close at hand."

DeWitt said, "The Hyatt is a block away."

They walked over to the Hyatt. But not exactly together. Not a foursome. More accurately a threesome and a singleton in a loose association, held together only by Reacher playing dumb enough to miss the hints he should get lost. The women were too polite to make it more explicit. But even so the walk was excruciatingly embarrassing. Out of the grounds, across Constitution, onto New Jersey Avenue, across Louisiana and D Street, and then they were there, at the Hyatt's door. Reacher stepped up promptly and held it open. Because immediate action was required, right there, right then. Indecisive loitering on the sidewalk would have led to heavier hints.

They shuffled past him, first Vaz, then DeWitt, and finally Walker. Reacher fell in behind them. They found the bar. Not the kind of place Reacher was used to. For one thing, there was no bar. Not as such. Just low tables, low chairs, and waiter service. It was a lounge.

Walker looked at Reacher and asked, "What should we drink?"

Reacher said, "Pitchers of beer, but I doubt if they have those here."

A waiter came and the women ordered white wine spritzers. It was summer. Reacher ordered hot coffee, black, no sweeteners required. He preferred not to clutter a table with jugs and bowls and spoons. The women murmured among themselves, a trio, with occasional guilty glances at him, unable to get rid of him, unable to be rude to him.

He asked, "Do those meetings usually go like that? Apart from the thing with Colonel Richardson, I mean."

Vaz said, "Your first?"

Reacher said, "And hopefully my last, ma'am."

Walker said, "No, it was worth it. It was a good at-bat. They can't say no to everything. So we just made it fractionally more likely they'll say yes to something else, sometime soon."

"You like your job?"

"Do you like yours, sergeant?"

"Yes, ma'am, most of the time."

"I could give the same answer."

The waiter brought the drinks, and the women returned to their three-way private conversation. Reacher's coffee was in a wide, shallow cup, and there wasn't much of it. He was a couple of mouthfuls away from the next awkward moment. They hadn't gotten rid of him leaving the Capitol, and they hadn't gotten rid of him entering the hotel. The end of the first round of drinks was their next obvious opportunity. All it would take was an order: *Sergeant, you're dismissed.* No way of fighting that, not even under Plan B. *Captain, you're dismissed* worked just as well, when said by majors and lieutenant colonels.

But it was Darwen DeWitt who left after the first round of drinks. She was still not talking much, and she clearly wasn't enjoying herself. She was finding no catharsis. She said she had work to do, and she got up. There were no hugs. Just tight nods and brave smiles and meaningful glances, and then she was gone. Vaz and Walker looked at Reacher, and Reacher looked right back at Walker and Vaz. No one spoke. Then the waiter came back right on cue, and Vaz and Walker ordered more spritzers, and Reacher ordered more coffee.

The second spritzer loosened Walker up a little. She asked Reacher what he felt when he pulled the trigger on a live human being. Reacher quoted a guy he knew. He said recoil against his shoulder. Walker asked what was the longest kill he had ever made. Truth was about eleven feet, at that stage, because he was a cop, but he said six hundred yards, because he was supposed to be a sniper. She asked with what. Truth was a Beretta M9, but he said an M21, an ART II scope, and a 7.62 NATO round.

Alice Vaz asked, "Where was this?"

Reacher said, "Ma'am, I'm not at liberty to say."

"Which sounds like a special forces scenario."

"I guess it does."

"Six hundred yards is fairly close range for you guys."

"Practically point-blank, ma'am."

"Black bag for CIA, or legitimate for us?"

"Ma'am, I'm not at liberty to say."

And those twin denials seemed to create some credibility. Both women gradually abandoned their defensive body language. Not that it was replaced by personal interest. It was replaced by professional interest, which came across in a poignant way. Neither woman had a realistic hope in her lifetime of becoming a battlefield commander. Both were forced to take a different route. But both seemed to look across the divide with concern. In an ideal world they would be fighting. In which case they would want the best available weapons. No question about that. In which case simple ethics demanded the best available weapons for those currently doing the fighting in the less than perfect world. Simple justice. And simple preparedness, too. Their sisters might never get there, but their daughters would one day.

Walker asked Reacher his private opinion about the rifle design. Were there things that should be added? Taken away? Reacher said, "Ma'am, I think they got it about right," partly because that was the kind of thing a sergeant would say to an officer, and partly because it was true. Walker seemed happy with the answer.

Then both Walker and Vaz got up to use the restroom. Reacher could have used a pit stop, too, but he didn't want to follow directly behind them. That would have been too weird, right after the walk from the

Capitol. So he waited. He saw Vaz use a pay phone on her way. There was a line of them in wooden hutches on the lounge's back wall. Vaz used the center phone. Walker didn't wait for her. She went on ahead. Vaz spoke for less than ten seconds and then hung up and continued on her way to the restroom.

Walker never came back from the restroom. Vaz sat down alone and unconcerned and said Walker had gone back to the office. She had used the D Street door. She had a lot to do. And did Reacher want another drink?

Reacher and Vaz, alone together. Walker, on her own, on the loose.

Reacher said, "You buying?"

Vaz said, "Sure."

Reacher said, "Then yes."

"Then follow me," Vaz said. "I know a better place than this."

The better place was tucked in close to the tracks out the back of Union Station. It was better in the sense it had an actual bar. It was worse in every other way. In particular it was in a lousy neighborhood, full of ugly brick and ramshackle buildings, with dark streets and all kinds of alleyways and yards all over the place, with more wires overhead than trees. The bar itself felt like a waterfront establishment, mysteriously landlocked, low and wide and made a warren by subdivision into many different room-sized areas. Reacher sat with his back to a corner, where he could see both front and rear doors at once. Vaz sat next to him, not close, but not faraway, either. She looked good. Better than she had a right to. Class A uniform, female officer, was generally no kind of a flattering outfit. It was essentially tubular. Maybe Vaz's was tailored. It had to be. The jacket was waisted. It went in and out properly. The skirt was tight. And a little short. Just a fraction, but detectable by the human eye unaided.

Vaz said, "I hope not to be in this shop much longer."

"Where next?"

"War Plans, I hope."

"Do they cash this shop's checks?"

"You mean, can I take my credits with me? Absolutely. Politics and War Plans? They're practically the same thing."

"So when?"

"As soon as possible."

"But you're worried this business with Colonel Richardson will slow things down. No one likes a fuss, right? And the shop is understaffed now. Maybe they can't let you go."

"You're pretty smart, for a sergeant."

"Rank has nothing to do with being smart, ma'am."

"Tell me about yourself."

"You first."

"Nothing to tell," Vaz said. "California girl, West Point cadet, first I wanted to see the world, and then I wanted to control it. You?"

"Marine Corps boy, West Point cadet, first I wanted to see the world, and then I wanted to survive it."

"I don't remember many West Point cadets who became sergeants afterward."

"Some did. From time to time. In a way."

"I see."

"Do you?"

"You're an undercover operator," Vaz said. "I always knew the day would come."

"When what?"

"When you finally figured it out. As in, your procurement office is riddled with corruption, and has been for years. As in, you don't need a new sniper rifle. You know that. But those guys have already sold stock in the new model. Maybe the money is already spent. So they have to make it happen. Any way they can. I mean, did you hear some of the arguments they were making?"

"Where is their office?"

"Who? Procurement is a big department."

"The guy I saw today, for instance."

"His office is in the Capitol Building."

"With a fax machine?"

"Of course."

"Did any of the others know this?"

"In the political shop? We all did. Why do you think Walker made them go through the whole thing again today? Because she wanted to generate a third fax."

"Why?"

"An extra piece of evidence for you. We knew you'd catch up with it eventually."

"Why didn't one of you drop a dime before?"

"Not our place."

"You mean the cost-benefit ratio wasn't right. One

of you would have to step up, and it's conceivable she could lose. Because anything can happen in a military court. In which case she's out of the running right from that moment. Because she was once on the losing side. You couldn't risk that kind of mistake. Not having come so far."

"The running for what?"

"For whatever it is you all plan to be."

"For a spell we thought the previous sniper could be the undercover guy. The one you replaced. Like entrapment. He was letting the officer push him to want more and more. But in the end we thought he was just a sniper. So we'd have nailed you for the real undercover guy in about a minute, except no one was really paying attention this afternoon."

"Because of Richardson? What did she think was happening?"

"The same as we all did. Procurement is a swamp and you'd notice sooner or later."

"What is it you plan to be?"

"Respected. Perhaps within a closed community, but by someone."

"Has your life lacked respect so far?"

"You have no idea," Vaz said. She turned toward him, moving on the bench, her knees coming close to his, dark nylon over dark skin. She said, "I'm proceeding on the assumption that I can trust my impression that you're younger than me. And in a branch with much less generous and accelerated promotion. And that therefore I outrank you."

"I'm a captain," Reacher said. "Ma'am."

"Therefore if our chains of command were in any

way related, it would be inappropriate for us to have a close relationship. Therefore the question is, are our chains of command in any way related?"

"I think they're about as far apart as chains of command can be."

"Wait there," she said. "I'll be right back."

And she got up and threaded her way through the cluttered space, heading for the restroom corridor in back. Five minutes, minimum, Reacher thought. He followed her as far as a pay phone on the wall. The phone was a scratched old item and the wall behind it was dark with smoke and grime.

He dialed, and said his name.

Cornelius Christopher said, "Yes?"

Reacher said, "I'm done."

"What does that mean? You're quitting?"

"No, it means the job is done."

"What do you know?"

"Walker must be back at the Capitol by now. Any faxes yet?"

"No."

"You were wrong. No one is leaking to a foreign firearms manufacturer. No one ever was. Why would anyone need to? Everyone knows what a good sniper rifle should be. It's self-explanatory. It's obvious. The basic principles have been understood for a century. No one needs to gather secret intelligence. Because they already know."

"So what's the story?"

"I'm waiting for the final proof. I should have it in five minutes or less."

"Proof of what?"

"It's Alice Vaz," Reacher said. "Think about the transcripts. Her big-picture questions. She asked a couple more this afternoon. She wanted it spelled out exactly where this new rifle will be used. She asked what new environments it might face."

"So?"

"She was trying to get into War Plans through the back door. And the procurement guy fell for it. No details, but he gave plenty of weather clues. Anyone could reverse-engineer our entire slate of global intentions from what he said."

"Like what?"

"He said high altitude plus freezing mist."

"Afghanistan," Christopher said. "We're going to have to go there sooner or later."

"And extreme dry heat with sand infiltration."

"The Middle East. Iraq, most likely."

"And rain forest humidity and high ambient temperature."

"South America. Colombia, and so on. The drug wars."

"And in snow many degrees below zero."

"If we have to go to the Soviet Union."

"You see? She got a summary of all our future plans from the guy. Exactly the kind of oblique data that enemy intelligence analysts love."

"Are you sure?"

"I gave her two seconds to react and she came up with blaming procurement for being corrupt. It was almost plausible. She's very smart."

"Which enemy? Which foreign intelligence?"

"The Soviets, of course. A local fax number, probably in their embassy."

"She's their asset?"

"In a big, big way. Think about it. She's on the fast track. She's going right to the top. Which is what? The Joint Chiefs, at least. But maybe more. A woman like this could be President of the United States."

"But how did they recruit her? And when?"

"Probably before she was born. Her granddaddy was some big Red Army hero. So maybe her daddy wasn't a real refugee. Maybe the KGB shuffled him to Hungary so he could get out and look like a dissident. Whereupon his daughter could be born an American and become a real deep down sleeper. She was probably groomed for the fast track from birth. These people play a long game."

"That's a lot of assumptions."

"The proof will be here in about three minutes. Or not."

"But why risk wasting a super-high-value asset on this? Because if you're right, then this is useful, but it's not life-changing. This is not the hydrogen bomb."

"I think this was kind of accidental. I think it came up in the normal course of her duties. But she couldn't resist phoning it in. Habit, or a sense of obligation. If she's a true believer."

"What's the proof you're getting in five minutes? Or is it three?"

"It's two minutes now, probably," Reacher said. "She made a brief call from the Hyatt hotel. Think about it. She's a huge asset. Maybe their biggest ever. She's headed all the way to the top. Which could be anywhere. And right now she's stopping in War Plans next, which is a real big prize in itself. So she has to be protected. Like no one has ever been protected before. And she was suspicious of me somehow. Maybe routine paranoia. I was new. I was hanging around. So she called for help. She told the embassy's wet boys where I'd be, and when. And then she lured me into the trap. Right now I'm supposed to believe I'm about to get in her pants."

"Soviet wet boys are coming for you?"

"One minute now, probably. I'm about to be a mugging gone wrong. I'm going to be found dead on a street corner."

"Where are you?"

"In the badlands behind Union Station."

"I can't get anyone there in less than a minute."

"I didn't expect you would."

"Are you going to be OK?"

"That depends on how many they send."

"Can you arrest Vaz before they get there?"

"She's long gone. I'm sure she went straight out the bathroom window. You'll have to pick her up. She'll be heading for her office."

Then a man stepped in through the bar's rear door.

"Got to go," Reacher said. "It's starting."

Reacher hung up the phone. The guy at the rear door was compact and hard-edged, dressed in black, moving easily. He looked vaguely similar to Vaz in terms of ethnic background. But he was a decade older. Nothing in his hands. Not yet. Not inside a public bar.

Reacher guessed the point of the guy coming in the back was to chase him out the front, where the main force would be gathered. Easier to set up a mugging gone wrong on a public street, rather than in a private yard in back of a bar. Because it wasn't a great street. Not a great neighborhood. Broken lighting, plenty of shadows, plenty of doorways, passersby habituated by instinct and long experience to look away and say nothing.

The guy was scanning the room. Vaz had spent very little time on the phone. Very few words. Probably not more than *big guy, very tall, gray suit*. Reacher felt the guy's eyes on him. He practically heard the check marks. *Big guy, right there. Very tall, no question. Gray suit, here's our boy.* The guy started away from the door.

Reacher started toward it.

A wise man asked, what's the best time to plant a tree? A wise man answered, fifty years ago. As in, what's the best time to make a decision? A wise man answers, five seconds before the first punch is thrown.

The guy in black weighed maybe one-ninety, and he was doing about two miles an hour. Reacher weighed two-fifty, and he was doing about three miles an hour. Therefore closing speed was five miles an hour, and impact, should it happen, would involve some multiple of four hundred forty pounds a square inch.

Impact did happen.

But not at five miles an hour. Closing speed was dramatically increased by a sudden drive off Reacher's back foot and the vicious clubbing swing of his elbow. Which therefore connected with a real big multiple of their combined body weights. Reacher caught the guy on the perfect cheekbone-nose-cheekbone line and the cracking and splintering was clearly audible over the wooden thud of feet on the floor. The guy went down like a motorcycle rider hitting a clothesline. Reacher walked on by and stepped out the back door.

Nobody or somebody?

That was the only question. And there is no bigger difference than nothing or something. Had they posted all of the main force at the front? Or had they left a lone guy as backup?

They had left a guy. Dark hair, dark eyes, thicker coat than his pal. Smart as a whip, probably, but any human given instructions is at a disadvantage. *Your target is a big guy, very tall, gray suit.* And however smart you are, however quick, that lethal one, two, three question-and-answer drumbeat occupies precious mental milliseconds, at least *big guy check, very tall check, gray suit check,* like that, and the problem comes when the big guy in the gray suit occupies those same precious milliseconds by walking straight toward you and breaking your skull with his elbow.

Reacher walked on, to where an arch led from the yard to the alley.

The alley was wide enough for two horses and a beer cart axle. At the right-hand end was an arch to another private yard. At the left-hand end was the street. Reacher's shoes were quiet. Class A uniform shoes. Therefore man-made soles. No one wanted leather welts. More to polish. Reacher stopped short of the street and put his back against the left-hand wall. In a movie there would be a busted shard of mirror at his feet. He could edge it out and check the view. But he wasn't in a movie. So he inched around, and peered out, one eye.

Thirty feet away. Four guys. Therefore a total of six dispatched. Six wet boys in a foreign embassy. Permanently. For her. *Like no one has ever been protected before. A woman like this could be President of the United States.* They had two cars parked on the far side of the street. Diplomatic plates. Probably never paid their parking fines. The guys were in a rough arc near the bar's door, their backs to Reacher, just standing there semi-animated, like guys sometimes do for a spell, outside a bar.

There was no busted shard of mirror, but there was a broken quarter brick, about the size of a baseball. In no way reflective, but the need for a mirror was past. Reacher picked it up, and stepped out to the street, and turned left.

Thirty feet was ten paces, and Reacher kept a steady speed through the first five of them, and then he wound up and threw the brick fragment at the nearer car and accelerated hard so that the brick shattered the rear windshield and the four heads snapped toward the sound and Reacher's elbow hit the first of those heads all in a tight little one-two-three sequence, less than a second beginning to end.

The first guy went down, obviously, vertically beneath Reacher's scything follow-through, and then Reacher spun back off the bounce and drove the same elbow backward into the next guy's head. Which left two guys still on their feet, one close, one inconveniently distant, so Reacher feinted toward the farther one and then pivoted back and head-butted the nearer one, like he was trying to drive a fencepost into dry baked earth with his head. Which left one still on his feet, which the guy put to good use by running for it.

Reacher let him go. There were things Reacher didn't like to do. Running was one of them.

Twenty-four hours later Reacher was back in Frankfurt, where he stayed for a week, before moving on to Korea for a regular tour. Neither he nor anyone in the world heard anything more about Alice Vaz. He had no idea whether his analysis had been right or wrong, close or wildly inaccurate. But a month after his arrival in Seoul he heard he was being considered for a medal. The Legion of Merit, to be specific, and for no discernible reason, other than what might be gleaned from the notes in the manual: *Awarded for exceptionally meritorious conduct in the performance of outstanding services to the United States.*

Small Wars

In the spring of 1989 Caroline Crawford was promoted to the rank of lieutenant colonel. She bought a silver Porsche to celebrate. She had family money, people said, and plenty of it. A trust fund, maybe. Some eminent relative. Maybe an inventor. Her uniforms were tailored in D.C. by the same shop that made suits for the president. She was held to be the richest woman in the army. Not that the bar was high.

With the new rank came a new posting, so the silver Porsche's first trip was south from War Plans in the Pentagon to Fort Smith in Georgia. All part of the War Plans method. There was no point making plans that couldn't be executed. High-level on-the-ground liaison was crucial. With a little surreptitious behind-the-scenes observation mixed in. Every new light colonel's first rotation. Crawford was happy to do it. Even though Fort Smith turned out to be a small damp place in the woods, full of desperate characters. Special forces, of various types. No tailored uniforms. Which was OK. Promising, even. Raw material, possibly, for the kind of new units she was going to need. Input at an early stage could be vital. They might even name the units after her. She would make full bird within a year and a half. She would be fast-tracked to her first star. And she was entitled to have some input. Wasn't she? Liaison was a two-way street. She was entitled to suggest what they should do, as well as listen to what they couldn't.

The first week went well, even though it rained a lot. The rumor mill had it straight within an hour: she was unmarried and available, but not cool to hit on, because War Plans was serious shit. So relationships were cordial, but with enough of a hint of a buzz to be interesting, too. The visiting officers' quarters were adequate in every respect. Like a motel, but more earnest. The woods were always damp and stretched for miles all around, but there were roads through, some of them just forest tracks or firebreaks, others with lit-up signs on their muddy shoulders, eventually, an hour or so out, for barbecue sometimes, or bars with dancing. Life wasn't bad.

At the end of the first week she left Fort Smith in her tailored Class A uniform, in her silver Porsche, and she turned off the county road at the first big fork, which eventually led to a hidden not-quite-two-lane road-to-nowhere through the trees, mostly straight and sunlit, perfect with the windows down, with the wet smell of the rich mud on the shoulders, and the woody echo of the exhaust coming back off the bark, part throaty, part whine, part howl.

Then, a broken-down car up ahead. A sedan, stopped diagonally across the road, its front wheels turned all the way, its hood up, a guy peering in at the motor. A tall guy, obvious even from a hundred yards away. Not lightly built. Big feet.

She slowed, late and hard, just for the fun of it, changing down, the exhaust popping behind her like a fireworks show. The stalled sedan was a Detroit product painted army green. The guy under its hood straightened up and turned to look. He was tall indeed, maybe six-six, in standard battledress uniform, woodland pattern. He was all in proportion, and therefore far from delicate, but he held himself gracefully. He looked slender, except he wasn't.

She stopped the car. She rested her elbow on the door and her chin on her elbow, just looking, part quizzical, part resigned, part ready to help, maybe after some teasing. All those things, and not suspicious at all. The raised hood triggered some kind of ancient early-motorist instinct. Helpful, and sympathetic.

That, and the familiar uniform.

The tall guy walked closer. Big clumsy feet, in battered tan boots, but otherwise an elegant long-legged lope. No hat. Cropped fair hair, receding. Blue eyes, an open gaze, somehow both naïve and knowing. An otherwise unremarkable face, with features just the right side of blunt.

He had a full colonel's eagle on his collar. Above his right pocket his tape said: *U.S. Army.* Above his left pocket his tape said: *Reacher.*

He said, "Forgive me for interrupting your journey, but I can't push it out of the way. Can't turn the wheel. I think the power steering broke."

She said, "Colonel, I'm sorry."

He said, "I'm guessing your car doesn't have a trailer hitch."

"I could help you push."

"That's kind of you, but it would take ten of us."

She said, "Are you who I think you are?"

"That depends."

"You're Joe Reacher. You just got a new counterintelligence command."

"Correct on both counts," Joe Reacher said. "I'm pleased to meet you." He glanced down at her nameplate. Plastic, white on black, because of the tailored Class As. *The nameplate is adjusted to individual figure differences and centered horizontally on the right side between one and two inches above the top button of the coat.* He looked at her unit insignia and her badges of rank. He said, "You must be Caroline Crawford. Congratulations."

"You've heard of me?"

"Part of my job. But it's not part of yours to know who I am."

"Not part of my job, but part of my interest. I like to track the key players."

"I'm not a key player."

"Sir, bullshit, with respect, sir."

"Academic interest, or career interest?"

She half smiled, half shrugged, but didn't answer.

He said, "Both, right?"

She said, "I don't see why it can't be."

"How high do you plan to get?"

"Three stars," she said. "In the Joint Chiefs' office, maybe. Anything more would be in the lap of the gods."

Joe Reacher said, "Well, good luck with all of that," and he put his hand in his battledress pocket, and he came out with a standard army-issue Beretta M9 semi-automatic pistol, and he shot Caroline Crawford with it, twice in the chest and once in the head.

Also with a new posting the same week as Caroline Crawford was a military police major named David Noble. He was detaching from his current command and heading to Fort Benning, Georgia, from where he would oversee criminal investigations throughout the southeastern military districts. A brand-new reorganization. Someone's baby. Unlikely to last, but temporarily important work. Noble never got to do it. He was in a car wreck on the way. In South Carolina. An adjacent state. Nearly there. Not fatal, but he ended up at Walter Reed. He had a collapsed lung. He couldn't breathe right. So an emergency substitute was decided on and hunted down and pulled off his current maneuvers and hustled north to Benning. Just how it always was, for the army. Situation entirely normal. A big job, the second-best guy, a week late. On the bright side people said this new one was a fast study and a hard worker. He might catch up. If he got started right away.

So it was that the same moment Joe Reacher said, "I'm not a key player," his younger brother, Jack Reacher, walked into a brand-new office more than a hundred miles away, and then out again, in search of coffee, almost ready to begin overseeing criminal investigations throughout the southeastern military districts.

The Porsche was found early the next morning, by four soldiers in a Humvee, who were trying to find a shortcut back to Smith after a night exercise had gone all kinds of wrong in terms of navigation. They recognized the car from a distance. It was already famous on the base. The new War Plans lady. Hot, smart, and rich. Nothing wrong with any of that. Nothing at all. Maybe she had a flat tire. Maybe she was in need of assistance.

As they pulled closer they thought the car was empty.

Then they saw it wasn't.

They rolled by at walking speed and their high seating positions let them look down inside the Porsche, where they saw a woman in Class A uniform flopped over backward across the seats, shot twice in the chest and once in the head.

They parked nearby, and called it in on the radio. Then they sat tight. Crime scenes were not their problem. Within forty minutes an MP crew got there. From Fort Smith. With two JAG lawyers. Also from Fort Smith. They all took a look, and then they all stepped back. There was a question of jurisdiction. The road belonged to the county. Hence the county police had been informed. No choice. They were on their way, for a discussion.

Fort Benning heard about it almost immediately. A brand-new reorganization. Too fresh to be screwed up yet. Reacher had spent until late in the evening studying the new unit manual, and reviewing open cases, and reading files, and talking to people. Then he had grabbed a few hours of sleep, and gotten up again with a plan in his head. He figured he had a lot of work to do. The place was drowning in paper. And the NCOs were badly chosen. In his experience units ran either well or not depending on the quality of their sergeants. He wanted expert bureaucrats, but he didn't want them to be in love with bureaucracy. There was a difference. He wanted people who treated tasks like an enemy, to be dispatched fast and efficiently and ruthlessly. Or punitively, even. *They won't send me that form again.* The new unit didn't have such people. They were all too comfortable. A little soft. Like the guy who brought the torn-off telex first thing in the morning. A soft, comfortable guy. Hard to put in words, but he didn't have the spirit Reacher wanted. He didn't have the edge. He didn't look dangerous.

The telex said: *One repeat one (1) active-duty personnel found shot to death ten miles north of Fort Smith. Circumstances unknown.*

Reacher pictured a bar fight, a private or maybe a specialist, in some kind of an altercation with a local. Maybe a Harley fell over in the parking lot, or a glass of beer got spilled. Bars near bases were always full of local civilian hotheads with guns in their pockets and points to prove.

He said, "Bring me the details as and when they come in."

The soft sergeant said he would, and left the room.

Reacher picked up the phone and called his new CO. Among other things he said, "I need a better sergeant here. I need you to send me Frances Neagley. Before the end of the day, preferably."

The county sheriff who showed up in the woods knew the value of mud as an evidentiary medium. He parked way short and skirted the scene a yard off the road, pausing often to crouch and study the marks in the fine black tilth, which covered the blacktop more or less side to side, like a scrim, molecules thin in the center and inches thick on the edges. There were a lot of marks, some of them crisp, some of them oozing black water, some of them overwritten by the four soldiers rolling by in their Humvee.

The county guy made it all the way to the gaggle of Smith guys, and they all introduced themselves and shook hands and then stood around mute, maybe taking the legal temperature, maybe rehearsing their arguments. The county guy spoke first. He said, "Was she based at Fort Smith?"

A JAG lawyer said, "Yes."

"Any indication this was blue on blue?" Meaning, *Was there a professional dispute I don't need to know about? Is this all in the family?*

The JAG lawyer said, "No."

"Therefore she's mainly mine. Until I know for sure the shooter wasn't a civilian. I need to pay attention to a thing like this. I could have a crazy person running around in the woods. What was her name?"

"Crawford."

"What did she do at Fort Smith?"

"I'm afraid I can't tell you that."

"She was ambushed," the county guy said. "I can tell you that. The marks are clear. Someone faked a breakdown. She stopped to help. He had big feet."

The ranking MP said, "What next?"

The county guy said, "It's above my pay grade. Literally, in the township bylaws. I have to pass it on to state. No choice."

"When?"

"I already called. They'll be here soon. Then they can decide to keep it or pass it on to the Georgia Bureau of Investigation."

"We can't wait forever."

"You won't have to. Half a day, maybe." And then the guy crabbed back around the mud, to his car, where he got in and sat by himself.

The next telex came in an hour later. The same soft sergeant tore it out of the machine and brought it to Reacher's desk. It said: *Gunshot victim previously reported was LTC Caroline C. Crawford. DOA inside POV stationary on isolated forest road.*

POV meant personally owned vehicle. *DOA* meant dead on arrival. *LTC* meant lieutenant colonel. All of which together added up to an issue. Very few senior officers of Reacher's acquaintance fought to the death in bars. Especially not senior officers named Caroline. And even if they did, they didn't wind up inside their own private cars on remote woodland tracks. How would they?

Not a bar fight.

He said, "Who was she?"

The sergeant said, "Sir, I don't know."

Which was a case in point. A decent NCO would have detoured to a book or a phone and brought with him at least a capsule biography and a copy of current orders. Frances Neagley would have had all of that five minutes ago. Plus a photograph. Plus a lock of baby hair, if you wanted one.

Reacher said, "Go find out who she was."

The dispute over jurisdiction lasted longer than expected. The state cop who showed up let slip he wasn't sure if the woods were federal property. Fort Smith's acreage was, obviously. Maybe the undeveloped land all around was, too. The county guy said the road was maintained by the county. That was for sure. And the car was on the road, and the victim was in the car. The JAG lawyers said killing a federal employee was a federal crime, and a lieutenant colonel in the U.S. Army was assuredly a federal employee. And so on and so forth. Dark clouds gathered in the sky. More rain was on the way. The marks in the mud were about to get washed out. So a compromise was offered. The state police would be the lead agency, but the army would be fully accommodated. Access would be guaranteed. Acceptable, to the men in green. The autopsy would be performed by the state, in Atlanta. Also acceptable, because everyone already knew what the autopsy was going to say. *Otherwise healthy, except shot twice in the chest and once in the head.* The deal was agreed, whereupon immediately all three factions got into a flurry of crime-scene photography. Then a hard rain started to fall, and a tarpaulin was draped over the Porsche, and they all waited in their cars for the meat wagon and the tow truck.

Reacher looked up and saw his sergeant standing in front of him. A silent approach. The guy had a sheet of paper in his hand. But he didn't pass it over. He spoke instead. He said, "Sir, permission to ask a question?"

Which was a bad thing to hear, from a unit NCO. It wasn't what it sounded like. It was a whole different announcement. Like a girlfriend saying, "Honey, we need to talk."

Reacher said, "Fire away."

"I've heard you don't like my work and you're having me posted elsewhere."

"Incorrect on both counts."

"Really?"

"Likes and dislikes dwell in the realm of emotion. Are you accusing me of having feelings, sergeant?"

"No, sir."

"I assess your work coldly and rationally against a custom metric of my own design. Which is, Are you a guy I could call in the middle of the night with an emergency?"

"Am I, sir?"

"Not even close."

"So I'm to be posted."

"Negative."

"Sir, not to challenge your answer in any way, but I already know Sergeant Neagley has orders to proceed here without delay."

Reacher smiled. "The NCO grapevine gets faster all the time."

"She comes, I go. How else could it work?"

"It could work by you sticking around and learning something. That's what's going to happen. Neagley will report to me and you'll report to Neagley. At times she'll offer advice and encouragement about how to improve your performance."

"We're of equal rank."

"Pretend she comes from a planet with double the gravity. Her rank is worth more than yours."

"How long will she be here?"

"As long as it takes. You people need to think ahead. This reorganization is going to come out exactly ass-backward. You're not going to be up on a hill, peering down on all you survey. You're going to be deep in a hole, getting buried in paper. Because this is going to be the cover-your-ass unit. Everyone in the army is going to report everything, so whatever turns bad in the end is automatically our fault, because we didn't follow it up at the time. So you need to develop a very aggressive attitude toward paperwork. If you hesitate, it will bury you."

"Yes, sir."

"Therefore you also need to trust your intuition. You need to smell the ones that matter. No time for extensive study. Are you an aggressive person who trusts his intuition, sergeant?"

"Maybe not enough, sir."

"What's on the piece of paper you're holding in your hand?"

"It's a fax, sir. A history of Colonel Crawford's postings."

"Did you read it on the way in?"

"Yes, sir."

"And?"

"She's in War Plans. Currently liaising with the special operations school at Fort Smith."

"Which tells us what?"

"I don't know how to put it."

"In your own words, sergeant."

"She's a pointy-head."

"The pointiest of all. War Plans is special. Regular pointy-heads can't even get in the door. We're talking needle-sharp here. Shot to death. Should we be worried?"

"I think we should, sir."

"Intuition," Reacher said. "It's a wonderful thing."

"Any practical steps?"

"Start playing bad cop with the guys at Smith. Tell them we need more things sooner. In fact tell them we require a Xerox of everything. A complete file, as per protocol."

"I think that's one of the issues not yet decided."

"Fake it till you make it, sergeant. Get them in the habit."

"Yes, sir."

"And close the door on the way out."

Which the guy did. Reacher dialed his phone. The Pentagon. A number on a desk outside an office with a window. Answered by a sergeant, inevitably.

Reacher said, "Is he there? It's his brother."

"Wait one, major." Then a shout, muffled by a palm on the receiver: *Joe, your brother is on line two.* Then a click, and then Joe's voice, asking, "Are you still in Central America?"

Reacher said, "No, they pulled me out and sent me to Benning. Some other guy got in a car wreck. So I'm a day late and a dollar short."

"What's at Benning?"

"It's a new thing. A lot of incoming reports. Success or failure will depend on high-speed triage. Which is why I'm calling. I need background on a name at War Plans. It would take all day to get it anyplace else."

"What's happening at War Plans?"

"One of them died."

"What exactly is it you're doing at Benning?"

"The mission is to supervise all criminal investigations in the southeastern military districts. The likelihood is it will become a gigantic file cabinet."

"Who was supposed to get the command?"

"A guy named David Noble. Never met him. Fell asleep at the wheel, probably. Too eager to get here."

"So you got it."

"Luck of the draw."

"Who died from War Plans?"

"Caroline Crawford."

"So you'll be investigating that."

"I expect someone will, eventually."

"How did she die?"

"Shot on a lonely road."

"Who by?"

"We don't know."

"She was a big star," Joe said. "She was going all the way. Lieutenant general at least. The Joint Chiefs' office, probably."

"Doing what exactly?"

"There are three possible vectors for the Cold War. It could go hot, or it could stay the same, or the Soviet Union could fall apart under its own weight. Obviously a diligent planner looks at option three and asks, OK, what's next? And small wars are next. Against half-assed nuisance countries, mostly in the Middle East. Caroline Crawford was working on Iraq. She was starting early and playing a real long game. A big gamble. But the payoff was huge. She would have owned the Middle East doctrine. That's about as good as it gets, for a planner."

Reacher said, "I assume all of that was behind closed doors. I assume I don't need to go looking for Iraqi assassins."

"Conventional wisdom would say the Iraqis didn't know who she was. As you say, it was behind closed doors, and there were many of them, and they were all closed tight, and she was too junior to attract attention anyway."

"Any other external enemies?"

"External to what?"

"The United States. Either the army or the general population."

"I can't think of one."

"OK," Reacher said. "Thanks. Are you well and happy?"

"What are you going to do?"

"About what?"

"Crawford."

"Nothing, probably. I'm sure there's a jurisdiction thing. State police will claim it. I think they opened a new mortuary, up in Atlanta. They're proud of it. It's like a new theater getting the best plays."

"Yes, I'm well and happy. Do you have time to drive up and have dinner?"

"It's about a thousand miles."

"No, it's about six hundred and ninety-three. That's not far."

"Maybe I'll get there for a weekend."

"Keep me in the loop about Crawford. If anything weird shows up, I mean. Part of my job."

"I will," Reacher said, and he hung up the phone. His sergeant knocked on the door and came in with a faxed report and a short stack of photographs. The guy put them neatly on the desk and said, "This all is from the MP XO at Smith. It's everything they've got so far. We know what they know."

"Did you read it on the way in?"

"Yes, sir."

"And?"

"There are tire tracks and footprints. Probably a second vehicle was deployed as a barrier. The perpetrator seems to be a tall man with a long stride and large feet. Also noteworthy is the fact that JAG lawyers went with the MPs to the scene. And there were three gunshot wounds. Two in the chest and one in the head."

"Good work, sergeant."

The guy said, "Thank you," and walked out, and a minute later Frances Neagley walked in.

Neagley was about the size of a male flyweight boxer, and could have beaten one easily, unless the referee happened to be watching. She was in woodland-pattern BDUs, newly washed and pressed. She had dark hair cut short, and a solid tan. She had spent the winter overseas. That was clear. She said, "I heard about the dead pointy-head."

Reacher smiled. *The NCO grapevine.* He said, "How are you?"

"Grumpy. You pulled me out of an easy week at Fort Bragg. Practically a vacation."

"Doing what?"

"Security for the special forces command. They don't tend to need much. Not that it isn't good to see you."

"What do you know about Fort Smith?"

"It's their version of pointy-heads. The theory and practice of irregular warfare. They call it a school."

"Why would they have JAG lawyers permanently on base?"

"The theory, I suppose. Rules of engagement, and so forth. I imagine they're pushing the envelope."

"My brother says the dead pointy-head was staking out a whole new doctrine for the Middle East. She wanted to own Plan B. If we don't get the big war, we get a bunch of small wars instead. Starting with Iraq, maybe. She was rolling the dice. And I guess special forces were rolling them right along with her. They don't fit well with the big war. Their only play is small. Was anyone talking about that at Bragg?"

Neagley shook her head. "That kind of thing would have to start at Smith. It's like espionage. You have to infiltrate the intellectual heart. Or like a political campaign. You have to build a constituency. You need key endorsements."

"So if she wins, who loses?"

"No one loses. She wouldn't divert resources away from the big war. It would be extra spending. The president is a Republican."

"So she was a woman with no enemies."

"She was rich," Neagley said. "Did you know that?"

Reacher said, "No."

"People say it was family money. She bought a sports car to celebrate her promotion."

"What kind of sports car?"

"German."

"A Volkswagen?"

"I don't think so."

Reacher leafed through the faxed report.

"A Porsche," he said. "The POV she was found in."

He scanned the rest of the report. Words, maps, charts. And the photographs. Mud, marks, wounds. He passed it all to Neagley. She scanned it in turn, the same way, words, maps, charts, mud, marks, and wounds.

She said, "Two in the chest and one in the head. That's an execution."

Reacher nodded. "The woman with no enemies. But

not exactly. Because it can't have been random. It wasn't a robbery. Not just some punk. Even a hillbilly would have taken the car. He'd have driven it hard all night and burned it in the morning."

"Two in the chest and one in the head is standard military practice. Under certain circumstances, in certain units. You can look it up."

"Is it exclusively military?"

"Probably not."

"And there are plenty of vets in the state of Georgia. We shouldn't narrow it down too much. We shouldn't put the blinders on."

Neagley turned to the last page of the written report. She said, "We might as well put blindfolds on. It isn't our case. The state police has got it."

"How many rich people are there in the army?"

"Very few."

"How many are also smart enough to fast-track through one tough gig after another?"

"Very few."

"So does this feel random to you?"

"Not with the execution-style placement, no."

"So she was a specific target, deliberately ambushed."

"You can see the tire marks in the mud. The guy parked across the road. Sawed back and forth a bit, to make it look good. Then he got out to wait. Big feet. That's how to narrow it down. This guy wears size fifteen boots."

Reacher took the paperwork back from her. He flipped forward to the maps. Not the kind of thing for sale at the gas station. Detailed government surveys, of woodland and streams and roads and tracks of every description and purpose, all Xeroxed and tiled together on slightly overlapping pages.

He said, "But that road doesn't really go anywhere. Maybe it's just a firebreak. There's no logical reason to be on that road. You'd have to detour to get there, and then get yourself back on track again afterward. Wherever you were going. Therefore there's no logical way to predict she would use that road. The odds get worse and worse after the first big fork. She could have used any road. It's ten to one at best. And who sets up a deliberate ambush on a ten-to-one chance? So it must have been random."

"So let the state police have it. They'll chase it through the shoe size. This guy must be a basketball player. I mean, what size are your feet?"

"Eleven."

"Is that big or small?"

"I don't know."

"We need a larger sample. What about Joe, for instance?"

Reacher didn't answer.

Neagley said, "What?"

"Sorry, I was thinking."

"What about?"

"About Joe and his footwear habits. He's same as me, I think. Maybe eleven and a half."

"And he's an inch taller, as I recall, as well as better-looking, so if we ballpark it we could round it up and say a size twelve is about right for guys about your height, and we could push it up to size fourteen, maybe, to allow for some genetic variation, which has to mean a guy who wears a size fifteen is not going to be any smaller than you, at least, and probably bigger, which makes him some kind of ape man who lives in the woods. Should be easy to spot. Should be easy to eliminate suspects. The state police will handle it fine."

"We're supposed to supervise. The JAGs got us access."

"I believe we're already getting all of Fort Smith's paperwork."

"I think we need to be proactive."

"In what way?"

"In whatever way works. It had to be random, but it can't have been. There's a whole span of assumptions right there, and at least one of them can't be true. We'll have to figure it out sooner or later. Because the state police will ask. Also sooner or later. That's for damn sure."

"OK. We'll do what we can. Plus the autopsy will be happening."

Two hours later the autopsy reported exactly what everyone expected. Otherwise healthy. The fatal shot was probably the first, into the chest. Hard to be sure, for both pathologist and perpetrator, hence the two follow-ups. The vertical triangle. Chest, chest, head. Job done.

All three bullets had been recovered inside the Porsche. They were badly mangled, but they were almost certainly nine-millimeter Parabellum. The entry wound in the forehead was exactly nine millimeters wide. The angle was plausible, for a tall man firing downward into a stationary car. Which matched the earlier photographs. The big feet had walked close, then shuffled around, possibly during a moment of conversation, and then they had stepped back and braced. For the moment of truth. Recoil off the nine wasn't terrible, but a sound footing was always a good idea. Range about eight feet, Reacher guessed. Ideal. Chest, chest, head. Hard to miss, at eight feet. No brass in the photographs. The guy had picked up his shell cases. And driven away, in the decoy vehicle.

A skilled worker.

An execution.

Neagley said, "The career gossip sounds fairly normal, for a pointy-head. She was a classroom superstar at West Point. A decent physical soldier, but mostly a geek. Therefore always destined for the back rooms. Smooth acceleration all the way. Really blossomed in War Plans. It suited her somehow. She became her own person. She loosened up a little. Even started spending some of her money. Maybe she felt awkward before. That was when she first got the fancy uniforms."

Reacher said, "Do we know anything about the money yet? As in, where it originally came from?"

"You think this is a financial crime?"

"Who knows, with rich people? They're different from you and me."

"I've got a call in, to the family. Difficult today, obviously. With her being dead, and so on. There are protocols involved and procedures to follow. We'll probably end up talking to the family lawyer. But that's fine. These things can be complicated. We'll need him anyway."

"Anything useful from the state police?"

"They're looking for a tall guy with big feet. Not necessarily active-duty military. Their minds are open. They acknowledge they have a lot of veterans. Plus a lot of kids who have seen every execution style in history on cable TV. And who have guns. And vehicles."

"Motive?"

"They say robbery. Casting a net and seeing what showed up. Like fishing on a lazy afternoon."

"On a road to nowhere?"

"They say people take that road sometimes. She took it that day, obviously."

"Low probability."

"But a quiet and undisturbed location."

"They didn't steal anything."

"They panicked and ran."

"Does the state police really believe any of that?"

"No. It's a polite hypothetical. They're bending over backward to be fair, because JAG is right there at their elbows. But I hear deep down they're sure it's a soldier. They're assuming romantic, because they haven't been told exactly how pointy her head was."

"Could it be romantic?"

"There's no evidence of boyfriends past or present. Or girlfriends."

"The woman with no enemies. She wins, no one loses. Extra spending. It's all good. Except it isn't. One of those facts is wrong. Which one is it?"

"You said it was random, Reacher. It was a road to nowhere. You just told me that."

"What was the decoy vehicle? Do they know?"

"The tire tracks were generic Firestones. On a million domestic products. Up to mid-size cars, and mid-range pick-up trucks. And before you ask, yes, the army uses them extensively. I checked, and there's a set on the car I drove down in."

"You drove from Bragg?"

"It's not that far. Normal people like driving more than you do."

Reacher said, "They're going to ask us for a list of shoe sizes at Fort Smith. That's what's coming next."

"Smith is all special forces. Those guys run smaller than normal. I bet they're all size nine."

"That's not the point. We can't give them something like that. Not without lawyers. They'll be talking for months. This thing is going to turn into a nightmare."

Thirty minutes later the fine print from the autopsy came in on the fax machine, and then the telex chuntered into life with a new report from Fort Smith. The pathologist in Atlanta had weighed and measured and poked and prodded and X-rayed. Crawford had been slender but well toned. All her organs were in perfect working order. She had long-healed childhood breaks to her right collarbone and her right forearm. She had recent cosmetic dentistry. Toxicology was clear, and there was no evidence of recent sex, and she had never been pregnant. Heart and lungs like a teenager. Nothing wrong with her at all, except for the bullets.

The telex from Smith showed some initiative. The MPs out there had done some good work, on a timeline for Crawford's first week on post. Seven completed days. A lot of talking. A lot of meetings. Different agendas, different constituencies. Not just officers. She had talked to NCOs and enlisted men. She had eaten in the mess two nights, and gone out five. She had taken recommendations from the mess stewards. Which was smart. They had long-term postings, and could be relied upon to know the local joints. Which were mostly an hour away, at least, on the roads through the woods. Reacher checked back with the maps, and traced them all. Barbecue, bars, a family restaurant, and even a movie theater. No place had an obvious linear way to get there. Every destination could be arrived at by a number of different looping routes. The roads had been made for forestry purposes, not ease of transportation. There had been speculation that the low-slung Porsche wouldn't handle them well. But Crawford had reported no problems. She had gone out and come back safe, five straight times. A young staff officer, for once outside the D.C. bubble, making the most of things. Reacher had seen it before.

Neagley came in and said, "The protocol office can't find the parents. They think the father might be deceased. But they're not sure. And they don't have a number for the mother. Or an address. They're still looking."

Then the soft sergeant trailed in behind her, with a torn-off telex in his hand.

The Georgia State Police had made an arrest.

Not a soldier.

Not a military veteran.

Reacher called Fort Smith direct for the skinny. The suspect was a black man who lived alone in a cabin on the muddy shore of a lake forty miles north and west of the post. He was six feet seven inches tall, and wore size fifteen shoes. He drove a Ford Ranger pick-up truck with Firestone tires, and he owned a nine-millimeter handgun.

He denied everything.

Reacher looked up at the soft sergeant standing in front of him and said, "You're in charge now, soldier. Sergeant Neagley and I are going to Smith."

Neagley drove, in her pool car from Bragg. It was a green Chevrolet, with Firestone tires. The trip was about a hundred and ten miles, more or less due east from Benning. Most of the scenery was woods. New spring-green leaves flashed by in the sun. Reacher said, "So we'll call this the casting-the-net theory. Like fishing on a lazy afternoon. Once in a while the guy comes down from the lake and sets up on a back road and catches something. Like Robin Hood. Or an ogre from under a bridge. When the moon is full. Or whenever he needs to eat. Or something. Like a fairy tale."

"Or maybe he comes down every day. But catches something only once in a while. Either way is possible. These are the Georgia woods. Think about carjacking in LA. Or getting mugged in New York City. Routine. Maybe this is the local version. Adapted to the environment."

"Then why did the carjacker not jack her car? Why did he execute her very clinically instead?"

"I don't know."

"Why did she stop in the first place?"

"He was blocking the road."

"She didn't need to come close and talk to the guy. Being in War Plans doesn't make her a total idiot. She went to West Point. She's a woman driving alone. She should have stood back a hundred yards and made a threat assessment."

"Maybe she did."

"Yes or no?"

"Yes. She did. She was a woman driving alone."

"In which case we conclude the guy was no threat. She drove right up to him, with her window open. Would she do that, for a weird six-seven stranger she had never seen before? With a broken-down pick-up truck? I'm sure she saw all the movies. With the chain saws and the banjo music."

"OK, she felt safe with the guy. Maybe she knew him. Or thought she knew him. Or knew his type."

"Exactly," Reacher said. "Which would make him active-duty military. Probably in uniform. Possibly even with a military vehicle. Not too far below in rank. Or maybe equal or even higher. For her to feel truly comfortable. This was a whole complicated performance. I want to get the right guy. Otherwise what's the point? And I've always found a big part of getting the right guy is not getting the wrong guy."

"They're going to say this guy has the right tires."

"So do a million other people."

"He has the right bullets."

"So do a million other people."

"He has the right feet."

Neagley had read a lot of research into first impressions, those merciless subliminal split seconds where one human judges another, on a million different things, all at once like a computer, all leading to an instant and inevitable yes-no answer: Should I stay or should I go? Sadly the state police's suspect scored very low on that test. Neagley knew her own sense of threat assessment was likely to be more robust than Crawford's, by an order of magnitude, but even so she would have kept her distance and approached warily, and only after locking her doors and getting her gun out.

They saw the guy in a holding cell at the county police station, which was ten minutes from Smith. He had some kind of growth disorder. Pituitary, maybe. A hormone imbalance. He should have been average size, but the long bones in his arms and legs had been racked out way longer than nature could have intended, and his hands and feet were equally huge, and his face was very long, with a chisel of a chin below it, and a narrow-domed forehead above.

Reacher asked, "Has he lawyered up?"

The county sheriff said, "He waived. He believes innocent men don't need lawyers."

"That's groundwork for an insanity plea."

"No, I think he means it."

"Then it might be true. It sometimes is."

"He's got the feet and the gun and the tires. That's a rare combination."

"A guy with hands that big prefers a shotgun."

"He told us he owns a nine."

"He might. But does he use it?"

"Think I should ask him? What else is he going to say?"

"Did you match the footwear?"

"It was raining again almost immediately. Photographs were all we got. No casts. Not that we could have gotten casts anyway. Wrong kind of mud. More like liquid peat. Too spongy. I apologize on behalf of the state of Georgia for the poor quality of our mud. Not what you expect, I know. But spongy or not, we measured the prints with a ruler. They were size fifteen. Just like the boots he was wearing when they brought him in."

"So you can't match the tires, either. Not exactly. For nicks or wear."

"The photograph is clear as to brand."

"Has he said where he was at the time?"

"Home alone. No witnesses."

"So it's a closed case?"

"The state police is expressing considerable satisfaction in the outcome. But no case is closed until the grand jury says so."

"Are they still looking?"

"Not as hard. What's your problem, major?"

"This guy lives alone in a cabin. You know why that is? People are scared to look at him. He's repellent. That's all he's ever heard, ever since he was a little kid. These growth things start early. So when it came time to earn some coin, why would he choose the role of smooth-talking con man, lulling passing drivers into a false sense of security? Why would he expect to succeed at that, given the way he's been looked at all his life? I think he's ugly, but I think he's innocent. In fact I think he's innocent because he's ugly."

"Lots of people look a little funny. Doesn't stop them working."

"Does this happen often? Is it a big thing here? Sticking people up by faking breakdowns?"

"I never heard of it before."

"So this guy invented it, too?"

"He's got the feet and the gun and the tires," the county guy said. "That's a rare combination."

They gave Reacher Caroline Crawford's room, in the Fort Smith visiting officers' quarters. The MPs had taken all her possessions out, as part of the investigation, and the stewards had cleaned the place up. Some of the surfaces were still damp. Neagley was in NCO accommodation. They met first thing the next morning in her mess for coffee and breakfast, and then they headed to the MP office to look at maps. The local commander was a captain named Ellsbury. He was a squared-away individual running a tight ship, and rightly proud of it. He produced every kind of map there was, including the government surveys they had seen before, plus large-scale topographical sheets bound into an atlas, and even a Triple-A giveaway of the southern part of the state.

Reacher started at the far end of a random potential journey, at what the government survey labeled a bar, and what the much older topographical sheets called a Negro Night Club. It was about thirty miles out. An hour by car, probably, given the prevailing conditions.

There was no really direct way to get there. An intend-ing patron departing Fort Smith would have to leave the county road at the first fork, and then thread through the woods on any one of ten potential routes, all looping and curving, none obviously better than another. The road Crawford had used had nothing to recommend it. Not in terms of efficiency. It might even have added unnecessary distance. A mile or two.

Reacher said, "Why would the guy with the big feet set up there? He could go days without seeing traffic. And nine times out of ten what traffic he saw would be soldiers. From here. What kind of a business plan is that? He decides to make a living by mugging Delta Force and Army Rangers? Good luck with that career choice."

"Why would anyone set up there?" Ellsbury said. "But we know someone did."

"You think the guy they got did it? Two to the chest and one to the head? That's a learned technique. Cen-ter mass, skip left, center mass again, skip up, one to the head just in case they get over the chest wounds. It's relatively precise. It's been practiced."

"They practice it here. But no one is unaccounted for ahead of when she left. It wasn't one of ours lying in wait."

"And I doubt it was a guy with a skeletal disorder that probably hurts his fine motor control, either."

"He's got the tires and the gun and the feet. He's a weird black guy who lives alone in a hut. This is 1989, but it's Georgia. Sometimes it's still 1959. This guy will do. He won't be the first and he won't be the last."

"I want to see that road for myself," Reacher said.

Neagley drove, with Reacher in the front and Ellsbury in the back. Off the county road at the first fork, into the capillary network, and then finally onto a not-quite-two-lane blacktop ribbon through the trees, mostly straight and sunlit, bordered by fine black mud washed smooth again by the rain. Ellsbury peered ahead between the seats, and pointed Neagley to a spot about three hundred yards after a slight bend. He said, "That's the scene."

There was plenty of scope for a threat assessment. Neagley pretended to see the broken-down vehicle, and lifted off and coasted, and she could have stopped two hundred yards out, or a hundred, or fifty, or wherever she wanted. She came to rest right where Ellsbury said it happened. There was nothing to see. The mud was dull and flat and uniform, lightly pocked by rain spatter. But the marks in the photographs had told the story. A vehicle had been parked right there, across the not-quite-two traffic lanes, and a guy had gotten out and waited near the front, probably pretending to look under the hood.

They all got out, making fresh marks in the mud, deep and oozing where it was thick, and spongy and blotted where it wasn't. The air smelled of rain and sun and earth and pine. Reacher looked back, and looked ahead.

He said, "OK, I've seen enough."

Then he looked ahead again.

A car was coming. Black-and-white. A cop car. State police. A spotlight on the pillar, and a bubble on the roof, like a little red hat. One guy behind the wheel. Otherwise empty.

The car came to a stop symmetrical with Neagley's, nose to nose in the other traffic lane. The trooper climbed out. A young guy, with fair hair and a red face. Built like a side of beef. He had small deep-set eyes. They made him look mean.

He said, "The army is supposed to inform us before interfering with the crime scene."

Reacher said, "Are you working this case?"

"Just taking a look, out of curiosity."

"Then get lost."

"Get what?"

"Lost."

The guy stepped closer and looked at Reacher's chest. *U.S. Army. Reacher.* He said, "You're the boy who don't like our work."

Reacher said, "I'm the boy?"

"You think we got the wrong guy."

"You think you got the right guy?"

"Sure I do. It's scientific. Plenty of people have Firestone tires, and plenty have nine-millimeter ammunition, but not many have size fifteen feet, so when you put it all together it's like three cherries on a slot machine."

"Will the guy get a lawyer?"

"Of course. The public defender."

"Does the public defender have a pulse?"

"Of course."

"Doesn't that worry you? You think the three-cherries argument will stand up to the slightest scrutiny? Were you out sick the day they taught thinking?"

"Now you're being unpleasant."

"Not yet," Reacher said. "You'll notice the difference."

"This is a public road. I could arrest you."

"Theoretically possible. Like I could get a date with Miss America."

"You planning to resist?"

"Maybe I'll arrest you instead."

"For what?"

"I'm sure we could figure something out. A bit of this, and a bit of that. We could get three cherries of our own."

The guy said, "Try it."

He stepped up and squared his shoulders. *Local civilian hotheads with guns in their pockets and points to prove.*

Reacher said, "Sergeant, arrest this man."

Neagley stepped up.

Face to face with the trooper.

She said, "Sir, I'm going to lean forward and take your weapon from its holster."

The guy said, "Little lady, I don't think you are."

Neagley said, "If you impede me in any way, you will be handcuffed."

The guy shoved her in the chest.

Which was a mistake on several different levels. Military discipline could not allow assaults by detainees. And Neagley hated physical contact. No one knew why. But it was a recognized issue. She couldn't bear to be touched. She wouldn't even shake hands. Not even with a friend. Thus a glove laid on her in anger was beyond the pale, and liable to produce a reaction.

For the trooper the reaction resulted in a broken nose and a kick in the balls. She came off the back foot and drove the heel of her hand into the guy's face, from below, an arching blow like a flyweight boxer thumping the heavy bag, and there was a puff of blood in the air, and the guy skittered back on his heels, and she punted him another six feet with the kick, and he went down on his ass with his back against the front wheel of his car, huffing and puffing and squealing.

Reacher said, "Feel free to make an official complaint. I'll swear out a witness statement. About how you got your clock cleaned by a girl. You want that in the record?"

The guy didn't, apparently. He just flapped his hands, mute.

Get lost.

In the car on the way back to base Neagley said, "I agree the guy was an idiot."

Reacher said, "But?"

"Why me? Why didn't you do it?"

"Like they say in England, why buy a dog and bark yourself?"

Back on the base Ellsbury's sergeant had a phone message for Neagley. She returned the call and came out and said, "They found an address for Crawford's parents. Plural. Now they think the father is still alive. But the phone number doesn't get them past the servants' quarters. They can't even establish whether the Crawfords are home or not right now. I guess the butler is too discreet. They want someone to do a drive-by, to get the lay of the land."

Reacher said, "Where is it?"

"Myrtle Beach."

"That's in South Carolina."

"Which is an adjacent state. I think we should volunteer."

"Why?"

"Why not? It's a done deal here."

Neagley drove. An adjacent state, but still hundreds of miles. They took I-16 to I-95, and headed north, and then jumped off cross-country for the final short distance, in the middle of the afternoon. They had an address but no street map, so they asked at gas stations until they got pointed in the right direction, which turned out to be a ritzy enclave between an inland waterway and the ocean. A manicured road ran through it, with little dead-end streets coming off it left and right like ribs. The Crawfords' street was on the ocean side. Their house was a big mansion facing the sea, on a deep lot with a private beach.

It looked closed up.

The windows were shuttered from the inside. Painted surfaces, reflecting blindly through the glass. Neagley said, "They're obviously away. In which case we should go talk to the butler. We shouldn't take no for an answer. Evasion is easy on the phone. Face to face is harder."

"Works for me," Reacher said.

They drove in, on a long cobblestone driveway, their

Firestone tires pattering, and they paused briefly at the front door, but it was blank and bolted, so they followed the cobblestones around to the back, where a back door was also blank and bolted. The servants' entrance, currently not in use.

"So where is the servant?" Reacher said. "How discreet can one man be?"

There was a garage block. Most of the bays had doors, but one was a pass-through to a utility yard in back. There was a car parked in the pass-through. An old compact, all sun-faded and dinged up with age. A plausible POV for a butler.

There was an apartment above the garage bays. All dormer windows and gingerbread trim, slimy from the salt air. There was an external staircase leading to the door.

Reacher said, "This place is so upscale even the downstairs people are upstairs."

He went first, with Neagley at his shoulder, and he knocked on the door. The door was opened immediately. As if they were expected. Which they were, Reacher supposed. Their car had made a certain amount of noise.

A woman. Maybe sixty years old, and careworn. A housedress. Knuckles like walnuts. A hard worker. She said, "Yes?"

Reacher said, "Ma'am, we're from the U.S. Army, and we need to know Mr. and Mrs. Crawford's current location."

"Does it concern their daughter?"

"At this point, until I know their whereabouts, I'm not at liberty to say what it concerns."

The woman said, "You better come in and speak to my husband."

Who was not the butler. Not if the shows Reacher had seen on TV were true. This was a hangdog fellow, thin and bent over from labor, with big rough hands. A gardener, maybe.

Reacher said, "What's your phone number?"

They told him, and Neagley nodded. Reacher said, "Are you the only people here at the moment?"

They said yes, and Reacher said, "So I believe the army has already called you. For some reason yours is the only number we have."

The hangdog guy said, "The family is away."

"Where?"

The woman said, "We should know what this is about."

"You can't filter their news. You don't have that right."

"So it is about their daughter. It's bad news, isn't it?"

The room was small and cramped. The ceiling was low, because of the eaves. The furniture was plain, and not generous in quantity. Storage was inadequate, clearly. Essential paperwork was stacked on the dining table. Bills, and mail. The floor was bare board. There was a television set. There was a shelf with three books, and a toy frog painted silver. Or an armadillo. Something humped. Maybe two inches long. Something crouching.

"Excuse me," Reacher said.

He stepped closer.

Not a frog. Not an armadillo. A toy car. A sports coupe. Painted silver. A Porsche.

Reacher stepped over to the dining table. Picked up a piece of opened mail.

A bank statement. A savings account. Almost a hundred dollars in it.

It was addressed to H & R Crawford, at the address the army had, and the phone number was the same.

Not filtering the news.

Reacher said, "Sir, ma'am, I very much regret it's my duty on behalf of the commander in chief to inform you your daughter was the victim of an off-post homicide two evenings ago. The circumstances are still being investigated, but we do know her death must have been instantaneous and she can have felt no pain."

Like most MPs Reacher and Neagley had delivered death messages before, and they knew the drill. Not touchy-feely like neighbors. The army way was appropriately grim, but with the stalwart radiation of wholesome sentiments such as courage and service and sacrifice. Eventually the parents started asking them questions, and they answered what they could. Career good, luck bad. Then Neagley said, "Tell us about her," which Reacher assumed was a hundred percent professional interest, but which also played well in the psychological context.

The woman told the story. The mother. It came right out of her. She was the cook. The hangdog guy was a groundskeeper. The father. Caroline was their daughter. An only child. She had grown up right there, above the garages. She hadn't enjoyed it. She wanted what was in the big house. She was ten times smarter than them. Wasn't fair.

Reacher said, "She gave the impression she had family money."

The hangdog guy said, "No, that was all hers. She gets paid a fortune. It's a government job. Those people look after each other. Pensions, too, I expect. All kinds of benefits."

"No legacies? No inheritances?"

"We gave her thirty-five dollars when she went to West Point. It was all we had saved. That's all she ever got. Anything else, she earned."

Reacher said, "May I use your phone?"

They said yes, and he dialed the Pentagon. A number on a desk outside an office with a window. Answered by a sergeant.

Reacher said, "Is he there? It's his brother."

Joe's voice came on the line.

Reacher said, "Name a good steakhouse in Alexandria open late."

Joe did.

Reacher said, "I'll meet you there at nine o'clock tonight."

"Why?"

"To keep you in the loop."

"With Crawford? Is there something weird?"

"Many things. I need to run an idea by you."

Neagley drove. Back on I-95. Hundreds of miles. As far as from Fort Smith to Myrtle Beach, all over again. They stayed on the left of the Potomac and got to Alexandria ninety minutes after dark. They were five minutes late to the restaurant. There was a guy near the door, doing nothing. Plain clothes. Almost convincing.

Neagley went in and got a table for one. Then Reacher went in and sat with Joe. White linen, dim candlelight, ruby wines, a hushed atmosphere. There was another guy in plain clothes all alone at a table, on the other side of the room from Neagley. Symmetrical.

Joe said, "I see you brought your attack dog with you."

Reacher said, "I see you brought two of yours."

"Crawford is serious shit. Immediate action might be required."

"That's why Neagley is here."

They ordered. Onion soup and a rib-eye for Reacher, foie gras and a filet mignon for Joe. Fries for both, red wine for Joe, coffee for Reacher. Plus tap water. No small talk.

Reacher said, "I was worried about the road from the beginning. It doesn't go anywhere. Stupid place to set a trap. Can't have been random. But deliberate makes no sense, either. She had a choice of three or four destinations, and about forty different ways of getting there. Then I figured it out. A truly smart guy would ignore the destinations. He wouldn't try to predict how she would get from A to B or C or D. He would figure all roads were equal. At least in terms of transportation. But not equal in other ways. Not emotionally, for instance. Sometimes I forget that normal people like driving more than I do. So a smart guy would ask, which road would she use just for the hell of it? A young woman with a brand-new sports car? No contest. That was a great road. Straight-aways, nice bends, trees, sunshine, the smell of fresh air. Great noise, too, probably. A windows-down kind of a road. A smart guy would be able to predict it."

Joe said, "A smart guy with military training."

"Because of the triple shot? I agree. It's a high-stress moment. That was automatic. Muscle memory. Years at the gun range. The guy was one of ours."

"But which one of ours, and why?"

"This is where it gets highly speculative. She wasn't rich. I know that now. I should have known long ago. It was right there in the fine print from the autopsy. She had recent cosmetic dentistry. A rich girl would have had it years before. As a teenager. So, no family money. I met her parents. They had thirty-five dollars in her college fund. There are no rich uncles. They think she earned it all. Government job. They think she earned a fortune. But we know she didn't. Ten light colonels couldn't afford a brand-new Porsche. But she got one. With what?"

"You tell me."

"She was in War Plans. Suppose she was selling information to a foreign government? Iraq, maybe. They'd pay a fortune. She's writing the plan. They'd be getting it straight from the horse's mouth."

"Possible," Joe said. "Theoretically. As a worst-case scenario."

"Are we going to have a problem with Iraq?"

"Likely," Joe said. "He wants Kuwait. Next year, or the year after. We'll have to throw him out. Probably stage in Saudi, put the Navy in the Gulf. The whole nine yards."

"So he wants that plan. And he pays for it, word for word. From a woman who maybe didn't want to be poor anymore. Scuttlebutt says she came out of her shell in War Plans. Finally started spending some of her money. Except maybe it wasn't finally. Maybe that was the first money she ever had."

Joe said nothing.

Reacher said, "Counterintelligence must have been keeping an eye on such things. But for some reason they missed her, and so it went on for a long time. It became the legend. Family money. The richest woman. It was hiding in plain sight. Then something changed. Suddenly they figured her out."

Joe said, "How?"

Reacher said, "Could be a number of reasons. Could be dumb luck."

"Or?"

"Could be counterintelligence got a new commander. Maybe the new commander brought with him the missing piece of the jigsaw puzzle. Suddenly two plus two made four. Which would be dumb luck of a different kind. But it happens."

Joe said nothing.

Reacher said, "But let's freeze the action right there. Let's look at it from the new commander's point of view. Right then he's the only one with all the pieces. He's the only one who can see the whole picture. In the world. It's a lonely position. No one else knows. But it's all about who else knows. Because no one else must know. It's only Iraq, but who will believe that?

You'll have mass panic. Every plan will be called compromised. The Soviet strategy will fall apart. Nothing will be believed ever again. So it's vital no one else knows. Literally. Not ever. No one. Two can't keep a secret. But she has to be stopped. And treason gets the death penalty. The new commander concludes he has to do it himself. It's the only way to contain it. Almost a historic moment. The world will be saved. That big of a deal. But the world will never know. So it's ironic, and strategically astute, and noble and ethical. Like a patriotic duty."

Joe said nothing.

Reacher said, "I imagine a new commander of such a unit would be smart enough to figure out the thing with the sports car and the road."

Joe said, "The guy had size fifteen feet."

"He had a maximum size fifteen. You can't make your footprints smaller, but you can make them bigger. I figure I could put on a tennis shoe, something tight, and get my whole foot inside a size fifteen boot. Tight and solid. Not like clown shoes. I could stomp around making footprints like an astronaut on the moon. You know where I got that idea?"

Joe said, "No."

"The second time we lived on Okinawa. You were six. Maybe seven. You got into a thing where you would get up early in the morning and clump around in Dad's boots. I didn't know why. Maybe it's a first-born thing. Maybe you were trying to fill his shoes, literally. But I would hear you. And once you got him in trouble with Mom for making marks on the rug. That's where I got the idea."

"Lots of people must have done that."

"How many grew up to be recently promoted commanders of counterespionage units?"

Joe said nothing.

Reacher said, "Thinking back, you did pretty well on the phone. You must have been very shocked. But you didn't forget to ask the obvious questions, like who died. And you asked how, which was good, and I said shot on a lonely road, but then you should have asked shot on a lonely road how, because a sniper in the trees was just as plausible as a stationary ambush. On the back roads. But you didn't ask shot on a lonely road how. You could have scripted that part a little better. And you got nervous. You wouldn't let it go. You asked me what I was going to do about her. And you totally blew it with the six hundred and ninety-three miles. You're a pedantic guy, Joe. You wouldn't get it wrong. And I'm sure you didn't. You figured Benning was on a level with a distance you knew for sure. The same radius. And the distance you knew for sure was your office to Fort Smith. Because you'd just driven it. Twice. There and back."

Joe said, "Interesting hypothetical. What would a hypothetical policeman do about it?"

"He would feel hypothetically better without a guy in the lobby and a guy in the room."

"Just Neagley?"

"She's driving the car. She's entitled to eat."

"Crawford is serious shit."

Reacher said, "Relax. The hypothetical policeman doesn't see a problem. He's a real-world person. I'm sure his analysis would have been the same as the hypothetical unit commander's. But there's a problem. I suppose the hypothetical size fifteens were supposed to be a dealbreaker, a cold case forever, but they didn't work. They're railroading a guy. Size fifteen feet, the same ammo as the hypothetical unit commander doing it himself, and the same tires, all a pure coincidence, but they're calling it three cherries on a slot machine. The guy is going down."

"What should a hypothetical unit commander do about that?"

"I'm sure there's a code word. Probably through the office of the president. Things get shut down. Guys get let go."

Joe said nothing.

"Then cases stay cold forever."

Joe said, "OK."

Then he said, "You're a hell of a policeman, to figure all that out."

Reacher said, "No, I'm a hell of a policeman to not quite figure it out, but get you to confirm it for me anyway. And I'm proud of you. It had to be contained. No choice. You did well. Good thinking, and almost perfect performance."

"Almost?"

"The three shots were bad. An obvious execution. You should have made it messy. The throat, maybe. Everyone assumes a round in the throat is a miss from someplace else. Automatic amateur hour. You can add a head shot if it makes you feel better, but make it weird, like in the eye or the ear."

"That sounds like the voice of experience."

"What do you think I've been doing in Central America?"

They talked about other things for the rest of the meal. Gossip, people they knew, things they had read, politics, and family. Joe was worried about their mother. She wasn't herself.

Reacher and Neagley got back to Smith late the next day. Ellsbury's sergeant told them the state police's suspect had been released without charge, that day at noon, and driven home. The case itself had been withdrawn from all concerned, and assigned as a bedding-in trial for a brand-new investigative unit deep inside the Pentagon. No one had ever heard of it. Conclusions would be announced within a year or two, if available.

Then another telex came in. Apparently Major David Noble had recovered from his automobile accident, and was anxious to assume his intended command. Reacher was posted back to Central America. And Neagley back to Bragg, because Noble was bringing his own sergeant. The reorganization lasted less than a year. No one ever heard of it again.

Possibly the finest professional achievement of Joe Reacher's military career was to get the war plan for Iraq changed without ever revealing why. And a year and a half later, when boots hit the desert sand in Kuwait, it all worked out fine, all over in a hundred hours, Plan B or not.

James Penney's
New Identity

The process that turned James Penney into a completely different person began ten years ago, at one in the afternoon on a Monday in the middle of June, in Laney, California. A hot time of day, at a hot time of year, in a hot part of the country. The town sits comfortably on the east shoulder of the road that winds from Mojave to LA, fifty miles south of the one and fifty miles north of the other. Due west, the southern rump of the Coast Ranges is visible. Due east, the Mojave Desert disappears into the haze. Very little happens in Laney. After that Monday in the middle of June ten years ago, even less ever did.

There was one industry in Laney. One factory. A big spread of a place. A long low assembly shed, weathered metal siding, built in the sixties. Office accommodations at the north end, in the shade, two stories of them. The first floor was low grade. Clerical functions took place there. Billing and accounting and telephone calling. The second story was high grade. Managers and designers occupied the space. The corner office at the right-hand end used to be the personnel manager's place. Now it was the human resources manager's place. Same guy, new title on his door.

Outside that door in the long second-floor corridor was a line of chairs. The human resources manager's secretary had rustled them up and placed them there that Monday morning. The line of chairs was occupied by a line of men and women. They were silent. Every five minutes the person at the head of the line would be called into the office. The rest of them would shuffle up one place. They didn't speak. They didn't need to. They knew what was happening.

Just before one o'clock, James Penney shuffled up one space to the head of the line. He waited a long five minutes and stood up when he was called. Stepped into the office. Closed the door behind him. Sat down again in front of the desk. The human resources manager was a guy called Odell. Odell hadn't been long out of diapers when James Penney started work at the Laney plant.

"Mr. Penney," Odell said.

Penney said nothing, but he nodded in a guarded way.

"We need to share some information with you," Odell said.

Then he stopped like he needed a response out of Penney before he could continue. Penney shrugged at him. He knew what was coming. He heard things, same as anybody else.

"Just give me the short version, OK?" he said.

Odell nodded. "We're laying you off."

"For the summer?" Penney asked him.

Odell shook his head.

"For good," he said.

Penney took a second to get over the sound of the words. He'd known they were coming, but they hit him like they were the last words he ever expected Odell to say.

"Why?" he asked.

Odell shrugged. He didn't look like he was enjoying this. But on the other hand, he didn't look like it was upsetting him much, either.

"Downsizing," he said. "No option. Only way we can go."

"Why?" Penney said again.

Odell leaned back in his chair and folded his hands behind his head. Started the speech he'd already made many times that day.

"We need to cut costs," he said. "This is an expensive operation. Small margin. Shrinking market. You know that."

Penney stared into space and listened to the silence breaking through from the factory floor. "So you're closing the plant?"

Odell shook his head again. "We're downsizing, is all. The plant will stay open. There'll be some maintenance business. Some repairs, overhauls. But not like it used to be."

"The plant will stay open?" Penney said. "So how come you're letting me go?"

Odell shifted in his chair. Pulled his hands from behind his head and folded his arms across his chest, defensively. He had reached the tricky part of the interview.

"It's a question of the skills mix," he said. "We had to pick a team with the correct blend of skills. We put a lot of work into the decision. And I'm afraid you didn't make the cut."

"What's wrong with my skills?" Penney asked. "I got skills. I've worked here seventeen years. What's wrong with my damn skills?"

"Nothing at all," Odell said. "But other people are better. We have to look at the broad picture. It's going to be a skeleton crew, so we need the best skills, the fastest learners, good attendance records, you know how it is."

"Attendance records?" Penney said. "What's wrong with my attendance records? I've worked here seventeen years. You saying I'm not a reliable worker?"

Odell touched the brown file folder in front of him.

"You've had a lot of time out sick," he said. "Absentee rate just above eight percent."

Penney looked at him incredulously.

"Sick?" he said. "I wasn't sick. I was post-traumatic. From Vietnam."

Odell shook his head again. He was too young.

"Whatever," he said. "It's still a big absentee rate."

James Penney just sat there, stunned. He felt like he'd been hit by a train.

"So who stays on?" he asked.

"We looked for the correct blend," Odell said again. "Generally, the younger end of the workforce. We put a lot of management time into the process. We're confident we made the right decisions. You're not being singled out. We're losing eighty percent of our people."

Penney stared across at him. "You staying?"

Odell nodded and tried to hide a smile, but couldn't. "There's still a business to run," he said. "We still need management."

There was silence in the big corner office. Outside, the hot breeze stirred off the desert and blew a listless eddy over the metal building. Odell opened the brown folder and pulled out a blue envelope. Handed it across the desk.

"You're paid up to the end of July," he said. "Money went in the bank this morning. Good luck, Mr. Penney."

The five-minute interview was over. Odell's secretary appeared and opened the door to the corridor. Penney walked out. The secretary called the next man in. Penney walked past the long quiet row of people and made it to the parking lot. Slid into his car. It was a red Firebird, a year and a half old, and it wasn't paid for yet. He started it up and drove the mile to his house. Eased to a stop in his driveway and sat there, thinking, in a daze, with the motor running. Then he heard the faint bell of his phone in his house. He made it inside before it stopped. It was a friend from the plant.

"They can you, too?" the friend asked him.

Penney mumbled his answer so he didn't have to say the exact words, but the tone of his voice told his friend what he needed to know.

"There's a problem," the guy said. "Company informed the bank. I just got a call asking what I was going to do about the payments I got. The bank holding paper on you?"

Penney went cold. Gripped the phone.

"Paper?" he said. "You bet they're holding paper on me. Just about every damn thing I got. House, car, furniture. They got paper on everything. What they say to you?"

"What the hell do you think?" the guy said. "They're a bank, right? I stop making the payments, I'm out on the street. The repo man is coming for the car right now."

Penney went quiet. He was thinking. He was thinking about his car. He didn't care about the house. Or the furniture. His wife had chosen all that stuff. She'd saddled him up with big payments on all that stuff, just before she walked out. She'd called it the chance for a new start. It hadn't worked. She'd gone and he was still paying for her damn house and furniture. But the car was his. The red Firebird. That automobile was the only thing he'd ever bought that he'd really wanted. He didn't feel like losing it. But he sure as hell couldn't keep on paying for it.

"James?" the guy on the phone said. "You still there?"

Penney was imagining the repo man coming for his car.

"James?" his friend said again. "You there?"

Penney closed his eyes tight.

"Not for long," he said. "I'm out of here."

"Where to?" the guy said. "Where the hell to?"

Penney felt a desperate fury building inside him. He smashed the phone back into the cradle and moved away, and then turned back and tore the wire out of the wall. He stood in the middle of the room and decided he wouldn't take anything with him. And he wouldn't leave anything behind, either. He ran to the garage and grabbed his spare can of gasoline. Ran back to the house. Emptied the can over his ex-wife's sofa. He couldn't find a match, so he lit the gas stove in the kitchen and unwound a roll of paper towels. Put one end on the stove top and ran the rest through to the living room. When his makeshift fuse was well alight, he skipped out to his car and started it up. Turned north toward Mojave and settled in for the drive.

His neighbor noticed the fire when the flames started coming through the roof. She called the Laney fire department. The firemen didn't respond. It was a volunteer department, and all the volunteers were in line inside the factory, upstairs in the narrow corridor.

Then the warm air moving off the Mojave Desert freshened up into a hot breeze, and by the time James Penney was thirty miles away the flames from his house had set fire to the dried scrub that had been his lawn. By the time he was in the town of Mojave itself, cashing his last paycheck at the bank, the flames had spread across his lawn and his neighbor's and were licking at the base of her back porch.

Like any California boomtown, Laney had grown in a hurry. The factory had been thrown up around the start of Nixon's first term. A hundred acres of orange groves had been bulldozed and five hundred frame houses had quadrupled the population in a year. There was nothing really wrong with the houses, but they'd seen rain less than a dozen times in the thirty-one years they'd been standing, and they were about as dry as houses can get. Their timbers had sat and baked in the sun and been scoured by the dry desert winds. There were no hydrants built into the streets. The houses were close together, and there were no windbreaks. But there had never been a serious fire in Laney. Not until that Monday in June.

James Penney's neighbor called the fire department for the second time after her back porch was well alight. The fire department was in disarray. The dispatcher advised her to get out of her house and just wait for their arrival. By the time the fire truck got there, her house was destroyed. And the next house in line was destroyed, too. The desert breeze had blown the fire on across the second narrow gap and sent the old couple living there scuttling into the street for safety. Then Laney called in the fire departments from Lancaster and Glendale and Bakersfield, and they arrived with proper equipment and saved the day. They hosed the scrub between the houses and the blaze went no farther. Just three houses destroyed, Penney's and his two downwind neighbors'. Within two hours the panic was over, and by the time Penney himself was fifty miles north of Mojave, Laney's sheriff was working with the fire investigators to piece together what had happened.

They started with Penney's place, which was the upwind house, and the first to burn, and therefore the coolest. It had just about burned down to the floor slab, but the layout was still clear. And the evidence was there to see. There was tremendous scorching on one side of where the living room had been. The Glendale investigator recognized it as something he'd seen many times before. It was what is left when a foam-filled sofa or armchair is doused with gasoline and set alight. He explained to the sheriff how the flames would have spread up and out, setting fire to the walls and ceiling, and how, once into the roof space, the flames would have consumed the rafters and dropped the whole burning structure downward into the rest of the building. As clear a case of arson as he had ever seen. The unfortunate wild cards had been the stiffening desert breeze and the close proximity of the other houses.

Then the sheriff had gone looking for James Penney, to tell him somebody had burned his house down, and his neighbors'. He drove his black-and-white to the factory and walked upstairs and past the long line of people and into Odell's corner office. Odell told him what had happened in the five-minute interview just after one o'clock. Then the sheriff had driven back to the Laney station house, steering with one hand and rubbing his chin with the other.

And by the time James Penney was driving along the towering eastern flank of Mount Whitney, a hundred and fifty miles from home, there was an all-points bulletin out on him, suspicion of deliberate arson, which in the dry desert heat of southern California was a big, big deal.

The California Highway Patrol is one of the world's great law enforcement agencies. Famous throughout America and the world, romantic, idealized. The image of the West Coast motorcycle cop astride his powerful machine is one of the nation's great icons. Smart tan shirt, white tee underneath, white helmet, mirrored aviator glasses, tight jodhpurs, gleaming black boots. Cruising the endless sunny highways, marshaling that great state's huge transient population toward a safe destination.

That's the image. That's why Joey Gunston had lined up to join. But Joey Gunston soon found out the reality is different. Any organization has a glamour side and a dull side. Gunston was stuck on the dull side. He wasn't cruising the sunny coastal highways on a big bike. He was on his own in a standard police spec Dodge, grinding back and forward through the Mojave Desert on U.S. 91. He had no jodhpurs, no boots, his white tee was a limp gray rag, and his mirrored shades were cheap Ray-Ban copies he'd paid for himself in LA, which he couldn't wear anyway because he was working the graveyard shift, nine at night until six in the morning.

So Joey Gunston was a disillusioned man. But he wasn't bitter. He wasn't that type of a guy. The way it worked with Joey, hand him a disappointment and he wouldn't fold up. He would work harder. He would work so damn hard that he would escape the dull side and get the transfer over to the glamour side. He figured it was like paying his dues. He figured he'd work U.S. 91 in a factory-beige Dodge with plastic CHP badging stuck on the doors as long as it took to prove himself. So far it had taken thirty-one months. No news about a transfer to U.S. 101 and a motorcycle. Not even a hint. But he wasn't going to let his standards drop.

So he carried on working hard. That involved looking out for the break he knew had to be coming. Problem was, the scope for a break on U.S. 91 was pretty limited. It's the direct route between LA and Vegas, which gives it some decent traffic, and there's some pretty scenery. Gunston's patch stretched a hundred and twenty miles from Barstow in the west over to the state line on the slope of Clark Mountain. His problem was the hours he worked. At night, the traffic slackened and the pretty scenery was invisible. For thirty-one months he'd done nothing much except stop speeders and about twice a week radio in for ambulances when some tanked guy ran off the road and smashed himself up.

But he carried on hoping. That Monday night at nine o'clock he'd read through the bulletins pinned up in the dispatcher's office. He'd copied the details into a leatherette notebook his sister had bought for him. One of those details concerned an APB on a Laney guy, James Penney, arson and criminal damage, believed to be on the loose in a red Firebird. Gunston copied the plate number in large writing so he'd be able to read it in the gloom of his car. Then he cruised sixty miles east and holed up on the shoulder near Soda Lake.

A lot of guys would have gone right to sleep. Gunston knew his colleagues were working day jobs, maybe security in LA or gumshoeing in the valleys, and sleeping the night away in their Dodges on the shoulder. But Gunston never did that. He played ball and stayed awake, ready for his break.

It arrived within an hour. Ten o'clock that Monday evening. The red Firebird streaked past him, heading east, maybe eighty-five miles an hour, maybe ninety. Gunston didn't need to check his leatherette notebook. The plate jumped right out of the dark at him. He fired up the Dodge and floored it. Hit the button for the lights and the siren. Jammed his foot down and steered with one hand. Used the other to thumb the mike.

"In pursuit of a red Firebird," he radioed. "Plate matches APB."

There was a crackle on the speaker and the dispatcher's voice came back.

"Position?" he asked.

"Soda Lake," Gunston said. "Heading east, fast."

"OK, Joey," the dispatcher said. "Stick with him. Nail him before the line. Don't be letting the Nevada guys get in on this, right?"

"You got it, chief," Gunston said. He eased the Dodge up to a hundred and wailed on into the night. He figured the Firebird might be a mile ahead. Conceivable that Penney might slew off and head down into the town of Baker, but if he didn't, then Penney was his. The break had maybe arrived.

He caught up with the red Firebird after three miles. The turn down to Baker was gone. Nothing on the road ahead except fifty-seven more miles of California, and then the state of Nevada. He eased the wailing Dodge up to twenty yards behind the Firebird's rear end and hit the blue strobes. Changed the siren to the deafening electronic pock-pock-pock he loved so much. Grinned at his windshield. But the Firebird didn't slow up. It eased ahead. Gunston's speedo needle was shivering around the hundred-and-ten marker. His knuckles tightened round the grimy vinyl wheel.

"Son of a bitch," he said.

He jammed his foot down harder and hung on. The red Firebird topped out at maybe a hundred and twelve. It was still there ahead of him, but the acceleration was gone. It was flat out. Gunston smiled. He knew the road ahead. Probably better than a guy from Laney did. The climb up the western slope of Clark Mountain was going to tilt things the good guys' way. The upgrades would slow the Firebird. But the Dodge had plenty of good Detroit V8 torque. New police radials. A trained driver. Fifty miles of opportunity ahead. Maybe U.S. 101 and a big bike were not so far away.

He chased the red Firebird for thirty miles. The grade was slowing both cars. They were averaging about ninety. The Dodge's siren was blaring the whole way, pock-pock-pock for twenty minutes, red and blue lights flashing continuously. Gunston's conclusion was this Penney guy had to be a psycho. Burning things up, then trying to outrun the CHP through the dark. Then he started to worry. They were getting reasonably close to the state line. No way was he going to call in and ask for cooperation from the Nevada boys. Penney was his. So he gripped the wheel and moved up to within feet of the speeding red car. Closer and closer. Trying to force the issue.

Ten miles short of the state line, a spur runs off U.S. 91 down to the small town of Nipton. The road leaves the highway at an oblique angle and falls away down the mountain into the valley. The red Firebird took that turn. With Gunston's police Dodge a foot off its rear fender, it slewed right and just disappeared straight out from in front of him. Gunston overshot and jammed to a stop, all four wheels locked and making smoke. He smashed the selector into reverse and howled backward up the shoulder. Just in time to see the Firebird cartwheeling off the road and straight down the mountainside. The spur had a bad camber. Gunston knew that. Penney hadn't. He'd taken that desperate slew and lost it. The Firebird's rear end had come unglued and swung out over the void. The red car had windmilled like a golf club and hurled itself out into space. Gunston watched it smash and bounce on the rocks. An outcrop tore the underside out and the spilling gasoline hit the hot muffler and the next thing Gunston saw was a belch of flame and a huge explosion rolling slowly a hundred feet down the mountainside.

The California Highway Patrol dispatcher told Joey Gunston to supervise the recovery of the crashed red Firebird himself. Nobody was very upset about the accident. Nobody cared much about Penney. The radio conversations back and forward between the dispatcher's office and Gunston's Dodge about an arsonist dying in his burning car on the slope of Clark Mountain carried a certain amount of suppressed ironic laughter. The only problem was the invoice that would come in next month from the tow-truck company. The protocols about who should pay such an invoice were never very clear. Usually the CHP ended up writing them down to miscellaneous operating costs.

Gunston knew a tow-truck operator out in the wastelands near Soda Lake who usually monitored the police bands, so he put out a call and got a quick reply. Then he parked up on the shoulder near the turn down to Nipton, sitting right on top of the skid marks he'd made overshooting it, and sat waiting for the guy. He was there in an hour, and by midnight Gunston and the trucker were clambering down the mountainside in the dark, pulling the truck's giant metal hook behind them against its ratchet.

The red Firebird was about two hundred yards down the slope, right at the end of the cable's reach. It wasn't red anymore. It was streaked a fantastic variety of scorched browns and purples. All the glass had melted and the plastic had burned away. The tires were gone. Penney himself was a shriveled carbonized shape fused to the zigzag metal springs which were all that was left of the seat. Gunston and the wrecker didn't spend too long looking at him. They just ducked near and snapped the giant hook around the offside front suspension member. Then they turned back for the long climb up the slope.

They were panting hard and sweating in the night air when they got back to the tow truck. It was parked sideways on the road, circled by Gunston's red danger flares. The steel cable snaked off the drum at the rear of the cab and disappeared down into the dark. The driver started up the big diesel to power the hydraulics and the drum started grinding around, reeling in the cable, hauling the wreck upward. Time to time, the remains of the Firebird would snag in the brush or against a rock and the truck's rear suspension would squat and the big diesel would roar until it dragged free.

It took the best part of an hour to haul the wreck the two hundred yards up to the roadway. It scraped over the concrete shoulder and the driver moved the truck to a better angle and sped the drum to haul the wreck up onto the flatbed. Gunston helped him tie it down with chains. Then he nodded to the driver and the tow truck took off and lumbered back west. Gunston stepped over to his Dodge and killed the flashing lights and fired up the radio.

"On its way," he said to the dispatcher. "Better send an ambulance over to meet it."

"Why?" the dispatcher asked. "He's dead, right?"

"Dead as can be," Gunston said. "But somebody needs to chisel him out of the seat, and I ain't going to do it."

The dispatcher laughed over the radio. "Is he real crispy?"

Gunston laughed back. "Crispiest guy you ever saw."

Middle of the night, and the sheriff was still in the station house in Laney. He figured a lot of overtime was called for. It had been a busy day. And tomorrow was going to be a busier day. There was a fair amount of fallout to deal with. The layoffs at the factory had produced unpredictable results. Evening time had seen a lot of drunkenness. A couple of pick-ups had been rolled. Minor injuries. A few windows had been broken at the plant. Mr. Odell's windows had been the target. A few rocks had fallen short and hit the mail room. One had smashed the windshield of a car in the lot.

And Penney had burned three houses down. That was the problem. But then it wasn't a problem any-more. The silence in the station house was broken by the sound of the telex machine starting up. The sheriff wandered through to the booth and tore off a foot and a half of paper. Read it and folded it and slipped it into the file he'd just started. Then he picked up the phone and called the California Highway Patrol.

"I'll take it from here," he told them. "This is Laney County business. Our coroner will see to the guy. I'll go out to Soda Lake with him right away."

The Laney County coroner was a young medic out of Stanford called Kolek. Polish name, but the guy was from a family that had been in California longer than most. Forty years, maybe. The sheriff rode east with him in his official station wagon. Kolek wasn't upset by the late call. He didn't object to working at night. He was young and he was new and he needed the money. But he was pretty quiet the whole way. Medical guys in general are not keen on dealing with burned bod-ies. The sheriff didn't know why. He'd seen a few. A burned body was like something you left on the barbe-cue too long. Better than the damp maggoty things you find in the woods. A whole lot better.

"We got to bring it back?" Kolek asked.

"The car?" the sheriff said. "Or the guy?"

"The corpse," Kolek said.

The sheriff grinned at him and nodded. "There's an ex-wife somewhere. She might want to bury the guy. Maybe there's a family plot."

Kolek shrugged and turned the heater up a click. Drove through the night all the way from Mojave to Soda Lake in silence. A hundred and thirty miles without saying a word.

The junkyard was a stadium-sized space hidden behind a high wooden fence in the angle made by the road down to Baker where it left the highway. There were gleaming tow trucks lined up outside the gate. Kolek slowed and passed them and nosed into the compound. Inside the gate, a wooden hut served as the office. The light was on inside. Kolek hit his horn once and waited. A woman came out. She saw who they were and ducked back inside to hit the lights. The compound lit up like day with blue lights on poles. The woman directed them to the burned Firebird. It was draped with a sun-bleached tarp.

Kolek and the sheriff pulled the tarp off the wreck. It wasn't bent very far out of shape. The sheriff could see that the brush growing on the mountainside had slowed its descent, all the way. It hadn't smashed head-on into a boulder or anything. If it hadn't caught on fire, James Penney might have survived.

Kolek pulled flashlights and his tool kit out of the station wagon. He needed the crowbar to get the driver's door open. The hinges were seized and distorted from the heat. The sheriff put his weight on it and screeched it all the way open. Then the two men played their flashlight beams all round the charred interior.

"Seat belt is burned away," Kolek said. "But he was wearing it. Buckle's still done up."

The sheriff nodded and pointed.

"Airbag deployed," he said.

The plastic parts of the steering wheel had all burned away, but they could see the little metal hinges in the up position, where the bag had exploded outward.

"OK," Kolek said. "Now for the fun part."

The sheriff held both flashlights and Kolek put on some heavy rubber gloves. He poked around for a while.

"He's fused on pretty tight," he said. "Best way would be to cut through the seat springs and take part of the seat with us."

"Is the body bag big enough?"

"Probably. This isn't a very big corpse."

The sheriff glanced in again. Slid the flashlight beam over the body.

"Penney was a big enough guy," he said. "Maybe better than five-ten."

Kolek grimaced. "Fire shrinks them. The body fluids boil off."

He walked back to the station wagon and pulled out a pair of wire cutters. Leaned back into the Firebird and started snipping through the zigzag metal springs close to where they were fused to the corpse. It took him a while. He had to lean right in, chest to chest with the body, to reach the far side.

"OK, give me a hand here," he said.

The sheriff shoved his hands in under the charred legs and grabbed the springs where Kolek had cut them away from the frame. He pulled and twisted and hauled the body out, feetfirst. Kolek grabbed the shoulders and they carried the rigid assembly a few feet away and laid it carefully on the ground. They stood up together and the body rolled backward, stiff, with the bent legs pointing grotesquely upward.

"Shit," Kolek said. "I hate this."

The sheriff was crouched down, playing his flashlight beam over the contorted gap that had been Penney's mouth.

"Teeth are still there," he said. "You should be able to make the ID."

Kolek joined him. There was a distinctive overbite visible.

"No problem," he agreed. "You in a hurry for it?"

The sheriff shrugged. "Can't close the case without it."

They struggled together to zip the body into the bag and then loaded it into the back of the wagon. They put it on its side, wedged against the bulge of the wheel arch. Then they drove back west, with the morning sun rising behind them.

That same morning sun woke James Penney by coming in through a hole in his motel room blind and playing a bright beam across his face. He stirred and lay in the warmth of the rented bed, watching the dust motes dancing.

He was still in California, up near Yosemite, cabin twelve in a place just far enough from the park to be cheap. He had six weeks' pay in his billfold, which was hidden under the center of his mattress. Six weeks' pay, less a tank and a half of gas, a cheeseburger, and twenty-seven-fifty for the room. Hidden under the mattress, because twenty-seven-fifty doesn't get you a space in a top-notch place. His door was locked, but the desk guy would have a pass key, and he wouldn't be the first desk guy in the world to rent out his pass key by the hour to somebody looking to make a little extra money during the night.

But nothing bad had happened. The mattress was so thin he could feel the billfold right there, under his kidney. Still there, still bulging. A good feeling. He lay watching the sunbeam, struggling with mental arithmetic, spreading six weeks' pay out over the foreseeable future. With nothing to worry about except cheap food, cheap motels, and the Firebird's gas, he figured he had no problems at all. The Firebird had a modern motor, twenty-four valves, tuned for a blend of power and economy. He could get far away and have enough money left to take his time looking around.

After that, he wasn't so sure. There wasn't going to be much call anywhere for a metalworker, even with seventeen years' experience. But there would be a call for something. He was sure of that. Even if it was menial. He was a worker. He didn't mind what he did. Maybe he'd find something outdoors, might be a refreshing thing. Might have some kind of dignity to it. Some kind of simple work, for simple honest folks, a lot different than slaving for that grinning weasel Odell.

He watched the sunbeam travel across the counterpane for a while. Then he flung the cover aside and swung himself out of bed. Used the john, rinsed his face and mouth at the sink, and untangled his clothes from the pile he'd dropped them in. He'd need more clothes. He only had the things he stood up in. Everything else, he'd burned along with his house. He shrugged and re-ran his calculations to allow for some new pants and work shirts. Maybe some heavy boots, if he was going to be laboring outside. The six weeks' pay was going to have to stretch a little thinner. He decided to drive slow, to save gas, and maybe eat less. Or maybe not less, just cheaper. He'd use truck stops, not tourist diners. More calories, less money.

He figured today he'd put in some serious miles before stopping for breakfast. He jingled the car keys in his pocket and opened his cabin door. Then he stopped. His heart thumped. The tarmac rectangle outside his cabin was empty. Just old oil stains staring up at him. He glanced desperately left and right along the row. No red Firebird. He staggered back into the room and sat down heavily on the bed. Just sat there in a daze, thinking about what to do.

He decided he wouldn't bother with the desk guy. He was pretty certain the desk guy was responsible. He could just about see it. The guy had waited an hour and then called some buddies who had come over and hot-wired his car. Eased it out of the motel lot and away down the road. A conspiracy, feeding off unsuspecting motel traffic. Feeding off suckers dumb enough to pay twenty-seven-fifty for the privilege of getting their prize possession stolen. He was numb. Suspended somewhere between sick and raging. His red Firebird. The only damn thing in his whole life he'd ever really wanted. Gone. Stolen. He remembered the exquisite joy of buying it. After his divorce. Waking up and realizing he could just go to the dealer, sign the papers, and have it. No discussions. No arguing. No snidey contempt about boys' toys and how they needed this damn thing and that damn thing first. None of that. He'd gone down to the dealer and chopped in his old clunker and signed up for that Firebird and driven it home in a state of total joy. He'd washed and cleaned it every week. He'd watched the infomercials and tried every miracle polish on the market. The car had sat every day outside the Laney factory like a bright red badge of achievement. Like a shiny consolation for the shit and the drudgery. Whatever else he didn't have, he had a Firebird. Until today. Now, along with everything else he used to have, he used to have a Firebird.

The nearest police were ten miles south. He had seen the place the previous night, heading north past it. He set off walking, stamping out in rage and frustration. The sun climbed up and slowed him. After a couple of miles, he stuck out his thumb. A computer service engineer in a company Buick stopped for him.

"Car was stolen," Penney told him. "Last night, outside the damn motel."

The engineer made a kind of all-purpose growling sound, like an expression of vague sympathy when the person doesn't really give a shit.

"Too bad," he said. "You insured?"

"Sure, Triple A and everything. But I'm kind of hoping they'll get it back for me."

The guy shook his head. "Forget about it. It'll be in Mexico tomorrow. Some señor down there will have himself a brand-new American motor. You'll never see it again unless you take a vacation down there and he runs you over with it."

Then the guy laughed about it and James Penney felt like getting out right away, but the sun was hot and James Penney was a practical guy. So he rode on in silence and got out in the dust next to the police parking lot. The Buick took off and left him there.

The police station was small, but it was crowded. He stood in line behind five other people. There was an officer behind the front counter, taking details, taking complaints, writing slow, confirming everything twice. Penney felt like every minute was vital. He felt like his Firebird was racing down to the border. Maybe this guy could radio ahead and get it stopped. He hopped from foot to foot in frustration. Gazed wildly around him. There were notices stuck on a board behind the officer's head. Blurred Xeroxes of telexes and faxes. U.S. Marshal notices. A mass of stuff. His eyes flicked absently across it all.

Then they snapped back. His photograph was staring out at him. The photograph from his own driver's license, Xeroxed in black-and-white, enlarged, grainy. His name underneath, in big printed letters. James Penney. From Laney, California. A description of his car. Red Firebird. The plate number. James Penney. Wanted for arson and criminal damage. He stared at the bulletin. It grew larger and larger. It grew life-size.

His face stared back at him like he was looking in a mirror. James Penney. Arson. Criminal damage. All-points bulletin. The woman in front of him finished her business and he stepped forward to the head of the line. The desk sergeant looked up at him.

"Can I help you, sir?" he said.

Penney shook his head. He peeled off left and walked away. Stepped calmly outside into the bright morning sun and ran back north like a madman. He made about a hundred yards before the heat slowed him to a gasping walk. Then he did the instinctive thing, which was to duck off the blacktop and take cover in a wild birch grove. He pushed through the brush until he was out of sight and collapsed into a sitting position, back against a thin rough trunk, legs splayed out straight, chest heaving, hands clamped against his head like he was trying to stop it from exploding.

Arson and criminal damage. He knew what the words meant. But he couldn't square them with what he had actually done. It was his own damn house to burn. Like he was burning his trash. He was entitled. How could that be arson? A guy chooses to burn his own house down, how is that a crime? This is a free country, right? And he could explain, anyway. He'd been upset. He sat slumped against the birch trunk and breathed easier. But only for a moment. Because then he started thinking about lawyers. He'd had personal experience. His divorce had cost him plenty in lawyer bills. He knew what lawyers were like. Lawyers were the problem. Even if it wasn't really arson, it was going to cost plenty in lawyer bills to start proving it.

It was going to cost a steady torrent of dollars, pouring out for years. Dollars he didn't have, and never would have again. He sat there on the hard, dry ground and realized that absolutely everything he had in the whole world was right then in direct contact with his body. One pair of shoes, one pair of socks, one pair of boxers, Levi's, cotton shirt, leather jacket. And his billfold. He put his hand down and touched its bulk in his pocket. Six weeks' pay, less yesterday's spending. Six weeks' worth of his pay might buy about six hours of a lawyer's time. Six hours, the guy might get as far as writing down his full name and address, maybe his date of birth. His Social Security number would take another six. The actual nature of his problem, that would be in the third six-hour chunk. Or the fourth. That was James Penney's experience with lawyers.

He got to his feet in the clearing. His legs were weak with the lactic acid from the unaccustomed running. His heart was thumping. He leaned up against a birch trunk and took a deep breath. Swallowed. He pushed back through the brush to the road. Turned north and started walking. He walked for a half hour, hands in his pockets, maybe a mile and three-quarters, and then his muscles eased off and his breathing calmed down. He began to see things clearly. He began to understand. He began to appreciate the power of labels. He was a realistic guy, and he always told himself the truth. He was an arsonist, because they said he was. The angry phase was over. Now it was about taking sensible decisions, one after the other. Clearing up the confusion was beyond his resources. So he had to stay out of their reach. That was his first decision.

That was the starting point. That was the strategy. The other decisions would flow out of that. They were tactical.

He could be traced three ways. By his name, by his face, by his car. He ducked sideways off the road again into the trees. Pushed twenty yards into the woods. Kicked a shallow hole in the leaf-mold and stripped out of his billfold everything with his name on it. He buried it all in the hole and stamped the earth flat. Then he took his beloved Firebird keys from his pocket and hurled them far into the trees. He didn't see where they fell.

The car itself was gone. In the circumstances, that was good. But it had left a trail. It might have been seen in Mojave, outside the bank. It might have been seen at the gas stations where he filled it. And its plate number was on the motel form from last night. With his name. A trail, arrowing north through California in neat little increments.

He remembered his training from Vietnam. He remembered the tricks. If you wanted to move east from your foxhole, first you moved west. You moved west for a couple hundred yards, stepping on the occasional twig, brushing the occasional bush, until you had convinced Charlie you were moving west, as quietly as you could, but not quietly enough. Then you turned about and came back east, really quietly, doing it right, past your original starting point, and away. He'd done it a dozen times. His original plan had been to head north for a spell, maybe into Oregon. He'd gotten a few hours into that plan. Therefore the red Firebird had laid a modest trail north. So now he was going to turn south for a while and disappear. He walked back out of the woods, into the dust on the near side of the road, and started walking back the way he'd come.

His face he couldn't change. It was right there on all the posters. He remembered it staring out at him from the bulletin board in the police building. The neat side-parting, the sunken gray cheeks. He ran his hands through his hair, vigorously, back and forward, until it stuck out every which way. No more neat side-parting. He ran his palms over twenty-four hours of stubble. Decided to grow a big beard. No option, really. He didn't have a razor, and he wasn't about to spend any money on one. He walked on through the dust, heading south, with Excelsior Mountain towering up on his right. Then he came to the turn dodging west toward San Francisco, through Tioga Pass, before Mount Dana reared up even higher. He stopped in the dust on the side of the road and pondered. Keeping on south would take him nearly all the way back to Mojave. Too close to home. Way too close. He wasn't comfortable about that. Not comfortable at all. So he figured a new move. He'd head west to the coast, then decide.

He put himself thirty yards west of the turn and stuck out his thumb. He was a practical guy. He knew he wasn't going to get anywhere by walking. He had to get rides, one after the other, anonymous rides from busy people. He decided as a matter of tactics not to look for rides from solid citizens. Not from anybody who looked like they might notice him or remember him. He had to think like a fugitive. A whole new experience.

After forty minutes, he came up with an ironic grin and realized he didn't have to worry about avoiding the solid citizens. They were avoiding him. He was standing there, thumb out, no baggage, messy hair, unshaven, dusty up to the knees, and one vehicle after another was passing him right by. Glancing at him and accelerating down the road like he wasn't even there. The sun wheeled overhead and dropped away into afternoon, and he started to worry about getting a ride at all. He was hungry and thirsty and vulnerable. Alone and on foot in the exact middle of the hugest and most contemptuous landscape he had ever seen.

Salvation arrived in the form of an open-topped Jeep, dusty and dented, a sandy color that really wasn't any color at all. A guy about forty at the wheel. Long graying hair, dirty tie-dye shirt, some kind of a left-over hippy. The Jeep slowed and plowed into the dust. Stopped right next to Penney and the driver leaned over inside and shouted across over the throb of the worn muffler.

"I'm going to Sacramento, my friend," he said. "But if you want the Bay, I can let you off in Stockton."

Penney shook his head, vigorously.

"Sacramento is great," he shouted. "Thank you very much."

He put his right hand on the windshield frame and his left hand on the seatback and swung himself inside exactly like he'd done with Jeeps in Vietnam.

"You just lay back and look at the scenery, my friend," the driver shouted over the muffler noise. "Talking is not an option in this old thing. Too loud, you know what I mean?"

James Penney nodded gratefully at him and the old hippy let in the clutch and roared off down the road.

The Laney County Medical Examiner's Office was just that, an office, and a fairly rudimentary one. There were no facilities for postmortem examination, unless Kolek wanted to clear his own desk and slice the carbonized lump open all over it. So he had taken the body bag down to the facility the county used over in northern Los Angeles. It was a big modern morgue, well equipped, and busy. It was busy because it sucked in all the business from the ring of small counties surrounding it, as well as handling its own substantial quota of unfortunates. So Kolek had parked the bag in the cold store and signed up for the first free visitor slot of the day, which was mid-afternoon. It was a half-hour slot, but Kolek figured that was going to be more than long enough. Not a hell of a lot of doubt about how Penney had died. All that was left was a routine ID through the dental data.

Laney itself had one dentist, serving the population of two thousand people. He had never seen Penney. But he was reasonably new, and the sheriff said it wasn't unusual for Laney people to forget about their teeth. The factory gave health insurance, of course, but not the best in the world, and dentistry required a contribution. But the surgery nurse was a stout old woman who had been there through three separate tenures. She went through the system and found the Penney file where it had been stored after his last visit, twelve years before. It was a thin packet of notes and film in a buff envelope. Kolek signed for it and threw it into the back seat of his wagon. Checked his watch and headed south for the morgue.

James Penney got out of the old hippy's Jeep right on the main drag into the southern edge of Sacramento, windblown, tired, ears ringing from the noise. He stood by the side of the road and waved and watched the guy go, waving back, long gray hair blowing in the slipstream. Then he looked around in the sudden silence and took his bearings. All the way up and down the drag he could see a forest of signs, bright colors, neon, advertising motels, air and pool and cable, burger places, eateries of every description, supermarkets, auto parts. Looked like the kind of place a guy could get lost in, no trouble at all. Big choice of motels, all side by side, all competing, all offering the lowest prices in town. He walked down to level with three of them. Figured he'd use the middle one. Hole up and plan ahead.

But then he decided to try something he'd read about once in a travel guide. Check in late, and ask for an even lower price. Late in the day, the motel would be keen to rent another room. They'd figure something is better than nothing, right? That was the theory in the travel guide. It was a theory he'd never tried, but now was the time to start. So he went straight out for a late lunch or an early dinner or whatever it was time for. He chose a burger chain he'd never used before and sat in the window, idly watching the traffic.

The waitress came over and he ordered a cheeseburger and two Cokes. He was dry from the dust on the road.

The forty-year-old leftover hippy with the long graying hair drove on downtown and parked the dusty and dented Jeep right up against a hydrant outside the Sacramento Police Department's main building. He pulled the keys and stepped out. Stood and stretched in the warmth of the afternoon sun before ducking inside.

The Drug Enforcement Agency's Sacramento office was located in a suite of rooms lent to them by the police department. The only way in was through the precinct hall, past the desk sergeants. Agents had to sign in and out. They had to collect internal ID badges to wear inside the building, and they had to leave them there on their way out. Two reasons for that. They tended to look more like criminals than agents, and the badges kept confusion inside the station house to a minimum. And because they were working undercover, they couldn't afford to slip their IDs into their pockets, absentmindedly or by mistake, and walk out like that. If they did, and they got searched by whatever new friends they were trying to make, there could be some very bad consequences. So the strict rule was the IDs stayed at the precinct house desk, every moment the agents weren't actually inside and wearing them.

The forty-year-old hippy lined up to sign in and collect his badge. He was behind a couple of uniforms with some guy in handcuffs. One desk sergeant on duty. A wait. He scanned the bulletins on the back wall. High risk of forest fire. Missing children. Then a face stared out at him. An APB Teletype. James Penney. Laney, California. Arson and criminal damage.

"Shit," he said. Loudly.

The desk sergeant and the cops with the cuffed guy all turned to look at him.

"That guy," he said. "James Penney. I just drove him all the way over here through the mountains."

The sheriff in Laney took the call from Sacramento. He was busy closing out the files on the previous day's activity. The DWIs, the broken windows, the smashed windshield, the small stuff. The Penney file was already in the drawer, just waiting for Kolek's formal ID to tie it up.

"Penney?" he said to the Sacramento desk sergeant. "No, he's dead. Crashed and burned on the road out to Vegas, last night."

Then he hung up, but he was a conscientious guy, and cautious, so he found the number for the morgue down in LA. He was stretching his hand out for the phone when it rang again. It was Kolek, calling on his mobile, straight from the dissecting table.

"What?" the sheriff asked, although he already knew what from Kolek's voice.

"Two main problems," Kolek said. "The teeth are nowhere near. Penney had a bridge across the front. Cheap dentures. These are real teeth."

"And?" the sheriff asked. "What else?"

"This is a woman," Kolek said.

Penney had finished his meal in the Sacramento burger shack when he saw the four police cruisers arrive. He had a dollar on the table for the waitress and was getting up, ready to leave. He had actually lifted off the sticky vinyl bench and was sliding out sideways when he caught sight of them. Four cruisers, playing leapfrog along the strip of motels. The cops were going into each office in turn, a sheaf of papers in their hands, coming out, sliding along to the next office. Penney sat back down. Stared out at them through the window. Watched them leapfrog south until they were out of sight. Then he stood up and left. Turned up the collar on his leather jacket and walked north, not quickly, not slowly, holding his breath.

The Laney sheriff was on the phone. He had tracked Penney to his bank. He was aware of the big cash withdrawal yesterday. He had looked at the road on the map, Laney to Mojave, and he'd guessed correctly about the northward dash along the flank of Mount Whitney. He'd called gas stations, one after the other, working north through the phone book, until he found a pump jockey who remembered a red Firebird whose driver had paid from a thick wad of cash.

Then he'd done some mental arithmetic, speed and distance and time, and started calling a thin cluster of motels in the area he figured Penney had reached at the end of the day. Second number, he'd found the right place, the Pine Park Holiday Motel up near Yosemite. Penney had checked in at about nine o'clock, car and all, name and plate number right there on the desk guy's carbon.

Beyond that, there was no further information. The sheriff called the nearest police department, ten miles south of the motel. No report of a stolen Firebird. No other missing automobiles. No knowledge of a woman car thief in the locality. So the sheriff called the Mojave General Motors dealership and asked for the value of an eighteen-month-old Firebird, clean, low mileage. He added that amount to the bank's figure for the cash withdrawal. Penney had rendezvoused at the motel and sold his car to the dead woman and was on the run with nearly fifteen grand in his pants pocket. A lot of money. It was clear. Obvious. Penney had planned, and prepared.

The sheriff opened his map again. The Sacramento sighting had been just plain luck. So now was the time to capitalize on it. He wouldn't be aiming to stay there. Too small, state capital, too well policed. So he'd be moving on. Probably up to the wilds of Oregon or Washington State. Or Idaho or Montana. But not by plane. Not with cash. Paying cash for an air ticket out of a California city is the same thing as begging to be arrested for narcotics trafficking. So he'd be aiming to get out by road. But Sacramento was a city with an ocean not too far away to the left, and high mountains to the right. Fundamentally six roads out, was all. So six roadblocks would do it, maybe on a ten-mile radius so the local commuters wouldn't get snarled up. The sheriff nodded to himself and picked up the phone to call the highway patrol.

It started raining in Sacramento at dusk. Steady, wetting rain. Northern California, near the mountains, very different from what Penney was used to. He was hunched in his jacket, head down, walking north, trying to decide if he dared hitch a ride. The police cruisers at the motel strip had unsettled him. He was tired and demoralized and alone. And wet. And conspicuous. Nobody walked anywhere in California. He glanced over his shoulder at the traffic stream and saw a dull olive Chevrolet sedan slowing behind him. It came to a stop and a long arm stretched across and opened the passenger door. The dome light clicked on and shone on the soaked roadway.

"Want a ride?" the driver called.

Penney ducked down and glanced inside. The driver was a very tall man, about thirty, muscular, built like a regular weightlifter. Short fair hair, rugged open face. Dressed in uniform. Army uniform. Penney read the insignia and registered: military police captain. He glanced at the dull olive paint on the car and saw a white serial number stenciled on the flank.

"I don't know," he said.

"Get in out of the rain," the driver said. "A vet like you knows better than to walk in the rain, right?"

Penney slid inside. Closed the door.

"How do you know I'm a vet?" he asked.

"The way you walk," the driver said. "And your age, and the way you look. Guy your age looking like you look and walking in the rain didn't beat the draft for college, that's for damn sure."

Penney nodded.

"No, I didn't," he said. "I did a jungle tour, seventeen years ago."

"So let me give you a ride," the driver said. "A favor, one soldier to another. Consider it a veteran's benefit."

"OK," Penney said.

"Where you headed?" the driver asked.

"I don't know," Penney said. "North, I guess."

"OK, north it is," the driver said. "I'm Jack Reacher. Pleased to make your acquaintance."

Penney said nothing.

"You got a name?" the guy called Reacher asked.

Penney hesitated.

"I don't know," he said.

Reacher put the car in drive and glanced over his shoulder. Eased back into the traffic stream. Clicked the switch and locked the doors.

"What did you do?" he asked.

"Do?" Penney repeated.

"You're running," Reacher said. "Heading out of town, walking in the rain, head down, no bag, don't know what your name is. I've seen a lot of people running, and you're one of them."

"You going to turn me in?"

"I'm a military cop," Reacher said. "You done anything to hurt the army?"

"The army?" Penney said. "No, I was a good soldier."

"So why would I turn you in?"

Penney looked blank.

"I don't know," he said.

"What did you do to the civilians?" Reacher asked.

"You're going to turn me in," Penney said, helplessly.

Reacher shrugged at the wheel.

"Well, that depends," he said. "What did you do?"

Penney said nothing. Reacher turned his head and looked straight at him. A powerful silent stare, hypnotic intensity in his eyes, held for a hundred yards of road.

"What did you do?" he asked again.

Penney couldn't look away. He took a breath.

"I burned my house," he said. "Near Mojave. I worked seventeen years and got canned yesterday and I got all upset because they were going to take my car away so I burned my house. They're calling it deliberate arson."

"Near Mojave?" Reacher said. "They would. They don't like fires down there."

Penney nodded. "I should have thought harder. But I was real mad. Seventeen years, and suddenly I'm shit on their shoe. And my car got stolen anyway, first night I'm away."

"There are roadblocks all around here," Reacher said. "I came through one south of the city."

"You think they're for me?" Penney asked.

"Could be," Reacher said. "They don't like fires down there."

"You going to turn me in?"

Reacher looked at him again, hard and silent.

"Is that all you did?"

Penney nodded. "Yes, sir, that's all I did."

There was silence for a beat. Just the sound of the wet pavement under the tires.

"Well, I don't have a problem with it," Reacher said. "A guy does a jungle tour, works seventeen years and gets canned, I guess he's entitled to get a little mad."

"So what should I do?"

"You got attachments?"

"Divorced, no kids."

"So start over, someplace else."

"They'll find me," Penney said.

"You're already thinking about changing your name," Reacher said.

Penney nodded.

"I junked all my ID," he said. "Buried it in the woods."

"So build a new identity. Get new paper. That's all anybody cares about. Pieces of paper."

"Like how?"

Reacher was quiet another beat, thinking hard.

"Easy enough," he said. "Classic way is find some cemetery, find a kid who died as a child, get a copy of the birth certificate, start from there. Get a Social Security number, a passport, credit cards, and you're a new person."

Penney shrugged. "I can't do all that. Too difficult. And I don't have time. According to you, there's a roadblock up ahead. How am I going to do all of that stuff before we get there?"

"There are other ways," Reacher said.

"Forgeries?"

Reacher shook his head. "No good. Sooner or later, forgeries don't work."

"So how?"

"Find some guy who's already created false ID for himself, and take it away from him."

Penney shook his head. "You're crazy. How am I going to do that?"

"Maybe you don't need to do that. Maybe I already did it for you."

"You got false ID?"

"Not me," Reacher said. "Guy I was looking for."

"What guy?"

Reacher drove one-handed and pulled a sheaf of official paper from his inside jacket pocket.

"Arrest warrant," he said. "Army liaison officer at a weapons plant outside of Fresno, looks to be peddling blueprints. Turns out to have three separate sets of bogus ID, all perfect, all completely backed up with everything from elementary school records onward. Which makes it likely they're Soviet, which means they can't be beat. I'm on my way back from talking to him right now. He was running, too, already on his second set of papers. I took them. They're clean. They're in the trunk of this car, in a wallet, in a jacket."

Traffic was slowing ahead. There was red glare visible through the streaming windshield. Flashing blue lights. Yellow flashlight beams waving, side to side.

"There's the roadblock," Reacher said.

"So can I use this guy's ID?" Penney asked urgently.

"Sure you can," Reacher said. "Hop out and get it. Bring the wallet from the jacket."

He slowed and stopped on the shoulder. Penney got out. Ducked away to the back of the car and lifted the trunk lid. Came back a long moment later, white in the face.

"Got it?" Reacher asked.

Penney nodded silently. Held up the wallet.

"It's all in there," Reacher said. "I checked. Everything anybody needs."

Penney nodded again.

"So put it in your pocket," Reacher said.

Penney slipped the wallet into his inside jacket pocket. Reacher's right hand came up. There was a gun in it. And a pair of handcuffs in his left.

"Now sit still," he said, quietly.

He leaned over and snapped the cuffs on Penney's wrists, one-handed. Put the car back into drive and crawled forward.

"What's this for?" Penney asked.

"Quiet," Reacher said.

They were two cars away from the checkpoint. Three highway patrolmen in rain capes were directing traffic into a corral formed by parked cruisers. Their light bars were flashing bright in the shiny dark.

"What?" Penney said again.

Reacher said nothing. Just stopped where the cop told him and wound his window down. The night air blew in, cold and wet. The cop bent down. Reacher handed him his military ID. The cop played his flashlight over it and handed it back.

"Who's your passenger?" he asked.

"My prisoner," Reacher said. He handed over the arrest warrant.

"He got ID?" the cop asked.

Reacher leaned over and slipped the wallet out from inside Penney's jacket, two-fingered like a pickpocket. Flipped it open and passed it through the window. A second cop stood in Reacher's headlight beams and copied the plate number onto a clipboard. Stepped around the hood and joined the first guy.

"Captain Reacher of the military police," the first cop said.

The second cop wrote it down.

"With a prisoner name of Edward Hendricks," the first cop said.

The second cop wrote it down.

"Thank you, sir," the first cop said. "You drive safe, now."

Reacher eased out from between the cruisers. Accelerated away into the rain. A mile later, he stopped again on the shoulder. Leaned over and unlocked Penney's handcuffs. Put them back in his pocket. Penney rubbed his wrists.

"I thought you were going to turn me in," he said.

Reacher shook his head. "Looked better for me that way. I've got an arrest warrant, I want a prisoner in the car for everybody to see, right?"

Penney nodded.

"I guess," he said, quietly.

Reacher handed the wallet back.

"Keep it," he said.

"Really?"

"Edward Hendricks," Reacher said. "That's who you are now, rest of your life. It's clean ID, and it'll work. Think of it like a veteran's benefit. One soldier to another, OK?"

Edward Hendricks looked at him and nodded and opened his door. Got out into the rain and turned up the collar of his leather jacket and started walking north. Reacher watched him until he was out of sight and then pulled away and took the next turn west. Turned north past a town called Eureka and stopped again where the road was lonely and ran close to the ocean. There was a wide gravel shoulder and a low barrier and a steep cliff with the Pacific high tide boiling and foaming fifty feet below it.

He got out of the car and opened the trunk and grasped the lapels of the jacket he had told his passenger about. Took a deep breath and heaved. The corpse was heavy. He wrestled it up out of the trunk and jacked it onto his shoulder and staggered with it to the barrier. Bent his knees and dropped it over the edge. The rocky cliff caught it and it spun and the arms and the legs flailed limply. Then it hit the surf with a faint splash and it was gone.

Everyone Talks

There are written rules and unwritten rules, and I hit one of each on my first day in the department. The unwritten rule said the new detective got the worst job. Which on that morning was to follow a written rule: City hospitals were required to report gunshot victims, and the department was required to investigate. Boring work, and likely fruitless. But rules were rules.

Times two for a woman in a man's world.

So off I went.

I got the worst car, obviously, with no GPS on the dash and no maps in the glove box, but I found the hospital easily enough. It was a large beige building southeast of downtown. I showed my shiny new shield and was directed to the fifth floor. Not exactly the ICU, they said, but the same kind of thing. A big enough deal that I had to turn off my phone.

A nurse met me there and took me to a doctor, who

had threads of silver in her hair and looked like brains and money. She said I had wasted a trip. The victim was asleep and wasn't going to wake up anytime soon, because he was sedated with a custom mix that sounded pretty good to me. But I was new, and I had a report to write, so I asked for her perspective.

"Gunshot wound," she said, like I was slow in the head. "In the left side, up under the arm, broke a rib and tore some muscle. Not very nice. Hence the painkillers."

"Caliber?" I asked.

"No idea," she said. "Not a BB gun, anyway."

I asked to see the guy.

"You want to watch him sleep?"

"I have a report to write."

She was cautious about infection, but she let me look in through a window. I saw a guy, fast asleep on a cot. A very distinctive guy. Short messy hair, plain features. He was on his back. The sheet was down at his hips. He was naked from the waist up. He had a pressure dressing high on his left side. He had tubes in the back of his hand, and a clip on his finger. I could see a sinus rhythm on his monitor. It was beeping away, strong and powerful. As it should. Because the guy was huge. Almost bigger than the cot itself. He was easily six-five and two-fifty. A giant. Hands like catchers' mitts. A slab of a man. He was ridged with muscle. Not old. But not young, either. He looked worn and battered. He had scars here and there. A big old thing low down on his gut, like a huge white starfish, with thick, crude stitches. An old bullet hole in his chest. A

.38, almost certainly. An eventful life. What doesn't kill you makes you stronger.

He looked to be sleeping quite peacefully.

I asked, "Any idea what happened?"

"Probably not self-inflicted," the doctor said. "Unless he's a contortionist."

"I mean, didn't he tell you anything?"

"He came in conscious, but he didn't say a word."

I asked, "Did he have ID?"

"His stuff is in a bag," the doctor said. "At the nurses' station."

It was a very small bag. Clear plastic, with a zipper. Like people use in the airport line. At the bottom was loose change. A couple of bucks. There was a wad of folding money. A couple of hundred, possibly. Maybe more. It would depend on the denominations. There was an ATM card. And a creased old passport. And finally a travel toothbrush, reversed for a pocket, with the bristles inside a plastic tube.

"Is that it?" I asked.

"You think we're stealing from our patients?"

"Mind if I take a look?" I said.

"You're the cop," the doctor said.

The ATM card was made out to *J. Reacher.* It had another year to run. The passport had expired three years previously. It was made out to *Jack Reacher.* Not John. Jack must have been on his birth certificate. No middle name, which was unusual in America. The photograph showed an approximate version of the face on the pillow. It was thirteen years younger, and animated with an expression halfway between patient and impatient, as if the guy was prepared to give the photographer the time he needed, but not a second longer.

No driver's license, no credit cards, no cell phone.

I asked, "What was he wearing?"

"Cheap things," the doctor said. "We burned them."

"Why?"

"Biohazard. I've seen better clothes on bums in the park."

"Is he a transient?"

"I told you, he didn't say a word. He could be an eccentric billionaire, for all I know."

"He looks in good shape."

"You mean apart from being bandaged up in a hospital bed?"

"I mean, generally."

"Healthy as a horse. Strong as a horse."

"When will he wake up?"

"Tonight, maybe. I dosed him like a horse, too."

I **went back** at the end of my shift. Unpaid, but I was new and I wanted to make a good impression. There had been nothing on the wires about a shooting incident. No rumors. No other victims, no witnesses, no 911 calls. Which I gathered was not unusual. The city was like that. The underbelly had a life of its own. Like Vegas. What happened there stayed there.

I spent some time with the databases, too. Reacher was not a common name, and I figured the Jack-none-Reacher combination was likely to be much less common. But there was no real data. Or to put it the other way, all the data was negative. The guy had no phone, no car, no boat, no trailer, no credit history, no home, and no insurance. No nothing. There were some military records, from way back. He had been an army cop, mostly in the Criminal Investigation Division, an officer, decorated multiple times, which at first gave me a warm fellow feeling, and then it worried me. Thirteen years' honorable service, and now he was homeless, getting shot in the side, wearing clothes so toxic the hospital had to incinerate them. Not what a new detective wants to hear, on her first day on the job.

It was dark when I got back to the hospital, but up on the fifth floor I found the big guy awake. I knew his name, so I introduced myself, to balance things up. To be polite. I told him I had a report to write. I told him it was required. I asked him what had happened.

He said, "I don't remember."

Which was plausible. Physical trauma can induce retrograde amnesia. But I didn't believe it. I got the feeling he was giving me a rote answer. I began to see why his file was so thin. A person has to work hard to stay under the radar. Which was OK with me, to be honest. I got my promotion because I'm a good interrogator. And I like a challenge. An old boyfriend said I should have it on my gravestone: *Everyone talks.*

I said, "Help me out here."

He looked back at me with clear blue eyes. Whatever painkiller cocktail they were using wasn't doing him any harm in the cognition department. His gaze was unworried and friendly, but also bleak and dangerous, wise and primitive, warm and predatory. I got the feeling he knew a hundred ways to help me, and a hundred ways to kill me.

I said, "I'm new on the job. Today is my first day. I'm going to get my butt kicked if I don't deliver."

"Which would be a shame," he said. "Because it's a very cute butt."

Which would have gotten him sensitivity training on the job, but I couldn't take offense. He was lying there wounded and helpless, half naked, radiating a lazy kind of charm.

"You were a cop," I said. "I saw your file. You worked in a team. Did you ever save someone's ass?"

"Time to time," he said.

"So save mine now."

He said nothing.

"How did it start?"

"It's late," he said. "Don't you have a home to go to?"

"Don't you?"

He didn't answer.

"How did it start?" I asked again.

He sighed and took a breath and said it started like things usually start. Which was to say they usually don't start at all. He said most places he went were peaceful and quiet. He said most places, nothing happens.

I asked him what he meant.

He said big cities, small towns, he went about his business and nobody knew. He said he ate his meals, and slept, and showered and changed, and saw what he saw. Sometimes he got lucky with an hour's conversation. Sometimes he got lucky with a night's companionship. But mostly nothing happened. He said he had a quiet life. He said he could go months between days worth forgetting.

But if it was going to happen, it was going to start with people. Usually with people in bars or diners or restaurants. Places where food and drink are consumed, and where a certain kind of community is expected, and where sipping and chewing make people unembarrassed about not talking.

Because no one ever says anything. They look instead. It was all about the looking. The looking away, to be precise. There can be a guy people are looking away from. Maybe alone at the bar, or alone in a diner booth or at a restaurant table. People are partly shunning him, but mostly they're scared of him. Some kind of a bully. Unpopular, and he knows it. He knows people go quiet around him, and he knows they look away, and he loves it. He loves the power.

"Is that how it started?" I asked. "Yesterday?"

Reacher nodded. There was a guy in a bar. Reacher didn't know the bar. He wasn't part of that community. He had never been in the city before. He had ridden the Big Dog all day and gotten out at the depot two blocks from First Street. He had walked over and found the bar. Not hard. That close to the depot, it was about the only game in town. He had walked in and taken a seat. He had figured he would rely on waitress service. He didn't want to belly up to the mahogany. He didn't want to get face to face with the barman. He wasn't looking for any kind of witty small talk.

I said, "Back up a minute. You came in on the Greyhound bus?"

He nodded. He had told me that already. I saw the same look on his face, like in his passport photograph. Patient to a degree, but he wanted the world to keep up with him.

I asked, "Where were you coming from?"

He said, "Does it matter?"

"Why were you coming here?"

"I have to be somewhere. I thought this place would be as good as any."

"For what?"

"For passing a day or two. Or an hour or two."

"The records show you have no permanent location."

"Then the records are correct. Which is reassuring, I suppose. From your point of view."

"What happened in the bar?"

He sighed again and took another breath and went on with the story, quite candidly. My interrogation mojo was working. Or maybe the painkiller cocktail was acting like a truth serum. He said the place was busy but he had gotten a seat with his back to a wall, so he could see the room and both its doors all at once. An old habit. Military cops do a lot of their work in bars. The waitress had scooted over and taken his order. He had asked for coffee and settled for beer. Rolling Rock, in a bottle. He was no kind of connoisseur. He was happy to take what places had to offer.

Then he had watched the man at the bar. He was a heavy-limbed guy, tall, with dark, vivid features, sitting there commandingly and complacently. With everyone else looking away from him. Reacher defaulted to his instinctive position, which was to hope for the best, but plan for the worst. And the worst with a guy like that wouldn't be too bad. He would come off the stool into a yard of clear space. There would be a certain amount of huffing and puffing. Bullies got by on reputation alone, and the worse the reputation, the less practice they got in actually doing anything. Because other people always backed off. Therefore a bully's skills were rusty and eroded. A simple cigarette punch would take care of the problem. Named way back in the day when everyone smoked. A guy's mouth would open, ready to load the next cigarette between his lips, an insolent and calculated little pause, maybe half a smile, and a vicious left uppercut under the chin timed just right would slam his mouth shut again, busting teeth, maybe making him bite through his tongue. Game over, right there, and if it wasn't, then a clubbing downward right to the side of the neck would close the deal, like driving a railroad spike with your knuckles. No major problem. Except that no one smoked anymore, at least not indoors, so you had to do it while they were talking, which was OK, because everyone talked. Bullies most of all. They talked a lot. All kinds of threats and taunts and *what are you looking at?*

But, hope for the best.

Reacher sipped the watery foam from his long-neck bottle and waited. The waitress was in a lull and came over to ask if he needed anything, which was clearly an excuse to chat a moment. Reacher liked her on sight. Maybe she liked him, too. She was a professional. Maybe forty years old. Not a college kid, not a young person planning to move on soon to something better. She was looking away from the guy, too. His needs were being met by the barman, and she seemed very glad about that. It was more than obvious.

"Who is he?" Reacher asked.

"Just a customer," she said.

"Does he have a name?"

"I don't know. I mean, I'm sure he has a name, but I don't know what it is."

Which Reacher didn't believe. A guy like that, everyone knows his name. Because a guy like that makes sure of it.

Reacher asked, "Does he come here often?"

"Once a week, every week."

Which was a strangely precise schedule. Which had to mean something. But the woman didn't want to talk about it. That was clear. She started in with the usual questions instead. New in town? From where? Doing what? Which were questions Reacher found hard to answer. He was always new in town, and he was from nowhere in particular, and he wasn't doing anything. He had been in the military all his life, first an officer's kid, then an officer himself, raised on bases all over the world, serving on bases all over the world, and then he had fallen out into civilian life and couldn't really settle down to the kind of existence normal people seemed to have. So he wandered the land, seeing the things he had never had time to see before, going here, going there, staying a night or two, and then moving on. No bags, no schedule, no plan. Travel light, travel far. At first he had expected to work it out of his system, but he had long ago given up on that ambition.

He said, "Anyway, how's business here?"

The waitress shrugged and made a shape with her mouth, and said business was OK, but she didn't sound convinced. And waitresses knew. They had a close-up view. Better than accountants or auditors or analysts. They saw the sad expression on the owner's face, exactly once a week, on payday.

Which had to mean something, too. The only bar near the bus depot should have been doing a roaring trade. Location was everything. And the place was crowded. All the tables were taken and people were shoulder to shoulder at the bar, except for a quarantine yard around the big guy on the stool. Bottles and glasses were slamming back and forth with regularity, and fives and tens and twenties were heading for the register like a raging river.

So Reacher watched a little longer, over the first beer, into a second, taking them slow, and he saw another guy step into the room, and he felt the atmosphere change. Like a moment of truth had arrived. Like the whole purpose of the evening had snapped into focus. The new guy was dressed one grade better than anyone else, and he moved in from the door with a proprietorial air. His place. The owner. He greeted people as he walked, a little vaguely, a little preoccupied, and then he ducked behind the bar and went in through a small door in back. The office, presumably. His domain.

He came out again two minutes later, carrying something in his hand. He stayed in the well behind the bar and squeezed past the bartender and stepped over to where the big guy was sitting on his stool. They faced each other, with nothing more than the mahogany slab between them. Everyone looked away.

Except Reacher. He saw the owner hand over the thing he was carrying. He did it fast and unobtrusive, like a magic trick. The guy on the stool took it and slipped it into his pocket. It was there, and then it was gone.

But Reacher had seen what it was.

It was a white office envelope, fat with cash.

Protection money, presumably.

The guy on the stool stayed where he was and finished his drink, ostentatiously slowly, rubbing it in. He had the power. He was the man. Except he wasn't. He was an underling. He was muscle. That was all. Reacher knew how these things worked. He had seen them before. He knew the envelope would go straight to some shadowy figure at the top of the chain, and the guy on the stool would get a cut, like a wage.

The waitress came back and asked if Reacher wanted a third go-round with the Rolling Rock. Reacher said no, and asked, "What happens now?"

"About what?"

"You know about what."

The woman shrugged, like a secret shame had been exposed, and she said, "We stay in business another week. We don't get smashed up or burned out."

"How long has this been going on?"

"A year."

"Has anything been done about it?"

"Not by me. I like my face the way it is."

"Me, too," Reacher said.

She smiled at him.

Reacher said, "The owner could do something. There are laws."

"Not unless something happens. The cops say they need to see someone beaten. Or worse. Or the place in flames."

"What's the guy's name?"

"Does it matter?"

"Who does he work for?"

She pincered her finger and thumb and pretended to zipper her mouth.

"I like my face the way it is," she said again. "And I have kids."

She collected his empty bottle and headed back to her station. The big guy on the stool finished his drink and put his glass on the bar. He didn't pay, and the barman didn't ask him to. He stood up and walked to the door, through a channel suddenly clear of people.

Reacher slid out of his chair and followed. First Street was dark, all except for a yellow light on a pole about a block away. The guy from the stool was fifteen feet ahead. Upright and mobile he looked to be about six-two and two-ten. Not small, but smaller than Reacher. Younger, but almost certainly dumber. And less skilled, and less experienced, and more inhibited. Reacher was sure of that. He had yet to meet the man who outranked him in those categories.

He called out, "Hey."

The guy from the stool stopped and turned around, surprised.

Reacher walked up to him and said, "I think you've got something that doesn't belong to you. I'm sure it was just a mistake. So I want to give you the chance to make it right."

"Get lost," the guy said, but he said it without the final few percent of conviction. He wasn't the total king of the jungle. Not right then and there.

Reacher asked, "How many more calls do you have tonight?"

"Butt out, pal. This ain't your business."

"So whose business is it?"

"Get lost," the guy said again.

"It's all about free will," Reacher said. "It's all about making choices. You want to know what yours are?"

"What?"

"You can tell me his name now, or you can tell me after I break your legs."

"Whose name?"

"The guy you picked up the money for."

Reacher watched his eyes. Waited for the decision. There were three possibilities. The guy would run, fight, or talk. He hoped the guy wouldn't run, because then he would have to run after him, and he hated running. He didn't expect the guy to talk, because of ego and self-image. Therefore the guy would have to fight. Or try to.

And Reacher was right. The guy fought, or tried to. He lunged forward and swung his left fist downward, like a sweep, as if there was a knife in it. An attempt at a distraction, nothing more. Next would come a big straight right, maybe a little overhand. But Reacher wasn't about to wait for it. He had learned to fight a long time ago, in hot dusty outposts in the Pacific, and cold damp alleys in Europe, and hardscrabble towns in the South, against resentful local youth and tribal military kids, and then his techniques had been broken down and built back up by the army, and he had learned the golden rule: *Get your retaliation in first.*

He stepped in close, falling forward, and threw a heavy elbow at the guy's face. Usually better to target the throat, but Reacher wanted the guy talking afterward, not choking to death on a smashed larynx, so he went for the upper lip, just below the nose, accelerating hard, which would break teeth and bone, which would make the subsequent conversation a little garbled, but at least the guy wouldn't be struck mute. The blow landed and the guy's head snapped back and his knees went weak and he sat down on his ass, right there on the sidewalk, eyes all over the place, blood all over his nose and his mouth.

Reacher was a brawler by nature, and a brawler's dream is to have the other guy on the floor, ready for the winning kick to the head, but he held back, because he wanted a name. He said, "Last chance, my friend."

The guy from the stool said, "Kubota."

Garbled. Missing teeth, and blood, and swellings.

Reacher said, "Spell it for me."

Which the guy did, fast and obedient. Not the king of the jungle anymore. Which Reacher was happy about. Because human legs are hard to break. Big physical efforts are required. He asked, "Where will I find Mr. Kubota?"

And the guy told him.

At that point Reacher stopped talking and took a breath and put his head back on the hospital pillow.

I said, "And then what?"

He said, "Enough for tonight. I'm tired."

"I need to know."

"Come back tomorrow."

"Did you find Kubota?"

No answer.

I said, "Was there a confrontation?"

No answer.

"Did Kubota shoot you?"

Reacher said nothing. And then the doctor came in. The same woman, with the threads of silver in her hair. She told me she was terminating the interview immediately, on medical grounds. Which was frustrating, but not fatal. I had plenty of valuable data. I left the building with visions of a major score in my head. A protection racket, busted, on my very first day in the department. Priceless. Women have to work twice as hard, to get half the credit.

I went straight back to the station house. Unpaid, but I would have paid them. I found a thick file on Kubota. Lots of leads, lots of hours, but we never had enough to get a warrant. Now we did, big-time. We had gun crime. We had his victim, right there in the hospital. Eyewitness testimony. And possibly even the bullet itself, in a stainless steel dish somewhere.

Solid gold.

The night judge agreed with me. He signed off on a big boilerplate warrant and I put a team together.

Plenty of uniforms, cars, heavy weapons, three other detectives, all senior to me, but I was leading them. My case. An unwritten rule.

We executed the warrant at midnight, which was legal-speak for busting down Kubota's door, and knocking him over, and bouncing his head off the tile a couple of times. We found the guy from the bar in a back room, in a bad way. Like he had been run over by a truck. I had him taken to a different hospital, under guard.

Then the uniforms hauled Kubota away to a holding cell and I and my three detective partners spent most of the rest of the night going through his place like we were looking for a tiny flake of chrome off the world's smallest needle in the world's biggest haystack.

His place was a treasure trove.

We found grocery sacks full of unexplained cash, and thirty different bank accounts, and notebooks and ledgers and diaries and maps. It was clear from our first glance the guy was making serious money from a hundred different establishments. According to his notes in the last six months three places had tried to resist, and we called in the dates and matched them to three unexplained arson attacks. We found temporary interruptions in two sets of payments, and when we checked the dates with the city's hospitals we found one broken leg and one slashed face. We had everything.

Except the gun.

But that made sense, in its way. He had used it, and

he had ditched it. Standard practice. It would be in the river, thrown from a bridge. Like his old cell phones, presumably. Pay-as-you-go burners. He had ditched the packaging and the paperwork, but for some dumb reason not the chargers. We found nearly fifty in a drawer.

At dawn I was face to face with him in an interview room. He had a lawyer with him, a slick guy in a suit, but I could tell by the guy's face he knew a defense was hopeless. On our side it was just me, all alone, but I guessed there was a crowd behind the one-way glass, to watch the mojo working. And it worked very well at first. I like to get a suspect in the habit of saying yes, one confession after the other, so I started with the easy stuff. I went through one bar after another, all the restaurants and diners, and I told him we had the notebooks and the ledgers and the diaries, and the cash and the bank statements, and he admitted them all. Ten minutes after I started we had enough on tape to put him away for a long, long time. But I kept him going, not because we really needed it, but because I wanted him warmed up for the big moment.

Which didn't happen.

He denied the shooting. He denied meeting Reacher the night before. He said he had been out of town. He denied owning a gun. He said he had never used one. I kept at him until the clock ticked around and my second day in the department officially began. Then my lieutenant came in, fresh from a night's sleep and a shower, and he told me to quit.

He said, "No harm, no foul. You've done great. We

have enough. He's going down for a long time. The goal has been achieved."

Which was the general opinion in the department. There was no sense of failure. Quite the reverse. The new girl had busted a racket, on her first day on the job. A major score.

But it rankled me. I didn't do the work I was supposed to do, and I dug deeper. I knew I would find something, and I did. But not what I was expecting.

The bar owner Reacher had seen was the doctor's brother-in-law. The woman with silver in her hair. They were family.

I was dizzy with fatigue, which helped, in a way. I made lightning connections a rational mind might have dismissed. Kubota's thick file, full of failed attempts to win a warrant. The endless quest for more. The need to see someone beaten, or worse. The relentless beep of Reacher's bedside monitor, too strong for a sick man. His clear eyes and his lucid mind, after opiates said to be strong enough to fell a horse.

I made my third trip to the hospital. Reacher's room was empty. There were no signs of recent occupation. The woman with silver in her hair swore she had treated no gunshot victims on the night in question. She invited me to check her records. Her records were blank. I sat down with the nurses, one at a time. No one talked.

Then I pictured Reacher, on the night in question, unable to find Kubota because Kubota was out of town. I pictured him heading back to the bar, handing back the money, working out a long-term solution with the owner. I pictured the owner, calling his sister-in-law.

I pictured the Greyhound depot at midnight. A tall figure getting on a bus. The bus rolling out. No bags, no schedule, no plan.

I went back to the station house. I walked in, and they gave me a round of applause.

Not a Drill

One thing leads to another, and in Jack Reacher's case, one warm and aimless August day, a hitched ride in an empty lumber truck led to East Millinocket in Maine, which led in turn to a decent mid-morning meal in a roadside restaurant near the highway, which led to a halting two-wary-guys conversation with the man at the next table, which led to an offered ride further north, to a place called Island Falls. The unspoken but clearly implied cost of the ride was the price of the guy's coffee and pie, but the establishment was cheap, and Reacher had money in his pocket, and as always he had no particular place to be, so he accepted.

One thing leads to another.

The guy's car turned out to be a softly sprung old Chevrolet, lacy with rust, and Island Falls turned out to be a pleasant little place on a lake, way in the north, where Maine sticks out like a thumb up Canada's ass, with Quebec to the left and New Brunswick to the right. But most of all Island Falls was pretty close to the north end of I-95. Which was tempting. Reacher had a collector's instinct when it came to places. He knew the south end of I-95 pretty well. More than nineteen hundred miles away, just past downtown Miami. He had been there many times. But he had never seen the north end.

He had no particular place to be.

One thing leads to another.

Getting out of Island Falls was easy enough. He had a cup of coffee in a hut next to a kayak rental slip, and stood in the buggy warmth of the lakeshore and took in the view, and then he turned his back on it all and walked out of town the same way the old Chevy had driven in, back to the highway cloverleaf. He set up on the on-ramp heading north, and waited. Not long, he figured. It was August, it was warm, it was vacation country. The mood was amiable. It was daylight. He was clean. His clothes were only two days old, and his shave was only three. Ideal conditions, overall.

And sure enough, less than ten minutes later an old-model Jeep SUV with New Brunswick plates slowed and stopped. There was a woman at the wheel, and a man next to her, in the passenger seat. They looked to be somewhere in their mid-thirties, clearly outdoor types, ruffled by the wind and tanned by the sun. Heading home, no doubt, after an active vacation. Maybe they had been kayaking. Or camping. Or both. The load space in the rear of the truck was piled up with stuff.

The guy in the passenger seat let his window down,

and the woman craned over for a look, too. The guy said, "We're only going to Fredericton, which isn't far, I'm afraid. Any good to you?"

Reacher said, "Is that in Canada?"

"Sure is."

Reacher said, "Then that's perfect. All I want is to get to the border, and then back again."

"Got something against Canada?"

"My passport expired."

The guy nodded. Gone were the days when a person could just stroll in and out of neighboring countries. Then the guy said, "But there's nothing much to see between here and there. Nothing much to see through the fence, either. You'd be better off staying where you are, surely."

Reacher said, "I want to see the end of the road."

The guy said, "That sounds heavy."

The woman said, "We think of it as the beginning of the road."

"Good point," Reacher said.

The guy said, "Hop in the back." He craned around in his seat and batted stray items aside. Reacher opened the door and slid in and used his hip to finish the job. He closed the door and the woman hit the gas and they took off, cruising easy through the last thirty-some miles of America.

The last exit was for a town called Houlton. Or the first exit, Reacher supposed, from the Canadian point of view. Then came a mile or so of hinterland, and a little queuing traffic, and barriers and booths and of-

ficial signs. Reacher stayed in the Jeep until the last
car's length, and then he said his thanks and his goodbyes and he slipped out, and he stepped ahead and put
his foot on the last inch of blacktop, directly under the
barrier pole.

The end of the road.

One thing leads to another.

He looped back and crossed to the southbound
lanes and set up again thirty yards from the barriers.
He wanted to give incoming drivers plenty of time
to see him, but not enough time to be already going
too fast to stop. Once again he anticipated no kind of
a lengthy delay. August, daylight, sunshine, vacation
country, warmhearted and relaxed Canadian drivers
full of generosity and goodwill. Ten minutes max, he
thought, maybe closer to five, and it wasn't outside the
bounds of possibility that the first car through would
be the one.

It wasn't. But the second car was. Which was more
of a minivan, really. But not the kind of thing a soccer
mom would be proud of. It was old and grimy, and
somewhat battered. Light blue, maybe, when it left
the factory, but now colorless, almost, faded by sun
and salt. There was a young man at the wheel, and
a young woman beside him in the front, and another
young woman in the back. The van had New Brunswick plates, and it was trailing a puff of oil smoke,
after pulling away from the customs post.

But Reacher had ridden in worse vehicles.

It slowed and stopped alongside him. The passenger window was already down. The woman in the
front said, "We're headed for Naismith."

Which was a place Reacher had never heard of. He said, "I'm not sure where that is."

The guy at the wheel leaned across and said, "The Allagash, man. About an hour west of Route 11. After going north for a bit. It's a little town. Where you get on the wilderness trail through the forest. It's a really cool place."

Reacher said, "North of here?"

The guy said, "Beautiful country, man. You should see those woods. Really primeval. Step off the path, and you could be the first human ever to set foot. I mean, literally. Ten thousand years of undisturbed nature. Since the last Ice Age."

Reacher said nothing.

The guy said, "Get it while you can, my friend. It won't be there forever. Climate change is going to take it all down."

No particular place to be.

Reacher said, "OK, sure, thanks."

One thing leads to another.

He looped around the rear of the van and the girl in the back slid the door on a rusty track and he climbed in. Behind him in the load space were two big backpacks and one hard-shell suitcase. The seat was some kind of nylon cloth gone greasy with age. He got settled and slid the door closed and the van moved off, puffing smoke again, from the effort.

"Thanks," Reacher said, for the second time.

The trio introduced themselves. The girl in the back was Helen, and the girl in the front was Suzanne, and the driver was Henry. Henry and Suzanne were a couple. They ran a bicycle store in a place called Moncton. Helen was their friend. The plan was Henry and Suzanne would walk the wilderness trail north from Naismith, to a place called Cripps, which would take four days. Helen would be waiting there with the van to meet them, having spent the same four days doing something else, maybe antiquing in Presque Isle and Caribou.

"I don't like the woods," she said, as if she felt an explanation was required.

"Why not?" Reacher asked, because he felt a response was expected.

"Too creepy," she said. "Too dark. Too full of bugs."

They puttered onward past Houlton, and then Henry turned off on 212, which soon joined Route 11 going north, which was a pretty road. Saddleback Mountain was ahead on the right, and on the left was an endless expanse of woods and lakes. The trees were green, and the water glittered, and the sky was blue. Beautiful country, just like Henry had promised.

"I don't like the woods," Helen said again.

She was in her late twenties, Reacher guessed. Maybe thirty, tops. She was paler than her friends, and sleeker, and more cared for. Indoor, more than outdoor. Urban, rather than rural. Like her luggage. She was a hard-shell suitcase, not a backpack. Henry and Suzanne were stockier, and tousled, and wind-burned. But not older. Maybe they had all been college friends together, still a threesome more than five but less than ten years after graduation.

Henry said, "The woods are actually awesome, Helen."

He said it kindly, full of enthusiasm. No hint of

confrontation or scolding. Just a guy who loved the woods, unable to understand why his friend didn't. He seemed genuinely intrigued by the possibility that he could walk where no other human had ever trod, in all of history. Reacher asked where they were all from originally, and it turned out that Henry and Suzanne were from the suburbs, of Toronto and Vancouver respectively, and it was Helen who was the real country girl, from what she called the trackless wastes of northern Ontario province. In which case he figured she was entitled to her opinion. She had earned it, presumably.

Then they asked where he was from, and his bio filled the next few miles. The Marine family, always moving, the dozen elementary schools, the dozen high schools, then West Point, then the U.S. Army, the military police, always moving all over again, some of the same countries, some new, never in one place long enough to notice. Then the drawdown, and the discharge, and the wandering. The hitched rides, the walking, the motels. The aimlessness. No particular place to be. Henry thought it was all very cool, Suzanne less so, Reacher thought, and he figured Helen didn't think it was cool at all.

They slowed and turned left onto a narrow rural two-lane that speared straight west through the trees. There was a rusted enamel sign that said *Naismith 40 miles*. It was possible the road had once had shoulders, but they were long overgrown with underbrush and broadleaf trees that reached forty feet tall. In places their branches met overhead, so that for hundreds of yards at a time it was like driving through a green tunnel. Reacher watched out the windows, left and right. Either side he could see not more than five or six feet into the vegetation. He wondered how much more primeval woods could get. Brambles and brush were tangled thigh-high, and the air looked dank and still. The ground looked soft and springy, densely matted with leaf litter, damp and fecund. The blacktop ribbon ahead had turned gray with age, and the heat it was holding made the air above it thick with tiny insects. After five miles the windshield was soupy with slime, from a million separate impacts.

Reacher asked, "Have you been here before?"

"Once," Henry said. "We walked south to Center Mountain. Which was boring, man. I like to stay below the tree line. I guess I'm a forest dweller."

"Are there animals in there?"

"Bears for sure. Plenty of small stuff, obviously. But the underbrush never gets eaten, so there's no deer. Which is interesting as to why. Predation, most likely. But by what? Mountain lions, maybe. Or wolves, but no one ever sees them or hears them. But there's something in there, that's for sure."

"You sleep in a tent?"

"Pup tent," he said. "No biggie. Double-bag your food, wash around your mouth in a stream, and there's nothing for the critters to smell. Bears like to eat, but if you don't lay out a picnic for them they'll leave you alone. But you know all this, right? I mean, doesn't the army train everywhere? I thought you got sent out in every kind of terrain."

"Not in a forest like this," Reacher said. "Can't move through it, certainly can't move vehicles through it, can't shoot through it. Clearing it with napalm and explosives would take forever. So we'd have to maneuver around it. Best kind of natural barrier there is."

They drove on, over a surface that got progressively worse. The encroaching brush had nibbled out fist-sized bites of blacktop on both sides, and then tree roots had punched out deeper holes, and the winter freezes had elongated the cracks, and the state's fixes had been infrequent and hasty. The old van's suspension creaked and pattered. Overhead the green tunnels became more or less continuous. In places leafy vines hung down and whipped the roof.

Then exactly an hour after leaving Route 11 there was a cleared length of shoulder with a board sign on it, which had words burned into it with a hot poker: *Welcome to Naismith, the Gateway to the Wilderness.* Which Reacher felt was about an hour too late. He felt that particular threshold had been passed long ago.

Henry slowed the van and the road curved to the left and came out in a clearing about the size of a football stadium. Dead ahead was a lake shaped like a crooked finger, first pointing north and then curling east. The road became a kind of Main Street leading straight to the shore. At the far end was a kayak pier, and left and right were low wooden buildings, with vacation cabins near the water, and a general store and a diner and small residences further from it. There were side streets made of the same battered gray blacktop. Naismith, Maine. A miniature town, in the middle of nowhere.

Suzanne said, "I'm hungry."

"I'll buy lunch," Reacher said. "That's the least I can do."

Henry parked the van in front of the diner and shut down the motor. The world went silent. They all climbed out, and they all stood and stretched. The air was somewhere halfway between fresh and heavy, the tang of the lake water mixed with the smell of the trees, and there was no sound beyond a subliminal drone from a billion tiny insect wings. There was no wind, no rustling leaves, no lapping waves. Just hot stillness.

The diner was all wood, inside and out, rough stained boards worn shiny in places by hands and elbows and shoulders. There were pies in glass cases and eight square tables draped in red checkered tablecloths. The waitress was a flinty woman of about sixty, wearing a pair of men's eyeglasses and carpet slippers. Two tables were occupied, both by people who looked more like Henry and Suzanne than Helen. The waitress pointed to an empty table and went to get menus and glasses of water.

The food was the same as Reacher had eaten in a thousand other diners, but it was adequate, and the coffee was fresh and strong, so he was happy. As were the others, not that they were paying much attention to what they were eating and drinking. They were talking amongst themselves, running through their plans. Which sounded straightforward enough. They were all going to spend the night in pre-booked cabins, and at first light Henry and Suzanne were going to set out walking, and Helen was going to drive back to Route 11 and look for whatever she could find. Four days later they were all going to meet again at the far end of the trail. Simple as that.

Reacher paid the check, said his goodbyes, and left them there. He didn't expect to see them again.

From the diner he strolled down to the kayak pier and walked out to the end of it, and stood with his toes above open water. The lake was a bright blue spear pointing north and then turning east into the distance, more than ten miles long, probably, but not more than a couple hundred yards across at its widest bulge. Overhead was a vast high bowl of summer sky, completely cloudless, unmarked except for wispy contrails eight miles up, from transatlantic jet planes heading to and from Europe, in and out of Boston and New York and Washington, D.C. Great Circle routes, way up over Canada and Greenland, and then dropping down again to London and Paris and Rome. Straight lines on a spherical planet, but not on a flat paper map.

At ground level the forest crowded in on both sides of the lake, unbroken, a continuous green canopy covering everything that wasn't liquid. There were hundreds and hundreds of square miles of it. Ten thousand years of undisturbed nature, Henry had said, which was exactly what it looked like. The earth had warmed, the glaciers had retreated, seeds had blown in, rain had fallen, and a hundred generations of trees had grown and died and grown again. Elsewhere on the giant continent people had cut them down to clear fields for farming, or for lumber to build houses, or to burn in stoves and steam locomotives, but some parts had been left alone, and maybe always would be. You could be the first human ever to set foot, Henry had said, and Reacher had no doubt he was right.

He walked back past the vacation cabins, which were all quiet. People were out and about in other places, clearly, doing whatever it was they were there to do. He found a turn to the left, which was basically north, where there was a hundred-yard side street, which he followed, and at the end of it he found a wooden arch, lashed together from bark-stripped trunks stained dark brown, like a ceremonial thing. A literal gateway to the wilderness. Beyond it the trail started. It ran straight for twenty yards, all beaten flat by booted feet, and then it turned a corner and disappeared. Next stop, the town called Cripps, four days away.

He stepped under the arch and stood still on the first yard of the trail. Then he moved forward, twenty paces, to the first turn. He took it and walked onward, another twenty paces, another twenty yards, and stopped again. The trail was about four feet wide. Either side the forest crowded in. The trunks were spiked with dead branches all the way to the canopy far overhead. The trees had grown tall and straight, racing for the light. They were two or three feet apart in some places, and more or less touching in others. Some were ancient and mature, all gnarled and burled and a yard across, and some were younger and slimmer and paler, exploiting the gaps, like opportunistic weeds. Below chest height the undergrowth was dense and tangled, a mess of dark-leaved thorny runners snaking among dry and brittle twigs. The air was still and completely silent. The light was green and dim. He turned a full circle. He was forty yards from the ceremonial arch, but he felt like he was a million miles from anywhere.

He walked on, another twenty paces. Nothing changed. The path wandered left and right a little. He guessed some kind of parks authority kept the underbrush trimmed back, and left it to passing feet to crush new seedlings. He guessed without that kind of human intervention the trail would close up in a year or two. Three, tops. It would become impassable. Reclaimed by nature. He guessed wider bulges had been hacked out here and there, for campsites. For the pup tents. Near streams, maybe. There was nowhere else to sleep at night.

He stood for a minute more, in the green filtered light and the eerie silence. Then he turned around and walked back to Naismith's token Main Street, and he followed it out the way they had driven in, to the board sign on the shoulder, with the welcome. But there was no traffic leaving town, and after a moment's reflection he realized there wouldn't be, not until the next morning. Presumably the checkout time for the vacation cabins was eleven or noon, which meant that day's exodus was already over. The diner and the general store would need occasional deliveries, but the odds were long that a returning truck would be passing by anytime soon. He stood in the heavy silence a minute longer, for no real reason other than he was enjoying it, and then he retraced his steps, through the town toward the lake.

The vacation cabins were laid out haphazardly, like a handful of dice thrown down. Reacher figured the location furthest from the water would be the least desirable, and sure enough found it was being used as some kind of a resident manager's accommodations, with a front room done up as an office, with one of its windowpanes converted to an opening hutch, which had a shelf behind it with a little brass bell and a ballpoint pen on a chain. He rang the bell and a long moment later an old guy stepped up, slowly, like he had arthritis. Yes, he had vacancies. The overnight charge was a modest sum. Reacher paid cash and signed his name with the pen on the chain, and got a key in return, to what turned out to be a tiny wooden house that smelled hot and moldy. Not a prime position, but it had a partial sideways view of the lake. The rest of the view was all trees, inevitably. There was a bed and two chairs, and a bathroom and kitchen facilities, and a short shelf with creased and battered paperback books on it. Outside in back there was a small deck with two folding chairs slung with faded and sun-rotted fabric. Reacher spent the rest of the afternoon in one of them, with his feet up on the other, reading a book from the shelf, warm, alone, relaxed, as happy as he could remember being.

He woke at seven in the morning but lay in bed a whole extra hour, stretched out like a starfish, to let the walkers and the boaters get through the diner ahead of him. He figured they would be looking for an early start. He wasn't. He figured about ten o'clock would be optimum, to catch the first wave of departures. A ride back to Route 11 was all he needed. To I-95 would be a bonus, and Bangor or Portland or anyplace further south would be the icing on the cake. He figured he would head to New York next. Yankees tickets would be easy to get. The dog days of summer, folks out of town, plenty of space in the high seats in the sun.

He showered and dressed and packed, which consisted of folding his toothbrush and putting it in his pocket. He saw the maid on her way between two other cabins, and told her his was vacant and ready for her. She looked like she could have been the waitress's sister, from the diner, and probably was. He walked on, thinking about coffee, and pancakes, and a corner table in a quiet empty room, and maybe someone's abandoned newspaper to read.

He didn't get the quiet empty room.

Henry and Suzanne were in there, with about nine other people, all milling about, all talking in a tense and agitated fashion, like a scene in a movie where folks find out the mining company has poisoned their water. They all turned to look at him as he stepped inside. He said, "What's up?"

Henry said, "They closed the trail."

"Who did?"

"The cops. State, I think. They strung tape across the entrance."

"When?"

"In the night."

"Why?"

"No one knows."

"They won't tell us," Suzanne said. "We've been calling all morning. All they'll say is the trail is closed until further notice."

Another guy said, "It's closed at Cripps, too. We started that end last year. I still have the motel number. Same situation. Tape between the trees."

Reacher said, "It's a four-day walk, right? There must be a bunch of people still in there. Maybe something happened."

"Then why won't they tell us?"

Reacher said nothing. Not his problem. All he wanted was pancakes. And coffee, more urgently. He looked for the waitress, and caught her eye, and found an empty table.

Henry followed him straight to it. "Can they do that?"

Reacher said, "Do what?"

"Close the trail like that."

"They just did."

"Is it legal?"

"How would I know?"

"You were a cop."

"I was a military cop. I wasn't a park ranger."

"It's a public resource."

"I'm sure there's a good reason. Maybe someone got eaten by a bear."

One by one the whole disgruntled group came over and gathered around. Eleven people standing up, Reacher sitting down. The guy who still had the number for the Cripps motel asked, "How do you know that?"

Reacher said, "Know what?"

"That someone got attacked by a bear."

"I said maybe. Like a joke."

"Bear attacks aren't very funny."

A guy said, "Maybe it's just a drill."

"What kind of drill?"

"Like a rehearsal. For a medical emergency, maybe. For the first responders."

"Then why would they say until further notice? Why wouldn't they say until lunchtime today, or some such?"

Another guy asked, "Who should we call?"

Suzanne said, "They're not telling us anything."

"We could try the governor's office."

Another woman said, "Like he's going to tell us anything, if the others aren't."

"It can't be bears."

"Then what is it?"

"I don't know."

Suzanne looked at Reacher and said, "What should we do?"

Reacher said, "Go for a walk someplace else."

"We can't. We're stuck here. Helen's got the van."

"She left already?"

"She didn't want to eat breakfast here."

"Can't you call her?"

"No bars."

"Bars aren't open yet."

"I mean no cell phone coverage here. We can't call her. We tried, from the pay phone in the store. She's off the network somewhere."

"So go kayaking instead. That's probably just as much fun."

Henry said, "I don't want to go kayaking. I want to walk the trail."

Eventually the small crowd wandered away again, out through the door to the parking lot, still mumbling and grumbling, and the waitress came by to take Reacher's order. He ate and drank in silence, and he got the check, and he paid in cash. He asked the waitress, "Does the trail get closed a lot?"

She said, "It never happened before."

"Did you see who did it?"

She shook her head. "I was asleep."

"Where's the nearest state police barracks?"

"The kayak owner says it was soldiers."

"Does he?"

She nodded. "He says he saw them."

"In the middle of the night?"

She nodded again. "He lives nearest the arch. They woke him up."

Reacher put an extra dollar on her tip and walked out to the street. He turned right and took a step in the direction of out of town, but then he stopped and went back and found the hundred-yard side street that led to the trail.

Henry and Suzanne were right there at the arch. Just the two of them. They had their backpacks on. The arch had tape tied across it, three lengths, one knee-high, one waist-high, and one chest-high, all two-inch plastic ribbon, blue and white, twisted on itself in places, saying *Police Line Do Not Cross*.

Henry said, "See?"

Reacher said, "I believed you the first time."

"So what do you think?"

"I think the trail is closed."

Henry turned away and stared at the tape, like he could make it dematerialize by willpower alone. Reacher walked back to Main Street, and onward out of town, to the welcome board on the shoulder. Ten minutes, he thought. Maybe less. He figured that morning's exodus would be brisker than normal.

But the first vehicle he saw was coming, not going. Into town, not out. And it was a military vehicle. A Humvee, to be precise, painted up in black and green camouflage. It roared past, all thrashing gears and whining tires. It took the curve and disappeared.

Four guys in it, hard men, all in the new army combat uniform.

Reacher waited. A minute later a car came driving out of town, but it was full. Two in the front, two in the back. No room for a hitchhiker, especially one as large as Reacher. He recognized people he had seen in the diner, disconsolate and complaining, boots on and ready, backpacks piled in the corner, no place to go.

He waited.

Next up was another Humvee, heading in, not out. Roaring engine, thrashing drive train, howling tires, four guys wearing ACUs. Reacher watched it around the corner and even at a distance he heard it slow, and change gear, and speed up again. A right-hand turn, he thought, and he would have bet the few bucks in his pocket it was heading for the wooden arch.

He stared after it, thinking.

Then another car came driving out of town. A sedan. Two people. An empty back seat. The driver was the guy who still had the number for the motel in Cripps. He slowed and stopped and the woman next to him buzzed her window down. She asked, "Where are you headed?"

Reacher said nothing.

She said, "We're going back to Boston."

Which would have been great. Three hours from New York. Multiple routes. Lots of traffic. But Reacher said, "I'm sorry, but I changed my mind. I'm going to stay here."

The woman shrugged and the car took off without him.

He walked back to the cabin rental office and rang the bell. His cabin was still available. He paid for another night, and got the same key in return. Then he headed for the arch, a hundred yards along the side street, and when he got there he found the two Humvees and their eight occupants. The Humvees were parked side by side, noses out, blocking the whole width of the road. Their occupants already had their boots on the ground. They were all armed with M16s. They were setting up an exclusion zone. Reacher knew the signs. Two squads, four hours on, four hours off. Military police, for sure. Reacher knew those signs, too. Not the National Guard, either. Regular U.S. Army. Not a drill. No one was going to get past them.

There was no sign of Henry or Suzanne.

Reacher said, "Sergeant?"

One of the grunts turned around. Chevrons on the tab in the center of his chest. Twenty years younger than Reacher, at least. A whole different generation. The military police has no secret handshake. No magic word. And no real inclination to shoot the breeze with some ancient geezer, no matter who he might claim to have been, one day long ago, way back when.

The sergeant said, "Sir, you need to step back ten yards."

Reacher said, "That would be a hell of a long step, wouldn't it?"

Two PFCs were hauling sawhorses out of a Humvee. A-shaped ends, and planks to fit between, marked *No Entry*.

Reacher said, "I'm guessing your orders are to keep people out of the woods. Which is fine with me. Knock yourselves out. But close observation of the terrain will reveal the woods start where the woods start, not a Humvee's length plus ten yards down the street."

The sergeant said, "Who are you?"

"I'm a guy who once read the Constitution."

"This whole place is woods."

"So I noticed."

"So back off now."

"Unit?"

"345th MP."

"Name?"

"Cain. Spelled *C, A, I, N,* with no *E.*"

"You got a brother?"

"Like I haven't heard that one before."

Reacher nodded. He said, "Carry on the good work, sergeant," and he turned and walked away.

He went back to the cabin rental office, and rang the bell again. The old guy stepped up, creakily, and Reacher asked him, "Are my friends still here? The people I came in with? Henry something and Suzanne something?"

"They checked out early this morning."

"They didn't come back again?"

"They're gone, mister."

Reacher nodded, and headed for his hut, where he spent the next four hours on the back deck, sitting in one lawn chair, his feet up on the other, watching the sky. It was another beautiful day, and he saw nothing except bright blue emptiness, and wispy contrails arching way overhead, eight miles up.

In the early afternoon he headed to the diner for a late lunch. He was the only customer. The town felt deserted. No trail, no business. The waitress didn't look happy. Not just about the lack of revenue. She was on the wall phone, listening to someone, concern on her face. A tale of woe, clearly. She hung up after a long minute and walked over to Reacher's table.

She said, "They're sending search parties south from Cripps. For the walkers. They're grabbing them and hustling them out. Real fast."

Reacher said, "Soldiers?"

She nodded. "Lots of them."

"Weird."

"That's not the worst of it. They're holding them for questioning afterward. They want to know if they saw anything."

"Soldiers are doing that, too?"

"Men in suits. My friend thinks they're the FBI."

"Who's your friend?"

"She works at the motel in Cripps."

"What are people supposed to have seen?"

"All we have is rumors. A bear gone rogue, maybe. A man-eater. Packs of wild coyotes, mountain lions, bigfoot monsters. Or some vicious murderer escaped from the penitentiary. Or wolves. Or vampires."

"You believe in vampires?"

"I watch the television, same as anyone else."

"It's not vampires," Reacher said.

"There's something in those woods, mister."

Reacher ate a tuna melt and drank coffee and water, and then he headed back to the arch for a second look. The sawhorses were in place, ten yards upstream of the parked Humvees. Four grunts were standing easy, weapons shouldered. A show of force. *No entry.* Not a drill. Pleasant duty, overall, given the season. Winter would have been much worse.

Reacher walked back to town. Just as he hit Main Street the colorless minivan came around the corner. Helen was at the wheel. She pulled over next to him and buzzed her window down.

She said, "Have you seen Henry and Suzanne?"

He said, "Not since breakfast time."

"People say the trail is closed."

"It is."

"So I came to pick them up."

"Good luck with that."

"Where are they?"

"I think Henry is a hard man to dissuade."

"They went anyway?"

"That's my guess."

"After it was closed?"

"There was a brief window of opportunity. After the tape went up, before the soldiers arrived."

"I heard about the soldiers."

"What else have you heard?"

"There's something bad in the woods."

"Vampires, maybe," Reacher said.

"This isn't funny. I heard it might be escaped prisoners or rogue military units. Something very dangerous. Everyone is talking. It's on the local AM station. There are anchors in Cripps already."

"You want a cup of coffee?"

Helen parked in front of the diner, and they went in together, to the same table Reacher had used before. The waitress brought coffee, and then hustled away and got on the wall phone again. To her friend in Cripps, presumably. For updates, and gossip, and rumor.

Helen said, "Henry is an idiot."

"He likes the woods," Reacher said. "Can't blame him for that."

"But there's something in there now, obviously."

"I guess there is."

"Which he must have known. It's not brain surgery. He's an idiot, but he's not an *idiot*. But he went in anyway. And dragged Suzanne in with him. He is an idiot. Both sorts."

"Suzanne could have said no."

"Actually, she's just as bad. No impulse control. I heard they have search parties moving south from Cripps."

Reacher nodded. "I heard that, too. Straight from the horse's mouth. Or slightly secondhand, I suppose. Our waitress has a friend up there."

"What are they searching for?"

"People like Henry and Suzanne. They're getting them out and asking questions about what they saw."

"But they'll miss Henry and Suzanne. Won't they? It's inevitable. They're expecting a three-day pipeline. They'll stop when they get all the people who started out yesterday morning. Henry and Suzanne will be twenty-four hours behind them. They'll leave them in there. With whatever else is in there. This is not good."

"It's a big woods."

"The thing could be roaming and hunting. Or if it's escaped prisoners they'll stick close to the trail anyway. They would have to. Henry and Suzanne will be in there alone with them."

Reacher said, "It's not escaped prisoners."

"How do you know?"

"I went to see the soldiers at the arch. They're military police, like I was. But technically what they're doing isn't entirely kosher. The military can't perform civilian law enforcement duties. There are all kinds of rules about that. But their sergeant told me his unit number with no hesitation at all. And then he told me his name, just as fast. He even spelled it out for me. *Cain,* with no *e.*"

"What does all that mean?"

"It means he's not afraid of anything. So he can get right in my face. Which means he has a solid gold get-out-of-jail-free card. Which must be urgent orders from somewhere very high up. From an unimpeachable source. As in, if some citizen like me makes a fuss, I'm going to get crushed by the machine. He's going to get a medal. Which makes this a national security issue. It's showing all the signs. And people escaped from the penitentiary isn't national security. That's a state affair."

Helen was quiet for a second.

Then she said, "A national security issue could be a rogue military unit. Or a band of terrorists. Or escaped prisoners from Homeland Security. Or some kind of mutant has gotten free. Like a genetic experiment. Or someone else's genetic experiment, *set* free. On purpose. Maybe this is an attack. And they're right there in it."

"It's none of the above," Reacher said.

"How do you know?"

"Because I sat in a chair all morning and watched the sky."

"Which told you what?"

"No circling spotter planes, no drones, no helicopters. If they were hunting a warm-blooded creature or creatures, they'd have been up there all day with heat-seeking cameras. And air-to-ground radar, and whatever other fancy things they have now."

"So what do you think they're looking for?"

"They aren't looking. I told you that. No aerial surveillance."

"Then what aren't they looking for?"

"Something with no heat signature, and too small to show up on radar."

"Which would be what?"

"I have no idea."

"But something they don't want us to see, obviously. Something we can't know about."

"Evidently."

"It could be a cold-blooded creature. Like a snake."

"Or a vampire. Are they cold-blooded?"

"This isn't funny. But OK, maybe it's not a creature at all. Maybe it's a piece of secret equipment. Inert, somehow."

"Possibly."

"How did it get in there?"

"That's a great question," Reacher said. "I think it must have fallen off an airplane."

They got refills of coffee, and Helen worried away at the problem in her mind, and eventually she said, "This is very bad indeed."

Reacher said, "Not really. Henry and Suzanne don't have much to fear from a piece of inert equipment. It's not going to jump up and bite them in the ass."

"But it is. That's exactly what it's going to do. Figuratively speaking. They're in the woods illegally, twenty-four hours behind anyone else. That looks secretive. Like their job is to find the thing and smuggle it out. Suppose it's a bomb or a missile? That happens, right? Bombs and missiles fall off airplanes. Accidentally. Sometimes, right? I read it in a book. But more likely deliberately. Like it's one big conspiracy. What do we do if Henry and Suzanne are taken to be the designated retrieval party? It wouldn't take much imagination. They sneak in through the tape, they're all alone in a deserted twenty-four-hour time window, their job is to grab the missile ahead of your government, and pass it on down the chain, until one day an airliner comes down at JFK and it's 9/11 all over again."

"Henry and Suzanne are hikers. Wilderness enthusiasts. It's the summer vacation. They're Canadians, for God's sake."

"What does that mean?"

"Nicest people in the world. Almost as good as being Swiss."

"But whatever, they'll check them out."

"Names and numbers, in a couple of databases. Nearest thing to doing nothing at all."

"Suzanne has a history."

Reacher said, "What kind?"

"She's a lovely person. You have to understand that. She has sympathy for everybody."

"Is that a problem?"

Helen said, "Of course it is. Because *everybody* means everybody. Plain English. Which means if you focus the spotlight one particular way, you can see sympathies going where your country doesn't want them to go. Out of context and more than balanced by other things elsewhere and not at all fair, but facts are facts."

Reacher said nothing.

Helen said, "And she's very passionate politically. And very active."

"How active is very active?"

"It's what she does. Like a job. Henry runs the bike shop on his own most of the time."

"So she's in more than a couple of databases. A couple hundred, at least."

"Red-flagged in most of them, probably. I mean, she's not Che Guevara or Chairman Mao, but computer memory is very cheap these days, and they have to fill it up with something. She's in the top million, I'm sure. And I'm equally sure they have pre-programmed responses ready. The screens will light up like a Christmas tree and she'll be hauled off to Egypt or Syria. She'll be in the system. They might let her come home in a year or so, all weird and slightly off. If she lives through it."

Reacher said, "It might not be a missile. It might be some boring black box full of coded data. Maybe it fell off a satellite, not an airplane. No possible use to anyone else. Which makes the idea of a retrieval party insane to them. They're not going to be chasing shadows. If they see Henry and Suzanne coming around the corner, dressed like hikers, walking like hikers, and sounding like hikers, then they're going to call them hikers. They're going to give them a drink of water and send them on their way."

"You can't be sure of that."

"It's one of a number of possibilities."

"What are all the others?"

"I guess some of them could come uncomfortably close to the kind of thing you're worried about."

"How many of them?"

"Practically all of them, really. Bottom line is she's a foreign national with a history in the middle of a national security lockdown."

Helen said, "We have to go get them out."

Resistance was futile. Reacher knew that right away. He was a realistic man. A Stoic, in the original meaning of the name. A guy who accepted circumstances for what they were, and didn't seek to change them. He asked, "How fast do they walk?"

Helen said, "Not very. They're communing, not commuting. They're stepping off the path and making footprints in the virgin earth. They're looking at everything. They're listening to the birds and the wind in the trees. We should be able to catch up to them."

"Better to get ahead of them."

"How?"

They started in the diner's kitchen, where the bewildered day guy gave up two machete-like weapons. Cleavers, possibly, for cutting meat. Then they hustled down to the kayak dock and rented a slim two-place vessel. It was bright orange in color. It had waterproof fabric around the seat holes. To tie around the rower's waist, Reacher figured. Like wearing the boat like a pair of pants. To stop water getting in. Which he thought was overkill, on a fine day in August, on an inland body of water about as placid as a millpond.

Reacher took the back seat. It was a tight fit. Helen looked better, in the front. The rental guy let go of a rope and they paddled away, chaotic at first, then getting better. Much better. All about building up a rhythm. Long, steady, propulsive strokes. Like swimming. But faster than swimming. Faster than walking, too. Certainly faster than communing, and putting prints in the virgin earth, and listening to birds. Maybe twice as fast. Maybe more. Which was good. The lake turned like a crooked come-on finger, which gave them a natural outflanking maneuver, at first running parallel to the trail, and then cutting up and in, all the way to the far end of the finger, right to where the nail would be, which would be as near the trail as they could hope to get. Because after the turn the lake dug into the woods, just like Maine itself dug into Canada. Like a blade. Like a knife wound. The far tip might dump them just a couple hundred yards from the path itself. A quarter mile, maximum. The primeval part of the forest was not wide at that location. Because of the water. Like a bay. Like a river estuary.

They paddled on. Not a sprint. A middle-distance race. The mile, maybe. Black-and-white film of skinny gentlemen pounding around cinder tracks. Baggy white shirts. Grimaces. Digging in. Enduring. The machetes were between Reacher's feet. They slid backward and forward, backward and forward, with the pulse of every stroke.

The far tip of the finger was a rocky V tight up against tree trunks. Which made it easy to steady the ship prior to getting out. There were handholds everywhere. But it made it hard to move more than a foot ashore. It was all about squeezing through, leading with one shoulder, leading with the other, being careful with the trailing foot, like crossing a crowded room at a party, except with statues instead of people, all of them as solid as iron. And not in candlelight, but in a strange green glow, from the bright sun behind a billion still and silent leaves.

And any wider clearing was no real bonus, either, because they were all tangled with vines and brambles, which to some extent could be blundered through, but nine times out of ten the machetes were needed in the last yard or two, to release ankles all snarled up and fresh out of momentum.

Reacher asked, "You OK?"

Helen answered, "In what way?"

"You don't like the woods."

"You want to take three wild-ass guesses as to why? As in, right now this minute?"

They pressed on, Reacher leading, making a big hole in the vegetation, Helen coming through it close behind, both of them making prints where maybe no human had ever walked before. And then they sensed rather than saw the trail up ahead, a slit, a discontinuity, an absence. A hole in the woodland sounds. A change in the sky. A seam in the canopy. And then they came upon it, stepping over gnarled trunks bent like knees, turning, squeezing, and finally falling out on what was literally the beaten track. The air above it was damp and still, and noticeably cool.

Helen said, "So are we ahead of them?"

"I think so," Reacher said. "For sure, if they're sightseeing. Maybe not, if something spooked them and they hustled. But I'm pretty sure we made it. And when it comes to speculation, I'm a very cautious man."

"So we wait here?"

"The most efficient use of our time would be to move and meet them head-on. By definition we'd turn them around closer to Naismith than here."

"We might be walking away from them."

"Life's a gamble, I guess."

"It was a spooky situation from the start. Maybe they were hustling all the way. Just to be able to say they'd done the miles. They could have passed here thirty minutes ago."

"I'm guessing they didn't hustle. They seemed really into this stuff. I think they're strolling slow, stopping all the time, looking at this and that. All on their own. It's just them and the forest. I say they're thirty minutes in front of us."

"You've done this kind of thing before, right?"

"From time to time."

"Did you get them right?"

"Some of them."

She took a breath and said, "OK, we'll hope to meet them head-on. And if we don't, I'm going to call you some very un-Canadian names. Some with several syllables."

"Sticks and stones," Reacher said.

"I'll go first," she said.

The trail was much easier underfoot, and it was a straight shot, with no twisting or dodging, which meant they could pay a little attention to things more than a foot and a half away. Of which there were many. And which in the end slowed them down more than the tripwire brambles. Because there was a lot to look at. *Primeval* was the right word. Not necessarily Reacher's thing, but he couldn't deny some sense of primitive connection. It could have been that a hundred generations of his ancestors had lived in the woods. They had to live somewhere. The trees were spotty with lichen and smooth with light green moss, and they bent and twisted and jostled for light and space, and the gloomy shapes they made seemed to talk, just faintly, like a distant hum. *Perfect ambush location ahead and left, so take care. Two defensive positions ahead and right, so plan to use the first, with the second to fall back on if necessary.* A hundred generations, and by definition all of them survived.

They walked on, through cool air, like cellar air, still and damp and undisturbed. The trail itself was soft and springy, a dark, leaf-rich loam. Like carpet.

No hikers up ahead.

Not in the first five minutes, or the first ten. Which made each new minute more and more likely. Two couples on exactly opposite vectors, one moving fast, one moving slow, fifteen minutes already gone. The window in which the encounter would have to take place was getting smaller and smaller. If it was going to happen, it was going to happen soon.

It didn't.

Not in the next five minutes, or the next ten. Which was getting arithmetically difficult. It was hard to imagine Henry and Suzanne could be slow enough to make the big numbers work. Unless they had chickened out and turned around, straight back to Naismith. Second thoughts, maybe, and an honorable retreat. They might have stepped out behind Sergeant Cain at the exact same moment Reacher and Helen had paddled away from the kayak dock.

No way of knowing.

No hikers up ahead.

Helen said, "Reacher, you blew it."

He said, "Start with the polysyllabic examples. I'm always interested."

She said, "Maybe something already happened to them."

"But what? There are no search parties coming north out of Naismith. No other hikers. The missing equipment is not jumping up and biting them in the ass. Not actually. You can say so later, figuratively, but so far nothing much can have happened to them."

"Then where are they?"

"They must be static. Maybe they pitched their tent already. Maybe they found the perfect spot."

"I think they hustled and we missed them. I think we came in behind them. You blew the call."

"Life's a gamble," Reacher said again.

They moved on, speeding up a little, ignoring the sylvan glades to their left and right, every one of them a separate curiosity, like a room in a museum. There was a new breeze high above them, and the canopy was rustling, and tree limbs were clicking and groaning. Small furtive animals made darting sounds in the underbrush. Insects hung in tight clouds, to be avoided if possible, or batted through if not.

Then the trail jinked right and left around a huge mossy bole four feet wide, and up ahead in the gloom they saw two bright objects stacked side by side on the forest floor. Red and orange and yellow, nylon, straps and buckles.

Backpacks.

"Theirs," Helen said.

Reacher nodded at her side. He had seen the backpacks before, most recently at the wilderness arch that morning, hoisted into place and ready to go. They walked on and stopped next to the luggage. It was not abandoned. Both packs were set upright, leaning one on the other. They had been carefully placed.

"They stepped off the trail," Reacher said. "A little side excursion. No point hauling bags through the brush."

"When?" Helen said.

"Recently, I hope. Which would mean they're close by."

Behind the click and the hum of the living woods there was nothing but silence all around. No gasps, no calls, no feet ripping through the tangled undergrowth.

Nothing.

Helen said, "Should we shout?"

Reacher said, "Not too loud."

"Henry? Suzanne?" She said their names like a fierce stage whisper, louder than talking, but far from yelling, with an anxious questioning cadence rising on the ends.

No response.

"Suzanne? Henry?"

No response.

She said, "They can't be far away, surely."

Reacher studied the brush to the left and the right. Logic said if they had stepped off the trail, they would have done so near their bags. No sense in stacking the packs and then choosing an exit point a hundred yards away. So Reacher knew where to start looking. But he was no kind of an expert tracker. Not out in the wilds. Not like the movies, where the guy squats down on his haunches and ponders a moment and says, *They passed this way three hours ago, and the woman has a blister on her ankle.*

But there were broken shoots and torn leaves in one location. Easy enough to imagine a planted foot, and the sweep of a short, cautious stride, and the next foot, and a second person following behind, leading with one shoulder, then leading with the other, squeezing through the gaps.

Helen said, "Should we try it?"

Reacher said, "Call their names again."

"Henry? Suzanne? Where are you?"

No response. No echo off the trees.

Reacher pushed his way into the brush, scanning ahead, looking for disturbances, for kicked twigs, for sap oozing from crushed stalks. It was an inexact process. In most places there was no obvious new direction to follow. He was forced to stop every few yards, and examine a whole arc ahead of him, and choose the least-worst possibility from among a number of equally plausible angles. He figured rabbits and other small animals could sweep blades of grass aside just as easily as a brushing foot, but only human weight could break anything thicker than a pencil, so he based his guesses on the presence or absence of bright new wood on the inside faces of busted twigs. On and on, like an algorithm, yes and no and no and yes.

Deeper into the woods.

Every ten yards they stopped and listened, the backs of their brains filtering out the normal sounds and scanning for the abnormal. But hearing nothing, not on the first stop, or the second, or the third, but the fourth time around Reacher felt he could sense held breath nearby, a tense human vibe, which the ancient part of his mind interpreted as either predator or prey, and therefore of interest either way. A hundred generations, and they all survived. Then he heard a tiny sound halfway between a wheezing click and a whirring crunch, all spiky with tiny squeaks and whistles and mechanical resonances, and bathed in faint but cavernous echo. Like a Nikon camera, but not really. An electronic imitation, reedy and insubstantial.

A cell phone, taking a picture.

And another.

Reacher pushed on, stepping high to keep clear of vines, squeezing through gaps, and then suddenly seeing Henry and Suzanne, standing shoulder to shoulder not ten feet from him, looking down, taking cell phone snaps of the thing on the ground in front of them. *No heat signature, and too small to show up on radar.* That was for damn sure.

It was a dead human, a man, small, dark-skinned, lean and ascetic, in old orange prison garb. He was on his back, and the angle of his neck and his limbs made no kind of anatomical sense. He looked soft inside, almost liquid, as if his bones were smashed and his organs crushed.

Reacher said, "He fell out of an airplane. Not off an airplane, exactly. Out through the door. Way high up. So he blacks out because he has no oxygen, or maybe the sudden cold gives him a heart attack right then and there, but either way he falls like a rag doll, and he smashes through the canopy, and he hits the forest floor, where he's DOA for sure. The canopy bounces back, so there's nothing to see from above, and he's cooling fast, down to ambient temperature, so the infrared can't find him, and as far as radar is concerned, he looks exactly like a tree root or a little pile of broken branches."

Suzanne said, "I hope he had the heart attack from the cold."

Reacher said, "The question is, did he jump or was he pushed?"

"He jumped."

"Who is he?"

"He's a Canadian citizen. He was supposed to come down in Toronto. But he missed."

"And who are you?"

"Just another Canadian citizen."

"Who are the pictures for?"

"His family."

"Who is he?" Reacher asked again.

"I see both sides," Suzanne said. "I would do anything to stop another attack. But it's getting insane now. They fly these guys from Guantánamo to Egypt and Syria, where they get a good working over, and after a while the ones who survive have to come back, because the Egyptians and the Syrians can't have them hanging about forever, but you don't want them back, because what are you going to do with them? Guantánamo is always full, and you can't just say never mind and let them go, because they've all got stories to tell."

"So what do they do with them? And tell me how you know."

"There's a network, for people of conscience. Way down in the dark web. Certain facts are established. Your ground crews bypassed a couple of failsafes, and made it possible to open the airplane door during flight. At very low speeds, and very low altitudes, mostly over the far north Atlantic, in the radar shadows, where they would come down low and slow, and open the hatch. That's what they do with them. Problem solved."

"So?"

"So word gets around, and this guy knows he's either going to die under torture or get thrown out of the plane on the way home. There's no happy ending here. So he decides to jump out the door on the outward flight. To take them by surprise. Somewhere over Toronto. To make a statement. A sympathetic foreign press, a chance to apply some external pressure."

Reacher nodded. *Like a thumb up Canada's ass.* Toronto wasn't very far away. He said, "What went wrong?"

"Not very much. They have access to information and experts of every kind. They knew the route, which never changes, and they knew the timing. It's just a question of counting the minutes in your head, and then going for it. Which I guess can't ever be totally accurate. Although he trained for months. And a gust of headwind counts for a lot, I suppose. Small errors multiply."

"Who are the pictures for?" Reacher asked again.

"His family. There's nothing else to be done. None of this exists on paper. The denials would be instant and convincing. They'd say the photos were faked. Low green light, a little grainy. Foreign radicals with a bike shop. The whole thing wouldn't last a day."

"Would it have lasted longer in Toronto?"

"They thought so. Cities and suburbs are different. There are lots of witnesses, and cops, and TV. Things don't go away so easily. They thought it could be a watershed moment."

"You seem to know a lot about how they think."

"I try to learn how everyone thinks. It's the key to understanding. Not that this was some innocent sweetheart. He was a thug straight from the Middle Ages. He was a vicious killer. I was glad he was jumping out of the plane. But he had already told them what he knew. And they were sending him anyway. Just out of habit. It's insane now."

"How did you know where to look?"

"Postgame analysis from the experts."

"Why you?"

"We were closest."

"Out of how many choices?"

"Many."

"Including Helen?"

Helen said, "Of course."

Henry said, "It was her idea to pick you up and bring you along. At least that way we get an American witness. You've seen it now. You can't un-see it."

Reacher said, "We need to get back to Naismith."

But they didn't make it far. Not as a group. They retraced their steps. It was easy to follow Reacher's blundering trail in reverse. Then thirty yards short of the path he heard noises ahead, and he saw a blink of movement through the trunks. He held out his hand in warning, and Suzanne and Helen and Henry froze behind him. He crept on without them, leaning rather than moving, straining forward, peering ahead.

Four guys in ACUs. One of which was Sergeant Cain. They were all staring at the backpacks. Carefully placed. One leaning on the other.

Reacher eased back, and they all four ducked their heads together, and he whispered, "Stay in the woods another hundred yards. Loop around. Hit the trail south of them, and then leg it. Jump in the van and head straight for home. Best of luck all the way. Don't come back again."

They all shook hands, and the three of them moved off, and Reacher waited. He gave them three minutes, and then he moved toward the four soldiers, as noisily as possible, brushing things and snapping things at every opportunity. They heard him ten yards out, and they turned as one, and their M16s came up, and Reacher heard four quiet snicks as four fire selectors were turned up a notch. Clean precise sounds, hard and real, not like the phony photo shutter.

He said, "Long guns are a poor choice in the woods, Sergeant Cain. You can aim all you want, but there's always going to be a tree in the way. That's your first mistake. Let's hope it's also your last."

Cain called back, "Are those people with you?"

"Which people?"

"The infiltrators."

"They were hikers, from Canada. I haven't seen them since this morning."

"I don't believe you."

"Let it go, sergeant. Play it smart. There are no medals in this one. By tomorrow morning it won't have happened at all."

"They might have seen evidence of a covert operation."

"They saw what they were supposed to see."

Cain said, "What does that mean?"

"Like a magician onstage," Reacher said. "A big showy flourish with the left hand, attracting all the attention, while the right hand does the real work. There are activists in the world, Sergeant Cain. We can't wish them away. They're always looking for something to piss and moan about. So we give them something. A big showy flourish with the left hand. Something to get all agitated about. But not too agitated, because after all who really gives a shit about vicious killers straight out of the Middle Ages? Meanwhile, the right hand does the important stuff undisturbed. Classic misdirection."

"Who are you?"

"I was an MP once. I was your boss's boss's boss. And my brother did a spell in military intelligence. I met some of his people. Some sly minds there, sergeant. There was an old guy called O'Day. A buck gets ten this scheme is one of his. Think about it. Hundreds of people, a secret website, all kinds of planning and scheming. It's an energy sink. Like a sponge. It keeps them where we can see them."

No answer.

"Let it go, sergeant," Reacher said again. "Play your part, which is to look sinister next to your Humvees. No one's going to thank you if you screw up your lines. These things are very carefully orchestrated."

Then Reacher stepped back and shut up, and let Cain's career caution do his work for him. After a minute Cain gave the word and all four of them formed up and jogged back the way they had come. Reacher followed five minutes behind them, but he took the precaution of looping the last hundred yards through the brush, and coming out on a parallel street. Two minutes later he was back at the welcome board, waiting for a ride out of town.

Maybe They Have
a Tradition

It started on a freezing Christmas Eve night in New York City, in a bar on Bleecker Street, in the West Village. Jack Reacher walked by, huddled in his coat collar, and he heard the thump of interesting rhythms inside. He pushed through the door into warmth and noise, and found a saxophone player and two sidemen up on a stage about the height of an orange box. But more important he found a blonde woman alone at a table for two. She was following the music. Turned out she was from Holland. She was about thirty, and over six feet tall. They talked when the band took a break. She spoke English very well.

She was a cabin attendant for KLM, which was the Royal Dutch Airlines. She said she couldn't chat for long. In fact she had to leave in twenty minutes exactly. The crew bus was coming by. She was working the night flight to Amsterdam.

They talked some more, and after twenty minutes

exactly she asked him to come with her. To Amsterdam. No charge. She had a coupon. Like a staff benefit. It was Christmas Eve. There would be empty seats.

Reacher said yes. He had no particular place to go, and all the time in the world to get there. Christmas Day in Amsterdam would be fine. He had his passport in one pocket and his folding toothbrush in another, and his ATM card and a wad of cash in a third. All he needed. As ever, he was ready to go.

They got to the airport and she was called into an emergency pre-flight briefing, and that was about the last he ever saw of her.

The problem was a snowstorm. It was due to roll over the United Kingdom, and then hit the coast of Europe. Including Amsterdam. But not yet. The plane could probably beat it home. But it didn't. The storm sped up unexpectedly. It blanketed Britain and headed onward, while high over the Atlantic the airplane passed its point of no return. The computers said it was due into Schiphol exactly when the weather front would be at its worst. It would have to divert. It would have to stop short, on a runway already snowed-upon and already cleared. Best offer was a place called Stansted, in England, in the county of Essex. Reacher saw his new friend hustle by in the distance, and another attendant told him the plan. She said his friend was sorry, but she would have to stay with the plane. He was on his own for Christmas.

Reacher was through the Stansted airport before six o'clock in the morning. Christmas Day. It was well before dawn and still dark as night. There was one cab on the rank. The driver wore a turban. Reacher asked him what lay round about. The guy said a town called Harlow in one direction, and a town called Chelmsford in another, and Cambridge about twice as far away to the north.

"Cambridge," Reacher said. He had been there on U.S. Army business. Back in the day. It had a university. And air bases nearby. Which he might need. His KLM coupon was one-way only. England was a fine country, but he couldn't stay in one place forever.

"Roads are very bad, sir," the driver said. "We won't make it to Cambridge."

"How much snow?"

"Two feet in places."

"You got here this morning," Reacher said. "Let's try for Cambridge."

They set off, and did pretty well for the first twenty miles. All the way to the middle of nowhere. Then their luck ran out. The wind had smoothed the snow over roads and walls, into glittering crusted shapes that bore no relation to what lay beneath.

The driver said, "I'm turning back."

It was still dark. All around was snow. In the far distance was a light. A house, maybe, an upper-floor window, a bulb left on all night. Maybe two miles away. All on its own. A country residence.

Reacher said, "You can let me out here."

"Are you kidding?"

"I don't like to turn back. I prefer to keep moving forward. As a matter of principle."

"No cars will come. You'll be stuck here all day. You'll freeze to death."

"I could walk. There's a house in the distance. Maybe a stately home. I could knock on the kitchen door. Maybe they have a tradition. I could get Christmas dinner below stairs. A cup of coffee, at least."

"Are you serious?"

"Nothing ventured, nothing gained."

So eventually the taxi drove away, leaving Reacher all alone in the landscape. He stood in the dark for a moment, and then he set out walking, knee-deep through the drifts, some crusty, some powder, which exploded around him as he blundered through. There was a wind blowing, laced with eddies of snow. He found a road surface under his feet, and stuck with it, and saw it was going to lead him to the corner of a high estate wall, built of stone and powdered with snow. The road led along it for about half a mile, to what looked like a pair of fancy iron gates between tall stone pillars topped with carved statues of lions. Or mythical beasts. In the pre-dawn gloom it was hard to tell.

He slogged onward, one plunging stride at a time, and he made it to the gates, which were standing open, knee-deep in snow. There was a long driveway ahead, buried in untouched white, running between avenues of bare trees straight to the house. A hundred yards or more. No tracks, no footprints. Reacher was going to be the first visitor of the day.

The gates had wrought iron words welded in as part

of the design. On the left-hand gate was *Trout,* and on the right was *Hall.* The name of the house. There were more lights showing in the front windows. Regular yellow bulbs upstairs, and twinkling reds and greens below. Christmas decorations, lit up all night.

Reacher set off down the driveway, stepping high, a yard at a time, clumsily. At the bottom of every step he felt frozen gravel underfoot. He was hungry. He hoped the cook was in a good mood. Which was never guaranteed. He had seen TV shows from Britain about country houses. Sometimes the cooks reacted badly to unexpected circumstances.

He made it to the house. It was a big old pile made of stone. The kitchen door was presumably around the back, through more deep snow. Whereas the front door was right there, and it had an iron bell-pull handle.

Reacher pulled the handle. He heard a faint sonorous *bong* inside, and then hurrying feet, and the door was flung open. A woman looked out. She was maybe fifty. She looked rich. She was wearing a formal dress. Black velvet. She looked like she had been up all night. She looked like a difficult person.

She said, "Thank goodness. Are you the doctor or the policeman?"

Reacher said, "Neither."

"Then who are you?"

"My taxi turned back because of the snow. I was hoping to get a cup of coffee."

"Taxi to where?"

"Cambridge."

"Impossible."

430 | No Middle Name

"Apparently. Merry Christmas, anyway."

The woman stared at him. The moment of decision. He was not an ideal houseguest, at first glance. He was a huge guy, all bone and muscle, not particularly good looking, and not very well dressed.

The woman said, "Did you see the doctor or the policeman out there anywhere?"

He said, "I didn't see anyone. Do you have a problem?"

"I suppose you better come in."

She backed away into the gloom inside, and Reacher followed her, to a hallway the size of a basketball court. There was a Christmas tree at least ten feet tall, and a staircase at least ten feet wide.

The woman said, "Are you sure you're not a policeman?"

"I was once," Reacher said. "In the army. But not anymore."

"Our army?"

"The U.S. Army."

"I should introduce you to the colonel. My husband."

"Why do you need a policeman? And a doctor?"

"Because someone stole my diamond pendant and my stepdaughter is upstairs having a baby."

"On her own?"

"It's the Christmas holiday. The staff left yesterday. Before the snow. There's no one here."

"Apart from you and the colonel."

"I don't know anything about babies. I never had any. I'm only her stepmother. I telephoned for her doctor almost four hours ago. And the police at the same time. I thought you must be at least one of them."

A man came down the wide stairs, holding the rail, shuffling with fatigue. He was dressed in evening wear, apart from maroon suede slippers. He came all the way down, and stood up straight, and said, "Who are you, sir?"

Reacher gave his name, and told his brief story, stranded in the snow, a lighted window in a distant house, the hopes of a cup of coffee. The man introduced himself with the rank of colonel. Reacher said in the circumstances he couldn't presume to trespass on their hospitality, and would leave at once.

The woman said, "Mr. Reacher was a policeman in the army."

The colonel said, "Our army?"

"Uncle Sam's," Reacher said. "Half a dozen different MP units."

"I wish you'd been a medic instead."

"Is there a problem?"

"It's her first baby, and it came on fast. I imagine her doctor is having a problem getting here."

"Does her doctor know her well?"

"Has done for years."

"So he'll make an effort."

"She. Her doctor is a woman. She'll make an effort."

"Therefore she could be stuck somewhere," Reacher said. "She might have tried the last couple miles on foot, like I did. It's about the only way."

"She'll freeze to death. What should we do?"

Reacher glanced at the window. He said, "We should

wait fifteen minutes. For a little more daylight. Then scan from the upstairs windows. With binoculars, if you have them. We need to look for incoming tracks that stop dead, way out there."

The colonel said, "You must have been given medical training to some degree. Our MPs seem to get plenty."

"Ours didn't include childbirth," Reacher said. "I bet yours didn't, either."

The lady of the house said, "I can't go in there. It wouldn't be appropriate."

Fifteen minutes later the snow was lit up gray, and all kinds of natural detail was visible for miles around. They started in the colonel's own bedroom, at a window facing west. They saw nothing. No abandoned car, no wandering footsteps getting weaker, and then stopping.

They set up facing north, at a window in the upstairs hallway, and saw the same nothing all over again. The wind in the night had polished the drifts to a shine, and nothing was broken.

South was the same story. A blank sheet. No footprints.

East was a different story. The only good view out was from what was about to become the delivery room. Or the maternity ward. Or whatever else you wanted to call it. Hopefully not the ICU. The colonel wouldn't go in. He said it would be unseemly. His wife had already made her position clear.

So Reacher knocked politely, and heard a gasped

come in, so he did, keeping his eyes front, explaining as he went, raising the field glasses, seeing his own tracks from earlier, curving in from the right, starting way out, coming close to the wall, and in through the gate.

But also seeing a second incoming track. From the opposite direction. Starting level with his own, but way on the left, and then homing in with the same smooth curve, but suddenly stopping. Stopping dead, some way short of the wall.

A voice from the bed said, "Have you found her?"

He said, "I think so."

"Look at me."

He did. She was a flushed brunette, squirming with discomfort, the sheet pulled up to her chin.

She said, "Go and rescue her, please. Bring her to me. I can't do this alone."

"I'm sure your stepmother would come if you really wanted her to."

"Not her. This is her fault. I saw her wearing the diamond. That was my mother's pendant. I freaked out and went into labor. Now I need help."

Reacher nodded and stepped back to the hallway. The others followed him downstairs. He said, "Get hot water ready, and blankets. The doctor could have been out there a long time."

Then he set out. Back along the driveway, using his previous footholds in reverse, straining from one to the next. Then peeling away from the gates, the other direction, in a symmetrical curve, scanning ahead to a lower horizon, battling the wind, plunging through undisturbed snow, at first seeing nothing, then seeing a shadow, and the shadow becoming a hole, and beyond it staggering footsteps leading backward to where she had started.

Two sets of footsteps, in fact.

A big hole.

Reacher floundered on. Saw two people lying in the snow. A woman in a parka, and a cop in a bulky yellow police jacket. Both were shivering and both had their eyes closed. Reacher rolled the cop aside and hauled the doctor into a sitting position. Her eyes blinked open. Beside her the cop sat up. Reacher asked him, "How long have you been out here?"

The guy checked his watch and said, "Me, about two hours. I found her car abandoned and followed her tracks in the snow. I didn't get any further than she did." His words were all broken up by shivering. They came out in spurts of steam.

The woman was very cold.

Reacher asked the cop, "How close is your vehicle?"

"Further than the house."

"Only one choice then. I'll carry her, and you carry her bag."

"Why is she even here? I thought a diamond was missing. Is someone injured?"

"The daughter of the house is having a baby, all by herself. And the diamond isn't missing. But we'll worry about that later."

"Who are you?"

"I was passing by. I thought they might give me a cup of coffee. Or even Christmas dinner."

"Why would they?"

"I thought it might be a tradition."

"What did they say?"

"They were preoccupied."

Reacher lifted the woman into his arms. He stood up and turned around and set off back the way he had come. The cop floundered behind, shorter than Reacher, unable to use his pre-made footholds, and therefore slower. Reacher hustled hard, trying to generate surplus body heat, pressing the doctor close, trying to transfer it to her. She was coming around slowly. Reacher pounded onward. Then she woke up the rest of the way fast, and she started struggling in panic.

"We're on our way," Reacher panted. "She's holding out for you."

"What time is it?"

"About three hours later than you figured it would be."

"Who are you?"

"Long story. Starts with a Dutchwoman. But that part's not important now."

"Have the contractions started?"

"Little ones, maybe. But no screaming or yelling yet. But she's all alone."

"The stepmother has a phobia. I think she had a bad experience of her own."

"She said she never had kids."

"People like that usually don't."

Reacher turned in at the gate, and staggered for balance, and set off down the driveway, galumphing from one old footprint to the next, the policeman huffing and puffing twenty steps back. They made it to the door, which opened immediately, into a flurry of hot towels and warmed blankets. Eventually the doctor passed herself fit and hurried up the stairs. The house seemed to breathe out and relax. The colonel took up a position in the upstairs hallway, pacing back and forth in a traditional style, an about-to-be grandfather just as nervous as he must have been a generation before, as an about-to-be father.

The about-to-be step-grandmother got herself halfway up the stairs, holding the rail all the way, and then she stopped, unable to go further. But she kept on gazing upward. Just waiting.

The cop joined Reacher in the back corner of the downstairs hallway, and said, "Now tell me about the diamond."

Reacher said, "It was described as a pendant. It was the first wife's, not the second. As rich as these folks are, it must have been big enough and heavy enough to notice if it's not there anymore. So she didn't lose it when they went out to dinner, which they did, because they're in party clothes, and the cook left yesterday, before the snow. The daughter didn't go with them tonight, but she saw them when they got back, because there was a big hoo-hah about her mother's diamond, during which the stepmother no doubt took it off. Then later it's missing, and because it was a big hoo-hah she doesn't specifically remember taking it off, so she projects backward and thinks it was lost at the dinner party or a coat-check boy stole it."

"So where is it?"

"The daughter picked it up. Her mother's diamond. Partly a defensive instinct, but mostly because she was about to have a baby all alone, and she wanted the comfort of clutching something of her mother's. Like a good-luck charm. They wasted your time. You'll find it in her hand or under her pillow."

"Her baby's being born on Christmas Day."

"So are a third of a million others. Don't make a big deal out of it."

"You should go look in the kitchen. The cook will have prepared in advance. They won't be eating today. Too nervous. You could get your Christmas dinner after all."

And Reacher did, alone in Trout Hall's basement kitchens, while above him the others waited. Then he left, and he never found out who was born there that day.

Guy Walks into a Bar

She was about nineteen. No older. Maybe younger. An insurance company would have given her sixty more years to live. I figured a more accurate projection was thirty-six hours, or thirty-six minutes if things went wrong from the get-go.

She was blonde and blue-eyed, but not American. American girls have a glow, a smoothness, from many generations of plenty. This girl was different. Her ancestors had known hardship and fear. That inheritance was in her face and her body and her movements. Her eyes were wary. Her body was lean. Not the kind of lean you get from a diet, but the Darwinian kind of lean you get when your grandparents had no food, and either starved or didn't. Her movements were fragile and tense, a little alert, a little nervous, even though on the face of it she was having as good a time as a girl could get.

She was in a New York bar, drinking beer, listening

to a band, and she was in love with the guitar player. That was clear. The part of her gaze that wasn't wary was filled with adoration, and it was all aimed in his direction. She was probably Russian. She was rich. She was alone at a table near the stage and she had a pile of ATM-fresh twenties in front of her and she was paying for each new bottle with one of them and she wasn't asking for change. The waitresses loved her. There was a guy further back in the room, wedged on an upholstered bench, staring at her. Her bodyguard, presumably. He was a tall wide man with a shaved head and a black T-shirt under a black suit. He was a part of the reason she was drinking beer in a city bar at the age of nineteen or less. It wasn't the kind of glossy place that had a policy about underage rich girls, either for or against. It was a scruffy dive on Bleecker Street, staffed by skinny kids trying to make tuition money, and I guessed they had looked at her and her minder and taken a snap decision against trouble and in favor of tips.

I watched her for a minute, and then I looked away. My name is Jack Reacher, and once I was a military cop, with heavy emphasis on the past tense. I have been out nearly as long as I was in. But old habits die hard. I had stepped into the bar the same way I always step anywhere, which is carefully. One thirty in the morning. I had ridden the A train to West 4th and walked south on Sixth Avenue and made the left on Bleecker and checked the sidewalks. I wanted music, but not the kind that drives large numbers of patrons outside to smoke. The smallest knot of people was next to a place with half a flight of stairs leading up to its door. There was a shiny black Mercedes sedan parked on the curb, with a driver behind the wheel. The music coming out of the place was filtered and dulled by the walls but I could hear an agile bass line and some snappy drumming. So I walked up the stairs and paid a five-dollar cover and shouldered my way inside.

Two exits. One the door I had just come through, the other indicated at the end of a long dark restroom corridor way in back. The room was narrow and about ninety feet deep. A bar on the left at the front, then some upholstered horseshoe benches, then a cluster of freestanding tables on what on other nights might have been a dance floor. Then the stage, with the band on it.

The band looked like it had been put together by accident after a misfiling incident at a talent agency. The bass player was a stout old black guy in a suit with a vest. He was plucking away at an upright bass fiddle. The drummer could have been his uncle. He was a big old guy sprawled comfortably behind a small simple kit. The singer was also a harmonica player and was older than the bass player and younger than the drummer and bigger than either one. Maybe sixty, built for comfort, not for speed.

The guitarist was completely different. He was young and white and small. Maybe twenty, maybe five feet six, maybe a hundred and thirty pounds. He had a fancy blue guitar wired to a crisp new amplifier and together the instrument and the electronics made sharp sounds full of space and echoes. The amp must have been turned up to eleven. The sound was incredibly loud. It was like the air in the room was locked solid. It had no more capacity for volume.

But the music was good. The three black guys were old pros, and the white kid knew all the notes, and when and how and in what order to play them. He was wearing a red T-shirt and black pants and white tennis shoes. He had a very serious expression on his face. He looked foreign. Maybe Russian, too.

I spent the first half of the first song checking the room, counting people, scanning faces, parsing body language. Old habits die hard. There were two guys across a table with their hands underneath it. One selling, one buying, obviously, the deal done by feel and confirmed with furtive glances. The bar staff was scamming the owner by selling store-bought beer out of an ice chest. Two out of three domestic bottles were legit, from the refrigerator cabinets, and then the third came from their own cooler. I got one of them. A wet label and a big margin. I carried the bottle to a corner seat and sat down with my back to the wall. It was at that point I saw the girl alone at her table, and her bodyguard on his bench. I guessed the Mercedes outside was theirs. I guessed Daddy was a B-grade oligarch, millions but not billions, indulging his daughter with four years at NYU and an ATM card that never stopped working.

Just two people out of eighty in the room. No big deal.

Until I saw two other guys.

They were a pair. Tall young white men, cheap tight leather jackets, heads shaved by blunt razors that had left nicks and scabs. More Russians, probably. Operators, no question. Connected, no doubt. Probably not the best the world has ever seen, but probably not the worst, either. They were sitting far apart from one another but their twin gazes were triangulated on the girl alone at the table. They were tense, determined, to some degree nervous. I recognized the signs. Many times I had felt the same way myself. They were about to go into action. So two B-grade oligarchs had a beef, and one was protecting his kid with drivers and bodyguards, and the other was sending guys around the world to snatch her. Then would come ransom, and extortion, and demands, and fortunes would change hands, or uranium leases, or oil rights, or coal or gas.

Business, Moscow style.

But not usually successful business. Kidnaps have a thousand different dynamics and go wrong a thousand different ways. Average life expectancy for a kidnap victim is thirty-six hours. Some survive, but most don't. Some die right away, in the initial panic.

The girl's pile of twenties was attracting waitresses like wasps at a picnic. And she wasn't shooing any of them away. She was taking one fresh bottle after another. And beer is beer. She was going to have to visit the restroom, soon and often. And the restroom corridor was long and dark, and it had a street exit at the end of it.

I watched her in the gaudy reflected light, with the music shrieking and pounding all around me. The two guys watched her. Her bodyguard watched her. She watched the guitarist. He was concentrating hard, key changes and choruses, but from time to time he would lift his head and smile, mostly at the glory of being up on the stage, but twice directly at the girl. The first of those smiles was shy, and the second was a little wider.

The girl stood up. She butted the lip of her table with her thighs and shuffled out from behind it and headed for the corridor in back. I got there first. The sound from the band howled through it. The ladies' room was halfway down. The men's room was all the way at the end. I leaned on the wall and watched the girl walk toward me. She was up on high heels and she was wearing tight pants and her steps were short and precise. Not drunk yet. She was Russian. She put a pale palm on the restroom door and pushed. She went inside.

Less than ten seconds later the two guys stepped into the corridor. I guessed they would wait there for her. But they didn't. They glanced at me like I was a part of the architecture and shouldered in through the ladies' room door. One after the other. The door slammed behind them.

The music played on.

I went in after them. Every day brings something new. I had never been in a women's bathroom before. Stalls on the right, sinks on the left. Bright light and the smell of perfume. The girl was standing near the back wall. The two guys were facing her. Their backs were to me. I said, "Hey," but they didn't hear. Too much noise. I caught them by the elbows, one in each hand. They spun around, ready to fight, but then they stopped. I am bigger than the Frigidaires they had been dreaming about back home. They stood still for a second and then pushed past me and pulled the door and headed out.

The girl looked at me for a moment with an emotion I couldn't read and then I left her to do what she needed to do. I went back to my seat. The two guys were already back in theirs. The bodyguard was impassive. He was watching the stage. The band was finishing up. The girl was still in the bathroom.

The music stopped. The two guys got up and headed back toward the corridor. The room was suddenly crowded with people standing and moving. I headed over to the bodyguard and tapped him on the shoulder and pointed. He took no notice. He didn't move at all, until the guitar player started backing away off the stage. Then he got up, the two movements perfectly synchronized, and I knew I had gotten it all wrong. Not an indulged daughter. An indulged son. Daddy had bought the guitar and the amp and hired backing musicians. The boy's dream. Out of the bedroom, onto the stage. His driver at the curb, his bodyguard watching all the way. Not a team of two from his rival, but a team of three. An adoring groupie. The boy's dream. A classic honeytrap. A last-minute tactical conference in the bathroom, and then action.

I shoved my way through to the back and got to the street well ahead of the bodyguard, just as the girl was hugging the boy and turning him through a half circle and pushing him toward the two guys. I hit the first one hard and the second one harder and got blood from his mouth all over my shirt. The two guys went down and the girl fled and then the bodyguard showed up. I made him give me his T-shirt. Bloodstains attract attention. Then I left through the front. The obvious move would have been to turn right, so I turned left, and I got the 6 train at Bleecker and Lafayette, heading north, the last-but-one car. I settled in and checked the faces. Old habits die hard.

No Room at the Motel

It was snowing when Reacher got out of the bus, in a part of America where it didn't snow often. It was late in the afternoon, and the street lights were on. People looked both excited and anxious at the un-accustomed weather. There was about six inches of slushy pack on the ground, and the flurries were coming down hard. Some folks looked itching to go sledding or snowballing, and others looked convinced the power was about to go out and vehicular transportation was about to become impossible for months. *Context,* Reacher thought. What was a mere sprinkle by northern standards was a big deal in the South.

He sloshed his way across the sidewalk to a humped patch of what he guessed was grass. Like a village green, with a flagpole, which had a frozen and matted Stars and Stripes hanging limply from it. The town was a mile from the interstate highway, and knew it. It was all gas stations and fast food and inns and motels. A pit stop, nothing more, all geared to what random travelers wanted. Especially that day. Already cars were pulling off and splashing through the downtown slush, searching for a place to stay an unexpected night. Anything to avoid certain death in the raging blizzard ahead.

Context, Reacher thought again. *And melodrama.* He figured he better snag a room before the panic turned into a rush. He had seen news video from time to time, of stranded travelers sprawled in motel lobbies. No room at the inn.

Which made him remember it was Christmas Eve. December twenty-fourth.

He chose the cheapest-looking place, which was a falling-down motel next to a Shell station big enough for eighteen-wheel trucks. It was a twelve-room dump with ten already taken, which made Reacher think maybe the rush had already started. The place could have been no one's first choice. It wasn't The Ritz. That was for sure.

He paid cash and got a key and walked along the row to his room, all hunched under his collar to ward off the blowing snow. Ten rooms had cars parked outside, all rimed with snow and streaked with salt, all with plates from states to the south, all laden with luggage and packages. Families, Reacher guessed, aiming to get together for the holidays, their journeys interrupted, their plans ruined, their gifts undelivered.

He unlocked his door and stepped into his room, which looked adequate in every respect. There was a bed and a bathroom. Even a chair. He shook meltwater off his shoes and sat down, and watched the flurries through a fogged window, as they whirled through yellow halos of vapor light. He figured drivers would be chickening out in waves. But they would look for accommodation first, not food, which meant the diners wouldn't crowd out for another couple of hours. He switched on the bedside light and took a paperback book from his pocket.

Ninety minutes later he was in a diner, waiting for a cheeseburger. The place was filling up and service was slow. There was a kind of manic energy in the room, from a lot of forced high spirits. Folks were trying to convince themselves they were having an adventure. Eventually his food came and he ate. The place got more and more crowded. People were coming in and just standing there, somehow defeated. The motels were full, Reacher realized. No more room at the inn. People were eyeing the diner floor. Like in the news footage. He ordered peach pie and black coffee, and settled in to wait for it.

He walked back to the motel pretty late in the evening. The snow was still coming down, but lighter. Tomorrow would be a better day. He turned in at the motel office and stopped short, to avoid walking straight into a very pregnant woman. She was with a guy, huddled aimlessly, and she had been crying.

An idling car stood by, an old three-door, rimed with snow and streaked with salt, and full of luggage and packages.

No room at the inn.

Reacher said, "Are you guys OK?"

The man said nothing, and the woman said, "Not exactly."

"Can't get a room?"

"The whole town is full."

"Should have kept on going," Reacher said. "The weather is letting up."

"I made him pull off. I was worried."

"So what do you plan to do?"

The woman didn't answer, and the man said, "I guess we'll sleep in the car."

"You'll freeze."

"What choice do we have?"

Reacher said, "When is the baby due?"

"Soon."

Reacher said, "I'll trade."

"What for what?"

"I'll sleep in your car, and you can have my room."

"We can't let you do that."

"I've slept in cars before. But never while pregnant. I imagine that wouldn't be easy."

Neither the man nor the woman spoke. Reacher took his key out of his pocket and said, "Take it or leave it."

The woman said, "You'll freeze."

"I'll be just fine."

And then they all stood around for a minute more, shuffling in the cold, but soon enough the woman took the key, and she and her partner crabbed away to the room, a little embarrassed but basically very happy, wanting to look back but not letting themselves. Reacher called a happy Christmas after them, and they turned and wished him the same. Then they went inside, and Reacher turned away.

He didn't sleep in their car. He walked over to the Shell station instead, and found a guy with a tanker with five thousand gallons of milk in it. Which had a use-by date. And the weather was clearing. The guy was willing to go for it, and Reacher went with him.

The Picture of
the Lonely Diner

Jack Reacher got out of the R train at 23rd Street and found the nearest stairway blocked off with plastic police tape. It was striped blue and white, tied between one handrail and the other, and it was moving in the subway wind, and it said: *Police Do Not Enter.* Which technically Reacher didn't want to do anyway. He wanted to exit. Although to exit he would need to enter the stairwell. Which was a linguistic complexity. In which context he sympathized with the cops. They didn't have different kinds of tape for different kinds of situations. *Police Do Not Enter In Order To Exit* was not in their inventory.

So Reacher turned around and hiked half the length of the platform to the next stairway. Which was also taped off. *Police Do Not Enter.* Blue and white, fluttering gently in the last of the departing train's slipstream. Which was odd. He was prepared to believe the first stairway might have been the site of a singular peril, maybe a chunk of fallen concrete, or a buckled nose on a crucial step, or some other hazard to life and limb. But not both stairways. Not both at once. What were the odds? So maybe the sidewalk above was the problem. A whole block's length. Maybe there had been a car wreck. Or a bus wreck. Or a suicide from a high window above. Or a drive-by shooting. Or a bomb. Maybe the sidewalk was slick with blood and littered with body parts. Or auto parts. Or both.

Reacher half turned and looked across the track. The exit directly opposite was taped off. And the next, and the next. All the exits were taped off. Blue and white, *Police Do Not Enter.* No way out. Which was an issue. The Broadway Local was a fine line, and the 23rd Street station was a fine example of its type, and Reacher had many times slept in far worse places, but he had things to do and not much time to do them in.

He walked back to the first stairway he had tried, and he ducked under the tape.

He was cautious up the stairs, craning his neck, looking ahead, and especially looking upward, but seeing nothing untoward. No loose rebar, no fallen concrete, no damaged steps, no thin rivulets of blood, no spattered fragments of flesh on the tile.

Nothing.

He stopped on the stairs with his nose level with the 23rd Street sidewalk and he scanned left and right.

Nothing.

He stepped up one stair and turned around and looked across Broadway's humped blacktop at the Flatiron Building. His destination. He looked left and right. He saw nothing.

He saw less than nothing.

No cars. No taxis. No buses, no trucks, no scurrying panel vans, with their business names hastily handwritten on their doors. No motorbikes, no Vespa scooters in pastel colors. No deliverymen on bikes, from restaurants or messenger services. No skateboarders, no rollerbladers.

No pedestrians.

It was summer, close to eleven at night, and still warm. Fifth Avenue was crossing Broadway right in front of him. Dead ahead was Chelsea, behind him was Gramercy, to his left was Union Square, and to his right the Empire State Building loomed over the scene like the implacable monolith it was. He should have seen a hundred people. Or a thousand. Or ten thousand. Guys in canvas shoes and T-shirts, girls in short summer dresses, some of them strolling, some of them hustling, to clubs about to open their doors, or bars with the latest vodka, or midnight movies.

There should have been a whole big crowd. There should have been laughter and conversation, and shuffling feet, and the kind of hoots and yelps a happy crowd makes at eleven o'clock on a warm summer's evening, and sirens and car horns, and the whisper of tires and the roar of engines.

There was nothing.

Reacher went back down the stairs, and under the tape again. He walked underground, north, to the site of his second attempt, and this time he stepped over the tape, because it was slung lower. He went up the stairs just as cautiously, but faster, now right on the street corner, with Madison Square Park ahead of him, fenced in black iron and packed with dark trees. But its gates were still open. Not that anyone was strolling in or strolling out. There was no one around. Not a soul.

He stepped up to the sidewalk and stayed close to the railing around the subway stair head. A long block to the west he saw flashing lights. Blue and red. A police cruiser was parked sideways across the street. A roadblock. *Do Not Enter.* Reacher turned and looked east. Same situation. Red and blue lights all the way over on Park Avenue. *Do Not Enter.* 23rd Street was closed. As were plenty of other cross streets, no doubt, and Broadway and Fifth Avenue and Madison, too, presumably, at about 30th Street.

No one around.

Reacher looked at the Flatiron Building. A narrow triangle, sharp at the front. Like a thin wedge, or a modest slice of cake. But to him it looked most like the prow of a ship. Like an immense ocean liner moving slowly toward him. Not an original thought. He knew many people felt the same way. Even with the cowcatcher glasshouse on the front ground floor, which some said ruined the effect, but which he thought added to it, because it looked like the protruding underwater bulge on the front of a supertanker, visible only when the vessel was lightly loaded.

Now he saw a person. Through two panes of the cowcatcher's windows. A woman. She was standing on the Fifth Avenue sidewalk, staring north. She was wearing dark pants and a dark short-sleeved shirt. She had something in her right hand. Maybe a phone. Maybe a Glock 19.

Reacher pushed off the subway railing and crossed the street. Against the light, technically, but there was no traffic. It was like walking through a ghost town. Like being the last human on Earth. Apart from the woman on Fifth Avenue. Who he headed for. He aimed at the point of the cowcatcher. His heels were loud in the silence. The cowcatcher had a triangular iron frame, a miniature version of the shape it was backing up against, like a tiny sailboat trying to outrun the liner chasing it. The frame was painted green, like moss, and it had gingerbread curlicues here and there, and what wasn't metal was glass, whole panels of it, as long as cars, and tall, from above a person's head to his knees.

The woman saw him coming.

She turned in his direction, but backed off, as if to draw him toward her. Reacher understood. She wanted to pull him south into the shadows. He rounded the point of the cowcatcher.

It was a phone in her hand, not a gun.

She said, "Who are you?"

He said, "Who's asking?"

She turned her back and then straightened again, one fast fluid movement, like a fake-out on the basketball court, but enough for him to see *FBI* in yellow letters on the back of her shirt.

"Now answer my question," she said.

"I'm just a guy."

"Doing what?"

"Looking at this building."

"The Flatiron?"

"No, this part in front. The glass part."

"Why?"

Reacher said, "Have I been asleep for a long time?"

The woman said, "Meaning what?"

"Did some crazy old colonel stage a coup d'état? Are we living in a police state now? I must have blinked and missed it."

"I'm a federal agent. I'm entitled to ask for your name and ID."

"My name is Jack Reacher. No middle initial. I have a passport in my pocket. You want me to take it out?"

"Very slowly."

So he did, very slowly. He used scissored fingers, like a pickpocket, and drew out the slim blue booklet, and held it away from his body, long enough for her to register what it was, and then he passed it to her, and she opened it.

She said, "Why were you born in Berlin?"

He said, "I had no control over my mother's movements. I was just a fetus at the time."

"Why was she in Berlin?"

"Because my father was. We were a Marine family. She said I was nearly born on a plane."

"Are you a Marine?"

"I'm unemployed at the moment."

"After being what?"

"Unemployed for many previous moments."

"After being what?"

"Army."

"Branch?"

"Military police."

She handed back the passport.

She said, "Rank?"

He said, "Does it matter?"

"I'm entitled to ask."

She was looking past his shoulder.

He said, "I was terminal at major."

"Is that good or bad?"

"Bad, mostly. If I had been any good at being a major they would have made me stay."

She didn't reply.

He said, "What about you?"

"What about me?"

"Rank?"

"Special agent in charge."

"Are you in charge tonight?"

"Yes, I am."

"Outstanding."

She said, "Where did you come from?"

He said, "The subway."

"Was there police tape?"

"I don't recall."

"You broke through it."

"Check the First Amendment. I'm pretty sure I'm allowed to walk around where I want. Isn't that part of what makes America great?"

"You're in the way."

"Of what?"

She was still looking past his shoulder.

She said, "I can't tell you."

"Then you should have told the train not to stop. Tape isn't enough."

"I didn't have time."

"Because?"

"I can't tell you."

Reacher said nothing.

The woman said, "What's your interest in the glass part of this building?"

Reacher said, "I'm thinking of putting in a bid as a window washer. Might get me back on my feet."

"Lying to a federal agent is a felony."

"A million people every day look in these windows. Have you asked them?"

"I'm asking you."

Reacher said, "I think Edward Hopper painted *Nighthawks* here."

"Which is what?"

"A painting. Quite famous. Looking in through a diner's windows, late at night, at the lonely people inside."

"I never heard of a diner called Nighthawks. Not here."

"The nighthawks were the people. The diner was called Phillies."

"I never heard of a diner here called anything."

"I don't think there was one."

"You just said there was."

"I think Hopper saw this place and made it a diner in his head. Or a lunch counter, at least. The shape is exactly the same. Looked at from right where we're standing now."

"I think I know that picture. Three people, isn't it?"

"Plus the counterman. He's kind of bent over, doing something in the well. There are two coffee urns behind him."

"First there's a couple, close but not touching, and

then one lonely guy all by himself. With his back to us. In a hat."

"All the men wear hats."

"The woman is a redhead. She looks sad. It's the loneliest picture I've ever seen."

Reacher looked through the real-life glass. Easy to imagine bright fluorescent light in there, pinning people like searchlight beams, exposing them in a merciless way to the dark streets all around, except the streets all around were empty, so there was no one to see.

In the painting, and in real life, too.

He said, "What have I walked into?"

The woman said, "You're to stand still, right where you are, and don't move until I tell you to."

"Or what?"

"Or you'll go to prison for interfering with a national security operation."

"Or you'll get fired for continuing with a national security operation after it suddenly got a civilian in the way."

"The operation isn't here. It's in the park."

She looked diagonally across the wide junction, three major thoroughfares all meeting, at the mass of trees beyond.

He said, "What have I walked into?"

She said, "I can't tell you."

"I'm sure I've heard worse."

"Military police, right?"

"Like the FBI, but on a much lower budget."

"We have a target in the park. Sitting on a bench all alone. Waiting for a contact who isn't coming."

"Who is he?"

"A bad apple."

"From your barrel?"

She nodded. "One of us."

"Is he armed?"

"He's never armed."

"Why isn't his contact coming?"

"He died an hour ago in a hit-and-run accident. The driver didn't stop. No one got the plate."

"There's a big surprise."

"He turned out to be Russian. The State Department had to inform their consulate. Which turned out to be where the guy worked. Purely by coincidence."

"Your guy was talking to the Russians? Do people still do that?"

"More and more. And it's getting more and more important all the time. People say we're headed back to the 1980s. But they're wrong. We're headed back to the 1930s."

"So your guy ain't going to win employee of the month."

She didn't answer.

He said, "Where are you going to take him?"

She paused a beat. She said, "All that's classified."

"All that? All what? He can't be going to multiple destinations."

She didn't answer.

Now he paused a beat.

He said, "Is he headed for the destination you want?"

She didn't answer.

"Is he?"

She said, "No."

"Because of suits higher up?"

"As always."

"Are you married?"

"What's that got to do with anything?"

"Are you?"

"I'm hanging in there."

"So you're the redhead."

"And?"

"I'm the guy in the hat with his back to us, all alone."

"Meaning what?"

"Meaning I'm going to take a walk. Like a First Amendment thing. Meaning you're going to stay here. Like a smart tactical thing."

And he turned and moved away, before she had a chance to object. He rounded the tip of the cowcatcher and headed diagonally across the heart of the complex junction, moving fast, not breaking stride at the curbs and the painted lines, ignoring the Don't Walk signs, not slowing at all, and finally straight into the park itself, by its southwest gate. Ahead was a dry fountain and a closed-up burger stall. Curving left was the main center path, clearly following some kind of a design scheme that featured large ovals, like running tracks.

There were dim fancy lights on poles, and the Times Square glow was bouncing off the clouds like a magnesium flare. Reacher could see pretty well, but all he saw were empty benches, at least at the start of the curve. More came into sight as he walked, but they too stayed empty, all the way to the far tip of the oval, where there was another dry fountain, and a children's playground, and finally the continuation of the path itself, curving down the other side of the oval, back toward the near tip. And it had benches, too.

And one of them was occupied.

By a big guy, all pink and fleshy, maybe fifty years old, in a dark suit. A pouchy face, and thinning hair. A guy who looked like his life had passed him by.

Reacher stepped close and the guy looked up, and then he looked away, but Reacher sat down next to him anyway. He said, "Boris or Vladimir or whatever his name was isn't coming. You're busted. They know you're not armed, but they've gone ahead and cleared about twenty square blocks, which means they're going to shoot you. You're about to be executed. But not while I'm here. Not with witnesses. And as it happens the SAC isn't happy with it. But she's getting pressure from above."

The guy said, "So?"

Reacher said, "So here's my good deed of the day. If you want to turn yourself in to her, I'll walk with you. Every step of the way. You can tell her what you know, and you can get three squares a day in prison the rest of your life."

The guy didn't answer.

Reacher said, "But maybe you don't want to go to prison the rest of your life. Maybe you're ashamed. Maybe suicide by cop is better. Who am I to judge? So my super-good deed of the day is to walk away if you tell me to. Your choice."

The guy said, "Then walk away."

"You sure?"

"I can't face it."

"Why did you do it?"

"To be somebody."

"What kind of stuff could you tell the SAC?"

"Nothing important. Damage assessment is their main priority. But they already know what I had access to, so they already know what I told them."

"And you've got nothing worthwhile to add?"

"Not a thing. I don't know anything. My contacts aren't stupid. They know this can happen."

"OK," Reacher said. "I'll walk away."

And he did, out of the park in its northeast corner, where he heard faint radio chatter in the shadows announcing his departure, and a deserted block up Madison Avenue, where he waited against the limestone base of a substantial building. Four minutes later he heard suppressed handguns, eleven or twelve rounds expended, a volley of thudding percussions like phone books slammed on desks.

Then he heard nothing more. He pushed off the wall, and walked north on Madison, imagining himself back at the lunch counter, his hat in place, his elbows drawn in, nursing a new secret in a life already full of old secrets.

If you enjoyed *No Middle Name*,
read on for a preview of the next thrilling
Jack Reacher novel by Lee Child:

The Midnight Line

A Jack Reacher Novel

Now in hardcover and ebook from
Delacorte Press

Chapter 1

Jack Reacher and Michelle Chang spent three days in Milwaukee. On the fourth morning she was gone. Reacher came back to the room with coffee and found a note on his pillow. He had seen such notes before. They all said the same thing. Either directly or indirectly. Chang's note was indirect. And more elegant than most. Not in terms of presentation. It was a ballpoint scrawl on motel notepaper gone wavy with damp. But elegant in terms of expression. She had used a simile, to explain and flatter and apologize all at once. She had written "You're like New York City. I love to visit, but I could never live there."

He did what he always did. He let her go. He understood. No apology required. He couldn't live anywhere. His whole life was a visit. Who could put up with that? He drank his coffee, and then hers, and took his toothbrush from the bathroom glass, and walked away, through a knot of streets, left and right, toward the bus depot. She would be in a taxi, he guessed. To the airport. She had a gold card and a cell phone.

At the depot he did what he always did. He bought a ticket for the first bus out, no matter where it was going. Which turned out to be an end-of-the-line place way north and west, on the shore of Lake Superior. Fundamentally the wrong direction. Colder, not warmer. But rules were rules, so he climbed aboard. He sat and watched out the window. Wisconsin flashed by, its hayfields baled and stubbly, its pastures worn, its trees dark and heavy. It was the end of summer.

It was the end of several things. She had asked the usual questions. Which were really statements in disguise. She could understand a year. Absolutely. A kid who grew up on bases overseas, and was then deployed to bases overseas, with nothing in between except four years at West Point, which wasn't exactly known as a leisure-heavy institution, then obviously such a guy was going to take a year to travel and see the sights before he settled down. Maybe two years. But not more. And not permanently. Face it. The pathology meter was twitching.

All said with concern, and no judgment. No big deal. Just a two-minute conversation. But the message was clear. As clear as such messages could be. Something about denial. He asked, denial of what? He didn't secretly think his life was a problem.

That proves it, she said.

So he got on the bus to the end-of-the-line place, and he would have ridden it all the way, because rules were rules, except he took a stroll at the second comfort stop, and he saw a ring in a pawn shop window.

The second comfort stop came late in the day, and it was on the sad side of a small town. Possibly a seat of county government. Or some minor part of it. Maybe the county police department was headquartered there. There was a jail in town. That was clear. Reacher could see bail bond offices, and a pawn shop. Full service, right there, side by side on a run-down street beyond the restroom block.

He was stiff from sitting. He scanned the street beyond the restroom block. He started walking toward it. No real reason. Just strolling. Just loosening up. As he got closer he counted the guitars in the pawn shop window. Seven. Sad stories, all of them. Like the songs on country radio. Dreams, unfulfilled. Lower down in the window were glass shelves loaded with smaller stuff. All kinds of jewelry. Including rings. Including class rings. All kinds of high schools. Except one of them wasn't. One of them was West Point 2005.

It was a handsome ring. It was a conventional shape, and a conventional style, with intricate gold filigree, and a black stone, maybe semi-precious, maybe glass, surrounded by an oval hoop that had *West Point* around the top, and *2005* around the bottom. Old-style letters. A classic approach. Either respect for bygone days, or a lack of imagination. West Pointers designed their own rings. Whatever they wanted. An old tradition. Or an old entitlement, because West Point class rings were the first class rings of all.

It was a very small ring.

Reacher wouldn't have gotten it on any of his fingers. Not even his left-hand pinky, not even past the nail. Certainly not past the first knuckle. It was tiny. It was a woman's ring. Possibly a replica for a girlfriend or a fiancée. That happened. Like a tribute or a souvenir.

But possibly not.

Reacher opened the pawn shop door. He stepped inside. A guy at the register glanced up. He was a big bear of a man, scruffy and unkempt. Maybe in his middle thirties, dark, with plenty of fat over a big frame anyway. With some kind of cunning in his eyes. Enough to calibrate a response to his sudden six-five two-fifty visitor. Driven purely by instinct. He wasn't afraid. He had a loaded gun under the counter. Unless he was an idiot. Which he didn't look. All the same, the guy didn't want to risk sounding aggressive. But he didn't want to sound obsequious, either. A matter of pride.

So he said, "How's it going?"

Not well, Reacher thought. *To be honest.* Chang would be back in Seattle by then. Back in her life.

But he said, "Can't complain."

"Can I help you?"

"Show me your class rings."

The guy threaded the tray backward off the shelf. He put it on the counter. The West Point ring had rolled over, like a tiny golf ball. Reacher picked it up. It was engraved inside. Which meant it wasn't a replica. Not for a fiancée or a girlfriend. Replicas were never engraved. An old tradition. No one knew why.

Not a tribute, not a souvenir. It was the real deal. A

cadet's own ring, earned over four hard years. Worn with pride. Obviously. If you weren't proud of the place, you didn't buy a ring. It wasn't compulsory.

The engraving said *S.R.S. 2005*.

The bus blew its horn three times. It was ready to go, but it was a passenger short. Reacher put the ring down and said, "Thank you," and walked out of the store. He hustled back past the restroom block and leaned in the door of the bus and said to the driver, "I'm staying here."

"No refunds."

"Not looking for one."

"You got a bag in the hold?"

"No bag."

"Have a nice day."

The guy pulled a lever and the door sucked shut in Reacher's face. The engine roared and the bus moved off without him. He turned away from the diesel smoke and walked back toward the pawn shop.

Chapter 2

The guy in the pawn shop was a little disgruntled to have to get the ring tray out again so soon after he had put it away. But he did, and he placed it in the same spot on the counter. The West Point ring had rolled over again. Reacher picked it up.

He said, "Do you remember the woman who pawned this?"

"How would I?" the guy said. "I got a million things in here."

"You got records?"

"You a cop?"

"No," Reacher said.

"Everything in here is legal."

"I don't care. All I want is the name of the woman who brought you this ring."

"Why?"

"We went to the same school."

"Where is that? Upstate?"

"East of here," Reacher said.

"You can't be a classmate. Not from 2005. No offense."

"None taken. I was from an earlier generation. But the place doesn't change much. Which means I know how hard she worked for this ring. So now I'm wondering what kind of unlucky circumstance made her give it up."

The guy said, "What kind of a school was it?"

"They teach you practical things."

"Like a trade school?"

"More or less."

"Maybe she died in an accident."

"Maybe she did," Reacher said. *Or not in an accident,* he thought. There had been Iraq, and there had been Afghanistan: 2005 had been a tough year to graduate. He said, "But I would like to know for sure."

"Why?" the guy said again.

"I can't tell you exactly."

"Is it an honor thing?"

"I guess it could be."

"Trade schools have that?"

"Some of them."

"There was no woman. I bought that ring. With a lot of other stuff."

"When?"

"About a month ago."

"From who?"

"I'm not going to tell you my business. Why should I? It's all legal. It's all perfectly legitimate. The state says so. I have a license and I pass all kinds of inspections."

"Then why be shy about it?"

"It's private information."

Reacher said, "Suppose I buy the ring?"

"It's fifty bucks."

"Thirty."

"Forty."

"Deal," Reacher said. "So now I'm entitled to know its provenance."

"This ain't Sotheby's auction house."

"Even so."

The guy paused a beat.

Then he said, "It was from a guy who helps out with a charity. People donate things and take the deduction. Mostly old cars and boats. But other things, too. The guy gives them an inflated receipt for their tax returns, and then he sells the things he gets wherever he can, for whatever he can, and then he cuts a check to the charity. I buy the small stuff from him. I get what I get, and I hope to turn a profit."

"So you think someone donated this ring to a charity and took a deduction on their income tax?"

"Makes sense, if the original person died. From 2005. Part of the estate."

"I don't think so," Reacher said. "I think a relative would have kept it."

"Depends if the relative was eating well."

"You got tough times here?"

"I'm OK. But I own the pawn shop."

"Yet people still donate to good causes."

"In exchange for phony receipts. In the end the government eats the tax relief. Welfare by another name."

Reacher said, "Who is the charity guy?"

"I won't tell you that."

"Why not?"

"It's none of your business. I mean, who the hell are you?"

"Just a guy already having a pretty bad day. Not your fault, of course, but if asked to offer advice I would have to say it might prove a dumb idea to make my day worse. You might be the straw that breaks the camel's back."

"You threatening me now?"

"More like the weather report. A public service. Like a tornado warning. Prepare to take cover."

"Get out of my store."

"Fortunately I no longer have a headache. I got hit in the head, but that's all better now. A doctor said so. A friend made me go. Two times. She was worried about me."

The pawn shop guy paused another beat.

Then he said, "Exactly what kind of a school was that ring from?"

Reacher said, "It was a military academy."

"Those are for, excuse me, problem kids. Or disturbed. No offense."

"Don't blame the kids," Reacher said. "Look at the families. Tell the truth, at our school there were a lot of parents who had killed people."

"Really?"

"More than the average."

"So you stick together forever?"

"We don't leave anyone behind."

"The guy won't talk to a stranger."

"Does he have a license and does he pass inspections by the state?"

"What I'm doing here is legal. My lawyer says so. As long as I honestly believe it. And I do. It's from a charity. I've seen the paperwork. All kinds of people do it. They even have commercials on TV. Cars, mostly. Sometimes boats."

"But this particular guy won't talk to me?"

"I would be surprised."

"Does he have no manners?"

"I wouldn't ask him over to a picnic."

"What's his name?"

"Jimmy Rat."

"For real?"

"That's what he goes by."

"Where would I find Mr. Rat?"

"Look for a minimum six Harley-Davidsons. Jimmy will be in whatever bar they're outside of."

Chapter 3

The town was relatively small. Beyond the sad side was a side maybe five years from going sad. Maybe more. Maybe ten. There was hope. There were some boarded-up enterprises, but not many. Most stores were still doing business, at a leisurely rural pace. Big pick-up trucks rolled through, slowly. There was a billiard hall. Not many street lights. It was getting dark. Something about the architecture made it clear it was dairy country. The shape of the stores looked like old-fashioned milking barns. The same DNA was in there somewhere.

There was a bar in a standalone wooden building, with a patch of weedy gravel for parking, and on the gravel were seven Harley-Davidsons, all in a neat line. Possibly not actual Hells Angels as such. Possibly one of many other parallel denominations. Bikers were as split as Baptists. All the same, but all different. Apparently these particular guys liked black leather tassels and chromium plating. They liked to lie back and ride with their legs spread wide and their feet sticking out in front of them. Possibly a cooling effect. Perhaps necessary. Generally they wore heavy leather vests. And pants, and boots. All black. Hot, in late summer.

The bikes were all painted dark shiny colors, four with orange flames, three with rune-like symbols outlined in silver. The bar was dull with age, and some shingles had slipped. There was an air conditioner in one of the windows, straining to keep up, dripping water in a puddle below. A cop car rolled past, slowly, its tires hissing on the blacktop. County Police. Probably spent the first half of its watch ginning up municipal revenue with a radar gun out on the highway, now prowling the back streets of the towns in its jurisdiction. Showing the flag. Paying attention to the trouble spots. The cop inside turned his head and gazed at Reacher. The guy was nothing like the pawnbroker. He was all squared away. His face was lean, and his eyes were wise. He was sitting behind the wheel with a ramrod posture, and his haircut was fresh. A whitewall buzz cut. Maybe just a day old. Not more than two.

Reacher stood still and watched him roll away. He heard a motorcycle exhaust in the distance, coming closer, getting louder, heavy as a hammer. An eighth Harley came around the corner, as slow as gravity would allow, a heavy machine, blatting and popping, the rider laying back with his feet on pegs way out in front. He leaned into a turn and slowed on the gravel. He was wearing a black leather vest over a black T-shirt. He parked last in line. His bike idled like a blacksmith hitting an anvil. Then he shut it down and hauled it up on its stand. Silence came back.

Reacher said, "I'm looking for Jimmy Rat."

The guy glanced at one of the other bikes. Couldn't help himself. But he said, "Don't know him," and walked away, stiff and bow-legged, to the door of the bar. He was pear shaped, and maybe forty years old. Maybe five-ten, and bulky. He had a sallow tan, like his skin was rubbed with motor oil. He pulled the door and stepped inside.

Reacher stayed where he was. The bike the new guy had glanced at was one of the three with silver runes. It was as huge as all the others, but the footrests and the handlebars were set a little closer to the seat than most. About two inches closer than the new guy's, for example. Which made Jimmy Rat about five-eight, possibly. Maybe skinny, to go with his name. Maybe armed, with a knife or a gun. Maybe vicious.

Reacher walked to the door of the bar. He pulled it open and stepped inside. The air was dark and hot and smelled of spilled beer. The room was rectangular, with a full-length copper bar on the left, and tables on the right. There was an arch in the rear wall, with a narrow corridor beyond. Restrooms and a pay phone and a fire door. Four windows. A total of six potential exits. The first thing an ex-MP counted.

The eight bikers were packed in around two four-tops shoved together by a window. They had beers on the go, in heavy glasses wet with humidity. The new guy was shoehorned in, pear shaped on a chair, with the fullest glass. Six of the others were in a similar category, in terms of size and shape and general visual appeal. One was worse. About five-eight, stringy, with a narrow face and restless eyes.

Reacher stopped at the bar and asked for coffee.

"Don't have any," the barman said. "Sorry."

"Is that Jimmy Rat over there? The small guy?"

"You got a beef with him, you take it outside, OK?"

The barman moved away. Reacher waited. One of the bikers drained his glass and stood up and headed for the restroom corridor. Reacher crossed the room and sat down in his vacant chair. The wood felt hot. The eighth guy made the connection. He stared at Reacher, and then glanced at Jimmy Rat.

Who said, "This is a private party, bud. You ain't invited."

Reacher said, "I need some information."

"About what?"

"Charitable donations."

Jimmy Rat looked blank. Then he remembered. He glanced at the door, somewhere beyond which lay the pawn shop, where he had made assurances. He said, "Get lost, bud."

Reacher put his left fist on the table. The size of a supermarket chicken. Long thick fingers with knuckles like walnuts. Old nicks and scars healed white against his summer tan. He said, "I don't care what scam you're running. Or who you're stealing from. Or who you're fencing for. I got no interest in any of that. All I want to know is where you got this ring."

He opened his fist. The ring lay in his palm. *West Point 2005*. The gold filigree, the black stone. The tiny size. Jimmy Rat said nothing, but something in his eyes made Reacher believe he recognized the item.

Reacher said, "Another name for West Point is the United States Military Academy. There's a clue right there, in the first two words. This is a federal case."

"You a cop?"

"No, but I got a quarter for the phone."

The missing guy got back from the restroom. He stood behind Reacher's chair, arms spread in exaggerated perplexity. As if to say, What the hell is going on here? Who is this guy? Reacher kept one eye on Jimmy Rat, and one on the window alongside him, where he could see a faint ghostly reflection of what was happening behind his shoulder.

Jimmy Rat said, "That's someone's chair."

"Yeah, mine," Reacher said.

"You've got five seconds."

"I've got as long as it takes for you to answer my question."

"You feeling lucky tonight?"

"I won't need to be."

Reacher put his right hand on the table. It was a little larger than his left. Normal for right-handed people. It had a few more nicks and scars, including a white V-shaped blemish that looked like a snakebite, but had been made by a nail.

Jimmy Rat shrugged, like the whole conversation was really no big deal.

He said, "I'm part of a supply chain. I get stuff from other people who get it from other people. That ring was donated or sold or pawned and not redeemed. I don't know anything more than that."

"What other people did you get it from?"

Jimmy Rat said nothing. Reacher watched the window with his left eye. With his right he saw Jimmy Rat nod. The reflection in the glass showed the guy behind winding up a big roundhouse right. Clearly the plan was to smack Reacher on the ear. Maybe topple him off the chair. At least soften him up a little.

Didn't work.

Reacher chose the path of least resistance. He ducked his head, and let the punch scythe through the empty air above it. Then he bounced back up, and launched from his feet, and twisted, and used his falling-backward momentum to jerk his elbow into the guy's kidney, which was rotating around into position just in time. It was a good solid hit. The guy went down hard. Reacher fell back in his chair and sat there like absolutely nothing had happened.

Jimmy Rat stared.

The barman called, "Take it outside, pal. Like I told you."

He sounded like he meant it.

Jimmy Rat said, "Now you've got trouble."

He sounded like he meant it, too.

Right then Chang would be shopping for dinner, probably. Maybe a small grocery close to her home. Wholesome ingredients. But simple. She was probably tired.

A bad day.

Reacher said, "I've got six fat guys and a runt. That's a walk in the park."

He stood up. He turned and stepped on the guy on the floor and walked over him. Onward to the door. Out to the gravel, and the line of shiny bikes. He turned and saw the others come out after him. The not-very-magnificent seven. Generally stiff and bow-legged, and variously contorted due to beer guts and bad posture. But still, a lot of weight. In the aggregate. Plus fourteen fists, and fourteen boots.

Possibly steel capped.

Maybe a very bad day.

But who cared, really?

The seven guys fanned out into a semicircle, three on Jimmy Rat's left, and three on his right. Reacher kept moving, rotating them the way he wanted, his back to the street. He didn't want to get trapped up against someone's rear fence. He didn't want to get jammed in a corner. He didn't plan on running, but an option was always a fine thing to have.

The seven guys tightened their semicircle, but not enough. They stayed about ten feet away, with better than a yard between each of them. Which made the first two plays obvious. They would come shuffling in, slowly, maybe grunting and glaring, whereupon Reacher would move fast and punch his way through the line, after which everyone would turn around, Reacher now facing a new inverted semicircle, now only six in number. Then rinse and repeat, which would reduce them to five. They wouldn't fall for it a third time, so at that point they would swarm, all except Jimmy Rat, who Reacher figured wouldn't fight at all. Too smart. Which in the end would make it a close-quarters four-on-one brawl.

A bad day.

For someone.

"Last chance," Reacher said. "Tell the little guy to

answer my question, and you can all go back to your suds."

No one spoke. They tightened some more and hunched down into crouches and started shuffling forward, hands apart and ready. Reacher picked out his first target and waited. He wanted him five feet away. One pace, not two. Better to save the extra energy for later.

Then he heard tires on the road again, behind him, and in front of him the seven guys straightened up and looked around, with exaggerated wide-eyed innocence all over their faces. Reacher turned and saw the cop car again. The same guy. County Police. The car coasted to a stop and the guy took a good long look. He buzzed his passenger window down, and leaned across inside, and caught Reacher's eye, and said, "Sir, please approach the vehicle."

Which Reacher did, but not on the passenger side. He didn't want to turn his back. Instead he tracked around the trunk to the driver's window. Which buzzed down, while the passenger side buzzed up. The cop had his gun in his hand. Relaxed, held low in his lap.

The cop said, "Want to tell me what's going on here?"

Reacher said, "Were you army or Marine Corps?"

"Why would I be either?"

"Most of you are, in a place like this. Especially the ones who hike all the way to the nearest PX to get their hair cut."

"I was army."

"Me, too. There's nothing going on here."

"I need to hear the whole story. Lots of guys were in the army. I don't know you."

"Jack Reacher, 110th MP. Terminal at major. Pleased to meet you."

The cop said, "I heard of the 110th MP."

"In a good way, I hope."

"Your HQ was in the Pentagon, right?"

"No, our HQ was in Rock Creek, Virginia. Some ways north and west of the Pentagon. I had the best office there for a couple of years. Was that your security question?"

"You passed the test. Rock Creek it was. Now tell me what's going on. You looked like you were fixing to fight these guys."

"So far we're just talking," Reacher said. "I asked them something. They told me they would prefer to answer me outside in the open air. I don't know why. Maybe they were worried about eavesdroppers."

"What did you ask them?"

"Where they got this ring."

Reacher rested his wrist on the door and opened his hand.

"West Point," the cop said.

"Sold to the pawn shop by these guys. I want to know where they got it."

"Why?"

"I don't know exactly. I guess I want to know the story."

"These guys won't tell you."

"You know them?"

"Nothing we can prove."

"But?"

"They bring stuff in from South Dakota through Minnesota. Two states away. But never enough to get the Feds interested. And never enough to put a South Dakota detective on an airplane. So it's pretty much a risk-free system."

"Where in South Dakota?"

"We don't know."

Reacher said nothing.

The cop said, "You should get in the car. There are seven of them."

"I'll be OK," Reacher said.

"I'll arrest you, if you like. To make it look good. But you need to be gone. Because I need to be gone. I can't stay here all day."

"Don't worry about me."

"Maybe I should arrest you anyway."

"For what? Something that hasn't happened yet?"

"For your own safety."

"I could take offense," Reacher said. "You don't seem very worried about their safety. You talk like it's a foregone conclusion."

"Get in the car. Call it a tactical retreat. You can find out about the ring some other way."

"What other way?"

"Then forget all about it. A buck gets ten there's no story at all. Probably the guy came back all sad and bitter and sold the damn ring as fast as he could. To pay the rent on his trailer."

"Is that how it is around here?"

"Often enough."

"You're doing OK."

"It's a spectrum."

"It wasn't a guy. The ring is too small. It was a woman."

"Women live in trailers, too."

Reacher nodded. He said, "I agree, a buck gets ten it's nothing. But I want to know for sure. Just in case."

Silence for a moment. Just the engine's whispered idle, and a breeze in the telephone wires.

"Last chance," the cop said. "Play it smart. Get in the car."

"I'll be OK," Reacher said again. He stepped back and straightened up. The cop shook his head in exasperation, and waited a beat, and then gave up and drove away, slowly, tires hissing on the blacktop, exhaust fumes trailing. Reacher watched him all the way to the corner, and then he stepped back up on the sidewalk, where the black-clad semicircle re-formed around him.

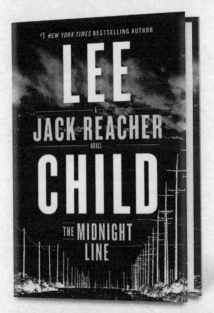